The Ba

Praise for *The Tea House on Mulberry Street*

'[A] heart-warmingly romantic novel in the spirit of
Maeve Binchy' *Woman's Own*

'A top read for snuggling up with on a chilly Sunday
afternoon' *Family Circle*

'A life-enhancing tale'
Woman & Home

'By the time I finished this book, I felt rather disappointed
that I couldn't step into the *Tea House on Mulberry Street*,
with its engaging, human characters and mouthwatering
recipes. Sharon Owens has a talent for drawing the reader
into her world. A book as warm and comforting as a really
good afternoon tea'   Jo Jo Moyes

ABOUT THE AUTHOR

Sharon Owens was born in Omagh in 1968. She moved to Belfast in 1988, to study illustration at the Art College. She married husband Dermot in 1992 and they have one daughter, Alice. *The Ballroom on Magnolia Street* is her second novel.

The Ballroom on Magnolia Street

SHARON OWENS

PENGUIN BOOKS

PENGUIN BOOKS

Published by the Penguin Group
Penguin Books Ltd, 80 Strand, London wc2r 0rl, England
Penguin Group (USA), Inc., 375 Hudson Street, New York, New York 10014, USA
Penguin Group (Canada), 10 Alcorn Avenue, Toronto, Ontario, Canada m4v 3b2
(a division of Pearson Penguin Canada Inc.)
Penguin Ireland, 25 St Stephen's Green, Dublin 2, Ireland
(a division of Penguin Books Ltd)
Penguin Group (Australia), 250 Camberwell Road,
Camberwell, Victoria 3124, Australia (a division of Pearson Australia Group Pty Ltd)
Penguin Books India Pvt Ltd, 11 Community Centre,
Panchsheel Park, New Delhi – 110 017, India
Penguin Group (NZ), cnr Airborne and Rosedale Roads, Albany,
Auckland 1310, New Zealand (a division of Pearson New Zealand Ltd)
Penguin Books (South Africa) (Pty) Ltd, 24 Sturdee Avenue,
Rosebank, Johannesburg 2196, South Africa

Penguin Books Ltd, Registered Offices: 80 Strand, London wc2r 0rl, England

www.penguin.com

First published 2006

1

Copyright © Sharon Owens, 2006

Set by Palimpsest Book Production Limited, Polmont, Stirlingshire
Printed in England by Clays Ltd, St Ives plc

For Dermot

Acknowledgements

Many thanks go to my Irish publisher and dear friend, Paula Campbell, and to all the team at Poolbeg in Dublin. A big thank you also to my Irish editor, Gaye Shortland.

Many thanks to my agents, Ros Edwards and Helenka Fuglewicz. And to everyone at Penguin, especially my American editor, Aimee Taub, and my American publisher, Carole Barron. Thanks also to my UK editor, Clare Ledingham, and all the team in London.

And finally, a major thank you to my husband, Dermot, and daughter, Alice. You both make everything worthwhile. And to all the readers who said such lovely things about *The Teahouse on Mulberry Street*. I sincerely hope you enjoy this story.

1. Hollywood Hogan

'But, three months! Johnny, that's not a holiday. That's crazy altogether!' Eileen might be eighty-four, but she wasn't an idiot. 'Nobody goes on holiday for three months, for pity's sake!'

'Gran, I told you I was only *thinking* about going. I need some time to myself. And I've always wanted to travel in America.'

'Huh! My two uncles worked on the railroads for forty years and died penniless in a boarding house in Chicago.'

'*Gran*, I know the story. You've told me it a million times.'

'Now, now,' said James, quietly, 'don't upset yourself, Eileen. Johnny is only thinking of taking a holiday. What's wrong with that?'

'That's right, Grandad. Thank you. I haven't had a good long holiday in twenty years.'

But Eileen had to have the last word. 'Are you thinking of retiring? Is that it? Are you trying to break it to me gently?'

God, but she was good, thought Johnny. She knew him too well.

'Not a bit of it,' he said quickly. But he *was* thinking of closing down the ballroom for good.

'Johnny,' said James, anxious to keep the conversation away from the proposed trip to America, 'you should think of doing something for older folk like us. There's nothing for retired people to do around here. What about proper ballroom-dancing, for example?'

'James, if you had your way, the ballroom would be full of old-timers like us, and nothing on offer but tea and cucumber sandwiches every night of the week.' Eileen laughed.

'I'm sure there's money in it.'

'Wouldn't do so well on the bar, Grandad.'

'Even so. It might be very popular. And a *lot* less trouble.'

Johnny and his grandparents stood sipping their drinks at the little office window, watching the crowd dancing far below. From time to time James and Eileen called in for a gin and tonic, just to see how things were going. They listened to the breathless, pot-bellied DJ Toni reading out some requests.

'Johnny, don't go to America,' said Eileen, suddenly. 'The ballroom is the best thing that ever happened around here. God knows we've had little enough excitement in this town.'

Johnny knew she was trying to talk him out of retiring. He smiled. Eileen could be very manipulative when she wanted to be.

'We'll be going now,' said James, interrupting Johnny's thoughts.

'Yes, pet. Goodnight,' added Eileen. 'Be careful, locking up.'

'I'll walk you down to the door,' said Johnny.

Johnny kissed Eileen on the cheek and saw her and James off in their car. On his way back in, he noticed Declan Greenwood coming in the main door, wearing a floor-length coat (army surplus) with what appeared to be several bullet-holes down one side. Anyone else's money would have been refused straight away, but Declan was Marion's boy so Johnny made an exception. He nodded his head in the direction of the cloakrooms, and Declan grinned and nodded, and slid the offending coat off his lean shoulders. Johnny would always allow the young fool admittance to his precious ballroom, because Declan's mother looked like Marilyn Monroe and because Johnny had loved her for twenty-five years. The lad will never get a girlfriend, though, dressed like that, Johnny thought sadly, as he picked a speck of dust off his own white jacket and checked his hair in one of the many gilt mirrors.

Johnny Hogan was a tall, powerful man, with thick black hair and dark brown eyes. He was handsome and sensual, and he could carry a tune and jive with the best of them. He had a dimple in his chin and, when he winked, girls forgot they had boyfriends. All the women of Belfast adored Johnny Hogan, but so far, Johnny had managed to remain single. The only woman he had ever loved had left him to marry another man, and Johnny had never recovered from the shock.

He was born in 1939, into a close family circle with conservative values. His parents were well liked in the district and the birth was celebrated for several days. All the women in the street knitted clothes for him. It was the beginning of a lifetime of female devotion. It took people's minds off the outbreak of war to fuss over such a handsome little fellow.

Meanwhile, people hung blackout blinds on the windows and began to panic-buy cigarettes, stockings and chocolate. The young men were enlisting in the army, and talking about the amazing capabilities of battleships and submarines; and the women only wanted to see the new baby on Magnolia Street. They all congratulated Johnny's mother on having the good fortune to have her baby before her man got sent away to fight. Everyone spoilt Johnny because he was a good baby and almost never cried. He lay in the sturdy wooden cradle that his grandfather had made for him, and he smiled up at everyone and they smiled down at him.

But the Hogan family was destined to become one of the countless casualties of that conflict. Johnny was only a year old when Magnolia Street was flattened in the Blitz and his devoted parents were found side by side in the rubble. They hadn't had time to gather up their baby son and make their way to the shelter that James had built for them with such devotion. Johnny's mother was clutching a bone-china teapot and his father was wearing his stiff, new soldier's uniform. They were both dead. But Johnny was alive and well in his solid, wooden cradle and his survival made the national press. He was the only person on Magnolia Street to survive the bombing.

Johnny moved to Eglantine Avenue where he was brought up by his paternal grandparents, Eileen and James, and he was a happy and contented child. He had never had a chance to get to know his parents, so he did not miss them very much, but he sometimes felt a kind of emptiness in his heart, especially at Christmas time. His grandparents understood this, and they were the most patient and considerate guardians that Johnny could have wished for.

4

Johnny grew up fast. He was the first young person in Belfast to wear blue suede shoes, a boast he never tired of making. In another time and place he might have become an actor in the theatre or a singer like Elvis Presley. He had a certain quality about him, an aura of celebrity that made people look after him in the street and wonder if he was famous. When he was still a child, people knew that he would amount to something. The miracle boy from Magnolia Street could never be allowed to fade away into obscurity, like so many other Belfast boys before him.

From the age of fourteen, he never missed a Saturday at the Odeon picture house on the Ormeau Road and the cinema staff soon began to call him Hollywood Hogan. The name stuck and Johnny kept it, even when he was grown up, on account of his big ideas and his outlandish dress-style. He combed his jet-black hair up into a steep wave and he wore tight trousers and long jackets long after they ceased to be fashionable. He cut a fine figure driving along the rain-washed streets in his imported pale blue Lincoln Continental.

And so, buoyed up by his local-celebrity status, and by his own vague ambitions, Johnny set out to find a purpose in life. Various jobs came and went. Salesman, office clerk, barman. He was very frustrated, watching the minutes crawling by in old-fashioned shops and offices; and far too spoilt to labour on the building sites. And he longed for something glamorous, a little bit of Hollywood sparkle. That's what he really wanted.

When he was twenty-three, Johnny fell in love. He saw a pretty girl, one sunny day on Royal Avenue in 1962, as

5

he waited for the lights to change. She had white-blonde hair and bright red lips, and Johnny waved her over to his car and asked her for her name and telephone number. She scribbled them down on the back of an old bus ticket and gave it to him, and he missed the green light and the other drivers beeped their horns at him. Johnny didn't care. Marion Evans was worth it. Johnny called her the following day. They went out on several dates, mostly to the cinema, and fell madly in love in the back row of the Odeon. Marion had a tiny waist and a rounded bust, and as the months went by she allowed Johnny to do things with her that she had never allowed other boys to do. Not even her teenage sweetheart, Eddy Greenwood. She worried about it afterwards, of course. But she was sure that Johnny was working up the courage to propose to her. He kept saying things about having big plans for the future.

The ballroom was the only one of his many business plans that ever made it off the ground. It was Eileen who had an idea about the big square of wasteland on Magnolia Street that had not been developed since the war. It was now up for sale. Eileen spent a few sleepless nights thinking about that piece of land. That was where Johnny's parents, and so many other people, had died so tragically during the war. In the end, she decided they would buy it and build a ballroom on it. As a sort of memorial to Johnny's parents, who had loved each other so much.

When the ballroom was finally opened to the public on a winter's night in 1967, it looked truly splendid. Multicoloured fairy lights twinkled on the huge Christmas tree in the foyer, and the rotating spotlights on the main ceiling turned the ballroom on Magnolia Street into an underwater paradise of blue and green floating circles. Several gas heaters had been running all day, to take the chill off the new building. The smell of drying plaster was barely detectable. All the staff wore velvet bow ties, red shirts and black trousers with a satin stripe down the side. The in-house DJ had just returned to live in Belfast following a very successful two-year stint in a Butlin's holiday camp in the north of England, and he prided himself on his popularity with the ladies. James thought this might have had something to do with the man leaving Butlin's in the first place, but Johnny said that DJ Toni had his own sound-system and disco-lights, and the gig was his, and that was the end of it. James muttered something about never trusting a person who spelt their name in a fancy way, but he knew when he was beaten. Johnny made a short speech at the main entrance and Eileen wore a fun-tiara and cut the ceremonial ribbon. There was a great turnout for the launch. The local press had a field day: MIRACLE BOY OPENS BALLROOM ON BLITZ SITE. Johnny told the spellbound crowd that the massive glitter-ball suspended on a chain from the ceiling was the largest of its kind in Western Europe. It was a lie.

And Johnny knew that he had found his niche at last.

2. The Sisters

In a tiny house on Cairo Street, Kate and Shirley Winters, still in their pyjamas, were gearing up for their favourite day of the week. Kate was pouring tea from a shiny brown teapot. Her long black hair hung round her face like curtains and her big blue eyes were still half-closed with sleep. Shirley was carefully making toast under the gas grill, using the last two slices of bread from the packet. Her jaunty 1920s' black bob was sticking out in all directions, and her eyes, large and blue like Kate's, were streaked with yesterday's mascara and eyeliner. Both girls were tall and slender, although Kate's glamorous satin pyjamas were in stark contrast to Shirley's homely flannelette ones. The morning sun was streaming through the net curtains at the kitchen window. Their parents had already gone to work in the hospital.

'This grill has had it,' said Shirley, as the dancing blue flame above the bread flickered and died. She relit the grill with a match, watching it burn down for a moment before she blew it out. But her elder sister wasn't listening.

'I don't know whether to buy the pink leather jacket in Top Shop or the white sheepskin boots in Dolcis,' sighed Kate, as she opened a fresh pot of strawberry preserve. 'What do you think, Shirley?'

'I think you should stop wearing animal skins,' said Shirley, gravely.

'Oh, good grief. Don't start on me so early in the day. Just because you once bought a couple of albums by the Smiths, you think you're going to save the world?'

'Every little helps, Kate. How can you afford leather jackets, anyway?'

'Never you mind.' (Kate had a massive overdraft and a bank clerk who fancied her.)

'I'm going to buy the new single by A Flock Of Seagulls,' announced Shirley, as she munched her toast. 'I absolutely *love* it.'

'And you think I waste money? Why don't you get your-self some new clothes instead?'

'I was thinking I might buy a new oven, before this piece of scrap explodes in the middle of the night and kills all of us in our beds. Mum would love a new one.'

Kate was quiet then for a few minutes. There was no possibility she might chip in for a new oven when there were pink leather jackets to be had in Top Shop.

'Are we still going to stalk lover-boy in Quigley's this morning?' asked Kate suddenly.

'No, I've changed my mind,' said Shirley. 'I'll buy my record somewhere else. And I'm not *stalking* him. And he's not my lover.' Not yet, she thought.

'Suit yourself. I'm away upstairs for a shower,' reported Kate, as she set her plate and mug into the sink.

'Righto, leave me some hot water,' warned Shirley, and she reached for the mail-order catalogue, to check the prices of various household appliances. Kate always took at least an hour getting ready in the morning.

They would spend until lunchtime trawling the shops for bargains, and in the afternoon they might have fish and chips in the city centre somewhere. Then they would return home – Kate to pamper herself in the bathroom, and Shirley might listen to a new record as she tried on her thrift-store discoveries. (In some stores, she could buy several outfits for less than ten pounds.) Then they would get ready for the Saturday-night disco in Hogan's ball-room. It was the in-place to go, so unfashionable that it had recently acquired cult status.

Shirley pottered around the house for a while, watched the news on TV, got dressed and then went to talk to Kate.

'I think that the men around here actually enjoy a good riot,' shouted Shirley above the noise of Kate's top-of-the-line hairdryer. Shirley was cross because she'd had to endure yet another cold shower.

'What are you talking about?' said Kate, switching it off.

'All that roaring and shouting. They're throwing whole *trees* at the police! Pure naked rage. Don't you think it's very *primitive*?'

'I never think about stupid riots. You think too much, Shirley. That's always been your trouble.'

'I was just watching the news. They burnt down a carpet shop.'

'Ah, no, the lovely carpets! And by the way, you're wearing outdoor shoes on my *white* carpet.' She wagged an accusatory finger at her younger sister. 'If there's oil on your shoes, this floor'll be ruined. And you can pay for a new one!'

Shirley sighed. She often wondered how Kate had managed to reach the grand old age of twenty-nine without ever having had one single, profound thought. Or how she could be germ-phobic and boy-crazy at the same time.

'You could take a PhD in missing the point, Kate. Do

you know that?' But she slipped off her shoes anyway, and held them up by the heels.

'Don't sit on the bed,' warned Kate, eyeing Shirley's latest outfit: a faded pink and orange silk skirt and blouse from the local thrift store. And horror of horrors, a waist-length necklace of red glass flowers, that even a half-blind maiden aunt wouldn't wear to the back door. Poor Shirley, only nineteen years old; she actually believed it was the ultimate in cool to wear *used* clothing.

'Oh, shut up, it's all been professionally cleaned,' said Shirley, 'and it's miles better quality than your trendy chain-store rubbish.'

Shirley Winters threw herself down on her sister Kate's pretty, cast-iron bed and studied Kate's extensive handbag collection, which was mostly kept hanging on the bedposts.

'Don't let that filthy purse of yours touch my pillow, for God's sake,' Kate cried.

Shirley laughed and lovingly rubbed the antique purse across her own face, while Kate shivered with disgust. Kate couldn't be too unkind to her little sister this morning, or she'd be left without an escort for her weekly visit to Hogan's ballroom.

Kate's room was a treasure trove of ladies' accessories. In fact, there were so many animal-print scarves, plastic belts and spike-heeled shoes everywhere, it resembled a well-stocked boutique. The room even boasted its very own mini-chandelier, complete with glass droplets.

'You're weird,' Kate sighed. Shirley's point-blank refusal to wear new clothes was impossible for her to understand.

'You buy a new handbag every time you go out with a new man. How weird is that?' Shirley said.

11

'Yeah, well. I'm sentimental.'

'You're a narcissist, Kate,' scoffed Shirley. 'That means you have no regard for other people's feelings, in case you didn't know.'

'I'm still looking for the perfect man–bag combination,' Kate said calmly, peering in the mirror of her dainty dressing table and rubbing on some blue eyeshadow. She didn't suffer from a guilt complex of any kind, that was true. And Kate thought that was a good thing. She'd once dumped a perfectly civil insurance salesman from Derry because he had committed the ultimate fashion-crime of having brown shoelaces in his black brogues.

Shirley counted the handbags. There were forty-three of them, made of velvet, denim, leather and suede. Some were very pretty – beaded or tasselled. Some were modern, minimalist and smart. Shirley wondered again if her big sister might have some sort of shopping addiction. No woman in her right mind could possibly need so many bags. (Or so many boyfriends.) Shirley had one handbag, and one handbag only; it was a small Victorian purse made of pale green silk, with pretty silver handles and a fine chain for carrying. She never let it out of her sight. It was her most precious possession, a once-in-a-lifetime find in an antiques store in the village of Helen's Bay. Kate was convinced the purse was full of deadly TB germs, and even the girls' mother wouldn't allow it in the kitchen, for fear it might contaminate the groceries.

Kate was now brushing her long, dark hair. 'Kevin McGovern asked me out last week,' she said, 'and he was wearing filthy overalls at the time.'

'He is a mechanic, Kate. He can hardly repair cars wearing a tuxedo.'

'We bumped into each other outside the newsagent's at the top of the avenue. I said, "Where are you taking me? To the garage to see your alloy-wheel collection?" We laughed it off, but really, the cheek of him.'

'Kate, he's nice.'

'Can you see me married to an oil-spattered Kevin?'

'Kevin and Kate? It has a kind of ring to it, don't you think? Kevin and Kate McGovern, of McGovern's Garage, Belfast. Solid and dependable, that sounds. Hasn't he kept that business going single-handedly since his father retired?'

'Oh, Shirley, you're away with the fairies. You probably would marry some stupid fella just because your names both started with the same letter.'

'Come to think of it, he's always inventing things to do with cars. He told our dad he was working on an anti-theft device, last time he saw him. Likely he'll be rich someday. You should have given him a chance, Kate. He might scrub up rather well, out of the overalls.'

'I doubt it. Anyway, name me one rich inventor. Pass me that can of hairspray, would you? The extra-strength one, there, in the metallic pink can, at the back of the shelf. With the purple lid.'

Shirley passed the container and stood back as the perfumed cloud enveloped her sister, waving away the strong-smelling fumes. They both held their breath until the fine, sticky mist finally settled on the white carpet.

'Where did I put that clutch bag with the sequin roses?' (She'd bought that particular bag after a two-week fling with a professional gardener who wrote love poems to her on the back of horse-chestnut leaves.)

'It's there, on the bed. On the pillow, under the denim shoulder bag.'

'Oh, yeah. Pass it over, would you?' Shirley passed it.

She stood behind her sister, peering into the mirror from over Kate's shoulder. She stole a blob of Kate's pink hair gel and used it to flatten down her blunt-cut fringe. The deadly purse swung from Shirley's wrist on its delicate chain, and caught Kate in the eye.

'For God's sake, I told you to keep that damn purse away from me!'

'Sorry.' Shirley tried to sound as if she meant it.

'Are you really wearing those old rags into town?' Kate moaned. 'You'll make a right show of me.'

'There's a matching hat, too,' laughed Shirley.

'Please tell me that's a joke. The hem is hanging off your skirt. People will think you've no money. Oh, Shirl-ee . . .'

'Okay, first, this is a genuine 1920s' garment, I'll have you know. It's supposed to look old because *it is old*. Secondly, I have no money *to spare*. A new oven won't come for free.'

'Yes, well. That's very nice of you, Shirley. But you've got to think of yourself. You'll not get a boyfriend, done up like that. You want to get a nice, leather dress, like my new one. Low-cut in front. Bit of body glitter on the old cleavage. Get the boys' eyes popping out, that will.'

'I don't want their eyes popping out. Or anything else, either. You shouldn't encourage them, Kate. They're barely able to control themselves at the best of times. A low-cut, leather dress could push them over the edge altogether.'

14

'You won't get far in your poverty-chic. That's all I'm saying. And those big buttons give me the creeps. Some old biddy could have died wearing that very blouse. Ugh!'

'I don't want *any* man,' said Shirley, softly. 'Just *one* man in particular. I want Declan Greenwood.' She thought of his dark brown, deep-set eyes and his blond crew cut, and wanted to hold him so much it was like a physical pain. 'That's what I'm trying to tell you. It's our destiny.'

'Destiny, nothing, Shirley. You fancy him. Don't try and dress it up as something from a higher level. You'll just have to attract his attention. Men are very visual creatures. Everyone knows that. Show him a bit of shoulder if you're too shy to show anything else. I've got a nice top you could borrow. Bananarama –'

'No, it's an elemental thing. It's something spiritual. As old as time. When two people are right for each other, when the chemistry is right, Mother Nature will know it, and she will bring them together. It's something in nature that pairs people off, you see – knowing they have complementary qualities that will help them to survive in the chaos of the world. That's my theory.'

'You're cracked, Shirley Winters. What about Bonnie and Clyde? Mother Nature slipped up badly the day those two met, didn't she?'

'It's not a perfect system. I'm not saying it's perfect.'

'I'm telling you, marriage is all based on physical attraction. Men marry women who are as attractive as they are, on a scale of one to ten. Beautiful people marry each other. Plain people marry each other. That's a scientific fact. Eventually, people become so plain that nobody at all will marry them. And the plain genes die out. See? I read about it in a magazine. It's just one big beauty competition out there.'

'Oh, please, Kate. That's total rubbish. An insult to human intelligence. Are you trying to tell me that nature cares about high cheekbones and long eyelashes?'

'It's true! Now, are you nearly ready?'

'Just the old eyeliner to apply.'

'In that case, Quigley's, here we come!'

'Kate, we're not –'

'You know, you should have your hair updated. Get some layers put in. That flat bob look was over five years ago. And buy some new clothes. You're like a mad granny in that old blouse. Is it meant to be that colour, or is it just faded? It's far too big for you. Here, put this belt over it. Cover up that missing button.'

'No, Kate. I like my clothes baggy. And pink plastic does not go with antique silk. I thought you were supposed to be a fashion expert?'

'Shirley, you're hopeless!'

'I mightn't bother going shopping now. Or to Hogan's, either. You've spoilt the mood for me.' Shirley did fancy herself as a mysterious, Bohemian, left-wing kind of girl, but it was a very fragile fantasy indeed, and didn't stand up to too much criticism.

'You're going into that record shop, and that's the end of it. You've been driving me crazy, moping over Declan Greenwood for months now. The sooner you ask him out, the better. And you'll be at Hogan's tonight as well, no matter what happens in Quigley's. I'll finally get to dance with Alex Stone tonight. I just know it.' She stood up and stepped into some silver sandals with see-through heels. Shirley was tempted to have a good sulk, but there was no point. Kate never paid attention to the moods of other people.

'Don't you mean *Standing Stone*?' Shirley said, playing with her strand of beads. 'That's what they call him. That's all he ever does: stand against the wall in Hogan's.'

'That's the beauty of it. I always know where he is. Not like some men. Up until now, all we've done is talk.'

'He talks to all the girls, Kate. He's just doing his job.'

'I want him, Shirley, and I'm going to get him.'

'Oh, dear, here we go again on the merry-go-round of love. Do you never get dizzy? He can't dance with you, anyway, Kate. Bouncers aren't allowed to romance the ladies while they're on duty.'

'They are if Johnny Hogan's not about.'

'Are you actually going to ask him for a dance?'

'Don't be silly, Shirley. He'll be the one doing the asking.'

'How? I don't get it. You'll have to spell it out for me.'

'Look, I told Alex something about that girl he fancies, that cheeky piece who works in the newsagent's. Louise Lowry.'

'What did you tell him?' Shirley asked, with a sigh. Kate's ambitious schemes usually ended in tears.

'Nothing much. Just that she has a glass eye.' Kate admired her ankles in the dangerously high sandals. 'Speaking of which, aren't these glass *heels* simply divine?'

'Kate! How could you! And it's a crazy thing to say. How many people have glass eyes? Louise'll find out what you said and come after you!'

'Who's gonna tell her?' asked Kate.

'She's got hands on her like two bricks. Have you

noticed that? She'll flatten you like a pancake. Even hardened shoplifters won't go in that shop.'

'How will she find out? Alex won't be talking to her now, will he? He'll avoid her like the plague. He almost threw up when I told him.'

'Did he really? How prejudiced,' Shirley gasped.

'He's *phobic* around disability. Phobic isn't the same as prejudiced,' Kate said firmly. Shirley shook her head. This was much worse than the time Kate had lied about her height on the stewardess application form, and then tried to convince them at the interview that their tape measure was faulty. And *then* calling the other girls nothing but a bunch of glorified waitresses when she was asked to leave the room. As if she could *ever* have convinced them that she wasn't six foot tall in her bare feet. Kate and Shirley were the tallest girls in Belfast, but that didn't stop Kate wearing high heels. Boys sometimes asked her if she needed oxygen up there, or if it was going to rain the next day.

'I don't believe you sometimes. You don't even like him that much. You just want him because Louise wants him,' said Shirley.

'Not true. I like him. He's taller than me, for one thing.'

'Oh, Kate! Anyway, he's only a bouncer. I wouldn't have thought he was your type. I thought you wanted a rich husband?'

'I do want a rich husband,' admitted Kate. 'But I do like Alex. A lot. He's only bouncing temporarily. Look, I'll tell you a secret, but you must keep it to yourself. Alex stands to inherit a chain of jewellery shops from his elderly uncle, but nobody knows about it.'

'Are you out of your mind? Come on, Kate. He's not one of *those* Stones.'

'He is. His mate, Jim, told me in confidence, but he swore he'd deny it if I let the word get out. So you see, I've got to be his girlfriend before the old uncle pops his clogs, otherwise Alex will think I'm only after his money.'

'Aren't you?' Shirley asked.

'Of course not. He's a walking dreamboat, or haven't you noticed?'

'No. A bit muscle-bound, for me. I like men who are slightly underweight and over-educated, not the other way round.'

'He's got lovely hair, though. You've got to admit, he's got a lovely head of hair. Natural blond. Thick as a thatch.'

'Him, or his hair?' Shirley laughed.

'His *hair*. Will you *stop* asking questions and do your face!' Kate almost shouted.

Shirley pulled a black eyeliner pencil out of her purse and traced a thick line across the delicate skin beneath each eye. Kate shook her head. No foundation, powder or blusher ever settled on Shirley's face. And she could do with it – she was as pale as death. They both were. Everyone in Belfast was; there were only five days of sunshine each year, on average.

'I'm sure you'll be very happy together,' said Shirley, smudging the black lines with her index finger. The blue of her eyes was greatly intensified. She smiled at her sister. 'Many's the lasting marriage was built on far less than a fine scalp. But, you know, I wouldn't believe a word that Jim says. Likely Alex put him up to it. For a laugh.'

'No, it's the truth. His uncle has the same first name,

so Alex won't even have to change the shop signs when he takes over. And I'm not going to wait for the bloody moon and stars to bring us together, either.'

A car horn tooted outside.

'There's the taxi! Quick, are you ready?'

'Wait! I think I'll wear some lippy.' Shirley took the lid off the silver capsule she also carried in her purse and quickly smeared on the sensual lip colour. Her lips were suddenly the lips of Joan Crawford about to murder some unfaithful man in a 1940s' melodrama. 'Just in case we decide to walk *past* Quigley's. Do you think Declan will notice me in this gorgeous lip colour? It's called Drama Queen.'

'He couldn't miss you if he was on the back of a runaway horse. Now put a smile on your fizzog and let's hit the shops.'

'Did Alex really believe that yarn? About the glass eye?'

'Yes. Especially when I told him it keeps falling out when she's weighing the sweets. Once, I told him, it was in the jar of mint imperials for two days before they found it again.'

'You witch! If he's that gullible, she's better off without him.' They both laughed. 'You've got a great imagination, Kate.'

'Here's a wee tip for you, Shirley. If you're going to tell a lie, make sure you tell a right old *whopper*. Add some detail, embroider it a bit. That way, it's far more believable than an ordinary old lie.'

'Thanks, Kate. I'll remember that. I'm sure it will come in very useful, sometime.' She dabbed her newly crimson lips with a tissue and looked at herself in the mirror. She was delighted with her new hairclip, 1950s' original dia-manté, only three stones missing. 'How many marks would you give me for attractiveness, on a scale of one to ten?'

'Five. Six. No, five. Hopefully, Declan has a poverty-fetish and he'll really dig the second-hand gear.'

The car horn sounded again. Kate snatched up her sequinned bag, purse, perfume, lipstick, tissues and her leather jacket. Shirley sighed and popped her T-bar shoes back on.

The two sisters went down the stairs, closed the front door behind them and then they were on the street, beside the waiting car.

'Quigley's, please,' Kate told the driver, as she settled herself regally on the back seat. Shirley watched him steal a lusty glance at Kate's denim-clad thighs, before the car pulled out from the pavement and into the line of traffic.

They didn't speak again until the taxi stopped outside Quigley's. Kate paid the driver while Shirley tried to see in through the small window. One fleeting glimpse of a military overcoat and she knew she would chicken out. And then she saw him standing beside the New Releases, looking absolutely fabulous in all-black with a low-slung leather belt with big metal studs on it. And black suede boots with pointy toes. She felt a hot flush of desire and drew back from the doorway. Kate, determined to get the two of them together, gave her a shove and suddenly Shirley knew she just couldn't go in. Her cheeks were on fire with embarrassment.

Shirley tried to reverse out of the shop, but Kate's elbow was in the way and a speeding train wouldn't have moved it. There was a slight scuffle as the two sisters pushed and shoved each other in the doorway, one trying to get in and the other trying to get out.

'Oi! No trouble in the shop! Take it outside, ladies!' The man behind the counter didn't want a punch-up near his precious cardboard cut-out of the Wham boys.

'No trouble. Just a woman in love,' said the long-haired girl, as she pushed her blushing companion down one of the aisles.

Declan Greenwood watched the two tall girls jostling each other as they stood beside the Singles rack. One of the girls was very glamorous in blue eyeshadow, a blue leather jacket, ripped jeans and glass stilettos. The other one was more artistically dressed, in a pink and orange skirt, red beads and a faded denim jacket with a huge pink silk rose pinned on the lapel. Her bob was paper-flat, and her blue eyes were circled heavily with black pencil. But he guessed they were sisters. They were very alike. He turned back to the display of LPs on the shelf in front of him.

He had been blessed with excellent hearing, something several years of listening to very loud music had not diminished. He could hear them arguing in angry whispers on the other side of the display.

'Ask him. Go on. Ask him. What have you got to lose?'

'No way. Are you completely mental?'

'Ah, go on. You're hopeless! Have you no guts at all?'

'That's rich coming from you! Why didn't you ask Alex out last week, instead of telling him outrageous lies about the opposition?'

'Tactics. Watch and learn, little sister. You've got to wound your rivals before you go in with the big guns. It's called propaganda.'

'Your head's cut. I can't believe *you're* trying to give *me* advice about men.'

'Listen! We're here now. Go on over.'

'No. I couldn't speak to him at the disco with three vodkas in me, and I definitely can't do it now. In broad daylight. Sober.'

'Well, then, I'll ask him for you. Honestly, the things I do for you!'

'You will *not* approach that fella.'

'I will. I'll give you a good mention. Don't worry.'

'Don't you dare!'

'Did you get that ring in a lucky bag, by the way? Take it off. It looks plastic.'

'Kate!'

'Let go of me. You're hurting my arm.'

'What are you going to say? My wee sister wants to marry you, she's got no savings, but all her own teeth? Let's throw in two goats and name the day?'

'Well, I *won't* tell him you're a nineteen-year-old day-dreamer who talks to the moon and thinks she's Louise Brooks.'

'If you go anywhere near him, I'll put all your hand-bags in the middle of the yard and I'll set fire to them. And that's a solemn promise.'

'Do you want to be On The Shelf, for ever?'

'Don't be ridiculous. You know I don't.'

'Right, then. You've got to get your hands on a red-blooded male. Now, listen to me. Act your age, walk right up to him and ask him out for a drink, like a normal human being. I haven't got time for this carry-on.'

'Please, Kate. You don't understand. This is too

important to me. I'd rather I never spoke to him at all than have him turn me down, right to my face. At least if I never know his answer, I'll still have my dreams.'

'You're definitely not going to ask him, then?'

'No. Definitely not. A refusal would just about kill me. Even a polite refusal. If you show me up in this record shop, I will never, *ever* go out with you to Hogan's again. I mean it. Or anywhere. Please, Kate.'

'Right. Come on, then. I've a ton of things to buy before tonight.'

The two girls left the shop and Declan looked around the room at the other customers and wondered who it was they were talking about. Hogan's ballroom, they had mentioned. He might go to Hogan's again, one of these days. Just to see if the girls were there. This was an intriguing little story, and the girl in the denim jacket was very nice-looking. Maybe, if this other fella she was after didn't show up, she might like to talk to him.

3. Johnny is a Hero

Johnny collected some holiday brochures from the travel agency and settled himself in his office, to spend a quiet afternoon making plans. He imagined himself and Marion, side by side on the plane, sipping champagne and smiling at the other passengers. Holding hands as they flew over the Atlantic Ocean.

Well, that's the way things should have turned out, and would have turned out, if it hadn't been for the robbery.

A few weeks after the grand opening, as James had predicted, a couple of gangsters came into the ballroom, looking for protection money. They were also big fans of the silver screen, judging by the way they spoke with cigars hanging out of the sides of their mouths. One of them looked very sly and one of them looked very stupid. They made their way past the thick blue rope, and the sign that said STAFF ONLY, and went quietly up the carpeted stairs. They cornered Johnny and Eileen in the office, and demanded a monthly payment in exchange for their 'protection'. The streets were becoming dangerous places to be after dark, they said. A person didn't know who might be lurking in the shadows.

The dopey-looking one clenched and unclenched his knuckles, as if he was longing to ruin Johnny's good looks. But nobody was going to threaten Johnny Hogan, right there on the street where he was born. Or his sixty-four-year-old grandmother, either. Johnny tried to stare them down, but the steely gaze of his tormentors never wavered. The sly one spoke with a soft voice that made Eileen's blood boil. They stated the terms of their business arrangements, and explained to Johnny that unless they were paid on the first Saturday night of every month, there would be trouble in the ballroom on Magnolia Street.

Johnny agreed at the time, not wanting to put his grandmother in any further danger, but he needed a plan to outwit the gangsters. He gave them code names: Knuckles and Sly. That's what James Cagney would have done. He paced around the ballroom, smoking cigarettes continuously, and ignoring his girlfriend, Marion, whose beautiful face had grown pale. He would have to split the gangsters up somehow, and catch them off their guard. He would floor the little, sly man with a couple of good punches, and then take on the big one in a fair fight. He'd give the two of them a pasting, Hollywood-style, and then they'd know it was useless to blackmail Johnny Hogan. They'd slide back into the shadows of the slum neighbourhoods where they belonged.

On Saturday night, at the promised hour, the gangsters crept up the stairs to Johnny's office and knocked on the door. He confidently called out to them to enter. Johnny was sitting behind his desk, casually smoking a cigarette. He was wearing his best, double-breasted suit. And a liberal helping of expensive aftershave.

'Come on in, fellas. Make yourselves at home,' said Johnny, with just a hint of a New York brogue. The two men stared at him.

'Are you ready to do business?' asked the smaller criminal.

'Or do you need a little persuasion?' added the big man. 'Such a shame to have to spoil those good looks of yours.' There was real intent in what he said.

'I'm ready,' said Johnny. 'Get back in your cage. Let's get this over with before someone comes.'

'A wise decision. Well, hand it over. We're busy men.'

'It's over there, in the cupboard,' said Johnny, pointing with his cigarette. 'I'll get it for you.' He stood up slowly, never taking his eyes off the two interlopers.

'Not so fast, Hogan,' said the one code-named Sly. 'We don't want no funny business. We'll get the money ourselves.'

Knuckles went straight over to the cupboard and tried the handle. It was locked.

'It's locked,' he said.

'The key's *in* the lock, you big monkey,' said Johnny. 'All you gotta do's turn it.'

'Don't call me a monkey,' snarled Knuckles, his face turning red.

'Shut up and hurry up!' Sly urged.

When Knuckles turned the key, Johnny ran his fingers through his hair in a confident gesture that seemed to unnerve Sly. Sly could smell a set-up, a mile away.

'Wait a minute. Give me the gun,' he said to Knuckles.

Johnny froze. He hadn't banked on that. He hadn't thought they would come armed. There was no money in the cupboard, only light bulbs, envelopes and ashtrays. As Knuckles fumbled for the gun in the pocket of his raincoat, there was a knock at the door and Marion came in, carrying a tray of tea and biscuits. Knuckles quickly withdrew the gun then returned it to his pocket.

'I'm sorry, Johnny, I didn't know you had company,' she said, setting the tray on the desk. 'I wanted to talk to you about something.' She coughed gently, and waved the cigar smoke away from her face.

'For God's sake, what kind of an operation are you running here, Hogan, letting *women* loose all over the place?' said Sly.

'I thought I gave you the night off, baby?' said Johnny, trying to sound casual.

'You did. One of the bar staff called in sick,' Marion said crossly. 'I had nothing else to do.'

'I wish you'd told me,' said Johnny. 'I would have got someone else to cover.'

'Never mind the staff rota! Sit over there, doll, and keep quiet, and you won't get hurt.' Sly was livid. 'Hurry up, you great lump, and get the money!' he shouted at Knuckles. 'I don't want to have to use the shooter.' After that, everything happened at once. Marion fainted clean away. She fell heavily on the floor, striking her forehead on a wooden chair. Johnny rushed to help her, causing Knuckles to lose his balance as he spun round to see what was happening. The big man landed in a heap, and there was a tiny hiss as he burnt his lips with the cigar.

'Well, that's nice,' said Sly. 'I hope you didn't hurt yourself.'

'Shut up, he made me do it, running about like that. I can't concentrate under these conditions.' Knuckles held the gun inside his pocket, his finger on the trigger. 'You said there would be no hassle.'

'Ah! You're useless! You couldn't rob sweets off a small child. Now, get the money before I lose my temper completely.'

Knuckles leapt up in a rage, slipped on the crumpled rug and there was a loud crack as the gun went off and he shot himself through the foot. He was silent for a moment, his eyes wide open in shock. As the pain began to tear at his bones, he let out a wail that made them all jump.

'*Ah, Jesus wept! Sweet Jesus! Why does nothing work out for me?*' he screamed, as he crawled around the floor of the office, in agony.

The noise roused Marion, who was cradled in Johnny's arms. Slowly, he helped her to stand up. She covered her stomach with her hands.

'Let me call an ambulance,' he said gently. 'This woman's not well. She's in shock. And we'll have to get that poor sucker to a hospital, too, I suppose. Give me that gun before you kill yourself.'

Johnny went forward to get the pistol. So did Sly. Sly got there first.

'*Look out, Marion!*' shouted Johnny, but it was too late.

Sly leapt forward, grabbed Marion in an armlock and the gun was in his other hand. 'Now, hurry up,' he snarled, 'before I do something we'll all regret.'

'All right. All right. I'll get the money,' said Johnny, pulling open a drawer in the desk. 'It's not as much as we agreed but it's all I can afford this time. Setting up this place has cleaned me out.'

Sly's greedy, green eyes lit up when he saw the thick bundle of tattered banknotes. Forgetting the empty cupboard, and his bleeding friend, he slowly reached for the money. Just as his fingers closed on the prize, Marion jerked herself out of his grasp and ran to the door. Sly saw her pull it open, and was so annoyed he wanted to shoot her. Women could never be relied upon to do what they were told. At the same time he felt something like regret, as he realized his finger had already squeezed the trigger. The gun exploded, taking two of his fingers with it. It fell from his rigid fingers, through the torn lining of his coat, and slid under Johnny's desk just as the door opened wide and Marion fled into the hall. Sly collapsed and lay trembling beside his accomplice. He closed his eyes.

Johnny grabbed the gun and turned to face the door.

Dozens of revellers, attracted by the noise of the first shot, had gathered outside the door. They struggled to get a good look at the two injured men, writhing in pain on the floor; and at the handsome figure of Hollywood Hogan, as he stood, looking magnificent, beside his fake marble desk, one eye closed to avoid the smoke from the cigarette he still held in his lips. He held the weapon up high above his head, to show them all that the trouble was over.

'Call the cops,' he said. 'Tell them I've got a couple of Christmas presents for them. And tell them not to worry about the gun. I have it here. There's been enough shootin' for one night.'

Of course, the police believed Johnny's version of what really happened in the office that night; that it was nothing more than a series of accidents and slip-ups, and good luck on his part.

But nobody else believed Johnny when he told them

he was nothing special. They said that he was not only a hero, but modest with it. Within days, the story was all over the city, richly embellished with every telling. Hollywood Hogan had taken on two of the city's most notorious gangsters and wounded them both with their own gun.

Sly and Knuckles were taken to the Royal Victoria Hospital and held under armed guard in a private ward. By the time their wounds healed, they would be ready to stand trial for armed robbery and extortion. Their misery was not mourned by the policemen of the city, who feared this was the beginning of a crime-wave, or by the outraged business community. A criminal investigation was duly launched, and Sly and Knuckles were charged under their real names of Eugene Lolly and Timothy Tate, respectively.

The story of the robbery blazed on for months. Timothy Tate was found to be a loner who lived with his mother in a run-down bedsit in the meanest area of the city; and it was revealed that he hadn't dated a woman in seven years. One of his ex-girlfriends came forward to sell her memoirs to the local newspapers. A modest bidding war followed. Unfortunately, when the bidding war ended in the high hundreds, she didn't have much to say except that Timothy Tate hadn't been a very skilled lover. Most of the time, she said, when they were in bed together, he preferred to watch cartoons on the television and eat sweets. Yellow bonbons, to be precise. And he was very selfish with the bonbons, too. He never offered her one from the little paper bag. Inevitably, Eugene Lolly and Timothy Tate became known as the Bonbon Gang.

Marion took two weeks off work to recover from the shock of the attempted robbery but when she came back to the ballroom it was only to tell Johnny that she would not be walking out with him any more. And that to make the split less painful for both of them, she was also giving up her job behind the bar. She said that she now realized that the business would always come first with Johnny, and that she didn't want to play second fiddle to an ugly great hangar full of smoke-damaged furniture. She gave him back the silver bracelet he had given her on their third date and kissed him gently on the cheek. Johnny was too shaken to say anything, so he put the bracelet in his pocket and simply watched Marion walk away. For a few moments, there was no sound at all in the main ballroom, except for the clickety-click of Marion's heels on the wooden floor. Then, there was the soft whisper of the heavy foyer doors closing behind her, and then Johnny was all alone.

Johnny was too proud to win her back. And so he did nothing. Marion would miss him, he decided, and come back to him when she was over the fright of the robbery.

He thought he still saw love in Marion's eyes when he spied her out walking in the vicinity one day, but when he crossed the road to speak to her, she announced that she was getting married to her childhood sweetheart, Eddy. They had set the date already. Johnny's knees went weak with the shock.

Eddy Greenwood! That dull stick. With his tweed sports jacket and beige slacks, and his untidy, curly hair! He couldn't even dance properly! All he could do was shuffle about in the one spot as if his shoes were made of lead.

It was the ultimate humiliation for Johnny, to be rejected by Marion for a man like that! What was she thinking of? She couldn't possibly love Eddy. She'd told Johnny a million times that he was the only man who'd ever made her heart flutter with excitement, and her body burn with desire. It was completely beyond his understanding.

Eddy, on the other hand, was only too glad to have the love of his life back again, and thrilled that he had won her away from Hollywood Hogan at last. When Eddy saw his chance, he did not rest for one minute until he had convinced Marion to marry him.

Pulling pints would not be a suitable job for the wife of a respected businessman so Eddy set Marion up in business on her own. A little bridal boutique, a few streets away from the ballroom, which she called Romance And Ribbons. Seven months later, she gave birth to a son. Marion and Eddy told everyone that the child was born early, because he was big and ready, and everyone believed them.

Johnny dated lots of women after that, but Marion was the one for him, and he couldn't believe that he had let her go. Thoughts of her invaded his dreams at night, and even when he was counting piles of money in the office he missed her bringing in the tea and sitting on his knee for a kiss. He missed dancing with her most of all.

Owning the ballroom lost a little of its shine for Johnny then, and all the women who loved him only made him more lonesome for the one that got away.

4. A Jar of Mint Imperials

Louise Lowry worked in a tiny, dusty newsagent's shop crammed to the roof with jelly worms, packets of dipping sherbet and boxes of chocolates, plastic water-pistols, tiny beaded purses and neon skipping ropes. The newspaper stand and twenty boxes of crisps prevented any daylight from coming in through the grime-covered window. A small fridge full of milk cartons and packets of butter hummed in one corner.

In the gloomy stillness of the shop sat two young women, deep in conversation. Louise was tall, blonde and well-built enough to look uncomfortable in a size-sixteen shell suit. Her friend, Mary, was a delicate freckly redhead, dressed in hippy rags and green leather sandals.

'Ah, now, Mary, I never heard such a tale,' said Louise, in a voice that was tinged with fear.

'I'm telling you, Lou, it's the gospel truth. She told him that your left eyeball was lying in a jar of mint imperials for two days. And that's why he never asked you out. That kind of thing gives him the creeps.' Mary pored over the confectionery display beneath the glass counter. 'Here, go on, give us a couple of those jelly frogs, Louise. No, not them wee ones – the big ones covered in icing sugar.'

'But it doesn't make any sense. My own eye? It falls right into a jar of sweets, and I don't even notice?' Louise couldn't take it all in.

'Yes,' said Mary wearily. 'The frogs?'

Louise passed them over. One red, one yellow.

'How could I *not* notice a thing like that?'

'I don't know. Maybe you can't actually *feel* a glass eye?' Mary began to lick the icing sugar off the red frog.

'Wouldn't I still have the other eye to *see* with, though? Oh, you couldn't lose a glass eye and not notice. Why would Alex believe a yarn like that? He must be completely brainless.'

'I wouldn't know about that. He's as smart as any other man in this city, I'm sure. I'm only telling you what I heard.'

'Who told you? I want names.' Louise took a frog herself and held it up to the light. 'You can see through the green ones, Mary.'

'His mate told me. The fella who bounces with him in the ballroom. I don't know his surname but they call him Jim. Sunny Jim, to be precise. I asked him, straight out. I said, "Why doesn't Alex ask my pal, Louise, from the newsagent's, on a date? She likes him, and he knows it."'

'That's just great! Talk about desperate.' Louise bit the head off her jelly frog, and sat down heavily on the battered wooden stool behind the counter. Mary checked to see that the boss wasn't around before hopping up on the counter, and reaching for another sweet.

'Sure, what's the harm in asking? Don't you walk past him a hundred times a night, when you're in Hogan's? Nobody goes to the toilet that often. Not even with a bladder infection. He's shy, Louise.'

'Is he? He's a bit too big to be shy, I'd have thought. And a bit too old.'

'Well, he is. All kinds of people are shy. Look, never

35

mind about that. Jim told me that Alex did notice you flaunting yourself before him, and he *was* going to ask you out, but then Kate Winters put the word out that you had an artificial eye.'

'The interfering, evil little –'

'And then *he* said that was the end of it. He wouldn't want a girlfriend with her vital organs rolling all over the street.'

'I'll swing for that Kate Winters, the rotten liar! Who does she think she is, going around telling barefaced *lies* about innocent people? Poor Alex must have been terribly shocked.'

'Are you going to let her get away with this, Louise? Are you going to give her a good dig in the beak? That's what I'd do, if I was you. Or tell him something rotten about her? Tell him she's got early onset osteoporosis, and can't have any bedroom-business.'

'I don't know, Mary. I'll bide my time, and think it over. I need to gather some information. See if he's really interested in her before I do anything stupid. Maybe he'll realize it's all lies, and ask me out after all. I don't want to lose my dignity.' Louise looked thoughtful as she dug a piece of jelly out of her back molar with a sherbet wand.

'God forbid,' said Mary gravely.

'Are you free tonight?'

'I guess so. I've no particular plans. Can I have a sugar mouse?'

'As long as the boss doesn't see me giving away the profits. He's due back any minute. Here. Why don't you go mad and buy a quarter of jelly beans? Or even a 10p mix-up?'

'All right, all right. So, are we going to the ballroom, or what?'

'Yes, we are. We'll get done up like a couple of film stars, and go in there as if we hadn't a care in the world. We'll not even speak to Alex. Men don't like to feel cornered.'

'Especially by women with glass eyes.'

'That's not funny, Mary. I'll dazzle him with my outfit. Something classy, mind. Nothing too common. Let's look through the magazines for some ideas.'

'Kate Winters had three-quarters of her bust on show last week, Jim said, like a prize marrow on a shelf. All covered in glitter it was, and her make-up was a real trowel job. I wish we'd been there to see it.' Unfortunately, Mary and Louise didn't always have the funds for a night out in Hogan's.

'Well, now! That's pathetic. Everyone knows men prefer women to have natural beauty.' Louise was adamant about that.

'And he said Shirley was like a bag of laundry. Some old rag with embroidery unravelling on the sleeves. Eyes like a panda, he said. No doubt it's a cool fashion thing.'

'Pretentious, you mean. She loves herself. They both do.'

'Kate loves herself. But Shirley's okay. Nothing like Kate. Just a bit eccentric.'

'Whatever. Did they get any men, I wonder?'

'No. Jim said they left on their own.'

'Ha! Let us examine the evidence, Mary, my dear. Tatty clothes and too much eyeliner equals cool. Cool scares the boys away. Right? A cleavage bared and covered in glitter equals sexy. But that doesn't work, either. Too sexy scares the boys away. Okay . . . We need something in between. Attractive, yet approachable. Yes?'

The two girls sat in silence for a while, sucking on raspberry lollies. They flicked through the pages of a fashion magazine. There did seem to be a lot of cleavage on display nowadays. Louise reached behind her for some chocolate raisins and caught sight of the jar of mint imperials sitting on a high shelf. Old-fashioned sweets. Only pensioners ever asked for them. The jar itself seemed to mock her, filled to the top with its miniature, minty eyes.

5. The Ballroom

Kate gave her cleavage another dusting of glitter, noting that the pot was nearly empty. Even though it was the height of summer, Shirley thought her sister's pale, sparkling bust resembled solid ice. She hoped Alex was fond of icy things. Shirley went to Kate's bedroom window, parted the white muslin swags, and looked up at the sky. It was a beautiful colour. The definitive shade of midnight blue, soft as chalk, and dotted with the hard whiteness of faraway stars. The moon seemed to pulse with a ghostly brightness.

'There's a full moon tonight. I'm sure that's a good sign. A clear sky. Plenty of stars. It's the kind of night when two people might fall in love.'

'Is the car here yet?' asked Kate.

'It's just turning the corner,' said Shirley, all ready in her fake-fur jacket and velvet gloves. 'Come on. Let's get this over with.'

Minutes later, they saw the lights of Hogan's shining through the darkness. A small queue was building up but they wouldn't have to wait too long. The taxicab pulled up to the pavement outside the concrete edifice that was Hogan's ballroom. Kate and Shirley clambered out, and Kate paid the driver while Shirley twisted her pewter-coloured bracelets round and round her wrist, in bitter-sweet anticipation of the night ahead. Would Declan

Greenwood be there tonight? (Hopefully, he hadn't noticed that embarrassing scene in the record shop earlier.) Would they gaze into each other's eyes, in the romantic haven that was the hot-food bar, as they both reached for the red sauce? (Still poured into plastic tomatoes, by popular demand.) Would he rush to protect her if a vicious scuffle broke out in the parking lot? Occasionally, things turned nasty in the queue for taxis. Maybe he would offer her his handkerchief when some gorilla spilt a pint down her back for a laugh?

Declan didn't grace Hogan's disco with his presence very often, as he dressed exclusively in army surplus, and the bouncers didn't think much of it. It was provocative and dangerous, they told him, given the tinderbox nature of the security situation. Granted, it was mostly Second World War overcoats (Allies, various) and sturdy marching boots that he wore; not exactly British army modern-day camouflage. But still. The bouncers in Hogan's ran a tight ship, and they didn't like army surplus, Celtic and Rangers football strips, or anything which might cause offence to anyone. (Three men ended up in hospital the night some wise guy wore a T-shirt to commemorate the visit of Pope John Paul II to Dublin.) And after that, Johnny warned the staff to be ruthless with the dress policy. Not because they couldn't handle themselves in a brawl. They certainly could, and enjoyed nothing more than a no-holds-barred melee on a Saturday night. But Johnny didn't like fights taking place on the premises, and Johnny was the big boss man, after all.

Kate and Shirley could see him now, in the foyer, chatting to some pretty girls. He was telling them a story of some kind, and waving his cigarette in the air, doing all the actions. The girls were in raptures. Shirley thought Johnny Hogan was quite attractive, for an older man. There was something about him that reminded her of Declan. Maybe she just noticed some men, the ones with dark brown eyes and very high cheekbones, more than others.

Kate dragged her sister into the ladies' toilets to do a last-minute make-up check and adjusted her black leather dress, smoothing out any wrinkles that had been occasioned by the taxi ride. Shirley gave her short bob a final press with her palms. It stuck to the sides of her face like a wet cloth. Both girls shivered in the stone-cold room. It was horribly chilly now, but the arctic atmosphere would be most welcome later on when the dancing crowds had driven the temperature in the ballroom up over thirty degrees.

'Did you see Hollywood Hogan, flirting with those stupid girls?' asked Kate, as she applied another layer of blue mascara. 'He's twice their age.'

'He's still pretty attractive, I suppose. Are you ready now, Kate? If you put on any more make-up, you'll need scaffolding round your chin.'

'I'm ready.' Kate zipped up her bag, and took a deep breath. 'Men of Belfast, here I come!'

'Hasn't Belfast suffered enough?'

'Oh, give over, you! Anyway, Alex is my man of the moment. Come on!'

They went out to the foyer again and the music wrapped itself around them as they made their way across the blue carpet to the ballroom proper. People were arriving in groups of five and six. Some girls were already dancing at the edges of the polished wooden floor.

'Hope we get good seats,' said Shirley. 'Looks like a fair crowd in, the night.'

'Yeah. I must go and chat with Alex for a minute or two.'

'Don't abandon me too soon, Kate, will you? Your current record is seven minutes, I think.'

'Come on, Shirley! I won't! I told you, Alex is my number-one target this evening, and he's going nowhere until the end of the night.'

They hurried into the ballroom, Kate leading the way.

Louise and Mary joined the back of the queue, and slowly edged their way towards the main entrance. Louise was outraged that Alex had not saluted her through the glass as she waited impatiently outside on the pavement. She knew that he must have seen her standing there. Her hairdo had doubled in size, thanks to a whole tin of expensive spray. She was wearing three necklaces and four different shades of eyeshadow. It was petty of him to ignore her like this.

She was consumed with the glass-eye story, and the consequences it might have for her romantic ambitions. She was convinced that Alex Stone was her soulmate and the true love of her life, and was determined to win him away from Kate Winters and her glittery bosoms, at any cost. No matter what she had to do to achieve that result, she was prepared to do it.

'The dirty rascal hasn't even looked at me yet,' she muttered, as Alex whispered something in Jim's ear and the two of them laughed so much they had to wipe their eyes. 'What the hell is so amusing, I'd like to know?'

Mary gave her friend a little rub on the arm, for moral

42

support. It was all very exciting. Even though Standing Stone was very good-looking, he could hardly be described as sexy. In fact, Mary thought he looked slightly camp – something about the way he held his cigarette up above his shoulder? Far too graceful for a so-called body-builder. The bouncers took up their usual spot along the back wall of the ballroom, just as Louise and Mary paid their entrance fee and made their way, as quickly as dignity would allow, to claim good seats. The DJ was playing 'Too Shy' by Kajagoogoo. Louise felt a rush of sympathy for her sensitive bouncer-love.

Sunny Jim waved at them as they made their way to a booth with high sides near the dance floor. Situated on a carpeted area and decorated with several tall, plastic palm trees, it gave them great privacy, while still providing an excellent view of the dancing area. The ballroom was slightly cold, and Louise shivered beautifully when she took off her jacket, her bosoms wobbling gently in a low-cut top with a graffiti pattern on it. She made a great show of settling herself into the seat, so that Alex would notice her. She flicked her freshly styled hair several times. The spotlights bounced off her tanned skin and her white top, and her blonde hair. Alex smiled over at them. He seemed pleased with what he saw.

'I'll go to the bar,' said Mary. 'Two pints of lager, is it?'

'Excuse me! *I'll* go to the bar,' said Louise. 'And we're having glasses of white wine. Ladylike, we are, tonight. Have you no sense of style?'

'Fair enough, Louise. You have wine. But I don't like wine. It makes me burp. I want a pint.'

'Shush. You just can't be seen sinking a pint. Right?

I don't want him thinking I associate with savages. Is he watching?'

'I'll see.'

'Mary, careful! Don't let him catch you looking, now.'

'He's not looking.' Mary was peering through her fingers, as she rested one arm on the table. 'Still not looking. Still not looking. He's looking now!'

'Right, I'm off.' Louise stood up, picked up her handbag and walked gracefully towards the bar. Mary kept watch. Louise would want to know if her journey to the bar had been noted. It had.

Just as Louise returned with the drinks, both girls saw Kate and Shirley Winters approach Alex and Jim. Louise held her breath but the sisters didn't get a chance to talk to Alex as a large crowd swept into the ballroom, and they had to retreat across the dance floor. Kate was the exact opposite of Louise in colouring, with pale skin and dark hair, and wearing a short black dress. The glitter that Mary had reported was also out in force. It caught the light and a thousand tiny spots of blue and silver danced on the cleavage of Katherine Winters. Louise had to admit, the effect was rather fetching. She inhaled deeply, and she could see her own tanned bosoms swell up to within two inches of her chin. The first four buttons on the white top had been left undone. The battle of the bosoms had commenced.

Alex nudged Jim and they both winked at Kate. Kate waved back and pointed to one eye, in a meaningful gesture that made Louise gasp.

'Don't hold me back, Mary, if I lose my temper,' snarled Louise, through gritted teeth. 'I'll tear that lying little tart limb from limb!'

'Steady on, Lou. Just sit tight, now. Sit tight.'

The seats were filling up. The record changed to 'Only You' by Yazoo. DJ Toni's rasping whisper came crawling through the loudspeakers on its belly.

'Yazoo! She's a big lass, that Alison Moyet. Oh, but what a voice, the voice of an angel. "Only You", ladies and gentlemen.'

Kate saw Louise and Mary sitting near the dance floor, and guided Shirley to the other side of the hall. Kate's face was hard to read but she had a defiant look about her. Shirley looked preoccupied, swinging a small purse on a chain, and biting her bottom lip hard.

Kate and Shirley made a couple of laps of the ballroom, talking briefly to anyone they knew, before finding vacant seats at the back of the hall, near the food bar. It wasn't ideal, what with the aroma of beefburgers drifting across to them, but it was either that or stand all night. They'd lost their good seats a few minutes earlier when they'd tried to get chatting to Alex. They settled themselves in and decided to make the most of it. Kate knew she was looking fantastic, and she felt absolutely ready to take on all love rivals. But first, a little liquid courage must be purchased. She nudged her sister towards the bar. Shirley looked almost bored as she set off across the carpet, in a long yellow dress and matching headband. She wore a black velvet choker and three long black necklaces, as well as several bracelets on each wrist. Combined with the yellow gloves and the fake-fur coat, it was quite a striking look. The entire ensemble had been an impulse-buy from a new charity shop, and she was beginning to think yellow wasn't really her colour. It didn't help when she saw Louise and Mary laughing at her from across the floor.

'My God, but Shirley's like a giant bumblebee,' observed Louise with huge satisfaction. 'She didn't get that little outfit in any normal boutique!'

Mary, watching Shirley rooting through her tiny handbag at the bar, began to feel some sympathy for Kate's younger sister. This couldn't be a lot of fun for her, either. Could this night really end up in a no-holds-barred cat-fight between Kate and Louise? For the first time, Mary began to feel uneasy about Louise's obsession with Alex Stone. Maybe she could talk Louise back to some kind of normality, and end this feud with Kate at the same time? She decided to bring up the delicate subject of Alex's inheritance. A rumour was going round the ball-room that he was about to come into money.

'Louise, are you sure that Alex has a rich uncle? I never knew he was well connected. And if he is in line for a big inheritance, why is he holding up the wall in Hogan's, and not working in the jewellery shops, learning the business?'

'Because. I don't know why. Does it matter?'

'Well, I think it matters. I think he's making it up. Aren't you even a bit curious? How old is he? Twenty-nine? Thirty? Why isn't he married already if he's such a great catch?'

'That's it, Mary. You're a genius! He's hiding his wealth until he finds the right woman. He doesn't want to be killed in the rush of greedy little gold-diggers like that Kate Winters. I wondered why she was interested in Alex, all of a sudden. Now I know. She must have heard the rumour too. *The hungry eye sees far* and all that. Keep a watch on my drink. I'm going up to the DJ.'

'What for?'

'To have a request played for Kate Big Liar Winters.' And she set off, at a quick marching pace.

'Lou, don't!' But Louise was already halfway across the ballroom.

Twenty minutes later, the DJ announced that he was playing a tune by popular band the Smiths, especially for Kate Winters, who was here tonight with her sister, Shirley.

'And this request comes from a good friend of yours, Kate, and she says you will know who it is. So here it is, apparently this is your favourite song. I can't say it's one of mine. Well, it takes all sorts!'

Kate's mouth fell open, and Shirley was glad she was standing far away from Kate at the crowded bar, as the plaintive sound of 'Bigmouth Strikes Again' filled the ball room. Standing Stone and his mate, Sunny Jim, were doubled over beside the foyer doors. Their laughter could be heard even over the sounds of the record. Kate tried to smile, as if she was enjoying the joke too, but the smile didn't quite reach her eyes. She couldn't believe Alex was laughing at her. How dare he! A common bouncer like him, having the barefaced cheek to laugh at a beautiful woman like herself? Suddenly, out of nowhere, Kate felt a most unpleasant sensation – as if she was falling down a very long slide. Her stomach lurched violently, and she felt very cold. More disturbing than that, was the realiza-tion that she wanted Shirley to be at her side, germ-ridden purse and all. Even though she usually treated Shirley as nothing more than her personal assistant, now she real-ized that she *needed* Shirley badly. She prayed fervently that her younger sister would hurry back with the double

47

vodka that would surely calm her down. But there was quite a crowd at the bar and Shirley would never push her way to the front, as Kate would have done.

A young man from the area, who was known to have psychiatric problems, ran on to the dance floor and began a frantic impersonation of the band's lead singer, Morrissey. He unbuttoned his shirt to reveal a snow-white, hairless chest and he pulled his oily hair up into a high point. Jerking his head and shaking one leg in the air, he leapt around the floor like a tethered firework. He knew the words to the song and he roared them out with all his strength. Thunderous applause broke out from the delighted audience, and someone threw a plastic flower from the balcony. The young man knelt down and picked it up with his teeth and continued the dance on his knees, and everyone in the hall laughed until their drinks came back up through their noses. To end his performance, he lay down on his back, and pushed himself to the edge of the floor with his feet. Both shoes had holes in the soles. Kate could not believe that one song could last so long. The humiliation seemed to have gone on for hours. Inside, she wept, but the smile stayed firmly on her face. A couple of the barmaids helped the young man up and took him to the cafe for a complimentary plate of chips as the clapping died away.

Kate was horrified to notice that her hands had suddenly become stone cold and were trembling slightly. She joined them together, very tightly, and, with every ounce of her remaining energy, willed Shirley to come back.

Louise and Mary made a high-five as they sipped their glasses of house white. The dance floor had emptied, as the song proved too challenging for the dancers to deal with. The DJ was very concerned about this state of affairs.

'Come on, Kate! Kate Winters and Shirley, where are you? Let's have you on the floor. Come on, now! "Bigmouth Strikes Again" – your favourite song in the whole world. "Bigmouth Strikes Again". It's nearly over! Come on, now,' coaxed the DJ.

But Kate was frozen to her seat with fear, and Shirley was wiping the tears from her eyes, safely hidden in the mob at the bar. She hadn't laughed so much in ages. Then, she caught the attention of one of the barmen. She dried her eyes, bought the drinks and hurried back to join Kate, feeling suddenly guilty about leaving her big sister all alone. As the song died away, the DJ took it off and replaced it with another one.

'It seems Kate is too shy to dance tonight, ladies and gentlemen. So here is another disco smash, it's Dollar and "Oh l'Amour"! Oh, I wouldn't kick that Thereza what's-her-name out of bed for passing wind! Come on!' The floor was heaving in less than ten seconds.

'You took your bloody time,' snapped Kate, as she grabbed for her glass. 'Why didn't you come back here and support me? I cannot believe what has just happened.'

'You told me not to come back without the vodka.'

'Well, that was before I was publicly disgraced. Have you no common sense?'

'I knew this would end in tears. They were laughing at me, too. I saw them.'

'You should have been here with me, Shirley.'

'I told you she would find out. Just be grateful you didn't get a fat lip to go with the request. You're playing with fire, Kate. You don't pick a fight with *anyone* in this town unless you're prepared to go all the way.'

'Oh, shut up! We'll stay for half an hour, for appearances' sake, and then we're getting out of here. I'm exhausted.'

'Suits me. There's no sign of Declan, anyway. Probably it's too early for him.'

'We're not staying till the end of the night, Shirley! I don't feel well.'

'All right! All right! You're the one who drags me in here every weekend, and now you want out again? Make your mind up, for heaven's sake!'

The two sisters sipped their drinks in stony silence – Shirley slumped in the seat like a half-full sack of potatoes, and Kate trying to stop herself from bursting into tears and wondering where her confidence had gone. Could she be developing some deadly illness that made her tremble like this? She must ring the doctor, first thing on Monday morning. If she was still alive by then. Her chest was almost hammering with tension. She held on to the table as a moment of dizziness came and went. The music seemed far too loud tonight. It made her jump. What was DJ Toni trying to do to them all, having the music so loud? Louise and Mary were out dancing now, laughing like crazy, the two of them. Kate watched them with a sense of mounting dread. Could it be nothing more than that silly Smiths song that had upset her, she wondered frantically. She looked at Shirley for reassurance, but Shirley was scanning the balcony for a sign of Declan Greenwood. Poor Shirley. Declan Greenwood was a middle-class medical student from a fancy house on the expensive side of the Lisburn Road. That road was full of mature trees and BMWs, and the people who lived there employed gardeners and cleaning ladies. That kind of boy, and that kind of life, was out of Shirley's league, and that's all there was to it. Kate patted her sister's arm, in a sudden rush of affection. Shirley's wide yellow headband and jet-black hair did make her look slightly anaemic, Kate thought, but she hadn't the heart to say it.

On the dance floor, Louise was having a great time. She even did a couple of twirls and one or two high-kicks. Lots of people were looking at them. Mary was mortified. She'd bet an entire vat of patchouli oil that this whole thing would end badly. Mary spied Kate's face through the crowd; it was a picture of distress. But Louise was absolutely delighted. When they sat down again, Louise nudged Mary so hard that Mary threw her wine glass over the back of the seat.

'Round Two to us, Mary!' said Louise, with the light of triumph shining in her eyes. 'I always knew that wimp Morrissey would be good for something.'

6. Romance and Ribbons

It was a sunny July morning. Marion smiled as she smoothed out the folds of a new gown in the window of the shop. It was incredibly expensive; much more expensive than the sort of gown she usually sold, but she just couldn't resist it when the supplier showed it to her. A retro-style with a high collar, long sleeves, a tiny waist and billowing skirts; all in white velvet. There were thousands of pearls on the hem, and even tiny flowers embroidered on the inside of the bodice. The dress was so beautiful that Marion decided it would look perfect on its own, without the gilt chair and the vase of fresh flowers she normally kept in the window. She carried the chair to the dressing room and placed the flowers on the counter of the shop. She went outside to study her work from the street. It really was a fabulous dress, but maybe she did need something to fill that space in the corner – something heavenly? Candles! She would buy a tall, heavy candlestick and some church candles this lunchtime. It really would be perfect, and very much in the style of understated elegance she was trying to promote.

After that, it was down to the real work; the bread-and-butter work. Selling budget gowns to pregnant teenagers, and plain gowns to elegant women over forty, who were getting married for the second time. Marion hoped that someday soon a pretty girl would come through the door of the shop who was just born to wear the gorgeous velvet gown in the window.

She vacuumed the white carpet until it was immaculate, polished the huge antique mirrors in the fitting rooms and ironed the gowns that were ready for collection, filling up the sleeves with tissue paper. She had two appointments for fittings that afternoon, so she brought several pairs of silk shoes from the store and left them in the dressing rooms, ready for the brides-to-be, who always seemed to turn up wearing black boots. Then, she checked that all the fabric-covered tissue boxes were well stocked. Most of the brides-to-be wept with joy when they found their perfect dress after weeks and even months of searching. She sometimes wondered if they gave as much thought to their choice of groom.

Marion thought of her own wedding day in January 1968. Eddy waiting impatiently in the porch, with a tiny red rosebud pinned to the lapel of his new suit, terrified in case Hollywood Hogan would turn up and cause a scene. All through the ceremony, Eddy never took his eyes off her, his love for her almost overwhelming. As soon as the priest declared them man and wife, she felt so relieved. The stress of hanging on to Johnny Hogan was over at last, and it felt like a huge burden had been lifted off her shoulders. She thought only once, during their quiet honeymoon in Galway, of Johnny Hogan in his white jacket. The man she had loved so desperately, the man she had once left her beloved Eddy for, the man who was Declan's real father. But she had waited a long time for him to propose, and even when the pregnancy was confirmed by her doctor, and she grew paler and paler, he didn't notice a thing. And if he'd loved her, he would have noticed, wouldn't he? Eddy knew she was unwell straight away, when she met him that morning in the street. He said she should eat something and he took her into Muldoon's Tea Rooms for an early lunch, and she had cried over the chicken and chips and told him everything.

'I love you, Marion,' Eddy had said, suddenly. 'I always have and I always will. Marry me and I promise you, you'll never be sorry.'

'I'd love to marry you, Eddy,' she'd said at once, with her eyes full of fat silent tears.

When the baby was born (thankfully with Marion's blonde hair colour), Eddy doted on him. That was when Marion started loving Eddy again. Because he loved Declan just as much as he loved his own daughters when they came along, over the years that followed: Emily, Eve and Eloise. The girls had the same dark curly hair and bright green eyes as Eddy, and the same gentle nature. They were the perfect example of a happy family unit.

Marion checked her make-up in the mirror. It was perfect. Eddy would be calling in soon to join her for lunch. They always spent Monday lunchtimes together. It was just one of the hundreds of little things Eddy did all the time to make her feel special. As soon as she thought of him, he was there, smiling and waving at her through the glass, carrying a huge bunch of white tulips in one hand and a small box of cream pastries in the other, tied neatly with string.

She went to open the door, and he kissed her gently.

'Hello, my darling, how are you?' he said.

'Fine, fine. What lovely flowers, Eddy!'

'You deserve them. Oh, I'd love a cuppa! What a morning I've had, it never stopped in the bakery. We ran out of eclairs and cream horns, and the soup got spilt over the wheaten bread.'

'Eddy, that's not like you.'

'We had a new girl starting with us, she's still learning the ropes,' laughed Eddy. 'No real harm done.'

'Was Declan in on time?'

'Yes, indeed he was. He's been serving behind the counter all morning.'

'Good. I don't want him lazing about this summer, even if he does deserve a rest after his exams.'

'Marion, don't worry about him,' said Eddy. 'He's fine.'

'Well, he told me that his degree is getting tougher by the day. He might drop out, or something, and settle for working in the family business.'

'If he wants to do that, sweetheart, we'll have to let him, okay?'

'No, no. He's going to be a doctor, definitely.'

'It's very hard work, Marion, to qualify in medicine. Would it be so bad if he worked for me? He could manage the restaurant section? A little bit of independence for him?'

'Listen, Eddy. All medical students consider dropping out from time to time. His tutors assured me he's got what it takes. Otherwise, I wouldn't push him.'

'Well, then. What's the problem?'

'You know what the problem is. He might . . . be like . . .'

'His father?'

'I'm sorry, Eddy.' She put her arms around his waist, and kissed his cheek; then leaned her head against the warm tweed of his jacket. 'I can't help worrying about him. I wish he was your son.'

'He is my son, pet. I've always thought of him as mine.'

'I love you, Eddy. I love you so much.'

'I know, darling, and I love you.'

'Are you glad we got married, Eddy?'

'Of course I am. I couldn't live without you, Marion. We've had a wonderful twenty years together since then. What's brought all this on? Have you seen Hogan?'

'No, I haven't. Honestly. It's just that I worry about Declan, he's restless.'

'All young lads are restless. It's their hormones.'

'I wish he'd settle down with a nice girl. The phone never stops ringing for him.'

'So that's it? You think he's going to be a heart-breaker?'

'Maybe. He's far too good-looking. Even with those awful clothes he wears.'

'Come on, darling,' said Eddy, laughing. 'He'll grow out of it. And he'll grow out of it a lot sooner if we pretend we aren't bothered either way. Young people are only looking for a reaction, most of the time. Let's put the kettle on. I'm gasping for a cuppa. Everything is going to be okay.'

'Promise me?'

'I promise,' he said.

Marion kissed him tenderly, then went to put the kettle on, her heart already feeling lighter.

7. Fantasies are Free

Shirley's daydream was always the same, perfected over recent months to a crystal-clear picture. She could begin to spin the reel in her head whenever she was bored, which was most of the time, if she was honest.

They would meet in the ballroom, in a dark corner, preferably. Yes, a dark, quiet corner; far away from the indignity of the plastic trees and the cigarette machine. He would be on his own, maybe on his way to the bar? Certainly not standing with a crowd of other boys. And she would have just come in with Kate. Her hair would be immaculately trimmed and wonderfully shiny, blow-dried poker-straight, and lightly waxed, the way the hair-dresser always did it. Kate would be busy checking in the coats, or talking to Alex at the foyer doors.

There they would be, Shirley and Declan. Together at last. She would be perfectly relaxed and confident. Yet still retaining an air of elegant mystery. He would smile shyly, pleased they had met. They would stand quite close to one another. He would admire her outfit, a beautiful gold and red brocade evening coat worn over black flared slacks, and an Art Nouveau bracelet with pewter fairies on it. *And* a fistful of silver rings set with semi-precious stones. A lock of her hair would fall into her eyes, and he would reach out, tenderly, and put it back. And then he would smile, because the huge gulf between them would have suddenly diminished. She would say something bright and breezy, something casual. 'Hello, there!' But he would know instinctively that she really liked him; more than liked him. And he wouldn't be worried that he was getting himself involved with a limpet-girl. He would be flattered and delighted that a lovely girl like Shirley Winters wanted to get to know him better. And of course, he would fancy her, too. He would have to close his eyes with the sheer strain of stopping himself from falling on her and tearing the brocade coat off her pale and tender shoulders, like a vampire seducing a willing virgin in a Hammer horror film.

She would like him to do that, of course, but he would wait. He was a gentleman. He would savour this time before any intimacy took place, because afterwards there would be no going back. They would be a couple for life. The gods would make sure of it. For the moment, they would begin their courtship in the usual way; they would dance.

What would they dance to? A selection of songs appeared in Shirley's head; a romantic jukebox of the mind. Japan would be the band. There was nothing to match their mixture of bitter-sweet longing. 'I Second That Emotion' would be the song. He would hold her hand, and lead her onto the floor as if they were professional dancers. They would melt into each other's arms and begin a smouldering dance together. Even the worldly Kate would be suddenly awestruck.

They would sway beautifully, still without speaking, their fingertips buzzing with chemicals, their eyes maintaining contact all the time, moving around the floor, his arm firmly around her waist, or a hand placed gently on her back, sometimes touching her face. She would be graceful and dignified; not the opinionated daydreamer she usually was. (Saying too much, too soon, and then running out of steam.) Afterwards, Kate would applaud them, then they would say goodnight to the ballroom and collect their coats, and walk along the streets of Belfast, holding hands. And there would be no one else on the streets; no drunks, hooligans, layabouts, wasters, troublemakers, clowns or losers of any description. And the streets would be clean of chips and cigarette butts and political slogans and hungry dogs. The council sweepers would have washed all the dust away, just for them. Everyone in the city would be happy for them. It was a fantasy, after all.

Where would they go? It was too common to kiss in the street, with the outline of house bricks pressing into your back. She couldn't bring him to her own tiny bedroom with its pink floral wallpaper, small single bed with a homely patchwork quilt on it, and the rickety dressing table piled high with junk jewellery, satin roses and diamanté clips in a cracked china dish. Not to mention the pop posters, which she was really too old for. The atmosphere would be all wrong, far too personal. And finally, there was her bossy mother, her nervous father, all the kitsch holy pictures from the mission stall, and the carpet that was threadbare at the top of the stairs.

His house? No. She would worry about his parents coming into the room. Wealthy people made her uneasy.

They might start talking about golf, exotic holidays or the stock market. Shirley didn't know the first thing about money. And if she had to drink tea out of expensive china cups, she'd be sure to drop hers and break it and disgrace herself.

They could go to the most lavish suite of the most expensive hotel in the city. The room would be booked already, and waiting for them, stocked up with fancy coffee and fresh flowers. Maybe that would be too intimidating? Okay, then, just an ordinary hotel; but with a friendly feeling about it? No. Still too *impersonal*.

A garden? Yes, a beautiful garden with a tall hedge all around it, full of rhododendron trees in full bloom. Shirley liked rhododendrons. The rich scent of them, and the sheer size of the flowers, made them seem somehow magical.

It would begin to rain. Suddenly. Heavily. Shirley loved rain. Rain made people scurry indoors and she had the streets all to herself. When it was raining, no young boys bothered to snigger at her lovely costume jewellery. They were far too busy trying to keep their cigarette butts dry. Shirley could just be herself, on rainy days.

Right. Back to the fantasy. Declan and Shirley, in a garden full of huge purple rhododendrons. It's raining heavily. Hollywood rain. They would have no umbrella. They would laugh about getting caught out in the downpour, and his face would be soaked, and it would suit him. He would look reckless. She would watch the raindrops trickle down the neck of his open shirt, and be sad that she could not see them running down his chest. Hand in hand, they would race across the lawn towards a niche cut into a box hedge. In some secluded part of the garden, where it was dark and quiet. And maybe there could be a statue or two, for dramatic effect?

He would press her against him, and kiss her softly. They would have their eyes open at first, and then, as they began to trust each other, they would close their eyes and give themselves up to the moment. As they fell into a hypnotic rhythm, their mouths opening and closing, he would unbutton her coat and put his hands on her back to warm them up. Where her face was numb with cold, he would kiss it with his warm lips. Slowly, ever so slowly, his hands would move around to her sides, and then rest there for a while, before resuming their gentle caresses upwards. She would touch his blond hair gently, and maybe even have a little feel of those narrow hips that moved so beautifully in charcoal coloured combats. A little rattle of thunder would be good at this point.

They were two young people. In love. So in love that wars around the globe would suddenly stop, as a mark of respect. He would find the top of the zipper of her black sweater, and kiss her again, and then . . . and then . . .

She wasn't sure what would happen then, but she was usually too exhausted with desire to even speculate. Would they kiss and talk for hours? Declan Greenwood, the one and only? And little old Shirley Winters herself? Against all the odds? A real, bona-fide romantic couple. Would it ever happen? Would she be able to cope if it did?

She had asked Kate's advice on what to do if she ever found herself in a heavily sexual situation. Kate wasn't too forthcoming on her own love life, except to say that if the two people involved were kind and considerate with each other, then the physical side of things just happened naturally. No need to worry at all. Booklets and instructions were okay on technical and health matters, but not very useful where attraction and true love were concerned. There were no reliable guidelines on those subjects. Kate always said that it was easy getting a man's interest and seducing him. The trouble was getting rid of him when you decided that the relationship did not have a future. Then, he followed you around the place with flowers and cards and pestered you with endless desperate phone calls. That was why she liked Alex Stone so much. Because he wasn't as easy to snare as the others had been. He dallied with all the girls, spoke to everyone, but spent most of his spare time working out with Jim at the Northside Gymnasium.

Shirley had her own theory about Kate choosing to remain single: she was simply too comfortable in her all-white palace of a bedroom, with clean laundry and hot meals provided by their hard-working mother. It was hard to picture Kate living in a home of her own.

And, even for Shirley, it was nice to just dream about kissing Declan Greenwood – much safer than going out into the real world and risking rejection, embarrassment and failure.

So! Declan's thumb and forefinger closed around the zip, and pulled. Shirley took a deep breath, held in her stomach and her breath, and then . . .

Beep-beep-beep-beep – the alarm clock went off: 8 a.m. End of fantasy. Shirley sat bolt upright in the single bed in her parents' house.

'Come on, Shirley, daughter,' called her mother, from

the bottom of the stairs. 'Do you want a slice of bacon before you go to work? All the hot water's gone again. That Kate one!'

8. The Dear Old Dole-ites

Kate and Shirley raced along Royal Avenue, to the government offices where they worked, reading and filing letters from the unemployed. The proper term for the office was the Department of Health and Social Services, or the DHSS. Or the 'dole'. People who were unemployed were described as being 'on the dole' or, as Kate liked to call them, 'the dear old dole-ites'. She insisted it was a term of endearment, but Shirley thought it was disrespectful. It wasn't the fault of the *dole-ites* that there weren't enough jobs to go round.

A lorry breaking down had caused traffic jams all over the south of the city.

'We're going to be late, again. Blast that bus!' grumbled Kate.

'They can't help it,' gasped Shirley, as she tried to keep up with her sister. 'What's eating you?'

'Well! That's four Saturday nights in a row that I never got to talk to Alex. Just when you think that Hollywood Hogan is safely holed up in his office, he appears behind the bar or in the foyer. How can I get close to Alex, with Hogan creeping around the place like some kind of a tiger?'

'Look on the bright side. Louise didn't get to talk to him, either.'

'Oh, don't bring up her name, Shirley.'

64

'Well, if you can't take the heat, get out of the kitchen, as they say. I told you Louise would find out.'

'I wonder who told her?'

'That Jim, I'll bet. He's stirring it, Kate.'

'Why would he bother himself?'

'I don't know. It must get pretty boring, hanging around the doors all night. Maybe they spread rumours just to pass the time?'

'Oh, no! There's Bingham going in the main door. She always checks the post table, first thing. Hurry up, Shirley! Take the other lift.'

The sisters ran straight to the post table in the main office and hid their coats in the stationery cupboard. The other staff in the section were polishing off some breakfast scones and cups of watery coffee, carried to their desks from the staff canteen.

'Old Battleaxe is on her way,' said Kate. 'Quick! Get busy. Let's see how many begging letters we have today from the dear old dole-ites. God bless their ragged little socks!'

'Kate Winters! We don't use negative words like that any more,' said the supervisor, coming into the room behind her. 'I think you'll find you mean, "Let's open today's correspondence from our valued customers."'

'Yes, Miss Bingham.'

'I hope you can develop a better attitude to those less fortunate than ourselves, Miss Winters. If you don't like your position here, you know what you can do about it. I'm sure one of the *dear old dole-ites* would be glad of it.'

'Yes, Miss Bingham.'

'Well, then. Hurry up and open the bag.'

Kate promptly loosened the string around the neck

of the sack, and emptied the huge bundle of letters onto the table. The tight-lipped clerks pulled slithering piles of envelopes towards them, opened them and began to read, sorting the letters into boxes, according to surname. Miss Bingham gave Kate a disapproving stare, and then marched on through to the Fraud department to see if anything interesting had happened on the weekend's spying operations.

Shirley opened one rather grubby letter. It was from Alex Stone.

Dear Sir,

I am shocked that you could even think I was doing the double. I declare truthfully that I was not working as a bouncer and claiming benefits at the same time. The person who informed on me must have been my ex-girlfriend; you didn't say who it was. She has been pestering me and phoning me for weeks now, so I think it was her. She is just trying to get me in trouble because we broke up. You know what women are like. They think they own you. I do not work as a bouncer in Hogan's or anywhere else. I go there a lot because I am a very sociable person. That is all.

Yours very truthfully,

Alex Stone

Shirley kept the letter in her pocket and showed it to Kate when they were having lunch. Kate was picking over a hefty portion of cod and chips, and didn't seem to realize the significance of the information.

'Are you not eating that?' said Shirley, nodding at the fat fish steak.

66

'It looked nice under the spotlights,' said Kate, absent-mindedly, 'but I've lost my appetite now.'

'Well, listen. This letter from Alex Stone – do you realize the situation he's in?'

'So what? Some jealous girl sent in a letter about him. And do you have to button that shirt right up to the neck? I'm suffocated just looking at you.'

'Kate, he's sexist. "You know what women are like."'

'Who cares? Not all women are perfect, you know. Just look at Louise Lowry. The big vicious lump!'

'You're missing the point, Kate. Again.'

'I'm not missing any point, Shirley. Half of Belfast is cheating the system. Everybody knows that. It's a low-wage economy, and a conflict-torn industrial waste-land to boot. How in God's name do you expect Alex to live on a bouncer's wages? We both live at home, don't we? We can't afford to move out and get places of our own.'

'It's not just the dishonesty.'

'Isn't it?' Kate set down her knife and fork. She felt nauseous and jittery.

'No, of course not. This is a very small city. He'll be caught.'

'Well, excuse me, Maggie Thatcher. When did you turn into a bloody Tory? You try living on the peanuts he gets at Hogan's. It's all right for them snobs in the government, with their country houses and their inherited millions. They don't know what it's like to be hungry.'

'That's not the *point*, Kate. If he'd told the truth about his situation, he'd still get something towards his rent. You know I'm no Tory, for God's sake. Everyone we know is struggling to make ends meet. But he could end up in court. They're cracking down on fraud, you know. Or have you missed this month's newsletter?'

'Who's the letter addressed to? Is Fraud really going to check this out?'

'I expect so. I have to pass it on to them today.' Shirley folded up the letter.

'Give it here, you little class-traitor,' snapped Kate. She put the letter in her pocket. 'I'll bin it later. They've little to do, so they have. Chasing poor Alex Stone, for a few measly quid!'

'You can't bin it,' said Shirley. 'It's been registered. Fraud sent him a letter in the first place, you idiot. Even if there's no reply, they'll still follow this up.'

'Oh, for heaven's sake! Right. Well, I'm glad you told me about this, Shirley. You've been a great help.'

'What are you going to do?'

'I'm going to warn him that they're on to him. That they might send someone round to check if he works in Hogan's. It will be the perfect opportunity to get to know him better.'

'I give up. You'll get into hot water if they find out. Sacked, for sure.'

'He's only getting by as best he can, Shirley, until the inheritance comes his way. This is the real world, you know. We can't all get by on daydreams and charity shop cast-offs, like you do.'

'Well, I hope you know what you're doing. Get someone else to tell him, at least, so you're not seen talking to him.'

'Ach! You're paranoid. Sure, no one will ever find out.

They're all half-dead in this godforsaken place. Any tea left in that pot? My stomach's in a right knot.'

Shirley shook her head and pushed the pot across the table.

9. Kate Gets Her Man

Louise Lowry's face was a picture. Mary was not able to console her friend, no matter how many times she told her it was all for the best. Alex Stone had his arm round Kate Winters's waist, and the two of them were talking away, their mouths going like machines. Even when Hollywood Hogan was spotted making his rounds, they went on talking. The staff all knew that Johnny Hogan had something on his mind these days; he was not as sharp with them as he usually was. Louise and Mary weren't to know, but Kate had just played her trump card, and Alex was very grateful indeed.

'You're a special kind of girl, Kate. That was very decent of you to tell me about those DHSS Nazis. No offence, now. Yes, very decent.'

'Well, Alex, I hate to see the low-paid suffer in this way. I can't just stand by and do nothing.'

'Ah, you're a great girl. You know, the humble circumstances are only temporary. I won't always be ducking and diving. No way.'

'Oh, I know, Alex. *I know*. And I won't always be stuck in that dump. It's not exactly my dream job.'

'Yeah, babe. You and me are destined for higher things.'

'Oh, I hope so, Alex. I'm tired of that place, and everybody in it.'

'So, what can I do to say thank you? Would you like to

go out for a meal sometime? Next Saturday night, maybe?'

At last, thought Kate. *At last.*

'I'd love to, Alex. Will you not be working?'

'No. I'll take a few weeks' holiday from here. There's another place I can work in till the heat's off me. Why don't you give me your phone number?'

'Well, I think I will. You won't forget, now? Will you?'

'Not at all. I won't forget.' She told him the number and he wrote it on his arm. 'Now, off you go before Johnny gets my length, that's a good girl.' And he patted her on the back.

Kate joined Shirley in the hot-food bar, where she was half-heartedly sipping a scalding coffee the colour of old tights. Kate dusted some burger-bun crumbs off a vinyl-covered chair and gently lowered her leather-covered backside onto it. She had to be very careful how she sat down sometimes, wearing skirts that were so shamefully short.

'Well,' said Shirley. 'Tell me all the gory details. Have you got a date? More importantly, have you had all your vaccinations, before you get up close and personal with that creature?'

'Give it a rest, Shirley.' Kate was in a better mood tonight than she had been for days, but she was still cautious and a little short-tempered. Her mystery symptoms might reappear at any time.

'Do you know any good vets?' Shirley laughed. 'Just in case?'

'Shut up, I said. He's going to ring me.'

'Okay. It's your life. I won't say another word about it.'

'Good. Louise Lowry is over there, watching everything.

She nearly fell over, trying to get a good gawp at us. She's fit to be tied. Oh, it feels good to be a winner. It feels good, good, good to get your man!'

'I wouldn't know.'

'I'll tell you something that'll put the fizz back in your bottle. Declan Greenwood is in the building.'

'Kate! Are you joking? Where is he?'

'At the main bar. He came in with another fella, while I was talking to Alex. He recognized me. I saw him looking at me as if he knew me. He must have seen us in Quigley's, that day. Why don't you swap that dishwater for a double vodka, and flirt with him?'

'Oh, God. I'm going to check my make-up. Wait here.'

'Hang on, don't go. Some sleazeball's coming over to us. Bloody hell, it's Kevin McGovern!'

'So it is. You wouldn't know him, out of the overalls.'

Kevin approached the table gingerly and asked the sisters if he could buy them a drink. Kate was temporarily lost for words. Kevin seemed to have had a makeover of some kind. Gone were the dull tartan shirts and grey drainpipe trousers of old. He was wearing a loose-fitting baby-pink suit, with the sleeves rolled up to the elbows, a bright blue shirt (no tie) and *white* patent shoes with Velcro straps and long pointed toes. To complete the outfit, he had (yes, it was true) a blue silk handkerchief dangling from his breast pocket. *And* a Simon Le Bon haircut, with blond highlights and a feathered fringe. What had happened to his flat brown hair?

'My God,' said Kate. 'Is it really you?'

'In the flesh,' said Kevin proudly. 'What do you think of the new threads?'

'Unbelievable,' said Kate.

'Thanks,' he said. He was delighted with himself. 'A drink?'

'Ah, ah, coffee? Maybe another coffee?' Shirley stammered. She was more than a little overwhelmed by Kevin's outfit. Even though *she* was wearing an antique, knee-length dress covered with black sequins, along with red tights and black suede ankle boots. And four bracelets she had made herself, from plaster of Paris and plastic gemstones.

'We'd like vodka, please. No ice. We'll split a cola.' Kate smiled up at Kevin, and elbowed Shirley in the side. 'We'll get a seat near the dance floor, while you're away.'

'Sure,' he said. 'I'll be right back.'

He hurried to the bar with a great sense of purpose. This was a superb development in his relationship with the lovely Kate, and worth the terrible teasing his brothers had given him for the new hairdo. But he had been friendly with Kate for a couple of years now, to no effect, so he had decided to up the ante slightly. And he had asked a very stylish shop assistant in London to give him some fashion advice. And the assistant had sold him a pink suit and told him to get his hair done. All the girls love a poser. Those were his exact words.

While he was waiting for the barman to assemble the drinks on a little tray, Kevin pulled a couple of strands of his gelled hair down over his eyes. Girls seemed to go for that kind of thing, he'd noticed. The 'pretty boy' look, it was called. Well, if it helped him to get a woman, he'd be as pretty as he could. Meanwhile, Kate and Shirley made themselves comfortable at a new table. Kate was hoping Alex might notice them and feel jealous. But not

73

so jealous that he might land over and hit Kevin. She hoped Kevin could handle himself in a fight. She supposed he must be stronger than he looked, what with all the mechanic-type things he did all day in the garage.

'Well, you've landed on your feet, you jammy thing!' said Shirley. 'He's mad keen on you, and you never even made an effort to be nice to him. What's your secret, Kate?'

'I'm gorgeous.'

'And modest with it.'

'No, it's because I'm gorgeous. Men are very basic creatures, I told you that before.'

'You'd better not be thinking of using him to get Alex's attention. Are you? Kate?'

'As if I would.' But she had the decency to blush.

'He's coming back. Be nice to him, won't you? He's okay,' Shirley whispered as Kevin sat down at the table, and set the drinks gently before the girls.

He had treated them to a cola apiece, and the vodkas were doubles. He'd even asked the barman to give him pretty glasses and slices of lemon. He smiled broadly at both girls before lifting a pint of ice-cold lager to his lips. They all smiled at each other. This was very cosy indeed. And to think the lads at the bar said no woman would be seen dead with him in a pink suit. In fact, they'd put money on it. And here he was, with two women, no less. Both of them stunning. What a result! Those pop-star guys on the television knew what they were doing, all right.

Shirley saw Alex and Jim watching them intently. The two bouncers stared from their place along the back wall, intrigued that Kate was being romanced by another man.

Kate was worried. She knew that if Kevin so much as brushed past another male on the dance floor, Alex would have him out of the door in a heartbeat; accused of disorderly behaviour. The bouncers in Hogan's had a lot of power. She decided not to dance with Kevin, if he offered. No need to upset Alex unnecessarily. She'd have to talk to the new improved Kevin, instead. And make it look as if they were just friends, sharing a friendly drink.

'So, tell me, Kevin, do you think we are all still influenced by the moon?' Kate asked. She was beginning to feel giddy. Maybe it was because she feared another meaningful request from Louise Lowry.

'I'm sorry?' Kevin leaned across the table, both to hear Kate, and to be closer to her magnificent cleavage. It was very hard for him to concentrate in the presence of such flawless beauty. He dabbed the perspiration off his forehead with a pink cuff.

'Never mind my sister, Kevin. She's had one too many vodkas, I'm afraid.'

'Oh, Shirley, I haven't! You're making me out to be an alcoholic! I've only had five or six drinks. That's nothing!'

'You're looking absolutely beautiful tonight, Kate. I really like your hair. It's very shiny.' Kevin was on a roll, and didn't want a sisterly row to get in the way.

'I've just had it trimmed.'

'It's lovely.'

'Thank you very much for the compliment, Kevin. You're not looking too bad yourself! I love the suit.'

'Really?' Kevin was delighted. 'I bought it in London.'

'Did you? What were you doing there?'

'I was taking my mother to get her veins done, privately.'

'Lovely. They've great clinics in London. How's the garage?'

'Going great, yeah. I'm snowed under with work. I might even take on an apprentice or two. I haven't bothered in the past – it's easier to do things yourself than to show somebody else.'

'I know what you mean,' giggled Kate. Shirley rolled her eyes.

'Would you like to dance, Kate?' Kevin stood up, and offered his arm to Kate, in a gesture that wouldn't have been out of place at a royal gala.

'Ah, I've a dodgy knee, Kevin. I banged it on a filing cabinet at work.'

'Oh, dear. I'm sorry to hear that.' He sat down again and began to twiddle the blue silk handkerchief between his muscular fingers.

'Shirley will dance with you. Won't you, Shirley?' Shirley choked on her drink and shook her head violently. She never danced until she was well oiled. Kate kicked her sister's foot, under the table, and nodded towards the watching bouncers. 'On you go, the pair of you. I'll mind the drinks.'

Kevin stood up again, and Shirley had no choice but to get up as well and follow him out to the dance floor. The current song was dying away. She prayed that DJ Toni could find something halfway decent in his eclectic record collection. It took her a while to recognize the song: 'The Land of Make Believe' by Buck's Fizz.

The DJ turned the volume down to make an announcement.

'A great little tune. Buck's Fizz. That's the name of a drink, you know. Champagne and orange, if I'm not mistaken. Six years since this classic was in the charts, ladies and gentlemen. Six years! Where does the time go, I ask you?' He turned up the music, then, even louder than before, and all hope of conversation was extinguished.

Kate drank her vodka, and Shirley's too. She felt moved by the song, with its sugary sentiments, and felt a longing for someone or something that she could not explain. She realized with horror that she was beginning to doubt herself. She was falling prey to Shirley's bad habit of thinking too much. What was she *doing* in this concrete ballroom, anyway? Did she like Alex enough to kiss him? To marry him? Was that a mild trembling she felt in her hands? Not again! She must get to a mirror. She reached for her bag and stood up too quickly, and the alcohol made her feel dizzy. She walked to the ladies' room with as much dignity as she could muster, and drew some comfort from its draughty chill. She went into one of the cubicles and locked the door. A weird feeling passed over her, like she was not standing in the cubicle any more, but was actually hovering just above herself. She closed the lid and sat down. Her hands shook so much she could not even manage to tear off a piece of toilet paper to dab her face with. Just then, Louise Lowry and Mary came bursting into the room. Kate held her breath behind the wooden door as she heard the girls talking by the sinks.

'It'll never last, Louise. Mark my words.'

'It might last. She's a nasty piece of work. He'll be like putty in her hands.'

'No. He'll be fed up with her in no time. Anyway, how do you know he asked her out? They were only talking for a few minutes.'

'Because I saw the look on her face, that's why. She'll be gloating over this for fifty years. I'll have to emigrate.'

'Oh, let it go, Louise! For heaven's sake! Look, I'll tell you something for nothing: he's just a boring, butch, body-building bouncer. He doesn't know his own strength – he'd crush you in the bed! Let Kate Winters have the big lug, and consider yourself lucky. I can't believe you, of all people, would be this pathetic.'

'Mary!'

'All the gold watches and fancy jewellery in the world wouldn't get me near that big oaf, Louise. You must have a screw loose, even thinking about it. He's as thick as two short planks!'

'Is that what you really think? Or are you just trying to make me feel better?'

'It's what I really think.' There was a long pause as Louise considered Mary's words. Maybe she should wait until Alex had inherited his uncle's fortune, and *then* nab him. Miss out on the hungry years.

'Aye, you're right. C'mon, the night is still young. Let's get out there and see if there's any new talent in Hogan's tonight!' She sounded as if she meant it.

'That's the girl. First, we're going to the food bar for a sausage supper, and a cup of tea. I missed my dinner, earlier.'

'Okay. Sausages and tea it is.'

'And don't you dare be giving Alex the glad eye. I'm warning you: if a fight breaks out between you and Kate, you're on your own.'

'No, I'm finished with all that. Kate Winters can have him. I wonder if he'll take his weights with him on the honeymoon?'

'Aye, he will surely, and when the *lovemaking* is over, he'll go and stand in the corner all night, with his arms folded.'

'Ha, ha! Here, I'm taking this strapless bra off. It's killing me. I'm cut to the bone with it.'

'Shove it in your bag, Louise, and come on – there's a jumbo sausage in there with my name on it.'

'You're a wild woman, Mary. I like your style.'

They went out, the sounds of their cackling laughter echoing round the tiled walls of the ladies' loo. Kate was left alone in her cubicle, suddenly feeling that she had won the booby prize at the Christmas raffle. She had emerged victorious from the battle of the bosoms, and now she felt trapped. What if Shirley was right about Alex? Was he really a lying scrounger with no rich uncle at all? As if she wasn't suffering enough already, another horrible little feeling started up in her chest. Like a little bird flapping its wings, just behind her heart. She began to breathe too quickly. Should she go and talk to Kevin, and ask him to take her outside for some air? And maybe hold his hand? She would like that. But would he take hand-holding as a sign they were going out together? There was only one thing to do: escape. Escape! She went to the public telephone in the foyer and dialled for a taxi to come at once. There was one right outside Hogan's, the man in the depot told her. He'd reserve it for her. She thanked him and clattered the receiver back into its cradle and took a deep breath.

Shirley and Kevin were having a great time on the dance floor. Kevin was turning out to be a very decent dancer, and Shirley had loosened up a bit and was actually enjoying herself with him. It was very dark where they were dancing, so the crowd couldn't really see them. And Kevin was the one they were all looking at, anyway. Not many men could wear a pink suit and get away with it. Alex Stone and Sunny Jim were having a heated debate about the suit. Jim thought Kevin must be a karate expert to be so brave. He could probably disable another man with a swift dig to the windpipe. That was Jim's conclusion. Alex said Kevin was just a total airhead who was so desperate to impress the girls that he didn't realize he was going to get a right kicking on the way home. From some *normal* local men wearing jeans and denim jackets. Hopefully. The DJ was playing 'Bedsitter' by Soft Cell, and Kevin and Shirley were giving a great performance. Shoulders going in and out. Hands up in the air. Shirley had temporarily forgotten about Declan Greenwood.

Even Kevin had forgotten that he was only dancing with the sister of the woman he adored. Not Kate herself. The huge glitter-ball, the coloured spotlights, and the hastily consumed alcohol had transported the two of them away to a magical place. The song faded seamlessly into 'Say Hello Wave Goodbye', and Kevin and Shirley danced on.

'Ah, Soft Cell,' said the DJ. 'You couldn't beat them with a big stick! I wouldn't fancy Marc Almond's chances in a game of hurley, but the same lad can carry a tune, and good luck to him. Live and let live, I say. Take it away, boys!'

Kate let her mechanic-suitor and her bizarrely dressed sister have their moment in the spotlight until the song was drawing to a close. Then, she hurried into the middle of the throng of dancers swaying to the beat like a school of fish, and grabbed Shirley by the elbow. She said goodnight to a very disappointed Kevin, and steered her sister outside to the taxi rank. It was cold on the street after the warmth of the ballroom. Shirley's teeth began to chatter.

'What are you doing, Kate? We're only in the door an hour ago!'

'I need to think. Here's the cab. Quick, get in!'

'But Declan was in there somewhere.'

'So? Were you going to do anything about it?'

'No.'

'Well, then. Anyway, I feel absolutely terrible.'

Kate began to cry softly then. She sat back on the leather seat, and her glittery shoulders heaved with a loud sob. She was confused and drunk, and she didn't feel beautiful any more. Louise Lowry was laughing at her new boyfriend. And Kevin McGovern was being so nice to her, and yet she didn't fancy him at all. She fancied Alex, with his big muscles and his chain of jewellery shops. Didn't she? It was all very upsetting. She must be going mad. Her parents were both half mad, so she must be carrying two sets of faulty genes that were just waiting to kick in when she turned thirty. She'd have a breakdown! They'd put her in the asylum and study her, and she would become a legend in the city. *The mad lady with all the handbags.* The fear washed over her like a bucket of cold water. A prickling sensation started up all over her scalp, and she clung to the door handle and gave herself up to a torrent of crying. The tears flowed down her face and washed all her lovely make-up away.

Shirley was alarmed. It was worrying when Kate was not her usual know-it-all self. Shirley usually disagreed with most of the daft things Kate said, but this display of vulnerability was much worse than Kate's normally rock-solid arrogance. It must be the drink, giving her hallucinations. Kate would just have to dry out, and then she'd be okay again. She put her arms round her big sister, gave the driver their home address and told him to hurry.

'It's all right, Kate,' she said. 'We'll be home in a minute, and I'll tuck you up in bed with a nice cup of hot milk. You'll be fine, I promise. You'll be absolutely fine.'

This warmth and kindness was just the last straw for Kate, who had always played the role of Big Sister with great enthusiasm. She wept until her sobs dissolved into silence. Shirley gave her a tissue, and prayed for a swift journey home.

The taxi-driver was the same one who had brought them to Hogan's earlier. He wondered if he could risk a friendly comment. Something to make the girls laugh and ease the tension? Too many drinks was all that was wrong with the crying one. He had seen it all before. Too many strong drinks, and a crush on some unsuitable fella. But, no, there was no point in cracking a joke. She was too upset, and the other one was too worried about her to pay any attention to him. He decided to say nothing, and drove the girls home as fast as he could. When the car arrived at the sisters' house, Shirley paid him and the two of them went in the front door with their arms wrapped round each other.

10. The Return of Eugene Lolly

Eugene Lolly was a desperate man. His latest spell in prison, for assaulting an Indian shopkeeper with a tennis racket, had cost him dearly. How many convictions had he now? He had lost track. Drink-driving, careless driving, driving without insurance, driving an illegal taxi, tax-evasion, fraud, robbery, burglary, selling stolen goods, not to mention possession of an illegally held firearm in 1967. (That old chestnut always bumped up the sentence a little bit. God knows, he had paid his debt to society for the Hogan's Ballroom Fiasco: two missing fingers, and a nine-year stretch at Her Majesty's Pleasure.) He sat now in a dimly lit back-street tavern on Maple Street and thought about the Bonbon Gang days again. The judge's voice had seemed very far away, that day in court.

Eugene Lolly knew he was going to jail for a long time. Everybody knew it; even the cleaners knew it as they quietly dusted the benches in the foyer. His wife, Virginia, was pulling on her gloves long before the sentence was handed down, her face perfectly composed. He looked across at her, his old charmer smile at the ready. *Will you wait for me? Will you wait for your old jail-bird?* But she did not smile back. She was already making plans that involved lots of white emulsion paint, some fresh flowers and a FOR SALE sign. He had lost his driving licence and his taxi-business. He had lost his gun, his savings and his few remaining friends. His wife had sold their Ormeau Road home and travelled abroad with the proceeds, while he was still settling into his cell. Within six weeks of his imprisonment, she was gone for good. A couple of years later, he heard she was doing very well for herself in Spain. He thought of following her there, when he was released, and trying to recover the money, but the house had been in her name, after all. It was legally hers to sell. He had arranged it that way, so it would be harder for the tax boys to get at him. How was he to know his treacherous spouse would sell the house, and everything in it, and not give him one blessed penny? And the word was, she had bought a small pub on the coast. And moved her two brothers in as barmen and bodyguards. The three of them were as brown as chocolate, that's what he was told. Out in the sun all day, wearing sunglasses and speaking the lingo as if they were real Spanish people. As happy as pigs in muck.

The resulting rage gave him headaches for months. Without a gun, he could not demand they give him the pub in Spain. The two brothers would flatten him and laugh in his face. Without money, he could not buy another gun. Without a gun, he would not be taken seriously by his old associates. Without associates, he could not commit more crimes. It was a problem that went round and round in his head, until he was nearly sick with the worry of it. But what else could he do? There was no legitimate work available to him, apart from cleaning jobs in the local factories. And even then, he would be very lucky to be let in the door. There were plenty of better men than Eugene Lolly cleaning floors in Belfast, with the economy going into free fall because of the sectarian unrest on the streets. He had no option but to commit more crimes. Housebreaking, and taking tools and golf clubs from garden sheds. Shoplifting occasionally. Charity scams, when things got really desperate. Smaller and smaller crimes, growing more pathetic with the passing years. His hand wound still pained him from time to time, twenty years on, just to remind him of what a failure he was.

He was currently living in a hostel for the homeless, on a rate of benefit so low it was an insult to him. To stand in line at the post office, waiting to cash his unemployment cheques, brought him out in a nervous rash. It was worse than being in jail, where the men took a certain pride in their punishment. Hard men, surviving on the edge, talking to their lawyers, going to court and on rehabilitation schemes. In jail, there was a timetable, things to do. Routine, gossip, and people to talk to. Living on the dole, however, was just miserable. Plain and simple. He had nothing to do all day and no release date to look forward to. He was even beginning to miss the prison officers; at least they had chatted with him as they went about their duties. And the dinners weren't that bad, either. Very nice sausage rolls.

Now, he was just a face in the crowd. No name in the paper, no mention on the local news. The staff in the post office stamped his book without looking at his face and swiftly slid the money under the glass partition. People who could not provide for themselves were too shameful to look at, obviously. He had become anonymous, a man of no importance, and that hurt him more than anything.

The hostel was built beside a six-lane motorway and the traffic roared past him twenty-four hours a day. The shadows of the biggest lorries blocked out the light, so that even reading the newspaper became an ordeal. No one from his former life would speak to him or let him in on a deal. Failure was contagious. The Bonbon Gang were legendary losers. 'Doing a Bonbon' was still slang for messing up. On bad days, Eugene thought of going straight, but that really would be the bottom of the barrel for him.

He ordered another pint of bitter and a corned-beef sandwich. He looked at the paper again. Nothing interesting. Maybe he would take a wee walk down to the bookies or the chip shop? But then he turned a page and his heart missed a beat. There was a picture of Hollywood Hogan, large as life in his white jacket, and – wait for it – he was announcing his *retirement*. And him only forty-eight! He must be worth a mint! Eugene read the article closely. Hogan was putting the ballroom up for sale and going to live in America. He was going to spend the rest of his days running a small pub and collecting vintage cars. At the end of the piece there was a list of events planned for the ballroom; including a Disco Extravaganza, spanning four decades of pop music. Well, well, well. Eugene Lolly put on his thinking cap.

And he thought of Timothy Tate, and of Johnny Hogan, and his dear old granny, Eileen, and the ballroom on Magnolia Street. And he smiled. Three months out of prison, and Eugene Lolly was back in business. That night, he lay back on his single bed in the hostel, watching the lights of the lorries flicker across the bare walls. Timothy Tate had yet to be punished for helping the police, back in 1967. Johnny Hogan had built his career and his reputation on the humiliation of the Bonbon Gang. Years' and years' worth of protection money had been lost to Eugene, when he was locked up. The flight of Mrs Lolly, and the loss of his beloved home and furniture, stuck in his throat like a chicken bone. He would devise a plan to wreak his revenge on Johnny Hogan, and he would get Timothy Tate to help him. He would make enough money to retire on, and maybe even get himself a replacement for Mrs Lolly. Some pretty little thing who wouldn't ask too many questions. Then again, he might not bother. For everyone knew, you could never trust a woman.

It wasn't too hard to find out where Timothy Tate lived nowadays. He had a job. A regular job. Caretaker of a gym, out by the M2 motorway. Live-in, it was. Timothy had found religion, too. He was a member of the local church, and never missed a service. He had kept his nose clean all these years. A real reformed character. The police would not be keeping an eye on him any more. Eugene decided to pay him a visit.

Timothy was mopping the floor when he saw Eugene standing in the doorway of the Northside Gymnasium. He looked away at once and resumed his mopping, hoping that his eyes had played a trick on him. Just because the man was short and menacing did not mean it was Lolly. But it was, and when he turned around and faced the door, Eugene was still there. He came in, and sat on the edge of the boxing ring.

'Haven't seen you in a month of Sundays,' he said.

'How've you been, Eugene?' Timothy was playing it cool.

'I've been better.' Eugene was playing it cool, also.

'You were inside, again?'

'Long time. I'm out now.'

'Well, that's great news, of course. Any jobs lined up?'

'You mean, proper jobs?'

'Yes.'

'What? Like you? Cleaning floors? That's not my style, Tim.'

'Honest work is its own reward.'

'Oh, Tim. What did they do to you?'

'I'm happy now, Eugene. I can sleep at night. I have a little flat, and a bicycle, and lots of friends here in the gym. It's not so bad.'

'How nice.'

'I don't know why you've come here, today. But if you're planning something, then leave me out of it.'

'I have a plan, as it happens. And you do figure in it. Quite a lot.'

'No. I won't tell on you, Eugene, but I'm not getting involved.'

'You owe me, Tim.'

'We were friends a long time ago. That's all behind me, now.'

'I got three years extra, inside. Because of what you told them. Jobs they didn't even know about. You told them everything.'

'You were going to shoot Hogan. I couldn't go along with that.'

'I wasn't going to hurt him. The tough talk was only for show.'

'I saw your face. You were going to do it. We could have been up for murder.'

'You never were much of a gangster.'

'I know. Is it money you want? I haven't any.'

'I want money, all right. But I want a lot more than a cleaner's wages.'

'You're not going to rob the gym?'

'Would it be worth my while?'

'No. They're behind with the bills, as it is.' There was a series of charity bouts coming up and some money would be coming in, but Timothy wisely decided to say nothing about them.

'I thought so.'

'Well, then, what?'

'I'm going to rob Hogan's place.'

'But that was a disaster last time! The two of us were taken out of it on stretchers. We were a laughing-stock. We still are, Eugene. The Bonbon Gang, and all that.'

'It's time the laughing stopped,' said Eugene quietly.

'How do you know he has any money?'

'Are you joking? After all these years? He must have millions. The lazy sod is retiring, and he's only forty-eight.'

'Eugene, Eugene, have you not tired of all this? Have you not learned your lesson, after all the time you spent incarcerated?'

'All I've learned is this: I'm finished with small-time stuff. Everything I had in the world is gone. Everything I worked hard for.'

'With respect, Eugene, most of it was not earned morally. Look on this as a fresh start. It's never too late to turn to the light. God is always there –'

'Don't start with all that holy rubbish. That's exactly what I am doing: a fresh start. A fortune I'll get from that fool, Hogan, in his ridiculous white jacket. I'm getting out of Belfast, permanently.'

'Where are you going?'

'You don't need to know. Somewhere warm, I'll tell you that. I won't need an overcoat, where I'm going.'

'I want no part of it. I'm sorry.'

'I need a look-out, some back-up muscle and an alibi.'

'I can't help you. I can't even run very fast, with my leg the way it is.' Timothy dipped the mop in the bucket, and swirled it round thoughtfully in the hot water. The smell of disinfectant wafted up to Eugene's nostrils. He flinched. It reminded him of prison.

'You owe me,' he said again. 'One last job. For old times' sake.'

Timothy didn't answer him. He didn't say yes or no. He would wait and see how things turned out. Maybe the plan would die a natural death. Eugene didn't have a weapon, he knew that much, although he could always pretend he had one. The old pointed-finger-in-the-pocket routine. They'd done that quite a few times in the past.

'I'll be in touch,' said Eugene. 'Few weeks from now. There'll be a few quid in it for you. You can donate your share to this dump, if you like.' He walked out as slowly as he had come in.

11. A Date with Destiny

Kate had no idea why she was going on a date with Alex Stone. The lust that had consumed her for months seemed to have disappeared without trace, and she simply could not understand it. She'd been to the doctor for a list of tests, and there was nothing wrong with her. Her blood count, thyroid, and sugar levels had been tested. Everything was fine. The advice was to get plenty of sleep, eat well and relax more.

'Shirley,' she said, as her sister passed the bedroom door, wearing spider's-web tights, an ankle-length skirt and a purple mohair sweater. 'Will you do me a favour? Will you tell Alex, when he comes to the door, that I have a headache, and I've gone to bed?'

'Sure, I will. Poor you! Will I tell him you'll see him another time?'

'I haven't really got a headache, you stupid lump! I have simply changed my mind about the man.'

'About time you saw sense. Why don't you just ask him to step into the hall and tell him the truth tonight? It's only fair.'

'Oh! How did I get myself into this mess? It was okay talking to him when he was up against the wall in Hogan's, when I could get away from him. But if he's walking around the place freely, there's going to be no escape.' The doorbell rang just then, with a little wobble. The battery was running low. Kate flinched. 'Wouldn't you know it! He's bang on time, the old slug! They always are, when you don't want them.' The two sisters looked at each other. Kate put her hand to her throat.

'Look, go for the meal,' advised Shirley, 'and let him down gently. Just talk about general things, and keep the mood light.'

'I suppose I'll have to. What if he gets frisky?'

'You'll be fine, Kate. After all, this is a first date. He can hardly think he's going to get any more than a quick kiss goodnight anyway.'

Kate blushed. Memories of other first dates flickered across her consciousness.

'Why am I so worried? This is not like me at all, Shirley. I could always handle myself, before. Am I getting old? Losing my touch?'

'I told you he was wrong for you, but you wouldn't listen.'

Listen to Shirley! Well, that was the absolute limit! Anger temporarily took over. 'Oh, shut up! What do you know about men? Let me past. I'm going to sort this mess out. And by the way, that outfit should carry a government health warning.'

'Suit yourself, *Bigmouth*,' snapped Shirley, and she went into her tiny bedroom and banged the door. Her fabulous tights and sweater were the height of fashion. Kate was just jealous of them, she decided. They were the first new things she had bought in years. There was just no pleasing some people. She lay on the bed, debating whether to read a book, listen to a record, or dream about Declan. She decided to do all three, and let Kate sort out her complicated love life on her own.

Kate went down the stairs with a heavy heart. Alex was waving in at her through the patterned glass at the side of the front door. Kate hated him for doing that. It was intrusive, to say the least. And he looked awful. Seen through the lumpy glass, it was as if he had fourteen eyes. She opened the door, and he stepped right into the hall, forcing Kate to take two steps backwards. She had intended telling him the date was cancelled, there and then, but he was already peering into the sitting room.

'Will I say hello to your parents, before we go?'

'No, no. They're watching television. We'll just nip out, quietly.'

But he was already in the front room, somehow, and shaking hands with her father and telling her mother she was only a 'young bit of a thing'. He took up all the space in the tiny room, with his big, broad shoulders.

'God, but that's a terrific fire you have there, missus,' he said, rubbing his hands before it. 'A great set-up, altogether! Alex Stone, at your service.' Laying it on like a player in some small-town third-rate theatrical production.

Mr and Mrs Winters beamed up at him, from their cosy sofa.

'Will you take a cup of tea, Alex?' said Kate's mother.

'I thought you'd never ask,' he practically roared, so enthusiastic was he. 'I'm as dry as the Sahara desert.'

Mrs Winters heaved herself to the edge of the chair, and attempted to get up off her nest of cushions, although it wasn't easy with Alex's great bulk towering over her. Kate was absolutely livid. Really, he was going on like they were engaged to be married. How dare he make himself at home like this! On a first date!

'There'll be no time for the tea-drinking,' she said, becoming a reluctant actor in this bizarre domestic theatre. 'We're off to a fancy restaurant, the two of us. Come on!' She put on her coat, a plain one that buttoned right up to the neck, and she selected a long umbrella for self-defence, from the hallstand. She would just have to break his heart over the chicken in white-wine sauce, instead.

'Come on,' she said again. 'Look lively! I could eat the leg clean off a wild horse.' Deliberately being crude and unladylike. She was determined to make sure the evening was a dismal failure.

They walked to the restaurant. Alex's car was broken down again, he explained. That figures, thought Kate, sadly. He probably hasn't even got a car, she suspected. Kevin McGovern would never have a broken-down car, she thought suddenly. Kevin was a mechanic with his own business. The thought of Kevin, driving along in his well-maintained car, cheered Kate up immensely. Alex saw her smiling and was pleased. They reached their destination in good spirits. Alex had chosen an Indian restaurant, which Kate thought was inconsiderate of him. He should have consulted her, first, before booking the table. Some people didn't like spicy food. (Or busy wallpaper.) A candle-lit French or Italian place would have been much more romantic. There were no other diners in the room. It was too early in the evening, probably. Alex ordered the hottest curry on the menu, lots of side dishes, two glasses of milk and two bottles of lager for himself. Then he asked Kate what she wanted.

'You can have anything you want,' he said. 'As long as it doesn't come to more than a fiver! Only joking!'

Kate smiled weakly. She ordered a vodka and cola, and a mild chicken curry with boiled rice. Then she changed her order to fried rice. And chips.

When they were left alone with their meal, Kate expected an awkward silence to engulf them. But Alex told her a very long and complicated tale about a body-building competition that he had once taken part in. And how he didn't win it because the whole thing was fixed. Kate had to cover her mouth with a slice of naan bread when she was unable to stifle a yawn. At one stage, he jabbed his fork into her plate and made off with seven fat chips that she had been saving for the end of the meal. In revenge, Kate called the waiter over, and asked for another drink. A double.

At no point did he ask her anything about herself, unless it was a question about her work. Did they get a bonus if they could think of a way to disallow a payment, for instance? (No.) Had anyone in the place ever been beaten up by a claimant? (No.) He laughed out loud when she told him that a clinically depressed gentleman had once arrived to sign on, in a drunken state and brandishing an antique sword. Was he arrested, Alex wanted to know. He was let off with a warning, Kate said. (Most likely, he had a few mates down the station.) And then, the narrow counter was swapped for one that was six foot wide, to give the staff some protection. Or at least, a head start.

'Ha! The yellow sissies!' he laughed, and drank a pint of milk in one go.

Alex burped right into her face as they stood at the cash desk to pay. He looked at Kate when the bill was presented to him on a little saucer full of mint imperials, but Kate kept her hands in her pockets and looked away. It was still only early in the evening. By right, she should have thanked him for the meal, and they should have parted as friends. After all, no formal announcement had been made that they were on a date. This meal was just to say thank you for the tip-off about the Fraud Squad. Right? Shirley would have been proud of her, if she had done that.

However, it was to Kate's eternal shame that she went straight home with Alex Stone to his miserable little flat. For a drink. And a nose around, if she was honest. If there was one thing that Kate loved as much as her hand-bags, it was having a good snoop around other people's houses. And she wanted to test herself; to see if she could be alone with a man and not start that awful trembling again. She might as well test the water with someone she didn't care about any more. She gripped her umbrella tightly, and went bravely up the creaking stairs of the dingy house on the Cromwell Road. Alex showed her round the place. It didn't take long. His bedroom was a terrible disappointment. A rather sad little bed, propped up on a brick at one corner, with only a very thin and faded quilt on the top of it. She began to feel a bit sorry for him. It was no picnic, living like this. Any available floor space was taken up with several large pieces of exercise equipment. Everything was covered in dust. There were sheets pinned over the windows with drawing pins, in place of curtains. Nothing nice anywhere. Somehow, Kate had pictured a Comfort-Zone boudoir of sheepskin rugs, zebra-print footstools and a well-stocked drinks trolley. Kitsch, but comfortable. Like Alex himself. Then she remembered, sadly, that he *was* actually unemployed. Any money he made in Hogan's must have been spent on the exercise equipment. And red-hot curries.

'It's very nice,' she lied, and they went into the living room.

Alex fetched a couple of cans of lager from the fridge and handed Kate one, without the benefit of a clean glass. He switched on the television, which was resting on a milk-bottle crate.

Kate took a sip and told herself she was a modern girl; that she did not like Alex enough to see him again, but that he did have fabulous hair and lovely muscles and surely she was entitled to one night of passion, to compensate for such a disappointing meal? She was on the pill, and not really getting the benefit of it. It was three months since her last romance. So! Alex was good-looking and available. Maybe she'd have a cuddle on the sofa, at least?

Soon, Kate was shivering to keep warm and glad she'd kept her coat on. It actually seemed to be colder inside the building than outside. There were no radiators in the flat. They finished their drinks, and then, with the empty can still in his hand, Alex leaned across to Kate and kissed her. It was an average kiss. No fireworks. A strong taste of vindaloo. Just as she was deciding whether to kiss him back or not, he asked her if she would like to see him in his competition briefs. Designer briefs from America, they were. Brand new. Kate was so shocked, she said yes.

Alex said he would just freshen up first. He went into the bathroom and switched on the shower. Kate began to think this night might not be so bad after all. She switched off the overhead lights in the flat as the sight of Alex's many pieces of training equipment was a bit of a passion-killer. Not to mention all the posters of his body-building heroes, which were Blu-tacked to the grey-painted woodchip. Kate couldn't bear the way all their veins bulged, as if they might pop at any moment.

She waited in the gloom for him to return. The minutes ticked by. Suddenly, he began to sing – 'The Final Countdown'. Which band, she couldn't say. They all sounded the same to her. Bon Jovi, was it? No. Europe, that was it. After a few more minutes, Kate knocked gently on the door.

'Are you going to be long in there?' she trilled, like some sort of girl-guide leader. She wanted to go to the loo herself.

'No, you're all right,' he replied. 'Be with you directly.'

'It's cold in the sitting room,' she ventured.

'What? There's an electric fire. You can switch it on, if you like. One bar, mind.'

'Gee, thanks, big spender!'

She stomped across the room to look for the switch. She approached the fire and bent over to turn it on, and froze when she saw six tiny black eyes peering at her from the grate. Mice. Three very cold little mice. They didn't even move when she jumped with fright and then whimpered a little bit.

'Alex! Alex! There're mice in here, and they're not even running away from me!'

'Don't worry about them!' he called. 'They're tame! They're only looking for a crumb.' And he resumed his singing.

'What the hell are you doing in there?' she shouted.

99

'You've been ages and ages. I'm bloody freezing, and there're mice in the fireplace.'

'For God's sake, will you hold your horses! I'm going as fast as I can. This oil is hard to apply, when you've just had a shower.'

But Kate had given up. Her heart was not really in this, anyway. And now, the moment was gone for ever. If he thought she was going to wait for him, like some kind of slave, while he pampered himself in there . . . And they weren't even on an official date. What must he think of her? A one-night stand? Suddenly, the thought of Alex Stone in his competition briefs scared the hell out of Kate Winters. She had to get out immediately. On her way, she left him a little gift.

'Sod the inheritance,' she said to the mice. 'I'm getting out of here, and if you'd any sense, you'd do the same.' She fled down the dingy stairs when she heard the bathroom door opening. She had left the little present under the quilt for Alex, when he did finally manage to drag himself away from the bathroom mirror.

Alex marched into the sitting room and struck up his best pose but Kate was not there to appreciate his biceps. She was not in the kitchen either. He realized she must be waiting for him in the bedroom. What a girl! He stood at the door of his darkened boudoir, wearing only several handfuls of body oil and a black satin posing pouch with fake diamonds on it. He twanged the elastic on his minuscule knickers, suggestively.

'I hope you've had your blood pressure taken recently,' he said, and he took a run at the bed, and leapt into the air. 'Paradise, here we come!'

Unfortunately, the slender bundle beneath the quilt was not the eager warm body of Kate Winters, but a small pile of stainless-steel hand-weights. And they were very cold and very hard. Luckily, Alex's handsome face landed on the pillow and was not marked in any way but he bruised his rhinestone pelvis quite badly.

'Ungrateful witch!' he yelled, as he rubbed his tender skin, and felt for the light switch. 'Ungrateful, bloody witch! Of all the mad, stupid, mad, crazy . . .' But he couldn't think of anything to say as the pain went right through him like a spear. Two of the diamonds had fallen off, as well. Fifty pounds down the drain: his best competition briefs were ruined.

12. Old Battleaxe Strikes Again

Kate was very subdued for a few days after that. She didn't go to Hogan's the following Saturday night. She didn't even go shopping for handbags on the Sunday, which led her parents to speculate that she might be catching a cold. It was the beginning of September, after all. Kate was normally a big devotee of the recently introduced Sunday shopping.

Mrs Winters made a big pot of chicken soup, and turned up the central heating. Her father bought some vitamin C tablets for the whole family, and left them on the kitchen window sill, so that nobody would forget to take one each morning. Shirley noticed that Kate's hands were a little bit unsteady, on Sunday evening, when she was buttering a slice of toast. She was filled with horror that Kate might be developing a drink problem. Shirley didn't say anything at the time, but she decided to try and reduce Kate's drinking opportunities. And that meant not going to Hogan's for a while, even if Declan Greenwood might be there. If Kate fancied a night out, Shirley would suggest they go to the cinema instead.

Monday morning arrived, and brought with it the Back-to-Work blues. Kate and Shirley sat on the bus in silence, each lost in her own thoughts. Shirley was daydreaming about Declan and wondering whether or not she should splash out on a new winter coat with fake-fur trim. There was a gorgeous one in Top Shop. Kate herself was also in a deep reverie. She was feeling very strange these days, as if she had lost her way somehow. The incident in Alex's flat had pulled the carpet out from underneath her, emotionally. She'd felt suffocated in that cold little sitting room with the mice and the dust and the body-building posters. Even the thought of Alex's beautiful body could not make her relax enough to spend another minute in the place.

There was a note on her desk, telling her to come right away to Miss Bingham's office. For the first time in ten years, she would not be opening the daily post from the dear old dole-ites. She made her way down the corridor, knocked nervously on Miss Bingham's door and went in. The supervisor was sitting behind her pristine desk, with her arms tightly folded. Kate noticed again that Miss Bingham had not personalized her office in any way. There were no family photographs or plants in the little room. Just one pot of very sharp pencils.

'Take a seat,' Miss Bingham said, and she slipped a red folder out of her top drawer. She shuffled through a few papers, stretching out the moments of tension. Then, she looked at Kate for a few further seconds before she spoke.

'I'm sure you know why you have been summoned here today.'

'Have I been promoted?' Kate asked, with a broad smile. 'Oh, goody!'

'You have *not* been promoted. Certainly not.' The older woman snorted a blast of air down her nose, like a race-horse on a cold day at Ascot.

'Well, then I'm afraid I'm at a loss.'

'There's no point trying to deny it, Miss Winters.'

'I'm sorry?'

'You alerted Mr Alex Stone to the fact that he was under observation by this department. A serious breach of —'

'Was he alerted? It wasn't me, honestly. I don't know where you got this information. Sure, he knew we were on to him, when he got the letter asking if he was working in Hogan's.'

'You were seen talking to him.'

'Where was I seen?'

'You know where. In Hogan's ballroom. You spoke to him for ten minutes. You were photographed.'

'Hell's bells! Is nothing sacred, any more?'

'Please don't use language like that in my office.' Miss Bingham was enjoying this interview immensely, and she wanted to make it last as long as possible. Before she told Miss Winters that her position here was at an end.

'Okay, I'm sorry. Look, I was talking to him, that's all. I didn't tell him anything about the investigation. It was just a casual, social chat.'

'We were already observing him, as it happens. He's done this kind of thing before, you see. We've been watching him for some time.' She puffed up with civic pride.

'I see, Miss Bingham. Listen, I'll contact him and make arrangements for him to pay back the amount he owes.'

'It's too late for that. He'll be summoned to appear in court.'

'Oh.' Kate felt sorry for Alex, now. But not too sorry, remembering his antics on the night she went back to his flat. 'I'm sure he was pretty desperate for money, to do what he did. And he doesn't have many qualifications. And he is a very good doorman.'

'He could get a full-time labouring job; there are plenty available. And still work as a doorman in the evenings, if he really wants to hang around such degenerate places. That is not my problem. Fraud are in control of that case, now. You, on the other hand, are in some considerable trouble, yourself.'

'Me?'

'You passed on confidential information to Mr Stone.'

'I did not.'

'I found the letter in your desk. It should have been filed in his case folder.'

'That doesn't prove I told him anything.' But her face was suddenly as red as a red-hot chilli pepper.

'I'm sorry, but a decision has already been made.'

'What decision?'

'Regarding your employment status.'

'I'll go to a tribunal. I will. This is just discrimination. You just don't like me because I'm young and a free spirit.' Somewhere, in the back of her mind, Kate knew what was coming. A song from the ballroom came back to her, suddenly: 'Damned Don't Cry' by Visage.

'Now, really. This is a serious situation. Talking to Mr Stone was only one thing on a long list.'

'What do you mean?' Kate's heart seemed to turn right over. She could feel the arteries and veins straining to hold it in place.

'Poor time-keeping, taking and making personal calls, a negative attitude to the customers, eating and drinking at your desk, lack of respect for senior management, not to mention careless filing, and playing tasteless practical jokes which contravene health and safety regulations.'

'What! Those things are not serious! Everybody in the building does things like that.'

'Oh, please! Stop trying to bring innocent people into this.'

'They do. They all do. We've drunk tea and coffee at our desks for years. Come on, now! It's not a high-tech lab we're working in.'

'We have very high standards here. You just don't make the grade for the civil service, I'm afraid.'

'The civil service is full of people who couldn't hack it in the private sector. We're very sensitive and delicate types. Except for you, of course, Miss Bingham.'

'How dare you!' Miss Bingham stood up, snorted air out through her nose again, and then sat down. 'You cheeky little – Oh, I won't say it!'

'No, you don't understand. I meant that as a compliment. That you're tough. You know? Tough as old boots! Oh, no; I didn't mean that the way it sounded.'

'Miss Winters, I regret to inform you that your position here has been terminated.'

'What? I thought I was getting a written warning, or something. You're sacking me?'

'Indeed, I am. How dare you slander the civil service!'

'All I did was state a true fact.'

'There are no slackers here. Besides yourself.'

'You've no compassion at all. Poor Mrs Kelly was in tears last week. Did you know that?'

'What rubbish!'

'It's true! Twenty-eight letters she had to send to one claimant, to recover a four-pound over-payment, because you wouldn't let it go. If you were a decent boss, you'd be nice to your staff, instead of prowling round the desks like a starving panther, picking off the weak and the vulnerable.'

'This interview is concluded.'

'Alex Stone calls this building Gestapo HQ. Put that in your secret file.' She called Miss Bingham a witch under her breath, too, but the outraged supervisor heard her.

'You may leave right away.'

'Is there no way to appeal this? What about my human rights? My loss of dignity?'

'Leave this building now, before I lose my temper. Go on, off you go. I thought you hated it here. What's your problem?'

'I will go, and gladly. I never liked you, if you want to know the truth.' There was the trembling. Check. And the palpitations. Check.

'Goodbye, Miss Winters. Don't bother to clear your paperwork.'

'I never liked this job. It's boring. I'm overqualified to be a clerk.'

'Goodbye, Miss Winters.'

'I've got ten O Levels, you know. You're just a horrible, hateful old witch! How many O Levels have you got? Or didn't they do exams in the Middle Ages?'

'Get up!'

But Kate couldn't get up. She felt dizzy. Her legs had turned to jelly. Even her feet were shaking now. She staggered to her feet, wobbled forward for a couple of steps and then tried to sit down again. But Miss Bingham had her by the elbow and was pushing her out of the door and into the corridor. She summoned a colleague from across the hall and told her to fetch Shirley Winters, as soon as possible, please. A white-faced Kate was helped into her coat, and escorted by a security guard to the front door, where he gently removed her security pass. He felt awful having to do it, but orders were orders. That old Bingham woman had no feelings, he knew. He smiled sympathetically at Kate to show her he was not enjoying his task. The sight of a friendly face helped Kate to recover slightly. She stepped out of the building and took a deep breath, her face turned upwards to the morning sun. The security guard stayed with her for a couple of minutes, talking gently about the weather. They both ignored Miss Bingham, who was pacing the foyer, spoiling for another argument. Kate's breathing returned to normal. She noticed that although the trembling had also stopped, her heart was still racing. Shirley came running, then, and Miss Bingham explained the situation.

'Oh, Kate. What have you done, Kate?' Shirley tried to put an arm round Kate's shoulders, but Kate turned away and began to walk in a crooked line, down the street. Miss Bingham was thrilled to have the troublesome Kate out of her way at last. She followed the sisters for a few moments, squeezing every second from this exciting small-scale drama.

'Take her home, dear. I think she should see a doctor. She's very emotional. I'll expect you back at your desk tomorrow morning, Shirley.'

Shirley nodded.

'It's not a crime to be emotional! Old witch! You've done me a favour, do you hear me?' Kate began to cry then, and several fat tears rolled down her cheeks. 'You and your stupid rules! I'll be rich one day. Because I've got a mind of my own. And I'll use it and I'll be rich! And you can go to hell!'

Miss Bingham went back inside, having safely seen a disgruntled ex-employee off the property, and with some choice gossip to report to the other supervisors. The two sisters were left standing on the street.

'Do you want to go home, Kate?'

'Sorry about that, Shirley, old bean. I think I said a couple of things out of turn, there. God, I feel weird. I thought I was going to crack up there, for a minute or two. Took a turn of some kind.'

'Never mind. You'll be okay in a couple of days, and then you can put all this behind you. I'm sure you can get a doctor's note to say you haven't felt so well recently, and fight the dismissal. Hormone trouble, or something.'

'I need a drink, Shirley.'

'Do you think that's wise, Kate? It's only half-past nine in the morning.'

'I can't go home and tell Mum I've lost my job.'

'Come on! When have you ever cared what she said? Look, I think the drink is making you unstable. To tell you the truth, Kate, I think you might have a little problem with the old firewater. To be perfectly honest.'

'Give me strength!'

'Don't be cross with me, but have you noticed that it makes you a little bit irritable? That could be the craving.'

'I *need* a drink. I've just been sacked by the most awful woman. Talk about solidarity among the sisterhood! She didn't even give me a verbal warning. Never mind a written one. I'm having a drink. And that's final.'

'Oh, God. Well, where do you want to go? We'll have to wait somewhere, until opening time. I take it you're not going to start drinking on the street?'

'Shut up. We'll go to the Crown Bar. I want to sit in a private snug and get quietly hammered.'

'Now, Kate. Think of your poor liver. It's taken a bit of a bashing over the years.'

'Are you coming with me, or not?'

'I'll come, I suppose. To keep you out of trouble.'

'Right. Come on, then.'

The two of them linked arms, and drifted aimlessly around the shops until eleven o'clock. Kate almost bought a pearl choker, but she couldn't summon up enough enthusiasm to get her chequebook out.

'Are you sure you wouldn't like to go home and relax in a hot bubble bath, Kate, and I'll make you something nice to eat? Shepherd's pie? You know, you love my shepherd's pie.'

'Shirley, if I want to be nursed, I'll go to hospital. Now, let's hurry before all the booths are taken.'

'Okay, but I want it on record that I think this is a big mistake.'

They walked in silence through the mid-morning shoppers, towards the dark and womb-like interior of the Crown Bar. They went in through the swing doors, their eyes taking a moment to grow accustomed to the lack of light. The bar staff were removing tea-towels from the beer pumps, slicing lemons and placing ashtrays on the tables. They nodded hello to their first customers of the day. Needless to say, there were still plenty of free booths available at that early hour, and Kate gave Shirley a twenty-pound note, as she sat down wearily on a leather-covered bench.

'A couple of doubles, Shirley. That's the girl.'

Shirley looked at her watch. It was three minutes past eleven. She couldn't believe that Kate was about to go on a bender so early in the day. What the heck would the bar staff think of the pair of them? As it happened, Shirley didn't have to go to the bar, as one of the barmen came to the booth to take their order. And Kate, who was deep in the throes of self-pity, still managed to wink at him. Although, to be fair, it wasn't up to her usual standard. She delivered her order with a huge yawn. The trauma of the morning was beginning to make her feel very tired.

'Just an orange juice, for me,' said Shirley, mutinously.

Three hours later, Kate was beginning to get over her humiliation. A plate of half-eaten chicken-and-bacon toasted sandwiches sat beside a small mountain of empty glasses. The lunchtime crowd had come and gone, and there was a blanket of cigarette smoke floating near the ornately carved ceiling. A few men sat at the bar studying the racing pages in the newspapers. The place had warmed up nicely, and Kate was feeling much happier.

'Shirley, you were right. I got the Boot, the Big E, the old Heave-Ho! It's all Alex Stone's fault. And he wasn't even worth it.'

'Don't be too hard on yourself, Kate.'

'You'd better watch yourself in there, I think they have the whole place bugged. Bingham was ferreting about in my desk, did I tell you that?'

'Never mind. Sure, you hated it, anyway.'

'True. But it was better than nothing.'

'Why don't you go into retail? Fashion, maybe? One of those fancy boutiques on Royal Avenue? It would be a real home from home for you.'

'What kind of a reference do you think they'll give me in the dole office? And the boutiques are a non-starter anyway. Those snobby managers want some dimwit teenager who won't talk back to them, or else they have to hire some dried-up old prune who's friends with the owner. It's not what you know that counts in this society, Shirley. It's *who* you know. It's hopeless. Besides, I don't want to be on my feet all day. I'm thirty-odd, for God's sake. I'll get varicose veins like Kevin's mother.'

Shirley blew a massive sigh, and struggled to her feet. She was a little bit cross with Kate for drinking money she could ill afford. If Kate kept this up, she would pass out, and then Shirley would be stuck with the problem of how to get her home. She would tell the barman to put only a drip of spirits in Kate's glass next time. But she didn't get the chance. The door of the booth opened, and a barman came in and stacked their empty glasses into a small tower, which he leaned against his shoulder while he wiped the table.

'Ah!' Kate smiled, drunkenly. 'Another round, my good man. And some loud music, if you please. My sister will be back presently, with some ready cash. There she goes! Hurry back, darling!' Shirley slithered out of the narrow door and left the pub. She didn't notice Declan Greenwood, who was standing at the bar. But he saw her.

'And some cigarettes, too. I think I'll take up smoking, again!' Kate called after the barman. 'A little smoke for a girl who's just been fired, ha, ha, ha!'

When the drinks arrived on a tray, they were not carried by the barman with the white apron over his black trousers, but by Declan Greenwood himself. He set the tray down gently on the mahogany table.

'I hope you'll let me pay for this. I'm Declan, by the way. Declan Greenwood.'

'Indeed you are,' said Kate, taking the box, pulling out a cigarette and striking a match. 'Cheers, and thank you very much. Will you have a drink, yourself?'

'There's a pint of Guinness settling.' A Stranglers tape crackled into life overhead, and the lights dimmed.

'That's the proper stuff, now. A bit of atmosphere, at last. So tell me, Declan Greenwood, how do you know me?'

'Oh, a friend of mine knows you. He told me your name. Actually I wanted to meet your sister. Shirley?'

'Aye, Shirley! She's a little pet! She's looking after me today. I just left my job.'

'I see. Celebrating, then?'

'Drowning my sorrows, actually. I was shown the door, so to speak. By a woman, would you believe? I thought we women were supposed to stick together. Unless there's a good-looking man involved, that is.' She yawned again, and thought of her lovely French-style bed.

'Well, never mind. You'll get something else.'

'Are you a working man yourself, Declan?'

'Well, I'm a student, and I help to run a small restaurant, but my father owns the place, so I can't boast.'

'Not at all. That sounds a hard enough job, to me. Anything to do with the public is a total nightmare. Always begging with their hands out. Or complaining about the service. I don't know which is worse.'

He shrugged. 'Must be hard on them, though, not having a job?'

'Well . . .' Kate had no interest in the private miseries of the unemployed.

'Has Shirley gone home?' asked Declan. 'I saw her leaving.' The barman brought his pint, and he stood up to pay. Kate poured her mixer into the glass very carefully. The glass seemed to be moving around the table on its own.

'Are you all right with that?' asked Declan. 'If you've had a few already, I can get you a mineral water?'

'I'm grand. Thanks again,' she said. But she decided not to drink it just yet.

'S'okay. Is your sister away then?'

'No. She went to the bank, that's all. Why? Are you interested?'

'Oh, just asking.'

'She's a lovely girl, is Shirley. Bit shy, but sound as a pound. You know, I shouldn't tell you this, but it's been a very weird kind of day so far, so I will. Shirley has a wee notion of you.'

'Does she? Right enough?' He smiled broadly.

'Aye, but she'd never do anything about it. She's a bit of a dreamer, you know. Fascinated by the Celts, she is. She talks to the moon, and the stars.'

'Don't we all, from time to time?'

'Well. She's very sensitive.'

'Is she? Tell me something else about her.'

'She's only young, nearly twenty, she doesn't know what she wants. Now, take me, I'm twenty-nine, and, blimey, I don't know what I want, either.' She began to laugh, then, and couldn't stop. She was still laughing when Shirley came back. 'Oh, Shirley, there you are. What kept you? Look who I bumped into? Your very own wee Declan! And he's bought us a round of drinks. Give me that bag, I'm going to powder my nose. That's a good girl.' Kate hurried to the bathroom, sure that her stomach was about to reject some of its liquid lunch.

Shirley sat down beside the door of the booth. Was it really him? Or were seven pure oranges playing tricks on her mind? She looked down at her shoes. They were very scuffed. Declan appeared to be saying something. She tried to listen.

'I saw you at the ballroom, a while back. With your sister.'

'Did you?'

'Yeah. You're not a bad dancer.'

Shirley blushed. 'You like music?'

'Definitely. I'm really into it. All kinds, really. I buy records every day. Thousands of them, I have. Limited editions. Extended editions. I'd love to be a DJ, maybe, some day. Play in a band. Something like that.'

'Would you?'

'Oh, sure. Music is a bit of an obsession with me. I have some great ideas, too: live gigs, theme nights. Entertainment is the best business to be in, everybody wants to enjoy themselves.'

'Do they?'

'Oh, yes. Entertainment is a great social leveller. No matter what a person's background, they all like to dance and socialize. That drink is for you, by the way.'

'Thanks. Sorry about Kate,' Shirley said quickly. 'She's had far too much vodka. She'll be falling asleep on me in a minute.' Shirley checked her watch again. 'I'll give her five minutes and then I'd better make sure she's not unconscious in there. I hate it when people drink too much. I never know what to do with them.'

But Kate came back at that moment. And, apart from a very pale complexion, she seemed steady enough on her feet.

'If you don't mind, I think I'll go home now, and lie down. Come on, Shirley.'

Declan stood up as Shirley reluctantly reached for her coat.

'Well, I'll just finish this and head on, myself,' he said. 'I just called in for a quick pint. Got to get back to work.' Declan smiled at Shirley. There was a hint of a smile on her face as well. He wanted to stay and talk to her but his father was expecting him at the restaurant.

'Well. Nice to meet you, Kate, Shirley. Maybe I'll see you again, in Hogan's sometime?'

'You will, surely. Cheerio, now. Mind how you go.' Kate was trying to light the wrong end of a cigarette. She had her coat on, inside out. The three of them went out into the street, and Declan said goodbye again, and turned towards the city centre.

'Bye,' whispered Shirley, watching him go. It was all she could do not to follow him.

Kate elbowed her sister, and peered expectantly into Shirley's eyes. It was quite hard to focus after several doubles. They began to walk in the other direction.

'Like, wow! What was that all about? Did you talk to him? Did you? Did you? I gave you as long as I could, on your own.'

'Thanks, Kate. That was big of you, considering the circumstances. Well, he talked to me a fair bit. I didn't say much.'

'What did you say? You must have said something.'

'Let me think. I think I said, *Did you? Do you? Do they? Is it?* He must think I'm a twit. Bloody questions, that's all I managed to come up with.'

'Oh, dear. You know what our trouble is, Shirley? We've been in that dole office too long. Our conversation has become very silted. I mean salted. I mean *stilted*.'

'He actually tried to talk to me, and I blew it.'

'No, you didn't. He likes you. He'll be back. Now, I think I'll go straight home, and have a nice big sleep. Telling old Bingham off has fairly taken it out of me.'

13. Past Passions

Marion and Eddy lay in their beautiful four-poster bed, in the big house on Derryvolgie Avenue. The street outside was very quiet and peaceful. Marion had decorated the bedroom in various shades of cream, and there was a luxuriously soft carpet on the floor, and even a small sofa at the foot of the bed. There was a framed watercolour of a rural scene in Galway, bought on their honeymoon. It was hanging above the dressing table, in a simple pine frame. They both looked at the picture and thought of when they had bought it. They had shared a bed in the small hotel beside the sea, but had only kissed and held hands when they went to sleep each night. Eddy said they didn't have to bother about the other stuff until after the baby was born, and Marion felt ready and relaxed with him. He wouldn't rush her. And when they did finally make love for the first time, almost a year later, she was amazed at how passionate he was. And how tender. He was a much better lover than she would ever have guessed. It was a wonderful surprise. He was such a sensitive man; she wished every woman in the world could be as blessed in her marriage as she was. She smiled at him and he kissed her softly.

Eddy was feeling very happy, too. This restful master bedroom was his favourite place in the house, although every other room was lovely as well. It was a source of great pride to him that Marion was so artistic, as well as being a super mother to their four children. He was a very lucky man, he told himself. Thank God he had waited for the right woman, when he could easily have given up and married somebody else. Marion and Eddy had left the bedroom curtains open so that they could watch the clouds drifting across the moon. Eddy had his arms round his wife, stroking the smooth skin on her shoulders, and her blonde bubble curls, and thinking how beautiful she still was. This was a very emotional time of year for Eddy; the big countdown to Christmas would be starting soon. The happiest of times for a contented family man like himself. On the first day of December, they would all go out for a special turkey lunch in the restaurant, and afterwards select a fresh tree from the local greengrocer's across the road. They would decorate it together, and take several photographs for the album. Declan and the girls loved this family tradition. Then, there was the shopping: himself and Marion would go browsing in the big stores for gifts for the children and each other. He sighed happily, and kissed his wife tenderly for the second time that night. She knew he wanted to make love but she could not concentrate on anything until she had told him about her meeting that day. She never kept any secrets from her husband. She took a very deep breath.

'I was talking to someone today, Eddy. Someone from the past.'

'Who was that, sweetheart?' As if he didn't know.

'Johnny Hogan.'

Eddy's heart missed a beat. 'What were you talking to him about?'

'Well, he called in to the shop, and took me out to lunch.'

'Why, pet? If you don't mind me asking.'

'He just wanted to say goodbye.'

'Is he ill?' Hope rose up in Eddy, like a tidal wave. People could get cancer in their forties, couldn't they? And Johnny was a chronic smoker. Eddy *hated* himself for even thinking something terrible like that, but he had never forgiven Johnny Hogan for stealing his lovely girl-friend away from him, in 1962.

'No, he's as fit as a fiddle. What a strange thing to ask. Actually, he's going away. To America. For three months. Six, if he likes it enough. He's going as soon as he can make the arrangements.'

'Is that all? A mere holiday! For heaven's sake, that's not worth a goodbye visit.'

'Johnny makes his own rules, Eddy.'

'Indeed he does. Did he want you to go with him?'

'No, you silly thing!' But she hesitated for a moment before she said it, and Eddy knew he was right. Under the bedclothes, he clenched his fists.

'I bet he did. He's got no right to ask you anything, not even to go out to lunch.' He lowered his voice to a whisper, in case any of the children heard him. 'I always thought he would work out that he was Declan's father. Did he mention anything about that? We were only married seven months when Declan was born.'

'No, no. He didn't. He's not the type to count up the days and months. He has no concept of time passing. Doesn't he still wear blue suede shoes? God knows where he gets them. He must have bought a stack of those shoes when they were the in-thing, and kept them in the attic all this time.' She knew she was babbling on to avoid the subject. 'He wouldn't want to be a father, anyway. That's not his style.'

'You say that as if you were paying him a compliment.'

'Eddy! You know only too well that Johnny would think bringing up a family was boring. He's just not the kind of man to go crawling around the floor, playing trains with a toddler. He's a night-owl.'

'Am I boring, Marion?'

'Not even a tiny little bit. How can you say such things?'

'When I find out my gorgeous wife is having a secret lunch with her old flame. That's how. What did he want? He must have wanted something. Please tell me the truth, Marion.'

'I have told you the truth, Eddy. He's going away, soon. And he wanted to say goodbye, personally. And to apologize for the way he neglected me, in the past. Laying old ghosts to rest. That's all it was.'

'Is that the truth?'

'Yes, darling. And I wished him well, and I told him not to worry about me. That I was very happy, with you. That I married the right man, in the end.'

'Did he say he still loved you?'

'No. Why would he?'

Eddy didn't believe her. Any man in his right mind would love Marion. Her baby-blue eyes, and bee-sting pout; her slender legs in dainty slingbacks. Her voice that was as gentle as a summer breeze.

'I'd do anything for you, Marion. You know I would. We've had a great life together, even though it wasn't full of drama and excitement.'

'Honestly, Eddy, I'd had enough of drama and excitement when you proposed to me. Drama's not all it's cracked up to be. It's very stressful.'

'Really?'

'Really. I wanted a quiet life, and security, and a man I could depend on. I've loved you for a long time, darling, and I always will. I promise.'

'I'm sorry for quizzing you, Marion. This is very difficult for me. He was your boyfriend for five years. Don't you think it's weird that he never married?'

'Not at all. He was too fond of the business to be a family man like you, darling.'

'But I run a business. It didn't stop me getting married. Or you.'

'Well, the late hours he always worked, it would be pretty hard on a wife.'

'There must be more to it. He never got over you?'

'Listen, Eddy. It hurts me to admit this, but Johnny only wanted me because I was pretty. A fashion accessory to his alter-ego as the local hero. We spent most of our time together dancing in the ballroom. Or sitting in the back row of the cinema. He liked to be seen in public with me . . . But hardly ever when it was just the two of us. We didn't go for long walks, like you and I do. We didn't spend hours making love, or really talking, you know? He didn't want to be lumbered with me on a full-time basis. He's selfish, Eddy.'

'So you didn't feel anything for him? No regrets at all?'

'Honestly, Eddy, there's nothing to worry about. Look, I only told you I saw him because we said we would have no secrets from each other. I've said what I had to say to Johnny and I won't see him any more. I'm sure he'll be so happy in America, he might even stay for good. Sure, he might as well be an American, the way he goes on. He's never fitted in here.'

'Don't say anything to Johnny about Declan. Do you hear me?'

'Are you mad? I've said nothing all these years. Not to a living soul. You're the only person who knows. Don't you remember the doctor's face, the day Declan was born? He was very dubious. A nine-pound baby after only seven months? And the woman who filled out the birth certificate? Didn't I lie to her as well?'

'Well, I know how emotional you are, Marion. You might feel sorry for Hogan. Going off to America by himself to sit gazing out over some lake, thinking what might have been. He still knows how to manipulate women. It makes me sick!'

'Oh, Eddy, how possessive you are. You still love me madly, don't you?'

'More than you'll ever know.' Eddy kissed her, then. A tender and gentle kiss. He said he was sorry for being so insecure; and promised not to mention Johnny Hogan ever again.

She was relieved that he was so understanding about everything. Apart from a little flash of jealousy now and then, Eddy was the perfect man. And she had to remind herself that it was only natural he should resent Johnny so much; he had spent five years waiting for her after she gave him back his engagement ring and went to jive with Johnny in the ballroom. She nestled up to Eddy, under the duvet, and told him she loved him again.

But Eddy was secretly very worried. There was a lump of ice in his heart; the rage that he had buried for so long was still there. He could not make love now, or even get to sleep. He was sure that Marion did love him, but also sure that Johnny was trying to take her away from him. The selfish brute wanted a companion to take care of him in his middle years. Someone familiar to grow old with, and listen to his ballroom stories. Never mind that Marion had a perfectly happy life already. Wasn't that just typical of Hollywood Hogan? Eddy wanted to go straight round to Magnolia Street and give Johnny Hogan the beating of his life; blacken those brown eyes of his. No decent man would blame him. But, knowing Hogan, he would have Eddy Greenwood thrown in prison for a couple of months, and use the time (and the bruises) to seduce Marion again. She'd promised she would never leave Eddy the first time, and yet she went off with Hogan the minute he asked her. She couldn't resist him. She wouldn't even talk to Eddy on the phone in case she hurt Johnny's feelings, she said. The frustration he felt during those five years almost drove him out of his mind. And he had only got her back because of the pregnancy. Because she was in desperate need of someone to take care of her. Could Eddy's life still come tumbling down around him like a house of cards? Stay calm, he told himself, a hundred times that night. Eddy knew that he had to be strong and sensible; that was what Marion wanted him to be. Think. Think!

If he couldn't take Johnny away from Marion, he would take her away from Belfast for two or three weeks, until Hogan had packed his bags and said his last goodbyes.

They would go on a winter holiday! And the girls would go, too. Marion wouldn't leave home for long without them. Declan could stay behind and run the business on his own. Three weeks at the helm should put the notion of being a businessman out of his head. Hopefully, he would be so exhausted by the time Eddy returned from holiday, that he would go running back to Queen's University for a rest. Marion would be delighted. Eddy closed his eyes then and dreamt of a luxury cruise that he would take his wife on, as soon as he could book it. He would show her that he could order cocktails, and kiss her under the stars, and find his way around new cities. And be a great father to the girls, too. He wouldn't fuss over them all the time, he'd let them go shopping on their own. He'd buy some really trendy clothes, and dance with Marion on the ship every night, even though he wasn't a fantastic mover. He'd show her that Johnny Hogan wasn't the only one who could do glamorous things.

Marion, too, lay awake for a long time. Yes, Johnny had offered to take her away with him. He'd told her he had very strong feelings for her, still. But, it was a declaration of love that was twenty years too late. And if he honestly thought she would leave her four children behind in Belfast, and spend the rest of her life sitting on a deckchair in Florida, then he really didn't know her at all. She was glad she had given him no encouragement as they sat in the cafe that day. Sometimes, she wondered what her life would have been like if she had stayed with Johnny. But he was so out of touch with the real world, he had no sense of responsibility at all. It would have been a disaster. Eddy was the one she wanted, thank God.

She wouldn't traipse off, after Johnny, to Florida, or anywhere else. She wondered if she should have told him the truth about Declan. Their son was a grown man now, there could be no ugly custody battle. And Declan? Did he have a right to know, too? It was impossible to know. Maybe Declan would not forgive her for keeping the truth from him, and go off with Johnny to America? She didn't want Declan to be distracted in any way until he got over this silly idea of his that a degree in medicine was beyond him. A shock like this would give her son the perfect excuse to go off the rails for a few years.

She was still awake when the moon faded away and the sun came up. She slipped out of bed, put on a warm robe, and made up a tray of breakfast for herself and Eddy. Toasted slices of soda bread, real butter in a glass dish, fresh orange juice, and two large cups of coffee with demerara sugar sachets in a pretty china bowl. And a pink rose in a tall vase, to show Eddy that he was the special man in her life, and that she was not thinking of past passions. Just the consequences of past passions.

14. Be Careful What You Wish For

As the weeks went by, Shirley soon realized that work was incredibly dull without Kate, who always cheered everyone up with her practical jokes. She was forever hiding plastic spiders in the filing cabinets, or shouting in to some new girl that there was a fire, just when she had sat down on the toilet. And when they held the office party each Christmas, Kate was always the first one out of her seat to dance, a party hat on her head and a string of old threadbare tinsel around her neck.

Back at home, Kate was not joking and laughing. In fact, she was crying at the thought of having to go into the unemployment office at two o'clock. As a *claimant*. It was going to be very hard for her to stand on the other side of the counter, now that she was a dreaded dole-ite herself. She should have gone in sooner but she was too embarrassed to face all her old colleagues. Mr and Mrs Winters had actually taken the news of Kate's dismissal very well. Her mother said it was a poor enough job anyway, and Kate should have done far better with the string of exams she had. And her father said that she was only a young girl with her whole life still ahead of her, and wouldn't she be wise to settle down and start a family? (They were the only over-fifties on the street with no grandchildren, a source of great shame for them.) But unfortunately, their well-intended remarks had backfired in a big way. And Kate ended up crying into her corn-flakes. It was Kate's thirtieth birthday at the end of October, and she was getting a bit sensitive about her age. Young, free and single? More like thirty years old, on the shelf and unemployed.

'Oh, thanks, Mum and Dad! It's great to know that you both think I have wasted ten whole years of my life in the DHSS. I'm sure I'll have no trouble getting in some-where new as an apprentice, *at my age*! Roll up! Roll up! Ladies and gentlemen, step right up and take a swipe at the middle-aged loser in the blue corner! Talk about kicking a person when they're down. I'd expect this kind of treachery off some people, but when it's your own parents, it really hurts! A useless job, they say! *Wallop!* And that was only the first punch! Now, it's *grandchildren* they want! *Crash, bang, wallop!* Is that the next of it? When you know rightly I haven't even got a boyfriend! God help me! What am I going to *do*? Is nothing good enough for the two of you? Will I run for election? For Prime Minister? With a pile of adopted weans strapped to my back? I'll get the campaign up and running as soon as I return from building a few orphanages in the Third World. Jesus Christ, look down on me!'

At that point, Mr Winters hurried out to the shed, to check that all his beloved Christmas decorations were in good working order. It was only October, but still. Mrs Winters scuttled to the upstairs landing to fold laundry at great speed. That was how they'd always handled Kate's teenage mood swings, and it was still the best idea they could come up with for avoiding confrontation. Kate never lost a fight. Ever. Therefore, there was no point in going through the motions with her. Last Christmas, she'd fought with Shirley for two hours over the last caramel sweet in the tin before Shirley conceded defeat and handed it over.

Shirley had left her big sister to wallow in her misery. She went to stand in line for the bus. It was incredibly boring, sitting in rush-hour traffic without Kate's constant chatter. She hoped that Kate would soon tire of the self-pity and get another job before the bills started arriving on the doormat. Shirley *did* say she would help out a little, but she didn't want Kate to get too comfortable with that arrangement. When she was hanging her coat on the back of her chair, Shirley was startled by a small commotion at the other end of the room.

'Shirley. Shirley! Personal call for you, over here.' One of the girls was waving from across the huge open-plan office. 'Hey, it's a fella!'

'Oh, fancy!' chorused the other women, thrilled with this small distraction from the daily tedium of crisis-loan application forms.

'Keep your voice down, will you?' said Shirley, rushing over to the phone. Miss Bingham was watching. 'This must be some mistake,' she said loudly. 'I never receive personal calls. Never.'

'Hello? Is that Shirley Winters?'

His voice was as deep as an underground gravel pit. Shirley felt her face begin to flush. A hot pink flush that would give her away in front of her supervisor. She muffled a squeak of excitement, and immediately despised herself for being such a fluffy-headed female. She took a deep breath and composed herself.

'It is.'

'This is Declan Greenwood here. Can I speak to you for a moment?'

Shirley was strangely calm. She saw Miss Bingham coming her way, and tried to sound normal.

'*Have you made a claim with this office before?*' she asked.

'What? I'm not claiming anything.'

'My boss is watching me,' she whispered.

'Oh. Well, I'll be quick, then. Will you come out with me, sometime?'

'*Just let me check those details . . .*'

'I didn't know how else to contact you. You haven't been at Hogan's recently.'

'*That is correct.*' Well, she would have been first in the door of the ballroom at 9 p.m. if she thought Declan would be there, but Kate wanted to avoid Alex Stone and his bruised pelvis.

'Can I call for you, take you out for a meal? Where do you live?'

'*I cannot give out that information on the telephone.*'

'What? Oh, yeah, your boss. Can I meet you outside your office, then? At five-thirty? Today? Tomorrow? Whenever you like.'

'*I think that will be satisfactory.*'

'Oh, great. Today? I'll see you at five-thirty. Bye.'

'Yes. Bye.'

Shirley stole a glance at Miss Bingham, who was hanging off the edge of a nearby desk, trying to listen in to her conversation. Shirley quickly turned and hurried away to the staff loo, to check her face for imperfections. She'd no make-up on, and none with her either. She would have to nip out at lunchtime, and buy another eyeliner in the chemist. She thought she had an old red lipstick in her desk, so that was okay. And why, oh why, hadn't she washed her hair that morning? And why hadn't she agreed to meet him the following day, so that she could come into work painted up like a circus trapeze artist? Honestly, she was such an idiot. Then, she began to feel a lovely warm glow inside her. She couldn't wait to see him again. She felt serene and in control. It was going to be so hard to concentrate on work for the rest of the day.

The letters seemed even more boring than usual, compared to the lovely floaty feeling she had about seeing Declan. Still, she'd better look sharp. There was always more work to do at this time of year when the cold weather drove big families to spend lots of time together in very small houses. As well as Santa Claus and mince pies, the festive season brought with it family feuds, love affairs, money worries, drink problems, and mid-life crises of all descriptions. And there was a general meeting this afternoon, to discuss possible strike action, as some of the administrative assistants were fed up with their workload. An ambulance would have to be called if the strike went ahead: Miss Bingham was a bit of a right-winger, and her heart wasn't as strong as it used to be. The morning dragged by, but after lunch a curious thing happened. The clock seemed to speed up. Every time Shirley looked up from her desk, huge lumps of time had gone by. She wished Kate was there to give her some useful advice.

At 2 p.m., she wanted to go down to the front desk and give Kate moral support while she registered herself as unemployed, but Miss Bingham sent her to photocopy five hundred forms instead.

Shirley was so preoccupied with her thoughts, that afternoon, that when she was asked for her opinion on the impending strike, she said, 'I'm never again going to leave the house without full make-up on,' and everybody laughed until their sides ached. Miss Bingham pursed her lips so tightly, they disappeared completely. The sheer incompetence of the Winters sisters backed up her theory that being useless was a genetic flaw that affected whole families.

In no time at all, it was five-thirty, and Shirley was skipping down the steps to the main entrance, hoping Declan wouldn't be there, and hoping even harder that he was. He was. He had changed his hairstyle, swapping his blond quiff for a black one. He was even more gorgeous than before. It was all she could do not to grapple him to the ground and rip off his black shirt. She laughed out loud. This was exhilarating stuff. Then she knew she'd have to say something to the poor boy. He seemed confused by her crazy laughter.

'Hi,' she said. 'You've changed your hair. It's black.'

'Ho! You don't miss much.'

'That'll be my job training.'

'Hope I didn't get you into trouble?'

'What?' Images of Declan unbuttoning her dress came into her mind. If any man could get her into trouble, it was Declan Greenwood.

'Calling you at work? I thought that would be okay in this day and age.'

'Oh! Well, most of the other supervisors wouldn't

mind, but Miss Bingham is a bit old-fashioned. She still thinks married women shouldn't be allowed to work in the civil service.'

'Well, I'm sorry about that. I mean, phoning.'

'That's okay. It was very nice of you. A nice surprise.'

They both smiled.

'Where would you like to go?'

'Anywhere.'

'Anywhere? You're easy to please! This is going to be easy.'

'What is?'

'You're a wild one for questions.'

'Sorry. Job training, again. You'd better decide, or I'll start quizzing you about how much money you have, and how many hours a week you have to work to get it.'

'I tell you what: we'll go for a stroll to that little French place on Shaftesbury Square, for a meal. And then, if you decide you still like me, we'll go for a drink. Okay?'

'Keep talking, cowboy. I like the sound of that. I'll just give Mum a ring and tell her not to keep me any dinner.'

And off they went, into the rush-hour crowd, chatting away as if they had known each other all their lives. And with Shirley wondering why she had called him a cowboy, to his face, after he had graciously invited her out for a posh French meal.

15. The Sibling Rivalry World Championships

When Shirley got home from her first date with Declan, it was after one o'clock in the morning. Her parents had gone to bed but Kate was still up. Surrounded by empty cups and Toffee Crisp wrappers, she lay on the sofa, flicking through some out-of-date magazines in a half-hearted sort of way.

'What are you doing up?' asked Shirley, as she passed by the sitting room on her way to the kitchen for a glass of water. Kate leapt up and followed her.

'What happened? Mum told me you were on a date. With Declan! You've been with him eight hours. I want all the gossip.' Kate filled the kettle and switched it on. 'Toast? Well, come on, tell me! I'm dying to know!' She slammed two slices of bread under the grill.

'Kate, I'm going to bed. I'm just worn out.'

'You're going nowhere until you tell me all about it. Sit down at the table.'

'Kate, I have to go to work in the morning. Remember work? That nasty place where I earn a living?' Shirley drained her glass and turned towards the kitchen door. They shouldn't have stayed out so late on a weeknight, but there was so much to talk about, they didn't notice the time passing.

'Shirley! I said: sit down! I'm making some tea. Now,

where did you go?' Kate pleaded. She looked very vulnerable and alone, in her old tracksuit and novelty furrypuppy slippers. Shirley took pity on her. She sat down and folded her arms.

'To the French restaurant beside Lavery's bar. That little place with the green arched window?'

'*Oh, la, la!* Money, money, money! It's dear, in there.'

'We had a lovely meal.'

'What did you eat?'

'Can't remember, but there was a lovely mural on the wall.' Declan had touched her hand as they waited for coffee. She would always remember the place where they had touched for the first time. Beneath a pretty mural in a French restaurant. How romantic! How perfect!

'Shirley! We can do this the easy way or the hard way. I'll ask you again. What did you eat? Beef, chicken or fish? I can't smell any garlic off you.'

'Okay. He had breast of chicken with tomatoes and cheese on the top. I had a crab. In the shell! I never ate a crab before. It was heavenly. I'll never forget it although Morrissey would be very disappointed in me. But I won't tell him if you won't. And then we had an assortment of sorbet balls in these pretty little spun-sugar baskets, and then really strong espresso coffee and then some fancy cocktails. Honestly, Kate. It was fantastic.'

'What sort of cocktails?' Kate's lip wobbled with pure jealousy. Trust Shirley to end up in a French restaurant on a first date, while she'd had to endure Alex Stone and his red-hot curry breath.

'I couldn't remember what the cocktails were called if my life depended on it,' said Shirley. 'We'd had wine by then, you see. They were pink. Or was it the glasses that were pink? There were glacé cherries on little plastic swords. I collected the swords and put them in my pocket. Look. Aren't they pretty? Pretty colours?' She showed Kate the little swords. They were transparent, under the kitchen light. Shirley burped a crabby burp, and giggled insanely. Kate had a horrible feeling that Shirley was totally smitten with Declan. Usually Shirley was interested only in Morrissey's latest single or Bette Davis films, or world politics.

'Who paid the bill?'

'Declan paid. He wouldn't let me chip in. I did offer.'

'Did he let you know how much it was?'

'No. He didn't look at the bill in front of me. He took it up to the counter, still folded.'

'Smooth operator. Where did you go after that?'

'A bar. I don't know the name of the place.'

'Shirley! You're doing this on purpose.' She set the cups on the table and sat down herself. Then she jumped up again to fetch the toast and the butter dish.

'I'm not, honestly. Some dark little wine bar in Stranmillas. There were real candles on the tables. And modern art pictures on the walls. It was very cosy. Let me see if I can remember the name of the place . . .'

'Forget it. Did you kiss him?'

'Maybe.'

'Did you?' Kate was almost in tears with frustration.

'Not in the wine bar. We talked a lot, though. There was a two-piece band; a girl singing. She was good.'

'Well, did he put his arm round you?'

'Afterwards, on the way home, he did.'

'Where?'

'Near the park. There was a crowd of fellas coming along the street, making lots of noise. Drunk, I suppose.'

'What else is new? What happened then?'

'We were standing beside this big rhododendron bush, and we just nipped into the middle of it until they went past. And we had a little kiss while we were waiting.'

'Let me get this right. You kissed Declan for the first time in the middle of a tree?'

'Yes. It's amazing how much room there is, inside a rhododendron. All the branches open outwards. It's very beautiful.' Her fantasy, come to life.

'That would explain why you have a leaf in the back of your hair. What was it like? Was it good?' Kate didn't want to hear that Shirley was in love, but she knew what was coming. It was inevitable. And very unfair when Kate had put so much more effort into the search.

'There was a lovely scent in the air, some kind of flower, I think. But then, we were near the park,' Shirley smiled. There was a sickening, faraway look in her eyes.

'Shirley! I meant the kiss. Did the earth move? Did your insides melt? Were you overcome with lust? Did you *want* him?'

'It was a really lovely kiss.' It was actually so good that it was hard to describe. So sensual, they were both speechless afterwards. Shirley felt so relaxed and sleepy that she fell over a tree root and landed on her back on the ground. (Hence the leaf.)

'Is he a good kisser? You're not going to wriggle out of this.'

'Like I said, he's really nice. I like him.'

'Well, don't be shy. Tell me about it. I want to know. Was he passionate? Smooth? A heavy breather? Did he close his eyes? Did your teeth knock together? I hate that.'

'You're very nosy, all of a sudden. I thought you were the man-eater in this house. Why should my humble love life be of any interest to an experienced woman of the world like yourself?'

'Are you going to tell me about this blasted kiss?'

'No, I'm not. It's private.' Shirley looked up at the clock, calculating how many hours it would be until she saw him again. Kate heaved a huge sigh. This was bad. Very bad.

'Are you seeing him again?' she asked, after a moment.

'Yes, as a matter of fact, I am.'

'When?'

'We're going to the cinema tonight.'

'That's a bit keen, Shirley. You should have made him wait a few days.'

'Oh, Kate! I'm not playing games with Declan. I really like him, and he seems to like me for some reason, and if it works out, then that's great. And if it doesn't, well, I'll get over it as best I can. I've decided it's better to love and lose, than never to love at all.'

'That's a very modern approach, I must say.'

'It's my approach. It feels right.'

'Now, Shirley, you aren't going to get serious with him, are you?'

'What do you mean, Kate?'

'You're too young to get serious. You'll make a fool of yourself.'

'I've told you. I'm going to go with my instincts on this. No games. No rules. No leading him on, no telling him lies. I don't care if he has rich parents, or good prospects, or a fancy car. Okay? I just like being with him.'

'Okay, keep your hair on. I just don't want you getting involved too soon, and ending up with a broken heart. You're only a kid.'

'I'll take my chances. Now, I'm going to lie down before I fall down. Goodnight, Kate.'

'Goodnight, Shirley.'

Kate watched her sister traipse happily up the stairs, and then she poured herself another cup of tea. She was not pleased about this latest development in Shirley's life. Shirley getting all precious about a guy? After just one date? Kate had dated countless men in the last fifteen years, and she had *never* felt the way Shirley seemed to be feeling tonight. She'd kissed rich men who owned high-performance cars, poor boys on the dole, a married man from Bangor, cool guys who were in local rock bands. She'd had flings with men from both sides of the religious divide, with a black student from Queen's University, with an American tourist who'd worked for a while in their favourite pizza parlour. She'd dated a policeman from Lisburn, and a teenager who had a criminal record for riotous behaviour. And, if she was perfectly honest with herself, she'd never, not even once, felt that she was falling in love. She cared more about her handbags. Kate began to panic. She couldn't possibly allow Shirley to go falling in love either.

The ticking of the orange plastic clock seemed very loud to Kate. She boiled the kettle again and rinsed the teapot under the tap. There was no point going to bed yet. She would not be able to sleep for hours.

Upstairs, brushing her teeth, Shirley was thanking her lucky stars that it was raining that evening. She was sure her fantasies of sleeping with Declan were about to become a reality. Declan had beautiful, soft lips and was a very good kisser indeed. So good, that had the ground been dry and soft, instead of wet and muddy, she might have lost her virginity inside a large rhododendron bush, at the gates of the Botanic Gardens. And it wasn't frightening at all. Not one little bit.

16. Desperate Times, Desperate Measures

Kate was no good at being unemployed. The days were long and empty. Several weeks in, and countless interviews later, and she still had not found work. She was too proud to do menial jobs but not well-enough qualified for a well-paid white-collar position. There was nothing worth watching on television, and it only took her three days to colour-coordinate her wardrobe. Her parents tried to be kind, but it made Kate feel even worse. Every time she ventured into the kitchen for a snack, they started on her. Her mother said not to worry about the silly old job, it was time she had a proper career. One that she would actually enjoy. One that would pay a decent wage, and she could buy a car and give her mother a lift to the supermarket occasionally.

Her father argued that some young women only went out to work and put a brave face on things, because they hadn't managed to nab themselves a husband. Who, in their right mind, would want some supervisor standing over them, when they could be sitting pretty in their own little place? Kate would be too old to have babies soon. She was a great-looking girl, there was no need for her to go to work at all. She should forget about college and get herself a man. Why not give that nice Kevin McGovern a call? He was asking after her, only the other day, in the newsagent's. He might still be interested.

Her mother was full of doubt about that scenario, and told her to do no such thing. Kate could stay at home for the rest of her life, if she wanted to, she said. Motherhood was a tough role, she told Kate. She didn't think she was cut out for it. She was too soft and spoilt. There were no crystal chandeliers in the maternity ward, she explained. Oh no. Red roses and moonlight sonatas counted for nothing there. Kate couldn't expect any sympathy from the busy doctors and nurses. Just pain and suffering and stitches, and very sore bits Down Below.

'Don't be putting her off childbirth, woman,' scolded Mr Winters. 'It's all over with, in a day or two.'

'Huh! Easy for *you* to say!' she declared. 'Kate, do you want to know where this boy was, the day you came into the world?'

'No.' Kate was trying to make a sandwich, and trying even harder not to think of her mother's lower regions spread-eagled on a hospital trolley.

'Martha, don't,' pleaded her husband. 'Not *again*.'

'*He* was filling his face with beer in the pub when half a dozen medical students were gawping at my modesty!' she said, pointing at her husband.

'How many times are you going to bring this up? That wasn't my fault. You went into labour early,' he said. 'Kate, she went into labour early.'

'It *was* your fault, Michael. I had to move that wardrobe myself because you had to go and watch a football match with your boozy mates.' She was shouting now.

'What the hell were you moving furniture for, at eight

months pregnant, woman? I didn't know you were going to move the bloody wardrobe!'

'I was dusting the rooms for the baby coming. Somebody had to do it! The visiting nurses are trained to look for dust.'

'Not behind the wardrobes, they aren't. They just want to make sure you aren't breeding dangerous dogs in the baby's cot. They would *never* have looked for dust behind a wardrobe.'

'A girl should be married by the time she's twenty, never mind thirty,' Mrs Winters ranted on, pointing at Kate's head. 'Before she's had a chance to get to know anything better. How can *she* settle down, now, when she's been gallivanting all this time? Off to Portugal with the girls every summer. She's had a life of ease and freedom. She can't even cook, for heaven's sake!'

'She can learn to cook, you daft woman!' shouted Mr Winters. 'It's only peeling a few spuds, for God's sake! Slapping a bit of steak on the pan. How could she go wrong?' He spread his arms out wide in desperation.

'Our Kate? Peeling potatoes? That'll be the day! And by the way, I hope you aren't trying to say housework is easy, because if you are, you're WRONG! You're a typical man.'

'Excuse me,' cried Kate. 'You can stop talking about me like I'm not here. Jesus H! And don't *ever* mention your modesty again, Mum. You're putting me off my food. Talking about stitches.' Kate pushed her plate away. She was going to have to get a job soon. Just to get away from these two lunatics. Cleaning out the city sewers with a toothpick would be more fun than putting in a full day with her mad parents. Even if she did love them both with all her heart.

'Look, there's no stigma attached to being an old maid, these days,' said Mrs Winters to her eldest daughter. 'No shame at all, being single and childless at twenty-nine. Shirley will give us the grandchildren, I'm sure of that.'

'Talk sense, Mum. Have you been at the cooking sherry, the day? Shirley's too quiet to be messing about with lads.' Well, up until now, she was too quiet.

'It's the quiet ones you have to watch,' said Mr Winters, wisely. He winked at Kate, and pointed at his wife's back. Kate giggled.

'Stop pointing at my back!' snapped Mrs Winters.

'I'm not pointing at your old back.'

'I know rightly, you are. Would you go into the front room and read the paper,' scolded his wife. 'You're making the kitchen look untidy.'

'I like them feisty,' he said, before scuttling down the hall in his old cardigan, like a big, woolly beetle.

Kate sulked in her bedroom for the rest of the day, only coming out to make a mug of hot chocolate, or to get a read of the evening paper. There were no jobs in it that she liked the sound of. Her father told her he could pull some strings for her in Casualty. There was a cleaning job going, if she thought she could handle the sight of blood. There were always a few broken bones at the weekend. Maybe a shooting or two. Kate refused to even dignify his suggestion with a reply. When her birthday arrived in October, she refused to open her birthday cards, so Shirley opened them for her. And the chocolate cake her mother presented to her after dinner, with thirty pink candles blazing on the top of it, made Kate's neck stiffen up with fear. Kate's friends were planning a birthday bash for her in Hogan's, and they said if she didn't turn up they would land round to the house and carry her there themselves. Kate tried to get out of it by telling them she was not speaking to Alex. There was no sign of Standing Stone, they told her, so that was all right. Sunny Jim told them he was working in a rough place near the docks for a while, until his court case was over. He would be off the scene for three months, at least. Louise Lowry, however, was still on the warpath, but they would make sure that Kate was not left alone in the ballroom. She would have plenty of support if Louise came over looking for a punch-up. Shirley and Kate avoided the newsagent's, and its one-eyed shop assistant with her brick-like hands, just in case. The birthday bash went ahead and it was a washout. (Kate didn't get a man.) Shirley spent all night dancing with Declan. Even when the slow songs came on, and DJ Toni did his sleaze-merchant heavy-breathing routine, they just laughed and went on dancing cheek to cheek. Kate was left sitting at the table, drinking vodka until her head swam.

Kevin McGovern was there, in a white suit and black shirt this time, but he didn't come over to ask her to dance. Kate smiled at him. He was wearing a metallic silver tie. A dance with Kevin was better than nothing, she reasoned. But Kevin thought that Kate was just being polite. After all, the first time he had tried to chat Kate up, she'd left him dancing with Shirley and then ran out of Hogan's in tears. He thought he would play it cool for a while. Play hard to get. He walked around the ballroom, nodding his head to the music, trying to look like an easy-going sex symbol. Let Kate Winters get a good look at the merchandise, he thought.

When December eventually arrived, Kate had been jobless for twelve weeks, and the bills were piling up on her bedside table. Shirley lent her fifty pounds but that was just a drop in the bucket. And Kate couldn't tell her family the truth about her debts because she had lied to them for years about the true cost of her purchases.

'This top?' she would say. 'A fiver in Primark.' When really it was forty pounds from a designer store. 'This perfume? Three pounds in the market.' Not true. Thirty pounds from Chanel. And so on. The chickens had come home to roost – was that the saying?

She was thirty years old, and felt every day of it. She felt ancient, over the hill. Was it legal to wear short skirts when you were thirty, she wondered. Or would people call you 'mutton dressed as lamb'? Did people still go to discos when they were thirty? To make matters worse, Shirley was wittering on about her precious boyfriend all the time. 'What should I buy him for Christmas?' she asked Kate, ten times a day. Kate suggested a white stick and a guide dog, and her mother slapped her on the arm.

'Make yourself useful,' she said. 'Go and get a nice tree for the front room, and get some new decorations while you're at it. Shirley is bringing her young man home to meet us at seven o'clock.'

'Why can't she do it? If it's for her boyfriend? And it's only the second of December. It's too soon for a fresh tree.'

'You have nothing else to do, you big idle lump! Go on. Get an artificial tree.' Mrs Winters snapped off the television and jabbed her thumb towards the front door. 'And get some mince pies and turkey slices. And a pot of cranberry sauce for the sandwiches. And fancy Christmas napkins as well. And check the fairy lights are working. We might need a new set. And –' But the front door had already banged shut. Kate was furious that she was reduced to running errands for Shirley's benefit. She would pick the worst tree in Belfast, and the tackiest decorations of all time. She would hang everything on one side of the tree, and pull the wings off the angel. And she would buy ham slices and strawberry jam instead of turkey and cranberry sauce. And plain pink napkins.

When the tree was finally switched on that afternoon, it was a total mess. Kate ran up to her bedroom in fits of hysterical laughter. In fact, she laughed so hard, she fell halfway up and accidentally tore off a small piece of the wallpaper. She threw herself down on her bed, on top of a pile of unpaid bills and laughed until her sides were sore. Now Declan Greenwood would know what kind of family he was getting involved with. A bunch of working-class idiots who couldn't even hang a few balls on a Christmas tree properly.

But when Kate came back downstairs two hours later, the old tree was in the yard, and a new one was in its place. A six-foot beauty with perfect branches, and sweet white lights shaped like snowflakes. And the decorations were beautiful; tiny angels with real feathers for wings, silver mirror balls and fat silver tinsel. Shirley was laying

147

out neat rows of turkey and cranberry sandwiches on plates covered with jolly Christmas napkins. And the whole house was filled with the smell of mince pies heating gently in the oven.

'Very funny,' said Shirley. 'We all enjoyed your little joke.'

Declan's first visit was a great success. Shirley was very nervous about bringing him to the house. But she reckoned it was time to let him meet her family. She warned her parents and Kate not to embarrass her in any way. But she needn't have worried. Declan complimented everything and Mrs Winters was soon simpering like a love-struck schoolgirl. She lapped it up when visitors admired her ornaments and crystal knick-knacks. She told him about each and every one, patiently going through the story of when and why it was purchased or who it was from. Declan was very easy to talk to, not stuffy or stuck-up at all. Mr and Mrs Winters thought he was lovely, and well worth the frantic dash to get the house ready for him.

The next day, Kate and Shirley had a big row. It all began when Kate asked Shirley for a small loan to buy some Christmas presents, and Shirley said that she was sorry but she had spent all her wages on some decent clothes for herself, as Declan had invited her to spend an afternoon with his family. And she wanted to look nice because the Greenwoods lived in a very posh area. And of course, she had to bring them a decent gift. (She'd bought some handmade wine glasses in a craft shop.) Shirley had also bought the long, purple coat she had admired all autumn, and Declan said she looked very sophisticated in it. Especially when she wore purple lipstick to match. She was like a witch. A beautiful witch. He found girls much more attractive when they were wearing elegant clothes and dramatic lipstick than when they were half-naked and plastered with eyeshadow and blusher. Kate was extremely irritated by these revelations, and jealous on so many counts that she lost her temper completely and called Shirley a bore.

'A bore, did you call me? A bore?'

'Yes! A bore. A *boring* little relationship-*bore* who can't do anything without consulting her *boring* boyfriend first. Declan this and Declan that! I'm your sister, Shirley, in case you've forgotten. And I'm out of work and broke. And you're throwing your money away on silly coats to impress your stuck-up boyfriend. You're way out of your depth.'

Shirley was very angry then and called Kate a miserable sponger who couldn't even be bothered to get a job and pay her own bills.

'You needn't think I'm slaving away at work all week, just to pay for the luxuries piled high in your precious boudoir. You bought them and you can bloody well pay for them. You're a fine one to lecture me about wasting money. The cheek of you!'

'You promised me you would help me to pay off the catalogues.'

'Well, stuff that.'

'You mean you're breaking a promise?'

'Yes, Kate. I am. Get over it. You big baby!'

'How dare you call me a baby!'

'You think you can twist me and Ma and Da round your little finger? Well, you can't, Kate. We're not afraid of you any more. If you're really as smart as you'd like to think you are, then why are you still living at home, at your age, jobless, and throwing yourself at gay bouncers?' Kate's face flinched as if she had been slapped.

'He is not *gay*. How dare you even suggest it!'

'He is surely gay. He practically walks on his tiptoes.'

'Are you a gay-basher, Shirley Winters? I cannot *believe* you, of all people, would turn out to be a gay-basher.'

'Not a bit of me. I think he's cute. But it doesn't alter the fact that he is a *gay man* and you are a straight woman. Are you blind as well as stupid?'

And then Kate called Shirley a silly tart.

'Don't lecture me on love, you silly tart!'

'What do you mean by that?' Shirley roared. 'I'm no tart.'

'Well, he's not going out with you for your brains, or your money, is he? Or your fashion-sense. Just what is he getting out of this so-called relationship? Would it be a little bit of *rumpy*, I wonder?'

'Oh! You're so *mean*, Kate! It's none of your bloody business if we sleep together or not. Who the hell do you think you are? We're in love, you big dope! You know? The L word? You're just jealous.'

'Oh, please! I've been in love before. A hundred times. Big swing! You'd think you were the only girl in the whole wide world, ever, to snog some fella and think: this is the real thing!'

'It *is* the real thing.'

'How do you know? How *would* you know? You've no experience of men. You think you're in love if a fella buys you a glass of lemonade. It's pathetic.'

'I just know he loves me. All right? You've had more

boyfriends than I've had hot dinners, and you haven't managed to hang on to a single one of them. And the only guy who was really nice was Kevin McGovern, and you treated him with contempt. So what the hell do you know about men? You're the silly one! Not me.'

'Aw, shut up!' Kate was tired now.

'You shut up!' Shirley was still outraged.

'Well, go on then, go and grovel to the big snobs on Derryvolgie Avenue. Leave me here, watching the blasted TV with Mum and Dad all night. Be sure you don't use the wrong knife and fork and I hope you have the time of your life!'

Kate stamped upstairs and slammed her bedroom door. She lay on her bed and had a little cry. Shirley would be up in a minute to apologize, she told herself. Kate waited and waited, dabbing at her face with a tissue. When Shirley didn't come upstairs to say sorry, Kate began to worry. Maybe her diva ways were beginning to lose their power. Even her parents weren't that bothered when she lost her job. The time was, they would have barged into the building and demanded to speak to the manager, and threatened to sue the entire department for upsetting their little girl. But they had mellowed a lot in recent years. They must be feeling their age, Kate thought. Age! She was thirty, unemployed and single. It was a chant in her head that would not stop. She sat up suddenly and dried her eyes with the sleeve of her velvet cardigan. She felt very alone. What could she do? The answer was simple: Kevin McGovern.

She got herself dressed up nicely on Monday morning and went for a walk past Kevin's garage. Kevin knew a lot of business people in the neighbourhood. He might know of a job going someplace, without Kate having to humiliate herself in the job centre again. He was sitting on a deckchair, just inside the garage doors, having a cup of tea and a cheese sandwich. He was almost afraid to speak to Kate, since she had run out on him in the ballroom, but Kate was the one who stopped and smiled this time. She leaned against the wall and waved in at him. Kevin almost dropped his sandwich onto the oily floor.

'Kate Winters! How are you doing?'

'Kevin, how's yourself?'

'Working away. The usual, you know. How's the office treating you?'

'I've left there, now. I'm looking for something else.'

'Is that right?' He stood up and rubbed his hands clean on the sides of his overalls. He did know of a few local jobs, as it happened. His brain went into overdrive. This was a great opportunity to help Kate. But he didn't want to waste the chance of getting close to her himself.

'Do you happen to know of anything going, in the area? I'm very flexible and open-minded.'

Kevin's mind exploded with this notion. He decided to offer Kate a job, even if he had to work an extra day each week to afford her wages.

'I'm looking for somebody, myself. That place is in an awful mess.' He nodded in the direction of his large, but dingy office, and looked at Kate, hopefully. 'I usually do my own paperwork at the weekends, but it's fairly piling up on me.'

'Well, look no further. I'm your woman. How would

you fancy me for your new office-girl?' Kevin's face blushed as pink as one of his London-bought suits.

'Aw, that's great. That's just great. Come on in, I'll show you round.'

'There's the small matter of references . . . I should tell you, there was a slight problem at my old place. A clash of personalities, as it were.'

'Not to worry! I'll not bother myself with references. When can you start?'

'Tomorrow morning?'

'That's just fantastic. It will save me from having to train up a stranger.' He led the way into the gloomy garage, and Kate knew, before she'd even seen the office, that she was soon to know what shoddy filing really was. Still, Kevin wasn't the worst of them. He'd be a nicer boss than old Bingham the Battleaxe. Kevin wouldn't know a time-sheet from a smack in the mouth.

'Here is the nerve-centre of the whole operation,' said Kevin, and he opened the door slowly.

'It's very nice,' said Kate, eyeing a scene of utter devastation. In the semi-darkness of the room, she could make out enormous piles of paper and car manuals, hundreds of car parts and even a few worn tyres. All of it, white with the dust of years.

'Anything you'd like to ask me?'

'Yes. I'll take the job on one condition.'

'Name it.'

'I want to revamp this office. Paint, carpet, desks, chairs. Proper storage, some pictures. Lighting. New kettle and mugs. About two thousand pounds should do it.'

'Sure.' He had his chequebook out in a second. 'I've

been meaning to get the place done up, but I don't have the time. Or the taste. Tell you what, just do whatever you want.'

'Righto,' said Kate.

I usually do, she thought. And she winked at him.

17. Angels' Wings, Engagement Rings

Kate's new job was an absolute godsend. She worked day and night on bringing Kevin's garage into the twentieth century. It was a great outlet for Kate's many talents, of which spending money was the most outstanding. She even had new windows designed for the old building, which made it much warmer. And she created a cosy little coffee area, with a lime-green sofa and pink scatter-cushions, a low table with a glass top and a pretty standard lamp of a 1950s' design. It was like a little oasis of style in the otherwise masculine dreariness, Kate liked to think. Anyway, it was gorgeous. She spent days sorting through the paperwork, some of it more than twenty years out of date. The tyres and car parts she consigned to the back of the garage.

The revamp of the office was a resounding success. Kevin was delighted. He surveyed the new filing system carefully, to show Kate how pleased he was. It would save him hours of time, he told her, being so organized. And even though the fancy coffee area wasn't strictly necessary, it was nice to have somewhere clean and stylish to enjoy his cheese sandwich at lunchtime. Kate placed her new desk beside the window, so that she could look out over the street. And Kevin loved to see her there as he talked to clients on the forecourt. She was like a princess in her tower, he thought, and he was her knight in shining armour. Well, her knight in oily overalls.

For the first few days, he waited politely for Kate to summon him for his lunchtime cuppa. Then, with his confidence increasing, he would just appear at the door of the office when the one o'clock news came on the radio. Kate would look up and smile and then get out of her seat to fill the kettle. It was never awkward between them. They could talk about the business for half an hour, with no fears about being alone together. And the phone never stopped ringing some days, so there was always the distraction of that. Sometimes it was quiet, and then they might discuss things like the price of holidays abroad or where they might like to live if the Troubles got much worse. A lot of their friends were emigrating, with or without legal papers. They said they might as well labour under a blue sky, as under a grey one; without the fear of violence hanging over them all the time. Kevin liked big cities like London but he was reluctant to leave his thriving business behind him and start all over again somewhere else. Kate agreed with him. She'd like to live somewhere hot and glamorous, but didn't want to strike out for foreign shores on her own. The two of them had some very pleasant chats about the world in general, on the green velvet sofa. Kate felt very relaxed with Kevin. Not crazy with lust, unfortunately; but then, no horrible trembling and palpitations either. All that business had stopped completely. Which made her so grateful she sometimes knelt down on the floor beside her bed and actually prayed properly for ten whole minutes before going to sleep.

When she had banked her first pay-cheque, Kate invited Kevin out for dinner, to thank him for the new job. He was growing on her, gradually; day by day, little by little. He was so easy to work with, she actually enjoyed hearing the alarm clock ringing in the morning. It wasn't too bad sitting behind a desk all day when you had some degree of freedom and independence. As long as all the paperwork was in order by the end of the day, Kevin didn't care how many coffee breaks she had or if she listened to the radio or if she had fresh flowers and little ornaments on her desk. He treated Kate like a human being, not as a human *resource*. Why didn't these so-called management gurus know that, she wondered. Hadn't they heard of words like *individuality* and *stress* and *PMT*? Kate felt so much better she decided she would even try to be nicer to her own family. She apologized to all of them for her recent bad humour.

Kate and Shirley made friends again. (Although they both knew it would take them a long time to forget the hurtful words that had been thrown in the heat of the moment.) Shirley told Kate that Miss Bingham was very upset when she discovered that Kate had a new job. She'd asked Shirley straight out why Kate hadn't turned up for her most recent 'signing on' and Shirley had told her that Kate was now the office manager of a thriving business. She wouldn't be claiming benefit any more; she was earning more money than in her old job. And Miss Bingham had been so annoyed she'd bent a teaspoon in half. So upset, in fact, she'd slammed a drawer shut in one of the filing cabinets without removing her fingers first. The sisters had a good giggle about that. Poor Miss

Bingham wouldn't get to gloat over Kate's unemployment after all.

Shirley also told Kate that she was getting on well with Declan. She didn't, however, tell Kate about meeting Declan's family, and that it hadn't been a nerve-racking experience at all. They were very warm and welcoming towards her despite their wealthy background. Even his mother, Marion, who might have been overprotective of her only son, could not have been nicer. Irish mothers could be cruel, sometimes; they could be even more snobbish than the English. But Mrs Greenwood went out of her way to make sure that Shirley enjoyed her dinner, and did not ask her too many awkward questions – like, where she worked or where she lived or what her father did for a living – knowing already that the answers would be very disappointing, that Shirley lived in a small, terraced house and her parents were both cleaners in the Royal Victoria Hospital.

Nor did she tell Kate that they had spent some heavenly afternoons in Declan's double bed when his parents had gone away on a cruise with their three daughters. Declan had a beautiful body and a fantastic record collection. She'd never be able to hear the Cure or the Stranglers again without blushing. Once Shirley had opened that button on Declan's shirt for the first time, there was no going back. And she was clear on that. She was the one who had started it, not him. 'Are you sure?' he'd asked her, that day. They'd been out for a lovely stroll in the park, followed by fish and chips and a cup of tea, in front of the television.

'Yes,' she'd said. 'I'm sure.'

They loved each other. They had both said it, several times. What was the point in waiting until they were in their thirties and could afford a fancy wedding? By the time they had saved up for something lavish enough to please Marion, they would be middle-aged.

Kate would be shocked that their relationship had progressed so much in just a few short weeks. But she would never understand how close Shirley felt to Declan, and that even though he was barely twenty years old, he was very mature and sensible. He didn't giggle when they undressed in the afternoons, with the bedroom curtains closed against the winter winds. And Shirley didn't tell Kate that all her fears and worries about taking off her own clothes hadn't been necessary, either. Most of the time, they barely paused to take off all of their clothes, anyway, and afterwards fell about the bed laughing, with shirts and sweaters wrapped around wrists, and socks and shoes half on. Shirley's time-sheets were in a state of meltdown: currently minus fifteen hours and twenty minutes. She could almost hear Miss Bingham shrieking the next time she carried out a spot check.

Declan was worth it, though. He was the sexiest man Shirley had ever encountered in real life. He had an easy-going charm that was not threatening or irritating, but warm and seductive. He told her funny stories that made her laugh until her eyes watered. He told her she was beautiful. Best of all, he was discreet. He didn't boast about his love life to his friends. Shirley knew that for a fact because they didn't snigger when they met her on the street. Some boys were so immature, they were really still children: laughing through their noses at words like 'breast' or 'orgasm'. Declan was a really special man; she knew he wasn't just pretending to be sensitive to impress her. Within days of meeting him, she felt that she had known him always. But Shirley couldn't tell her big sister any of that. Kate used her sexuality to reward expensive meals out, or gifts of gold jewellery. She enjoyed knowing that men desired her, but it wasn't an intellectual experience for her, or even an emotional one. She wouldn't understand that sacred feeling of bonding between two separate souls who had suddenly found each other and become one. Kate would say that Shirley had given out the goods too soon and that Declan would have no respect for her.

She had to be vague when she was talking to Kate about romance. She couldn't say that they had already carried out Shirley's fantasy of kissing in the rain until their clothes were soaked through. (Kate would think she was crazy.) Or that Declan had told her he wanted them to be together for ever. (He wasn't commitment-phobic, as so many men seemed to be these days.) Or that his skin was soft and clean and smelt of aftershave and toast. Or that the first time they slept together was very uncomfortable for Shirley. (That was to be expected.) But that after that, it was wonderful. He was a gentle lover, who kissed her shoulders and her face tenderly before, and after, they went to bed together. And now, it just felt so *right*, lying in his arms and falling asleep beside his deliciously warm body. The closeness of sleeping together was almost more special than making love. Sometimes, they stayed under the warm blankets all afternoon, drinking tea and eating biscuits, and gossiping about their friends and families. Poor Kate had never felt any of these things and so Shirley kept the depth of her new love a secret. Some things just had to remain private.

And then Shirley was writing her Christmas cards on the fifteenth of December, and wondering what the last day for posting was, and the thought suddenly came to her that she couldn't remember the date of her last period. She was determined to be calm as she got out her diary and flicked through the pages. Five weeks! What with the Christmas preparations, she'd forgotten all about it. She didn't breathe for about three minutes when the realization finally dawned on her. She'd never been late before. Not even when she was worried about important exams or a lack of money or the death of a close relative. Shirley put on a warm coat and walked to a chemist shop, well away from her own neighbourhood. She bought the pregnancy testing kit in a matter-of-fact way, as if she was buying it for someone else. When the friendly assistant told her it was the most accurate brand on the market, she said she would pass on the advice, thank you very much. She kept the little carton in the bottom of her wardrobe, hidden in a shoebox, for three whole days. Waiting and praying for her period to come. But it didn't.

And then she carried out the test. Such a simple and straightforward test, it was hard to believe it could really tell Shirley if her whole life was about to go into free fall. She checked the instructions over and over again, to make sure there would be no mistakes when the result came through. And of course, it was positive. She was pregnant. She was going to have a baby! She was so shocked, she couldn't even laugh or cry or panic or feel *anything*.

Time stood still. She tensed up completely, waiting for the sky to fall down heavily on her head. But amazingly, nothing at all happened. Nothing. She ate her supper with her family and they didn't even comment that her face was tight with tension or that she ate nothing and drank six cups of tea. She lay awake that night, so numb it was frightening, just looking up at the moon. Have I ruined everything, she wondered. Will Declan change his mind about me? Will my father have a heart attack? Will my mother chop down a tree on the avenue, fashion a rudimentary cross with it and quite literally *crucify* me? Will I end up in a hovel somewhere, living on economy cornflakes, with a greasy ponytail and wearing the same cheap anorak for the rest of my days?

Finally it was Christmas Eve. Shirley hadn't told anyone her news. Not her family, not her friends, not even Declan. She couldn't tell them, until she could come to terms with it herself. She refused to contemplate ending the pregnancy, that was all she knew for certain. It wasn't the baby's fault that she had been such an idiot. The baby was the only person in all of this that was pure and precious and blameless and innocent. And so, although she was tempted to go to London and book herself into a private clinic, like Kevin's mother and her varicose veins, she knew she would regret it for the rest of her life. She'd read all the magazine articles about how some women were suicidal for years afterwards, half mad with grief and regret. *This will pass*, she told herself, a hundred times a day, like a recovering alcoholic. *This will pass*. All the same, she knew that it was going to be a bumpy ride until things quietened down again. She felt nauseous at

162

the thought of it. Or was that the morning sickness starting already?

It was going to be so hard to deal with her mother's religious rants, her father's inevitable withdrawal to the shed, Declan's possible desertion, and Kate's smug lectures on birth control. So, she said nothing. And life went on as normal. Mr and Mrs Winters fussed over the food supplies, debating for hours about whether they should buy a posh and trendy fresh turkey or a good old-fashioned frozen one. In the end, they bought both. A cheaper frozen one for Christmas Day, and an expensive fresh one for the following day. They wanted to impress Kevin and Declan, who had both been invited for dinner. Mrs Winters had somehow got her ideas all mixed up and decided that Thanksgiving in America, and being middle-class in general, meant that nothing else but a fresh turkey would do when guests were invited to the house. And fresh cranberry sauce had to be made as well. The glass jar from the supermarket had been hidden at the back of the larder, along with the box of dehydrated stuffing mix and the cheap crepe-paper crackers. Mr Winters complained that such rampant snobbery would have him bankrupted, and that if any of the neighbours found out they had paid twenty pounds for a box of crackers, they would call the nearest mental hospital, and have them both committed right away.

'We're two-up, two-down people,' he kept saying. Which was incorrect, since they had three bedrooms. (Well, two, and a very small boxroom.)

Shirley was kneeling on the floor of the boxroom, after lunch on Christmas Eve, wrapping her gift for Declan.

After much deliberation, she had bought him a lovely pair of real leather gloves. (Probably some subconscious jab at him for not being careful enough with the condoms.) She tucked the corners of the parcel in neatly, and stuck a big blue bow on the top. Then, she fetched the matching gift-tag from the carrier bag and wrote *love from Shirley* on it. She had bought her mother perfume, aftershave for her father and a glittery handbag for Kate. (Even though she didn't need it or deserve it.) But anyway. Shirley was going to enjoy Christmas. She'd promised herself that. She'd revel in every traditional minute of it; eat lots of sweets and sandwiches, watch television until her eyes dried up, and then deal with the fallout from the pregnancy in the dismal anticlimax that was January.

The little bedroom became dark and when Shirley got up to switch on her bedside lamp, she saw the reason for the lack of light in the sky. As if the Christmas fairy had arranged it, it had begun to snow. Big fat clusters of dry snowflakes came scurrying down from the grey sky. At first, there were just a few, and then more and more began to fall until Shirley could barely see the houses on the other side of the street. Shirley was delighted to note that the snow was not melting on the ground, but piling up in corners as if it intended to hang around for a few days. A little bubble of excitement burst in her heart. She would get to kiss Declan in a new weather situation! Bliss. For a moment she even forgot about the baby.

She felt sorry for Kate, then, as she watched the fat flakes swirling past her windowpane. It must be very lonely for Kate, having no boyfriend at Christmas time. Shirley had been very sensitive over the last few weeks, deliberately not telling her sister how fabulous her new romance was. And now she resolved not to talk about Declan when she watched television with Kate later that evening. She was afraid she might let something slip about the baby. So they watched cartoons and munched their way through two jumbo selection boxes, and gossiped about harmless things. Shirley told her sister that Alex Stone was now dating Louise Lowry. He'd been found guilty in the court case but let off with a small fine. To celebrate, he'd spent the night dancing with Louise in Hogan's ballroom. As an ordinary customer. Kate was jealous, but not jealous enough to do anything about it. If Louise wanted him, she could have him. For a girl who spent her days surrounded by jelly frogs and sugar mice, Alex was probably an improvement. Just about.

'Do you fancy Kevin a little bit, even? I really think he would be good for you,' ventured Shirley the next day.

They were peeling vegetables in the tiny kitchen, giving their mother a day off the chores. The turkey was safely in the oven, the stuffing was ready in a separate dish, and the entire house had been scrubbed and polished until it was practically sterile. Mr and Mrs Winters had set off for midday Mass in great spirits, holding hands like teenagers. Mrs Winters was wearing the new coat her husband had bought her. And he was wearing the new boots that she had bought for him. Their squabbles over Kate's future had been forgotten. Kate was working again, and Shirley had a boyfriend, so the longed-for grandchildren could not be ruled out after all. In the long term, of course.

Kate shrugged her shoulders. The truth was, she had already kissed Kevin, twice, on the new, lime-green velvet sofa in the coffee area at the garage. Just to see if her libido had returned. It hadn't. And to see if Kevin still fancied her. He did. And they'd had a bit of a cuddle as well. And it hadn't been too bad. In fact, the second time, Kevin had taken off his oily overalls beforehand and it had been quite pleasant. He looked almost handsome in his blue jeans and a crisp white T-shirt. Purely in the interests of romantic research, Kate had kissed Kevin as passionately as she could. A little bit of heavy breathing, for effect, and a quick run of her fingers through his hair. He was absolutely thrilled, and caressed her back so much with his big, strong hands that it warmed up considerably; she could have fried an egg on it. Kate threw caution to the winds then, and undid a few buttons on her new red cardigan, to reveal a matching bra underneath. The contents of the red bra put in an appearance for a couple of minutes and Kevin could barely restrain himself. He said, '*My God!*' seven times and touched the magnificent mounds with his eyes closed. And then with his eyes open. And then closed, again. And then he leapt up off the sofa and put the overalls back on, and stumbled down the stairs to the half-stripped car engines. Kate was very pleased that she still had the power to get men hot under the collar. She buttoned up her cardigan, boiled the kettle and brought him down a mug of tea. Kevin offered to buy her an engagement ring a few days after that, so there was no question of this being just an office fling for him. He was crazy about her. And Kate thought he wasn't a bad catch, either. He was very talkative, and attentive, and quite a competent kisser. But she didn't feel any fireworks when they were alone together.

Kevin was pushing her for an answer to his proposal, claiming it wasn't too soon as he had been in love with her for ages. And Kate was thirty and Kevin was thirty-five. What was the point of hanging about? Kate actually gave his proposal serious consideration. Her father would be pleased, and Kevin would make a better husband than most. But she couldn't say yes, or no, just yet. She wanted to think about it for a while. They were not even a couple, officially. It was very complicated. Then again, if there was any danger that Shirley was going to have a serious relationship with Declan, she might just get engaged after all. She could not possibly be upstaged by her baby sister, who owned not one item of designer clothing or even a drop of designer make-up. And who left important decisions of the heart up to silly things like *instinct*. And so, she went out with Kevin for a drink after work occasionally, or shopping maybe, or just for a Sunday walk. The two of them were more or less dating. They had been out for dinner several times and both of their families were curious. Kevin and Kate brazened it out. They weren't ready to discuss their relationship with anybody. They were still trying to work it out themselves.

'I'm delighted that you asked me to marry you, Kevin,' she told him one day, as they lay on the sofa together after their lunchtime cup of tea. 'And when I'm able to give you an answer, I will. And I promise you there is no other man on the horizon.'

On Christmas night, Declan called round to go for a stroll with Shirley. The snow was so thick on the ground they made lovely scrunching sounds when they walked.

He was delighted with his gloves and put them on straight away. He gave Shirley a tiny present in a fancy box, which she just knew was jewellery. It turned out to be a beautiful silver necklace with a little diamond heart on it. The little diamond sparkling under the street lights made her feel very vulnerable and small. She wanted to cry. Shirley decided there was no point in holding the news about the baby to herself any longer. Whatever he said or did now, would not alter her decision to keep the baby. She looked around to make sure they were on their own.

'Declan, look, there's no easy way to tell you this. I wasn't going to tell you until January but I can't keep it to myself any longer. I'm going to have a baby. I know we've just met, and I didn't do this on purpose, and you probably think I did, but anyway I'm keeping the baby and you don't have to stay with me, and I'm sorry if your parents go mad, and my parents will definitely go mad, and I don't know what I'm going to do.'

'Shush, Shirley,' he whispered, putting his arms round her, in the middle of the footpath. His face was full of concern. 'Are you absolutely sure about this?'

'Yes. I've been to the doctor for a proper test.'

'How long?'

'About six weeks. It must have happened the first time we slept together.'

'I'm so sorry, Shirley. This is all my fault.'

'It's okay. These things happen all the time. That's what the doctor said. No method is absolutely foolproof, she said. I'm not sad.'

'Are you not?'

'No. I'm scared stiff. But I'm not sad. Are you?'

'No. But I'm sorry for all the trouble this is going to be for you, pet.'

'Do you want to break up?' There was a lump in her throat, but she wanted to know right away. She couldn't bear it if he said he would need some time to think things over. She'd never speak to him again, if he said that. It was all or nothing for Shirley. But she needn't have worried.

'No, you idiot,' he laughed. 'Why would I want to break up?'

'Because, if you do, that's fine with me. As I said before, I didn't do this on purpose to hang on to you or anything. I still have my pride. I can get through this on my own.'

'Shirley, I love you. And I love being part of a happy family. My parents have a fantastic marriage. Do you want to get married? Will you marry me?'

'What? Aren't we too young? Too inexperienced?'

'Well, yes and no. Why not? I'm willing to take a chance if you are.'

'Take a *chance*?'

'I mean, you might decide you don't love me in a year's time, but I'm pretty sure I'll still love you. In fact, I know I will.'

'Won't your family think I'm too common for you?'

'Not at all. They're from common stock themselves, you know. They just worked their way into that big house.'

'Still. I'm sure they'll be disappointed.'

'I'll sweeten the pill for them a little bit.'

'What do you mean?'

'I'll tell them I'm going to stick at medical college after all, now that I have serious responsibilities. I was considering chucking it for a while, recently.'

She began to relax, and breathe properly for the first time in days. If Declan wasn't going to do a runner, it would be easier to tell her parents.

'That's great news, but it'll take years before you graduate. I earn next to nothing. How will we live?'

'We'll rent a flat. I'll work weekends in the restaurant.'

'We'll live together?'

'Yes – aren't we going to get married?'

'Before the baby comes?'

'Yes. You don't mind?'

'Of course I don't mind. I had some notion I was going to keep the baby in my room at home.'

'You said it was the boxroom.'

'It is. It's tiny.'

'You couldn't fit a crib in there, could you? Or a playpen and toys? You wouldn't believe how much stuff you need with babies.'

'Oh, God! A crib! Declan! What have we done?'

'It's okay, Shirley. Everything is going to be okay. I promise you. I have three sisters younger than me; I know all about stairgates and baby rice. Now, say after me: *Everything is going to be okay.*'

They walked for two hours and by the time Declan eventually kissed Shirley goodnight at her front door, they had made a pact to tell everyone right away and arrange the wedding before Shirley's bump made the keepsake photographs just too embarrassing. They looked at the beautiful angel perched on the top of the tree in the bay window, smiling down on them through the frosty glass.

'Do you realize that getting engaged at Christmas is the Holy Grail for romantic women everywhere?' whispered

Shirley. She wasn't sure but she thought she felt happy and maybe even a tiny bit excited. At least, it wasn't the catastrophe it had seemed in the beginning.

'I'm glad you're getting used to the idea,' said Declan. 'I really love you, Shirley. It's not just the baby. I do love you. We'll be okay.'

'I think this child will be in university before I get used to the idea,' said Shirley in a quiet voice. 'But I'll tell you one thing.'

'What?'

'Kate is going to go *ballistic* when she finds out that I'm getting married. And I do mean ballistic. Nuclear melt-down hissy-fit bonkers. In fact, I think we'd better have the men in white coats standing by with rhino-sedatives when we make our big announcement. She'll have to be restrained with ropes.'

'Every cloud, eh?' Declan said, and they both laughed for the first time that evening.

'When will we tell your parents?' he asked quietly.

'We'll tell them tomorrow evening,' she said. 'When they're too full of turkey and wine to do anything but shout.'

The minute Declan came through the front door, dusting fresh snow from his shoulders, Marion knew that something important had happened. Her beloved son's face was flushed and bright with excitement. She watched him from her comfortable armchair in the sitting room for a few moments, as he lingered by the coat rack, straightening the arms of his jacket. She knew that if he had some news to tell her, he would bring up the subject himself, in his own way. Marion was a good listener. She prided herself on her approachable nature. Eddy had nodded off on the sofa under a cosy woollen blanket. Declan came into the room, and she smiled her brightest smile at him.

'Mum,' he whispered, spying his softly snoring father. 'Can we go into the kitchen? I have to tell you something. Sorry I'm a bit late getting home. Were you waiting up for me?'

'Not at all, sweetheart,' she said. 'Come on.' She got up and placed the fire screen in front of the flames. They tiptoed past Eddy and went into the kitchen with their arms round each other.

'I was just going to make some hot chocolate, actually,' said Marion. 'I hate going to sleep at all at Christmas time, it seems such a waste! Now, what is it?'

'Mum, I know you're going to be very disappointed with me,' he began, running his fingers through his hair in a way that reminded her of Johnny.

'Declan, I won't be. Honestly.'

'I've been a bit careless, you see.' He looked very embarrassed.

'Just tell me, son, whatever it is,' she said gently. 'I'll understand.' She held his hands and waited, praying he wouldn't tell her he was hooked on drugs.

'Shirley is . . . We're having a baby, Mum. Shirley's pregnant.'

'Is that all, pet?' She laughed with relief. 'I thought you were going to give me bad news. A baby? Why, that's just wonderful. Wonderful!'

'Really? You're not angry with me?' Declan was amazed.

'Not one bit. I don't expect it was planned, my darling.

But these things happen when you're young, and in love. How is Shirley coping?'

'She's a bit shaken, of course. A bit worried.'

'She's keeping the baby, isn't she? I presume she is, if you're telling me about it?'

'Oh, yes, we're keeping the baby, surely; and we're going to get married right away.'

'A wedding! Oh, Declan! This is fabulous altogether. I'm so proud of you for proposing. Naturally, I'll help you both in any way I can.'

'I love Shirley, Mum. We're not just getting married because of the baby. I really love her. She's special. She's smart, and she likes the same things as me, and we never get bored with each other. We're like you and Dad.'

'I know, son. I've noticed how happy the two of you are together. I'm not blind, you know.'

'And you don't think we're too young to get married?'

'There's no ideal age to be married, pet. Some people wait until they are much older than you are, and then they are too set in their ways to share their life with another person. If Shirley is the one for you, why wait?'

'I can't believe you're taking it so well, Mum.'

'I'm delighted, really I am. I adore children. It will be heavenly to have another little one to coo over again. I'll be a doting grandmother, just you wait and see. It will be poor Shirley who will have the morning sickness and the labour pains to deal with.'

'We might have to move in together quite soon. She won't get much support from her own family. They're a bit old-fashioned.'

'Give me a hug,' Marion said. 'I'll miss you so much,

pet, when you go. But you must, of course. You must get a place of your own and take good care of Shirley. You will be good to her, won't you, Declan? No matter what the women's libbers say, it's impossible to bring up a child without lots of help and support.'

'I will, Mum. I promise.'

'Good boy. And in the meantime, Shirley is very welcome to stay with us. It's so important not to be upset when you're expecting a baby. How far on is she?'

'Just a few weeks.'

Marion thought of her own first pregnancy. No one sympathetic to tell, and no comfort in her parents' cold little house on the edge of the city cemetery. No one at all to help her, until Eddy came to the rescue. She took a deep breath and composed herself.

'Come on,' she said. 'Get some cups and saucers on a tray. And some chocolate biscuits and Christmas cake as well. We'll tell your father right away. And the girls, too. They'll be raging if we keep this wonderful news to ourselves for any length of time.'

'Tonight? You're going to wake them all up, tonight?'

'Indeed I am. We'll have a little party to celebrate!'

18. For Unto Us a Child is Born

The great formal dinner was under way. The good dining table had been pulled out from the wall and extended until there was barely room to walk round it. It was covered first with two protective blankets and then a new crimson tablecloth, and *then* a gold runner. There were quilted placemats, green wine glasses, blue water glasses; and salt and pepper shakers in the form of ceramic Santas. There were china dishes of assorted nuts and sugar-coated jellies and fancy almond biscuits and home-made cranberry sauce. There were crackers criss-crossed up and down the table and tea lights in red-glass holders. It was really very cosy when it was finished and the overhead lights were switched off. The turkey was cooked to perfection and was resting on the draining board before being carved. Shirley was in charge of minding the vegetables while Kate was slicing up fresh fruit and mashing raspberries and icing sugar for the starters. Mrs Winters was stirring the gravy, made to her own secret recipe: four spoonfuls of Bisto gravy powder, with a dash of red wine and a sprinkling of black pepper thrown in. The women fussed happily in the kitchen and Mr Winters left them to it and went to put his feet up, in front of a hearty fire in the lounge. There were few things sweeter in life, he decided, than dozing in front of a good fire while the women clattered pots and pans in the kitchen. The aroma of the golden-brown turkey took him right back to his happy childhood, spent on an isolated poultry farm in deepest Armagh.

Shirley had bought the number-one single, 'Fairytale of New York', and had set the record player to spin it over and over again, until her mother lost her temper and threatened to throw the whole contraption in the fire. Kate said Shirley was mad to buy the record, number one or not, because it was sung by an ugly man with most of his teeth missing. Shirley said Kate wouldn't know art if it jumped up and bit her on the nose.

'Just keep an eye on the sprouts, Shirley,' scolded Kate. 'You don't want them going soggy.'

The doorbell rang at one o'clock precisely. Mr Winters leaned out of his chair to see who it was. He always did that, even when he knew already who was coming.

'Well, I owe your mother a tenner,' he called out to his daughters. 'They've actually turned up, by God. They're braver than they look, then, the pair of them. I suppose I'd better let them in.' He heaved himself up out of the armchair, yawned and stretched himself. The heat of the fire had made him quite drowsy.

Declan and Kevin had arrived on time. They stood nervously on the doorstep, clutching bottles of wine, and pulling at their shirt collars. The two sisters preened themselves in the dining-room mirror while their father dragged himself to the front door and let the boys in with a scowl on his face. Despite his wish to see his daughters married off and settled down with families of their own, he was a little bit unsettled by the arrival of two new males into his private territory. They were ushered inside, greetings were exchanged, coats were hung up on the already overflowing coat rack and the festive table was praised, and praised again. Kate kissed Kevin on the cheek, to the amusement of the rest of her family; and everyone sat down, taking great care not to pull the gold runner out of place. Kate went into the kitchen and came gliding out, Delia Smith-style, with a tray full of pretty-looking starters.

'Kate made the *cool-iss* herself, Kevin,' said Mrs Winters, proudly.

'*Cool-ee*, Mum. Honestly! Don't show me up!'

'Let's say Grace first,' declared Mr Winters and the boys froze, terrified that half an hour of solemn prayer was about to ensue. A bead of sweat appeared on Declan's forehead. Any mention of religion made him worry about how news of the baby would be received. Kevin was also uncomfortable with group prayer. He lived alone and didn't pray very often. He wasn't sure he could remember the words to the rosary if things got out of hand and he was called upon to lead. But, it was only Mr Winters enjoying his favourite joke. They all bowed their heads for ten long seconds, waiting for someone to speak.

The silence was broken by the girls.

'*Grace first!*' shouted Shirley and Kate, and they all burst out laughing.

The party mood was in full flow after that, and the fresh-fruit platters disappeared within two minutes. Kevin opened the wine and filled up every single glass on the table to the brim. Including the water glasses. Declan drank his in one go, but only Shirley noticed. They exchanged looks. *It's going to be okay*. Shirley took a sip of her wine, then remembered about the baby and put it down again.

Mrs Winters was wearing a pink cardigan trimmed with a feather boa, and the feathers kept going in her mouth when she was eating.

'Oh my word, do pardon me, I do beg your pardon,' she kept saying to Declan, who was sitting beside her. Which made them all laugh every time.

Mr Winters kept drawing everyone's attention to the lavish crackers he had provided, and the high-quality stainless-steel screwdrivers and key rings that had fallen out of them. He managed to mention the high price of crackers several times, as well as many examples of how he could have spent the twenty pounds on something better. Eventually, Kate had to kick him under the table to get him to stop it.

Everyone clapped when the enormous golden-brown turkey was carried in by Mrs Winters, on a huge plate that had once belonged to her grandmother. She set the plate in front of her husband and withdrew respectfully. He stood up to carve it with a bow of his head and a little flourish of the carving knife. Kate chatted to Kevin about how well the garage was doing while Shirley was left to work her way round the table, doling out steaming vegetables and stuffing-balls. The turkey was delicious, but then again, it *was* a fresh bird.

Mrs Winters told Declan she'd 'never, never, ever' let a frozen turkey in or near the house, in her entire life. The very thought of doing such a thing gave her the creeps. And he told her they used frozen turkey in the restaurant every year. They had to, in case they ran out of supplies of fresh. Mrs Winters went bright red and ate a few more feathers off her boa. Kevin didn't say much but he ate two helpings of dinner and three helpings of mince pies and cream. Kate had told him that she did most of the cooking while Shirley was messing about with her precious records, and he wanted to show her that he appreciated her domestic efforts.

'Well, Kate, those pies were truly splendid,' he gasped. His face was red with overeating. He wanted to unbutton his trousers but, with Kate's father watching him like a hawk, he wisely decided against it.

'There's nothing to cooking,' Kate smugly declared, as they passed the jug of fresh cream round the table. 'I don't know what Mum made such a fuss about, all these years.'

Mrs Winters was quite indignant about that outrageous remark, but she said nothing, for the sake of peace. That cheeky madam, Kate, was as lazy about the house as anyone could imagine. She'd rather live on biscuits and tea, than venture near the cooker. But she was well able to rouse herself to throw a bit of tinfoil over the turkey and jam it into the oven when there was a young man to impress. Yes, indeed! And as for the mince pies! Kate had used frozen pastry and mince from a jar. Huh! Let's see her put up a different dinner each day, every day, for forty years, she fumed to herself. Let's see her bake a meat-and-potato pie when she's trying to stop two young children from playing with the fire in the front room. Still. It was all going so well, it would be a sin to spoil it now with a big row. It was a dream dinner party. She bit her lip, smiled at Declan for the hundredth time, and announced she would clear the plates and bring in some coffee and chocolates. And she pronounced chocolates properly as well, in honour of the occasion. Not in the usual Belfast way: *chac-lits*.

But then, near the end of the feast, when they were all so full that they could not force down even one more bite of a wafer-thin mint, Shirley nervously announced that she was pregnant with Declan's baby, and that his parents had been told about it and that everything was going to be okay. Mr Winters looked terribly confused, as if someone had just asked him to explain the social and historical background to the Reformation. Mrs Winters turned bright cerise pink, as pink as her floaty feathers, and stared at Shirley's abdomen as if she could see the child within, growing and taking shape. Shirley placed her arm across her baby to protect it, and to stop her mother's eyes boring into it.

'Say something, Mum,' said Shirley softly, and she began to weep.

Declan put his arm round Shirley and kissed her gently on the cheek. He prayed they would not be too hard on her. What they said now would affect his opinion of them for ever.

'We're getting married right away,' he said, and he held Shirley's hand on the tablecloth that was covered with pictures of holly sprigs. 'We're buying the ring tomorrow. My parents are very pleased for us. I'm sorry if this has come as a big shock to you all but I love Shirley very much.'

Kate was so merry on Black Russian cocktails that she thought she was hallucinating when Shirley dropped her baby bombshell. Kevin was taking her out to the disco that evening and she had decided to inform him that they could start telling people they were a couple. And now, Shirley (wee, simple Shirley with her rubbish clothes) had to go and steal Kate's thunder with this earth-shattering news.

Kevin was the only one who seemed impressed by the revelation. He looked at Declan with admiration in his eyes. Then he slapped him on the back, shook his hand and cried, 'Well done, yourself, ye boy ye! And you too, Shirley, of course. Congratulations to you both! For unto us a child is born! Top class altogether!'

Mr Winters dropped his glass of whiskey onto the good rug, and said a swearword they'd never heard him use before. He left his seat at the head of the table, wandered aimlessly into the lounge, switched off the television, and began cleaning out his ears with a Twiglet.

'Are my ears deceiving me?' He coughed. Then his voice returned. 'Martha! Martha! Did you hear what this daughter of yours has just said!'

Mrs Winters just mouthed the words, 'Holy Mother of God, help me,' over and over again, like a positive chant. Shirley was struck with how pagan the ritual of repeating prayers sounded. On the other hand, it seemed to work well. Her mother was very calm.

'Now, Shirley,' said Kate, slowly, 'are you sure you're pregnant? Have you had a proper test? Or is this just some crazy notion of yours?'

'Yes. Yes. And no, to your questions.'

'How could you be pregnant? In this day and age? Did you not use protection?'

'Well, obviously we did.' Shirley patted down her fringe and Declan adjusted his tie. This was very embarrassing indeed, even though they had prepared themselves for a reaction like this. They looked at each other, as if to say: *The worst is over. We've told them. The recriminations will be over soon also.*

'The pill, was it? Which brand?'

'Arrah! I'll be in the shed, if there's going to be this kind of talk in the house at Christmas time,' said Mr Winters and he hurried out of the house and down the garden path with a yellow paper hat still on his head.

Kate looked at her sister as if she had just beamed down from another planet. 'Well, Shirley, how did this happen? We're waiting.'

'I'd rather not discuss that side of things, Kate, if you don't mind. It wasn't planned, suffice to say. I'm sorry, Mum. I really am.'

'Shirley, I . . . tell me this is just a dream.' Kate was feeling faint.

But no, Shirley was indeed 'with child'. And Declan was holding her hand and smiling at her, and she didn't look like a little sister any more. She was a young woman, in a relationship, pregnant, and the father was still around. Sometimes, the fathers of unplanned Belfast babies went running to the ferry port without stopping to put on their coats. But Declan seemed okay with the idea. In fact, he had proposed. They were buying a ring; telling people about their baby. Shirley was all grown-up at last. Kate's heart started to hammer like a chain gang laying railways. Damn it! She'd thought that awful scourge was all behind her. Her hands were shaking too, so she sat on them. Kevin put his arm round Kate when he noticed that her face had suddenly drained of all colour except for two slashes of bright orange blusher.

'Kate,' he said. 'Are you all right? Kate?'

Kate blinked her heavily made-up eyes wide open, and the faces of her mother and sister swam into focus. She had to say something. They were all looking at her.

'I *was* going to tell you all today that Kevin and I have been dating, and that we are getting engaged to be married, but of course Shirley had to go and ruin everything,' she cried. 'The little drama-queen!'

'Are we en-engaged?' stammered Kevin. 'I'm spoken for at last! Woah! Some Christmas this is turning out to be!' He drummed his fingers on the table to celebrate.

'What the hell is this? How can you be engaged? You're not even courting.' Mrs Winters was totally confused now. She wondered how many glasses of wine she'd had. Maybe it was the alcohol making her think she was about to become a grandmother. God knows, she hadn't had four glasses of wine since last Christmas.

'Yes, we bloody are engaged! We have been courting. I mean, *dating*. I've just told you we've been dating, but of course you never listen to me.' She turned to Shirley with tears in her eyes. 'You're not the only girl on the planet with a boyfriend, Shirley. No, you're not. But that's not good enough for you. You have to have a bun in the oven as well. And you're no age. Who the hell do you think you are?'

'I didn't do it on purpose,' wept Shirley. 'I thought you'd be happy for me. Just once, I thought that you could take a back seat and be happy for me; but no, you have to get engaged too, just to copy me.'

'I am getting engaged, Shirley, because I am the *proper* age to do so.'

'Bully for you! Have you set the date? Because we have. Engaged means *nothing* if you haven't set the date.' Shirley blew her nose on a paper napkin and sighed deeply. The last thing she wanted, when she was feeling so vulnerable, was a row with her sister. But Kate could be very irritating when she wanted to be.

'Calm down, Shirley,' said Declan. 'Think of the baby. You mustn't get upset.' And he hugged her again. He looked crossly at Kate.

Kate was almost hysterical with indignation and alcohol, but she could smell defeat. An engagement ring was little more than a pretty lump of glass unless the wedding venue and reception had actually been booked. It was just a sad attempt to put a thin veneer of respectability on sex before marriage. Only a completely gullible female would trade the comforts of her young body for a cheap engagement ring from the local jeweller's. (That was the opinion of the older generation, anyway.) Kate looked at Kevin with panic in her eyes.

'When are we getting married?' she gasped at him.

'Whenever you like, Kate,' said Kevin, very quickly.

'Well, now, as Shirley said, we're getting married in the spring. And I'll do everything I can to make Shirley happy,' said Declan, trying to diffuse the situation.

'I think you've done enough,' muttered Mrs Winters. 'And by the way, what's the rush with you two? Is this one preggers and all?' She poked Kate in the arm with a serving spoon that still had some cream on it.

'I am not *preggers*! How dare you?' shouted Kate. 'You're getting cream on my best dress. Honestly! I'm not clueless enough to get myself up the duff to a mere *schoolboy*.

Of all the insulting things to say to me on the day I announce my engagement! You see, Kevin? I told you they were all mad.'

'Well, it's a miracle you never did have a baby before now,' cried Shirley. 'You needn't think you're getting away with playing the innocent virgin. Don't you *dare* look at me like that. And I'm not *up the duff* to a schoolboy. I'm in love with Declan, he's my first and only lover, and we're getting married. And yes, we went to bed together, and I'm not ashamed of it. It was lovely, if you must know! So there!'

Declan blushed furiously and Kevin winked at him and nodded his head to a job well done.

'Don't you bloody well lower yourself with talk like that on a holy day,' cried Mrs Winters. 'We don't require that level of information, thank you very much! What is the priest going to say about this?'

'Oh, God! Stop the clock! I wondered when the poor priest would be dragged into this. Won't he be made up, there's another little Christian baby in the world? The birth rate is collapsing in the West, don't you know? Anyway, I only did what was natural and normal. I didn't start a war! You wanted a grandchild! Didn't you? Well?'

'Oh, my poor heart! *Lord God, I have failed thee!*' Mrs Winters blessed herself three times.

Declan wished he could beam himself and Shirley out of the room altogether, like they did on *Star Trek*. He decided to give the discussion five more minutes, and then he was going to take Shirley home to his place. His mother had told him he could do that, if things got too heated.

'Well, what can I do about it now, Mum?' said Shirley,

calming down a little. 'We're trying to make the best of things. Please be reasonable.'

'I'll have to ask Father Damien's advice,' sniffed Mrs Winters.

'Ask him why there are no women priests, while you're at it,' Shirley muttered. 'Second-class Christians, we women. Obviously, with our hormones all over the place, we aren't capable of saying Mass without bursting into tears.' And then she ruined her great speech by bursting into tears again.

'Oh, yes, always the clever madam! Always knowing better than the rest,' said her mother, bitterly. 'If you're so clever, why are you in this mess? Tell me that!'

'Right! That's enough! Shirley, pet, can you get your coat and some night-things. I'm taking you out of this house tonight.' Declan stood up and set his napkin down on the table.

'Where to?' Shirley was confused now, and very tired.

'You can stay with us until we get a place of our own,' he told her. 'There is just no need for all this fuss. I'm sorry, Mrs Winters, but there isn't. Shirley's carrying a child, for God's sake. Don't shout at her.'

'Sit down, would you?' said Mrs Winters, quietly. 'What did you expect me to say? You know what they're like round here. They love a bit of scandal. We'll be the talk of the street.'

'It's not a scandal, Mrs Winters. We're getting *married*. Anyway, it's Shirley you should care about. Not the neighbours. If you don't mind me saying so. Why can't you support her, like my parents are doing?' He thought of how reasonable they'd been when he told them the news last night. Marion had just hugged him and said she would do everything she could think of to help, and Eddy said he was glad Declan was doing the responsible thing by his girlfriend. They told him not to worry; to enjoy Christmas, and then in January they would start to make plans for the wedding.

Mrs Winters wasn't used to being spoken to so directly. These middle-class types were very forward, she decided. Well, Shirley would fit right in with people like the Greenwoods if this was their shocking attitude to morality.

'Is this true, Declan Greenwood?' she asked him, after a minute's silence. 'Are you going to make an honest woman out of our Shirley? What age are you anyway? You're only a cub yourself.'

'Please don't worry, Mrs Winters. I'm twenty. My parents are already helping with the plans. My mother, Marion, said that she would take care of everything. Weddings are her speciality. You won't have to worry about a thing.'

Mrs Winters mentally cancelled her own plans to emigrate. Maybe this wasn't the fiasco it had looked a moment ago. If his parents were helping with the arrangements, there was more chance he'd go through with it.

'Why's a young lad like yourself so eager to venture up the aisle?' asked Kate, now more composed, and ever curious to the workings of the male mind. 'You're only a pup, like me ma said.'

'My own parents are very happily married. I'd love to have a marriage like theirs,' Declan said, quietly. 'I did plan to get married some day. To be as happy as they are.'

'How do you know it will be happy?' asked Kate, and

Shirley wanted to punch her sister in the face. Hard. 'How do you know it *will* work out?' she persisted.

'I just do,' said Declan. 'We'll make it work. We're both *reasonable* people.'

There was another silence. Whatever Kate and her parents claimed to be, it was not reasonable. Suddenly, there was a loud burp, and they all turned to Kevin, whose face was a picture of relief.

'Better out than in,' he gasped. 'Sorry about that, everyone. Are we really getting married, Kate?' Kevin was still in shock.

Kate sighed and rolled her eyes. 'Yes. We are. Definitely.'

He punched the air with delight.

'Will you fetch my husband in here, Kevin, please, or we'll be going to a friggin' funeral, not a wedding.' Mrs Winters had started to weep with relief. The Christmas napkins were working overtime, mopping up all the tears.

'Two weddings,' said Kate smugly, as Kevin bolted out of the door.

'Sweet Jesus and His Holy Mother,' sobbed Mrs Winters. 'What a Christmas this is turning out to be. If your father thought he was robbed for a box of crackers, what's he going to say when he has to cough up for the nuptials of you two eejits? I'm going upstairs to lie down. Tape the soaps for me, Shirley, would you? Hilda Ogden's leaving *Coronation Street*.' She left the room muttering another prayer to herself. Shirley was relieved. Her parents hadn't coped too badly, after all.

'Well, well, well,' said Kate, looking from Shirley to Declan and back again. 'Talk about dark horses.'

'Dark horses, yourself. I didn't know you were even dating Kevin.'

'There's a lot of things you don't know about me,' said Kate, mysteriously.

'No, there isn't. You stupid twit! I even know what you owe. Eight thousand pounds, would you believe, Declan?'

'You nosy cow!'

'Well, you shouldn't leave your statements on the bathroom floor.' Shirley yawned. She was so tired, she wanted to lay her head on the table and sleep on the remains of the dinner.

'How dare you interfere in my private affairs,' scolded Kate. 'And by the way, I'm the eldest, so Daddy will be funding *my* wedding as a priority. So don't be getting any fancy ideas for *your* wedding.'

'Get real, Kate. What do you mean, the eldest? It's not the eighteenth century, you know. It's first come, first served, nowadays.'

'You're wrong. *I am the eldest*, and therefore entitled to the biggest wedding.'

'Look! Brain donor! It'll be turkey and ham for forty at the very most, no frills whatsoever. And you can buy your own dress in Smithfield market, second-hand. Dad's a cleaner, for God's sake. What's he going to do? Rob a bank?'

'Actually, Mum and Dad said they'd be happy to host *our* reception at their restaurant at their expense. And provide your wedding dress too, Shirley. Mum has hundreds of them in her store.'

'Declan!' Shirley was in raptures. 'Oh, that's lovely of her! Tell her I'm really delighted. Not that I'll take something very expensive. I definitely won't.'

Kate's jelly legs returned with a vengeance, at the very idea of Shirley showing off in a fancy gown from Mrs Greenwood's bridal boutique. The world had changed too much, too quickly.

'I was going to tell your parents not to worry about all the expense, but they left the table too soon,' said Declan.

Just then, Mr Winters and Kevin returned from the garden. Mr Winters was shivering violently.

'Daddy, Declan just said his family are going to pay for Shirley's wedding.'

'Well, isn't that the best news I've had in a long time? Cheers, Declan.' Some colour returned to the older man's face. He removed his yellow hat and sat down again.

'So,' continued Kate. 'That means there's more money in the kitty for my big day. Daddy dear, brace yourself! Kevin and myself are also getting hitched.'

Silence descended upon the room. Everyone froze. Only the candles in their red-glass holders flickered and wavered in the draught. Mr Winters was bug-eyed from whiskey and shock. They all stared at him, praying his heart would be able to take the strain.

'If I'd known there was two weddings coming up, I wouldn't have bought them blasted crackers,' he said, eventually. 'Twenty pounds would have paid for six plates of egg mayonnaise.'

'Oh, Daddy!' Kate was in agony, knowing that Shirley was correct about the money situation. Her poor father would drop dead if he knew the list of things Kate wanted to buy. The best champagne, enormous bouquets of hot-house roses and trailing ivy, a silver Rolls-Royce to the church. It just wasn't going to happen. Not if her father was paying. And how could she fund a fairytale day on her own, with eight thousand pounds of personal debt already? And half that amount again, she owed to the bank. She bit her lip.

Mr Winters noticed that his wife was not sitting at the table.

'Where's your mother?' he said quietly.

'Upstairs. Lying down. But Daddy . . .'

'I think I'll just go and join her,' he said, shuffling out to the hall.

The two couples listened to the stairs creaking beneath his slow ascent. Kate glared at Shirley. Her father hadn't formally agreed to pay for *her* big day, and she was in debt to her ears. She couldn't pay for it herself. She'd have to save up. She didn't want to wait for five years until she had savings of her own. She wanted to set the date right away, preferably before Shirley's shotgun marriage took place. She wondered what to call a wedding that was *quicker* than a shotgun wedding. A rocket wedding? She wanted a rocket wedding. The two of them could fly to Las Vegas and get married at the weekend in the Little White Chapel. Anything that would prevent Shirley from tying the knot first.

'Well, that was a lovely meal,' said Kevin, brightly. 'Will we wash the dishes, Kate?' He lifted a few plates and began collecting napkins. 'Lovely mince pies.'

'Leave the dishes, Kevin; let's go out for a walk. It's far too warm in here. I'll get our coats.' She hobbled out to the hall, holding on to the backs of chairs. The others hardly noticed her distress. They were all caught up in their own thoughts.

Kevin decided he would ask Kate to move in with him. He had a three-bedroom house in Finaghy all to himself and although it was neat and tidy, it was not a cosy home. It needed a woman's touch.

Declan was working out sums in his head, wondering if he could afford to rent a flat on the outskirts of the city. Well away from this claustrophobic little street. Shirley would never cope with her pregnancy in such a hysterical household. She needed plenty of peace and rest.

'Kevin!' Kate summoned her boyfriend, like he was a dog. 'I'm ready!'

'Fair enough.' He pushed a couple of dishes along the table, to show that he was willing to tidy up but that there was no time, and followed Kate out to the hall. He smiled at the other couple on the way past. 'Congratulations again, Declan and Shirley. I wonder which of us will be married first.'

'I wonder,' said Shirley, knowing full well that Kate was prepared to marry a homeless drunk off the street rather than let her sister have her big day first. She might have known that something like this would happen.

When the front door closed, Declan hugged Shirley tightly and told her not to worry any more.

'She's a spiteful cow, Declan. She never said congratulations to me. Not once. She's just raging that I beat her to it. And Mum and Dad are going to be totally useless. It's hysteria or depression with them, and nothing in between. I told you it would be like this.'

'I know it's hard work, love. But it won't be for much longer. I'll rent a flat right away. I promise. Soon we'll have a cosy little place of our own, where no one can bother us, and we'll have lovely nights just curled up together in bed, listening to music, and making our plans for the future.'

'I hope so. I hope so.' Shirley went into the kitchen to make tea. On the way she bumped into the stereo, and the record that Mrs Winters had threatened to burn dropped onto the turntable and crackled into life.

'I love that song,' said Declan. 'Come on and we'll dance!'

'There's not enough room.'

'Then we'll stand very close together. Come here.' He put his arms round her, and they swayed gently in each other's arms beside the brightly coloured debris on the dining table. 'I love this time of the day when things are winding down and the place looks lived in.'

'I love you. You're too good to be true. I'm so lucky.'

'I am not, Mrs Greenwood-to-be. I'm the lucky one. And by the way, I love you, too.'

Then, the ugly man with no teeth sang the most beautiful love song of the decade and Shirley felt utterly at peace. Kate and her parents could rant and rave and moan and complain all they liked about the new baby. But they couldn't touch it or take it away from her. Shirley finally had something that was hers and hers alone. Well, hers and Declan's. Kate might move heaven and earth to make her wedding more spectacular than Shirley's, but she was surely not prepared to have a baby as well, was she? Shirley didn't think so. She smiled a huge smile. She was completely happy.

January arrived, and the Winters' home was a flurry of excitement. Mrs Winters had finally emerged from her holy statue-laden boudoir and was on a manic high. She had prayed non-stop for days and had consulted with the priest and several relatives and friends, and everyone seemed to be okay about the baby. So, she was okay, too. She was on the phone constantly, telling everyone that both of her beautiful daughters were engaged to be married. Both of them! And what a total surprise, she gasped, a thousand times, at British Telecom peak rate. They were dating their young men for only a month or so before Cupid shot his arrow. She even told the young man from the department store about it, when she called in to return a skirt. He was fascinated. Well, she explained, it was a family tradition, that wedding proposals came quickly to the women.

'I'm pregnant,' Shirley casually told the girls at work, one morning over scrambled eggs and toast in the canteen.

'Holy guacamole! Is it Declan's?' squeaked Amanda.

'Of course it's Declan's,' said Julie.

'You know it's Declan's,' said Shirley. Indignantly. 'I'm not a prostitute in my spare time, you know.'

'Oh, my God!' cried the girls. '*Oh. My. God.*'

'I know it's a bit sudden, but there you are,' said Shirley. 'I'd be very grateful if you could all support me in this. I'm feeling a bit delicate.' She looked at the faces of her stunned colleagues, and tried hard not to laugh.

'Is this young pup going to marry you? That's what I want to know.' Amanda had read too many hard-luck letters to think like an optimist any more.

'Don't be so old-fashioned,' said Shirley, keeping them in suspense.

'Is he, pet? We only want to know, so we can buy a present,' soothed her friend. 'We're not making moral judgements.'

'Yes, we *are* getting married. Sorry for teasing! In April. You're all invited, of course. I may need one of you to be my bridesmaid, now I come to think of it. Kate is acting very strangely these days. She may be committed by April.'

'She'll get over it. What did your da say?' Julie asked.

'He keeps saying, "I'll be in the front room, counting my life savings, if anyone wants me."'

'Aw, typical father!' said Amanda. 'They're all the same.'

Marion told Eddy to start house-hunting for the young couple. Somewhere far enough away from Derryvolgie Avenue, so that Declan could feel independent. But near enough for Marion and Eddy to pop in every day to help out a little bit when the baby came, if they were needed.

'Don't you see?' she said to Eddy, late one night. 'This will be the making of him. Now that he has responsibilities.'

'She's a nice girl, isn't she? Pretty enough. They'll be happy, won't they?'

'Oh, yes. They'll be very happy. Shirley is a sensible girl.' And Eddy left it at that. Marion was delighted, and that was all that mattered to him.

Johnny Hogan had not been in touch again, and he should be jetting out of their lives for ever, any day soon. The ballroom was up for sale at last. There were notices in all the local papers. Eddy was sleeping better than he had for a long time. And Declan was going to be a doctor, after all. A little stint as general manager in the restaurant had put him off the hospitality business.

Shirley continued to tell everyone she knew at work that she was expecting a child. She thought it was better that way, to be honest from the start. And just in case she might suffer from a touch of morning sickness. Miss Bingham collapsed in the toilets when she heard the news. She dropped the china mug she had been rinsing in the sink, and it shattered into a hundred pieces. She had to be held up by two women from Self-Employed, and have cold water splashed on her face.

'Well, I'm not surprised,' she managed to whisper, when her blood pressure had returned to normal. 'She's got no manners. Like her sister, Kate. I had to sack her, you know. The language of her, when I told her! I blame the parents. My God! No doubt, Shirley'll be in to the Housing Executive, looking for a free house off the taxpayer.'

'Oh, not at all,' said the first woman, whose name was Beryl. 'She's engaged to some stunner, I believe. Some big, tall fella. I haven't seen him, but they say he's gorgeous. And his parents are very well off, and they're buying them a house and paying for the wedding.'

'I don't believe it,' said Miss Bingham.

'Shirley's landed on her feet and no mistake. Oh, yes!' added Beryl's friend, Kathy. 'We'll not see her in here with her hand out. I'm sure she'll be handing in her notice, to tell you the truth.'

'Oh, don't tempt me!' muttered Beryl. 'Who, in their right mind, would work here if they didn't have to?' The women knew all the details. And Miss Bingham collapsed again. She wasn't feeling right for days afterwards.

Neither was Kate. Shirley had destroyed the whole system and proper order of things. If Shirley went up the aisle first, it would make Kate look like an old maid, like a woman who had been passed over. And that was why she had decided to get married as well. She told Kevin they could set the date, after another few passionate afternoons on the lime-green sofa.

Kevin was so pleased with himself, he couldn't concentrate on the garage, and didn't get any cars fixed for two days. Kate told her parents she was getting wed immediately, and they began to plan for the expense. They told Shirley and Declan about it over supper one night. Declan didn't want them to worry, especially since he felt partly responsible for this new development. He kindly suggested they have a double wedding.

Kate was initially against the idea, but in the end, she reluctantly agreed. She'd wanted a dream wedding with a fleet of limousines and expensive champagne and six bridesmaids; but her father had informed her that all he could provide was turkey and ham for forty. No frills. All the extras were up to herself and Kevin.

Marion Greenwood, on the other hand, was already up to her eyes in planning. She was having a lavish hot-and-cold buffet, ice sculptures, and a string quartet. (She was a big fan of the television show *Dallas*.) When Declan told her that he had offered to share his big day with Kevin and Kate, she was mildly disappointed. But Kevin didn't have many relations, as it turned out, and they were all very shy; they could be squeezed in at another couple of tables near the back of the room. It was all agreed. Thankfully, the invitations had not yet been printed.

Kevin said he'd pay for a lovely honeymoon for Kate and himself, the suits for all the gents, and the wedding cars. Eddy shook his hand and said he was a good man. Marion Greenwood wasn't exactly delighted that her only son's glorious wedding was being hijacked by Shirley's bossy sister, Kate. She had met Kate only twice and disliked her intensely. However, that was the only fly in the ointment, so she decided to be gracious.

Shirley wasn't exactly pleased that Kate was sharing her big day either, but she didn't have the energy to fight about it. On the positive side, it took the spotlight off her a little bit; and the pregnancy scandal was submerged in the terrific excitement of the double wedding. No one could remember any such thing happening in the district. And it had made her father very happy, to be relieved of the expense of the reception. Shirley sometimes resented Kate for the way she was turning the whole wedding into a drama-laden pantomime. But she kept quiet, and daydreamed of a little flat where she and Declan could be alone together at last.

She watched a programme about space, one Saturday morning, when she was alone in the house. The programme was designed for children, but Shirley found it fascinating. It explained how the universe did not have a top or a bottom, and, therefore, neither did the planets. It was quite a huge concept to take in. Shirley found the information more perplexing than enlightening. What exactly was it that kept all the planets and suns spinning along merrily in the black emptiness of the universe? A universe that had no top, and no bottom. And if it *was* God and he was so powerful, then why couldn't he have helped her father and mother to find better jobs, and not spend the best years of their lives cleaning toilets and floor tiles? And smelling of very strong pine-scented disinfectant and eye-watering bleach?

Then she had to rush to the bathroom for another hearty session of morning sickness, and that put an end to her musings for the day. She knelt beside the toilet bowl, her shoulders heaving with the effort, unable to concentrate on anything except her body's immediate physical needs. She was astonished at the power of her own body. It was like she had no control over it. Afterwards, she lay on the floor sweating, exhausted, purged and calm. Being sick was a little bit like making love, she thought sadly.

After a few minutes, Shirley began to shiver. She dragged herself to the sink and splashed some warm water onto her face. And even though she could hardly be bothered to, she brushed her teeth as well. It would be horrible later, if she didn't. Her face in the pretty seashell mirror was grey and terrified. She wondered if she'd look this awful on her wedding day. She wanted to look nice for her family. Weddings were for the bride and groom's families, really, she thought. She and Declan had made their vows to one another in other places, in other ways. She padded down the hall to her tiny bedroom and lowered herself delicately onto her little bed, drawing the patchwork quilt over her shoulders. She always felt cold when the morning sickness subsided. She wouldn't think so much in the future, she decided. She'd try to be more like Kate, who was a complete idiot, but very happy most of the time. She tried to concentrate on the background noises of the street. A dog barking, some builders hammering, a police siren. But it was hard to stop thinking when you were all alone in an empty house, and your stomach muscles were aching from nausea. Would Kevin and Kate be happy, she wondered. Would *she* be happy with Declan, for that matter? Would Declan get bored with her? Would he dump her in September for a clever fellow student with blonde hair and tight jeans? Would their eyes meet over the cadavers in the dissecting hall, and would that be the end of Shirley Winters and her big ideas about love? 'Stop it,' she told herself. 'I'm just run down because of the nausea, and it's making me morbid,' she confided to her old teddy bear. 'Declan loves me. He does.'

Even though the room was bright, Shirley closed her eyes and drew the quilt tighter around herself. The shivering stopped and she relaxed. She slept for a while and dreamt that all the planets were held up by string, and that her parents won the lottery and threw away their stinky mops for ever.

Kate told everyone she was getting married on the same day as her sister, in a shared ceremony, because she'd been madly in love with Kevin McGovern all along, and just hadn't realized it.

The date was set for 21 April. Shirley's morning sickness would have settled down by then, and the bump would still be only tiny. Mrs Winters went shopping for hats on a full-time basis, breaking for lasagne in Maguire's coffee shop at lunchtime. Mr Winters spent a lot of time putting up more shelves in the shed. In time, he came to terms with the shock and was happy that his unpredictable daughters had finally managed to snare themselves some decent men. And secretly very pleased that they were having a joint wedding. It would save him a fortune, although that wouldn't be a nice thing to say out loud. The Greenwoods were paying for the food, Declan and Shirley's honeymoon, even the iced fruitcake. And Kevin was forking out his share too, praise the Lord. So all he had to pay for was Kate's dress. He was in seventh heaven, until Kate decided she would like a designer gown, specially created just for her. And he was plunged into worry once more.

Kevin bought Kate an engagement ring the size of a grapefruit, and gave her his chequebook, so she could start remodelling his 1930s' semi on the Lisburn Road.

Miss Bingham spent hours looking up the rule books for some way she could fire an unwed mother. But, unbelievably, all that sort of thing seemed to be done away with. Not only would she *not* be fired, but she would be entitled to paid leave when the child was born. Nobody on the senior staff wanted to gossip about the scandal at lunchtimes. They only wanted to talk about their foreign holidays; and whether or not they should downsize their mortgages to put the children through university, or encourage their offspring to find part-time jobs instead. Miss Bingham didn't have a family of her own to talk about, so those conversations didn't interest her at all. Nobody in the office batted an eyelid when Shirley nipped out to the toilets every morning for a quick heave. Unplanned pregnancies were bread-and-butter to them. The more, the merrier. And most of the staff were open-minded mothers themselves. They knew that the joy they felt when they held their precious baby in their arms was far more important than whether or not they were married. It was marvellous to have a loving husband at the side of the bed during the delivery, of course. Holding their hand and sharing the experience of the birth. But all mothers were alone, really, in their joy and in their labour pain, and in their worries for their children.

They held a secret collection, and bought Shirley a lovely buggy from Mothercare, and wheeled it into the office with a big bow tied on the handle. Everybody clapped and cheered, and Shirley stood up and took a bow. It was sickening to watch.

Declan's friends teased him to death about the wedding. They said he was well and truly whipped and trapped and tied down, and what a fool he was to be trailed up the aisle so young. They said they would never be dumb enough to be caught like that. But he amazed them all by saying that he really did love Shirley, and that he couldn't wait to be a married man with his own home and child. And no, they could *not* come round all the time for beer and videos and parties. The baby would need peace and quiet. And Shirley's privacy must be respected, too. He would see them in the pub once a month, or so. If Shirley didn't mind. He also turned down the offer of a stag night in a private room in a club. Drink by the lorryload. Strippers, even. But, no. That would be very hurtful for Shirley, he told them, when she was feeling so tired. Only a waster of the lowest order would abandon a pregnant woman for a night of seedy entertainment like that. The boys were stunned by Declan's pompous attitude, but he only laughed at them and said they were unbelievably old-fashioned and that was why they were all still single geeks, and living at home with their parents.

The gifts poured in. A double wedding was a rare and special thing. Hand-painted tea sets and gilt mirrors and steel saucepans were delivered to the house on a regular basis. Crystal glasses and bone-china ornaments, and clocks covered with painted shamrocks, and rugs with long, heavy fringes. Shirley was thrilled with each new gift. Kate thought some of the designs were a little vulgar. Mrs Winters warned Kate that if she tried to swap any of the items for something more stylish, she would bring bad luck on the whole enterprise. Some people wanted to buy gifts for the baby, but worried about offending Shirley, so they gave cash inside a greeting card instead.

Kate was jealous of her little sister. She had planned to steal the show with her designer gown, but how did that compare with a new life coming into the world? New babies were still a big event, nowadays, no matter what they said about having a career. Running a garage was nothing, when people were buying you strollers and clapping for you at work. Even the dinner ladies in the canteen wanted in on the celebrations. They made a big chocolate cake with yellow icing on it saying *CONGRATS*, and bought Shirley a cuddly toy rabbit. Kate was devastated to see that Shirley was actually very well liked in the community. Even her parents were being reasonable, for the first time in living memory. Mrs Winters wouldn't let Shirley do any housework.

Kate told Kevin that she felt a little left out of things.

'Don't worry,' he told her. 'When we're married, we'll pop those babies out like peas. We'll have two children to every one of theirs.'

Then Kate had nightmares about pushing a shopping trolley full of screaming children around the supermarket, all of them rubbing chocolate biscuits into their hair. Kevin was frantic to begin the baby-making process and Kate wondered how she would endure it. She seemed to lose her passion when the thrill of the chase was over. It was very strange, because that was the sort of thing that usually happened to men. According to the glossy magazines, anyway. She was fed up with those 'How to Keep Your Man Interested' articles. She needed something to keep Kevin's mind *off* sex.

She thought of pulling out of the wedding, but then decided to stay on board. She could just about bear the regular sexual relations on the green velvet sofa, but there was no way she wanted children. (If she had to, she could always feign fertility problems.) Kate devoted all her spare time to the house renovation. She chose a beech kitchen with state-of-the-art handles, and double-glazing with Georgian bars for Kevin's home. She decided not to move in with Kevin just yet, however. That way, she would avoid all the dust and the noise the home improvements would cause, as well as Kevin's rampant libido; and she could still enjoy her mother's home cooking for three more precious months. Kate Winters wasn't your average romantic.

19. Kidnapped

It was the first week of February and the citizens of Belfast were feeling the pinch of winter winds and post-Christmas pockets. The city walls and windows were looking very drab now that all the decorations and lights had been put away for another year. Johnny was feeling pretty flat and colourless himself, and had been ever since Marion had told him that she did love Eddy Greenwood. Truly loved him, on a deep and profound level that went beyond looks and superficial things. Johnny had harboured some vague notion that Marion was only punishing him with her long marriage to Eddy, and that when she was ready, she would come back to him. Marion was afraid when she heard Johnny talk like that. She thought he might be unstable in some way. After all, it was twelve hours before they found Johnny Hogan in the rubble and the darkness, lying in the cradle that James had made for him. Did he suffer so much trauma, in that dark cradle, that he had grown up with his thinking pattern distorted, she wondered. Was that why he liked to be in the middle of all the fun and the music and the crowds? Because he had lain in the dark all night, cold and hungry, and afraid that no one would come? She was gentle with him, holding his hand, and saying that she would always care for him as a dear friend, but that friends was all they could ever be.

Johnny worried that he might back out and not go to America on his big trip after all. What would everyone think of him then? That he was just a big baby, that's what. With a heavy heart, he decided to leave Ireland at the end of April.

The very day Johnny booked his flight to Florida, a tourist was attacked by a crocodile there. The man survived, but needed two hundred stitches in his legs. It was the main story on the local news stations all day. Lots of Ulster people were going to Florida on their holidays; and even though they lived their lives under the constant threat of sectarian murder, and no-warning bombs going off in the town centres, they were scared stiff of stray crocodiles lurking in suburban swimming pools. Johnny thought it was a bad omen. He slipped the ticket into his wallet and half-hoped he would never use it.

The disco was packed to the doors every night with people eager to visit the famous nightspot before it closed down for good. Sunny Jim and the recently returned Standing Stone were very depressed. Working in the ballroom was the best job they had ever had. They would miss the sense of importance they felt, standing with their backs to the crowd before the doors were opened each night. DJ Toni was already scouting for another gig, but he doubted he would find one where he got half-price cocktails and all the free fish suppers he could eat. Sometimes, he read out requests with his mind on something else, and Louise Lowry and Kate Winters took full advantage of that. Louise had a song played for her friend Kate, 'whose hobbies are knitting socks, singing hymns and collecting spoons'. Kate retaliated by having a Smiths song played for Louise: 'Last Night I Dreamt that Somebody Loved Me'. Louise then had DJ Toni inform the crowd that Kate Winters was receiving counselling for being agoraphobic, and the crowd clapped their support, and Louise had to barricade herself in the ladies' toilets for her own protection. Johnny Hogan had to give Toni a stiff lecture about being more alert to the pranks of the young people, and Toni sulked for a while in his little booth and played too many sad love songs.

Timothy Tate was feeling more forlorn than most. He had been on his knees for two hours, praying and praying for an answer to this huge problem that faced him. Eugene Lolly had at last contacted him and would be outside the door of the gym in thirty minutes, ready to take Timothy on his first criminal outing in twenty-odd years. Timothy wondered if it was too late to put on his anorak and hurry down the road, and go to the park, or anywhere. Just hide until Eugene gave up on him, and found somebody else to be his sidekick. Without thinking, he had his coat on, and had switched off the lights in the main hall. As he fumbled with the bunch of keys, there was a footstep behind him, and Eugene was there, eyes bright and shining with excitement.

'I decided I'd get here early, like. Why not, I said to myself, seeing as I'd nothing else to do.'

The weasel, thought Timothy. He knew that I would try to hide.

'I thought you might have changed your mind,' he said, not looking at Eugene, 'when it took you so long to get back to me.'

'No, not at all. It just took a while longer than I figured to study the lie of the land. Now, come on, we'll talk on the way. I've got a car. It's parked on a side street beside the ballroom, since yesterday.'

'So, you're really going through with it? You're going to rob the ballroom? Then what?'

'We go to your flat, and wait for a few days.'

'I told you, not there. Not my home.'

'They'll never think of looking there. Too long ago, since you and me were a team, since you were on their books. And anyway, they'll never know it was me – we'll keep our faces well covered. We'll watch a bit of telly, have a curry and a few beers. You'll go to work, as normal. When they've stopped checking the ferry terminals, I'll sail to England, and freedom. I can catch another boat to anywhere I like. South of France, anywhere.'

The two men set off walking towards the park.

'You don't think Johnny Hogan will have that kind of money in his back pocket, do you? It will take weeks to sell the place; any developer thinking of buying will need to secure planning permission to knock down the hall, before he coughs up. And what if Hogan hasn't got the money on the premises? No bank will give him a big lump of cash like that. Just over the counter. No questions asked.'

'Of course he'll have cash there. Bags of it. Tax evasion and all that. Do you know nothing about dance halls? He'll have it, or else.'

'Or else, what? Has it come to this, Eugene? Terrorizing a back-street disco? Are you crazy?'

'Now, you listen to me, Tate. I'm sick of you, and that's the truth. If it wasn't for you, I might be in Spain now, letting the wife take care of me in my retirement. You do what you're told, or I'll do what I should have done years ago. Shut you up for good!'

'But, my flat, my job? I can't go back to my old life when all this is over. They might see my face, find out where I live. They'll never trust me again in the gym.'

'Just a minute. Step in there, I want to check something,' said Eugene, and he elbowed Timothy into the Palmhouse. There were a few people inside the main body of the gracious old building, exclaiming at the huge size of the leaves on the exotic plants. To the right, the cacti on the hot side had also attracted some visitors. Eugene and Timothy went into the cool side of the greenhouse, where hundreds of potted plants were laid out in neat rows.

'Go on, down to the end. There's something there I have to collect.'

Timothy hurried down the path, behind the display shelves, to a little space where empty flowerpots were stacked neatly. The floor was damp and covered with moss. He could see nothing, no bag or package.

'There's nothing here,' he said.

Eugene only smiled. He reached in behind a large flowerpot and drew out a long knife with a fancy handle. The blade was thin and evil-looking. He turned it over a few times, so that it caught the light shining in through the mottled glass of the greenhouse.

'This is what I was looking for, Timothy. Now, unless you want to go a couple of rounds with my good friend here, you spineless fool, you'll do what I tell you.'

'Please, Eugene.' There were tears in Timothy's eyes.

Then the smaller man had him by the collar, and was

shouting up into his face. 'I am not telling you this again, Tate. All you have to do is keep watch, maybe thump Hogan a couple of times. I cannot *stand* any more of this whining. I'm going outside for a cigarette, and when you have pulled yourself together, you will come out, and you will shut up, and we will complete this operation.' He pushed him backwards then, roughly, so that he fell over the flowerpots and lay still on the damp moss.

Eugene's retreating footsteps were soft on the mossy path. The door closed behind him, with a tiny squeak. Timothy sat up on the path, and laid his face against the cool glass, letting the condensation soothe his hot skin. The window moved out slightly, and he realized it was loose in its frame. He gasped, and before the thought had formed itself properly in his tormented mind, he had gently pressed it out of the frame, and crawled through the hole. It was a tight fit but he made it. He was free! Quickly, he reached in and slid the glass back into place. The condensation had been wiped away, but still, Eugene might not notice. Timothy crawled into the shrubbery at the side of the Palmhouse, and lay down. He could not, and would not, go through all this kind of thing again.

Eugene reappeared soon enough, as Timothy knew he would. He was shaking with agitation at Timothy's failure to meet him at the door. Timothy saw his tormentor scratch his head, and look up and down the path, and then out of the windows, at the visitors strolling by. But there was no sign of Timothy. Eugene Lolly lost his temper, then, kicking at the display, knocking some pots down on the floor and stamping on them. Timothy closed his eyes and smiled, and thanked God for the broken window, and for Eugene's nicotine addiction. Timothy wanted to stay in the well-tended shrubbery for ever, like a garden statue, but he knew that was not possible. Slowly, he crept out of his hiding place, and set off walking in the other direction. He nipped into a phone box near the museum, and asked the operator for the number of Hogan's ballroom on Magnolia Street. With a sudden feeling of calm, he dialled the number and asked the girl who answered to put him through to Mr Hogan.

'It's urgent,' he said. 'Please hurry.' After a short time, the receiver was handed over to James.

'Yes? James Hogan here. Can I help you?'

'I can't say who I am, but there's a man on his way to the ballroom. He's going to do a bad thing.'

'Who is this? What's going to happen?'

'A robbery.'

'What?'

'That's all I know. Goodbye.'

'Wait. Who is this?' But the line went dead. James Hogan replaced the receiver and hurried down the stairs to find Eileen, who was having a coffee at the bar. The bar staff were setting up and preparing for that evening's function, a twenty-first birthday party.

'Quick,' he shouted. 'Lock all the doors, and search the storerooms. I've had a tip-off. We're about to be robbed. Call the police right away. Everyone stay in small groups. No one is to search by themselves. Eileen, you come with me.'

'What is going on, James? Have you lost it?' But he had her by the arm, and was gently guiding her to the main doors. Trust Johnny to be out at a time like this.

'I'm taking you home, pet, and we'll let the police deal with this. Remember what happened last time?'

'We can't leave the staff here on their own, James. They're only bits of youngsters, for heaven's sake. What if they panic? We'll stay with them until the police come.' And she stopped walking and held on to the door handle.

'Will you, for once in your life, listen to me? You don't want to get a big shock at your age, Eileen.'

'What do you mean, my age? I'm perfectly fine. We should stay with the young people, to help them. We're responsible for them.'

'You really are the most annoying woman! Wait! There's Marion Greenwood, coming along in her car.' He hurried into the road with his hands up in the air. 'Stop! Marion, stop!'

Marion jammed on the brakes.

'James Hogan, are you trying to get yourself killed?'

'Listen, Marion, will you do me a huge favour? Will you take this madwoman of mine to your house and keep her there for a while? We've had a call that there's going to be a robbery.'

'A robbery? At the ballroom? Not again! I don't believe you.'

'Yes. Now, it's probably a crank call. I don't believe it, myself. But the police are on their way and I'd like Eileen to be kept away from all the excitement. Just in case. Please, would you do this for me? I'd be so grateful.'

'Surely, I will. Get in, Eileen. I'll just call into the shop, tell my assistant I'll be out for a while, and we'll go back to my place for a cup of tea. Let the boys take care of this one. Okay?'

Grumbling, Eileen clambered into the passenger seat, and folded her arms. She looked up at James.

'What about you, old man? Don't you think you should come with us poor, defenceless womenfolk? We'll all go back to the parlour and starch our petticoats.'

'I'm going to wait here, to let the police in. Don't worry, I'm not planning any heroics. Off you go.' He closed Eileen's door gently and tapped the roof of the car. Marion and Eileen sailed up the avenue in Marion's stylish saloon with its gleaming windows. As they disappeared round the corner, James breathed a sigh of relief, went back inside and checked that the doors to the ballroom were firmly locked. The staff had checked the building. It was declared secure. Johnny had been contacted. Two police cars were in the area and an ambulance was on its way. Just as a precaution. They all sat down to wait.

Eugene saw everything from the newsagent's shop at the top of the road, where he stood peeping out from behind a magazine. The woman in the Mercedes looked familiar. It came to him. She was Hogan's girlfriend, from all those years ago.

'Are you buying that magazine?' asked the shop girl, crossly. A big, tall strap of a girl, with brassy blonde hair and very big hands. She was eating a chocolate hammer. Eugene closed the magazine and placed it back on the shelf.

'No, thanks. I've just remembered I've got to be some-where.'

He ran out of the shop and away from the ballroom as the first police car turned in at the top of the street. He stood in the doorway of a working-men's club, wondering if it was safe to walk to his car.

First, Timothy Tate does a runner like the big, yellow chicken that he is, thought Eugene. And secondly, he tips off Hogan. Anyone would think there was a conspiracy against me.

Eugene would have to think of something else now. He was not going back to that dingy hostel, and the long empty days and the even longer, lonely nights. Besides, Tate had probably given the cops his name by now. He had to keep going forward. There was simply no going back. He would select another business and rob it instead, although he had planned to gloat over this robbery for the rest of his life. It made him feel sick to think that the Hogan clan had got the better of him once again. How that cheap playboy, Johnny Hogan, had done nothing at all, but sit in his office for twenty years, while the hard-working people of Belfast poured their money into his breezeblock cattle-market of a dance hall.

Just then he noticed the Mercedes belonging to Hogan's girlfriend parked outside a bridal salon. With Eileen Hogan sitting alone in it. And he saw his chance. Kidnapping! He'd take the old woman prisoner, and get the cash out of Hogan that way instead. He darted up to the car, realized that the doors were not locked, and gently opened the back door. The knife was in his hand. He jumped in.

'What the hell is this!' Eileen was outraged.

'Don't move a muscle, or you're dead,' said Eugene. 'I've got a knife, and I promise you, I'm not afraid to use it.' A surge of adrenaline shot through him. It was good to be back in the crime business.

'Oh, for pity's sake, I'm not standing for this. Take the bloody car and leave me alone! Far too old to be stealing

cars, you are! Are you sure you're not from the asylum?'
She fumbled at the door handle, but it was new to her
and she didn't know whether to pull it upwards or outwards. Just then, Marion came dashing out of the shop
and jumped into the car.

'Right, Eileen, let's get you home,' she said brightly, and
then the words died on her lips. She saw the thin evil-
looking knife, inches away from her throat. 'It's you.
Eugene Lolly.' Marion's face was as white as chalk.

'Correct. Now, drive,' he commanded.

'Where?' she whispered.

'I don't know yet. Just drive.'

'Don't listen to him, Marion. He's a bloody fool and
he won't touch us.'

'I said, drive!' shouted Eugene.

'Not an inch, you ugly slug!' Eileen turned round in
her seat to give Eugene Lolly a withering look. If she had
the strength, she would have reached for the man and
wrung his neck like a chicken. But sadly, she was about
fifty years too old for that. She made slight jabbing movements with her elbow, to show Marion that she could try
to disable Lolly with a sharp dig in the neck. But Marion
shook her head.

'I said, drive! I've got nothing to lose – I'll kill the two
of you, I swear it.'

Marion started up the engine, and the car moved out
from the kerb and went down the avenue at a snail's pace.
Looking straight ahead, Marion drove the car without
thinking, feeling or speaking.

'Oh, Marion! You shouldn't be afraid of this ne'er-do-
well. He was no use when he had a gun and a henchman.

How far does he think he's going to get with a bread-knife, for pity's sake?'

But Marion *was* afraid. She was absolutely terrified. And that vicious knife was like no bread-knife she had ever seen.

Back at the ballroom, Johnny and James were congratulating themselves on a well-conducted emergency procedure. The warning call was eventually declared a hoax by the investigating officers, but they were all pleased with the way that things had been handled. All of the staff had been calm and cooperative under pressure. Johnny and James went round to Marion's house in Johnny's pale blue Lincoln Continental to collect Eileen. But she was not there. Neither was Marion. One of Marion's daughters told them that her mother had not been home since breakfast. They began to worry, but assumed that Marion had taken Eileen to a cafe somewhere. By early evening, there was still no sign of them. Eddy had to be notified. He came back to the house, still wearing his baker's apron, with a smudge of flour on his face. They phoned every person they could think of. Marion's friends, Eileen's friends. Hospitals even, in case Eileen had been taken ill. Marion's assistant had seen her only briefly.

Eileen was gone. Marion was gone. Nobody knew where they were. It was getting dark. James was grief-stricken. Johnny was guilt-ridden. Eddy blamed the entire Hogan family for Marion's disappearance. Everything they were connected with seemed to attract danger. He would have attacked Johnny Hogan there and then, but he didn't want to frighten his tearful daughters. They had never even heard him raise his voice before. And right now, they needed his support. Declan and his sisters were worried sick about their beloved mother.

The police began organizing a search party, and a press conference. Johnny helped them. The bar staff were told to cancel the birthday party, and go straight home but they hung around, whispering in corners, for a long time. James kept vigil in the office, staring at the wall, waiting for some information to come through.

20. Dark Days

'I should have been here,' said Johnny, for the hundredth time that night. 'I should have been here to prevent this.'

Marion and Eileen were still missing, without any word at all, from them or anyone.

'Don't blame yourself, Johnny. You can't be here all the time.' James was sipping a small brandy. He hadn't eaten since the disappearance of his wife, and the brandy went straight to his head. He blinked, and set the glass down, unfinished. No point getting tipsy with the cameras about to roll.

'I just can't believe it,' said Johnny. 'Where can they be?'

'They're about to film the appeal, Johnny. Are you sure you can face this?'

'I am.'

James patted him gently on the back. Just then, Eddy Greenwood came into the office. He looked his old love rival in the eyes and a lump of ice formed in his heart. The Hogan men had no right to involve Marion in their low-grade business affairs. When this was all over, Eddy was going to sort Johnny out, big-time.

'Any word here? I've heard nothing.' Eddy had decided to dispense with the small talk.

'Eddy, I'm so sorry. This is just the worst thing.' James went forward to shake Eddy's hand. 'Isn't it awful?'

'Awful isn't the word,' said Eddy. And he looked at

Johnny when he said it. Eddy hated Johnny Hogan more at that moment than he had ever hated him. He'd been nothing but trouble, all of his life. What kind of man would stay single all these years, just to spin disco records in a concrete warehouse like this? Knowing that the entertainment business was a honey-pot attraction for criminal types? What had he got himself mixed up in, this time?

'Will you have a cup of tea?' Johnny asked, trying hard to be civil. He knew that Eddy didn't like him, but he couldn't figure out why. Sure, he had taken Marion away from Eddy when they were kids. Men did not forget that kind of thing. But Eddy was the one who had married her in the end. And had four children with her, for heaven's sake. So why was he still sore? It wasn't Johnny's fault that the women were missing, although some irrational part of his brain told him that it was.

'No, I've just come for the appeal. I want to get back to the children.' Eddy was anxious to go home and sit beside the telephone. As well as that, he'd been crying a lot in the last few hours, and the last thing he wanted to do was cry in public. Just when Marion was so happy – planning for Declan's wedding and the new house and the new baby – she was dragged into the living nightmare that was the Hogan family, all over again.

'Let's go downstairs, then, and get it over with,' said James. They trooped down the staircase in silence.

The three men sat in a row behind the table, and the spotlights were adjusted. Johnny spoke to the camera with the polish of a seasoned presenter. He gave details of Eileen's appearance and also Marion's. He didn't notice the flash of anger in Eddy's eyes when he described Marion as a very attractive woman.

'Don't be afraid to show some emotion,' the sergeant had told Johnny. 'We find it helps to jog memories, if the public see how upset people are. Just be as direct as you can. We'll help you out if you get stuck.' So, when Johnny had finished speaking, he wiped his eyes with the back of his hand and sighed deeply.

James was still too shaken to say much. He shook his head and nodded to Eddy to say his part. Eddy smoothed down the collar of his jacket, looked into the camera, and waited for the signal to begin. He spoke quietly and tenderly about his beautiful wife and how much her distraught children were missing her. Then Johnny wound up the appeal.

'Please, please,' he began, when the cameraman pointed to him. 'If anyone out there knows anything about the disappearance of my grandmother, Eileen Hogan, or where she is now, please come forward, or call the police. Eileen is a very special woman, and I know she will be bearing up well, but she is over eighty, and we want her back. Gran, if you can hear me, we all love you, and we miss you terribly.' He held up a picture of Eileen, and wiped another tear from his eye. 'By the way, I'm offering a six-figure reward for any information that will help us find Eileen and Marion.' The police were in two minds about that, but Johnny had insisted.

Eddy showed a fairly recent picture of himself and Marion on the cruise together, with the wind blowing his wife's hair away from her face. She looked just like Marilyn

Monroe in the picture, in a white raincoat and with large sunglasses perched on top of her head. One of the detectives read out a telephone number, and urged the public to keep a look-out for the two ladies.

Just as they were about to stop filming, James said, 'Please, Eileen, come home. And Mrs Greenwood, too. I love you more than anything, Eileen, if you can hear me. We'll find you soon. Very soon.'

'Yeah,' said the cameraman. 'We got that. Should be in time for the ten o'clock news.'

James Hogan was at home. He sat staring at the telephone. Waiting. He rubbed his eyes. Johnny was keeping vigil in the ballroom, just in case a telephone call came through there. But James had a feeling that he was the one who would be contacted, and he was right. The shrill ringing made him jump, and a yawn died in his throat. He snatched up the receiver.

'Yes? James Hogan here.'

'Mr Hogan. I presume you know what this is about? I've got your wife.'

'Is she all right? Have you harmed her?' James could hardly form the words. A headache began to prickle across his scalp. He rubbed his head gently.

'She's fine. There's no time for small talk.'

'What do you want?'

'Money, I'm afraid. I've no imagination.' Eugene read out his demands, and heard James gasp at the other end of the line. 'I'll be in touch. Two days' time.'

'Let me talk to my wife!'

'No time for small talk.'

'Please —'

'No funny business.' And he hung up.

Listening to the ten o'clock news that night was one of the highlights of Eugene Lolly's career.

After, he smiled and turned off the car radio.

'There, did you hear that?' he said. 'We're famous.'

'They're out looking for us, already,' Eileen said to Eugene. 'You'll be back in prison before too long, mark my words.'

Marion did not speak. She had said very little throughout the journey. Fear and unhappy memories kept her thoughts too busy to even try to make casual conversation. Without Lolly's attempt to rob the ballroom in 1967, she might not have had the courage to leave Johnny and marry Eddy. Was history about to repeat itself, and change her life again? This time, would Lolly's return bring her tragedy? They had crossed the border into Donegal hours ago, and were parked in a leafy lane near the coast. A fresh breeze streamed in through the window. It was pitch-dark, and windswept bushes flicked the sides of the car. Marion just wanted to curl up somewhere warm and dry and go to sleep. She had never wanted Eddy more than she did at that moment. Eileen, however, was in the mood for an argument.

'You haven't got a hope, Lolly, have you? There's a reward for your capture now, you *outlaw*!' She spat out the words, giving him her most intense stare.

'Good,' he said, not in the least perturbed. Eileen Hogan was positively ancient, and no threat to him whatsoever. And Marion Greenwood was no heroine either. This was going to be so easy, it was embarrassing. 'I'm glad to see you're so popular. That means you're worth more.'

'I guessed this was about money,' hissed Eileen. 'Tell me something I don't know.'

'It's always about money. Isn't that all that matters in the end?' said Eugene, philosophically. 'Money is the only path to freedom.'

'You ought to be ashamed of yourself. Kidnapping two defenceless women.'

'Shame is a luxury I can't afford, I'm afraid, Mrs Hogan.'

'A man in good health has plenty of options, in my opinion. The only thing wrong with you is you've got a very plain face.'

'Ha! Always the smart answer. The story is this: you are a hostage, your family is wealthy, you will be returned when a sum of money has been paid. It's not rocket science.'

'How much?'

'I don't know yet. Half a million?'

'You're out of your mind, Eugene Lolly. We haven't got that kind of cash flow. The site is worth something, I dare say, but unless you want a building site for your trouble, you'll get nothing for me. And I'm not scared of you, either. You're a hateful coward.'

Eileen folded her arms and stared straight ahead. Eugene smiled.

'Same old Hogan bravado. They'll pay up for you, all right. No one gets the better of me. Not twice, anyway.'

'You buck-eejit! Call yourself a kidnapper? You, that shot off half your own hand! Good God, look down on me! I've been abducted by a fool with butterfingers. Mother of God, be merciful!'

'That's right, say a little prayer.'

'You're a bitter man, Mr Lolly.'

'Not bitter, Mrs Hogan. Just in need of some hot sunshine.'

'What do you want that for? Don't you know there's a price to be paid for sunshine? Snakes and spiders biting the backside off you? Lions and tigers eating the people wholesale? Did you not hear about the crocodile that attacked that poor man in Florida, and him only off the plane two hours?'

'Be quiet. I'm thinking,' he commanded.

'Oh, God above! He's *thinking*. God help us altogether!'

'I said, stop talking! I'm tired of talking. And no more religion either. I'm an atheist and proud of it.'

'You'll change your mind when you're older. When you're my age. You'll be grateful for the simple things in life. Fresh air. Flowers.'

'I said, be quiet!' said Eugene.

'Yes,' persisted Eileen. 'You'll be grateful for any day you feel halfway healthy.'

'Women talk too much, I've always said it,' Eugene snarled.

'Eileen, please,' whispered Marion, and silence enveloped them.

The luxury car waited patiently in the Donegal landscape, as the three occupants pondered the existence of God, the universe in general, and the financial health of the Hogan family in particular. Then, Eugene told Marion to start the engine again and make for a lone farmhouse he remembered spotting some years ago. It was too nicely painted to be owned by local people; likely it was a holiday home belonging to some moneybags blow-in from Dublin or Belfast. It might well be empty at this time of year.

'As if we'll ever find it in the dark.' Eileen was very frustrated, and starving too. 'And when are we going to get something to eat?'

'There's plenty of holiday homes around this area. We'll break in and get set up, comfortable like. And wait until it's time to call the ice-cream man again.'

'Who?'

'Johnny Hogan, in his famous white coat. That's who. And I'm warning the two of you, when we move from this car to an empty property hereabouts, if there is one false move, I won't hesitate to use this knife.' He pointed the knife at Eileen but she snorted her contempt for him.

'Oh, shut your mouth,' she snapped. 'Where could we go in the dark? In the cold? It's not you and your stupid knife we're afraid of. We could die of exposure on a night like this. Or *boredom*.'

21. Eugene Lolly is Licked

Eugene Lolly was at his wits' end. Eileen Hogan was driving him crazy. Just a few days with her and he was feeling psychotic. The old bat had far too much energy for a woman of her advanced years, and she was using every drop of it to torture him. Maybe it was a vitamin deficiency that he was suffering from, but he could have sworn she was using psychological warfare against him. She was constantly piping up with daft questions, distracting him when he was trying to make plans for a luxury retirement in some quiet holiday resort in South America. He had to lock the two women in an ensuite bedroom, eventually, just to get a bit of peace. And even then, Eileen demanded that he give them bottles of fresh water to drink, and a fire extinguisher, just in case there was an electrical fault in the room. Complaining about everything, she was: the house was either too cold, too warm or too dry. She wanted him to turn up the heating, turn down the heating or give them another blanket.

And when they were in the kitchen together, for meals, she never let up either. He was tempted to keep them in the room all the time, but he hated cooking. That was women's work, after all. And Eileen Hogan cooked a mean steak. Which was why he hadn't stabbed her before now.

In any case, he was worn out from lack of sleep. He was confident he would be instantly awake at the first sound, should they try to break out of the bedroom, but that meant his snatched scraps of shut-eye were light, edgy and broken. Eugene checked that he had the house keys in his pocket. He had. How nice of the owners to keep a spare set in the shed. Under a flowerpot, too! Some people just deserved to be burgled. Or, in this case, to have their home occupied by squatters. Eugene checked again that his prisoners were safely locked in their room. He put his feet up on the sofa in the sitting room, and settled down for forty winks.

In the bedroom, Eileen dipped a couple of teabags in two mugs, and added powdered milk and three sugar lumps to each one. (She had created a mini-kitchen on the bedside table.) She handed a mug to Marion who was sitting quietly by the window, hoping that someone would pass by on the road and rescue them. They had thought of trying to smash the triple-glazed window but rejected the idea. He would be upon them at the first sound and then no doubt would tie them up. Tape their mouths, even. They couldn't bear that. Besides, they were pretty sure the window was unbreakable.

'Don't worry, Marion,' Eileen said. 'We'll be out of here by this afternoon. I promise. But you've got to pull yourself together, dear. I need you to help me.' Eileen just hoped that when they did escape, Marion would be capable of driving back to Belfast, even if she had to do it on auto-pilot. Otherwise, they'd have to flag down a lift.

Eileen's plan was going nicely. She might be old but she was not stupid; she was very quick to notice that Eugene Lolly was a bag of nerves and starved of sleep, and she had used that fact to her advantage. Keeping him on edge, so that he was nearly exhausted. He was barely able to keep awake today, and she decided that it was now time to take control. Eileen had also demanded that the central heating be turned on as high as it would go. Few people could stay alert in a sweltering house and Eugene's eyes were heavy with lack of sleep. She'd give him ten minutes and then she'd bang on the bedroom door and call him.

Eugene Lolly was an idiot. Any idiot would have known that Johnny couldn't come up with half a million in cash in two days. These amateur criminals hadn't a clue. All they knew was what they saw in the movies. It took years to make that kind of money, building up assets. And months to turn assets into cash again. Large sums of money meant large amounts of paperwork.

She was becoming quite fond of this house with its huge windows and its blinding-white walls. A linen sofa, a leather armchair and lots of paintings on the walls – that's all there was in the sitting room. Big, abstract watercolours of seascapes, great washes of blue and green, dark at the bottom, fading to the merest hint of colour at the top. No people, no details in the paintings. Still, the house was very clean and tidy. And so bright when the sun was shining, such a change from the shadowy world of the ballroom. She wondered if they were keeping the ballroom closed, or open. Eugene Lolly wouldn't let her see the news on television or listen to the radio. The pint-sized little demon! It was a great pity they had done away with hanging in 1953, she thought bitterly. She took another biscuit from the barrel on the table. And she listened carefully for any sounds from Eugene Lolly. There were none.

'Are you ready, Marion? Come on, now. Just do what I told you and we'll be home in no time. Good girl. Be brave, okay? Five minutes is all it will take.'

'Are you sure, Eileen? I'm frightened.'

'It will work like a dream, I promise you. He thinks the two of us are useless. Come on, now, lie down on the bed and close your eyes. Try and look ill.'

Marion did as she was told. It wasn't difficult to look distressed; she was barely able to stay rational. 'Get on with it, then,' she whispered. 'If I don't do this right now, I never will.' She thought of her lovely home in Belfast, and how much she wanted to be back there. She closed her eyes and nodded.

Eileen put on her cardigan, took a deep breath, and thumped on the door.

Eugene Lolly was out for the count. Snoring, with his mouth wide open. Days' worth of stubble on his jaw, and red rims round his eyes from all the wine he had drunk the night before. There were beads of perspiration on his forehead. The room was very hot. He became aware of a commotion somewhere in the house. Then Eileen began hitting the bedroom door with her shoe, and he went staggering down the corridor in a stupor.

'*Help! Help! Mrs Greenwood's collapsed! Help!*'

Eugene unlocked the door and barged in. Marion was collapsed on the bed with her eyes closed. Eugene ran over to her and began gently slapping her face while Eileen hovered behind him. Eileen was delighted to see that he had left the knife elsewhere in the house and that she wouldn't have to resort to Plan B, which was to hit him over the head with the electric kettle.

'I think she's in a shock-induced coma,' she cried. 'She's a nervous wreck at the best of times. Now you're in trouble! If she dies, you'll be hailed a murderer.'

'Shut up! Give her some water.'

'There's none left in the bottle.' Eileen had poured it down the sink.

'Use the bathroom tap.'

'I will not. It's not for drinking.'

'Go to the kitchen, then, you stupid woman!' he roared.

'Don't shout at me. I'll get it. You try and get her to sit up. I don't think she's breathing!'

Eileen rushed to the sitting room and found the knife on the floor next to the sofa. When she came back, Eugene was struggling to sit a moaning Marion up.

Eileen came up behind him and held the thin sharp blade against his neck.

'Don't move a muscle, you little rat!'

He flinched, and made to turn around but she pulled the knife across the back of his neck and left a red mark that made him gasp.

'Just a flesh wound. Hurry up, Marion.'

The other woman jumped up off the bed like a grasshopper.

'Get the keys,' ordered Eileen, pressing the knife harder into Eugene's unshaven neck.

Marion reached into Eugene's pocket, and felt the cold steel of the keys. She held them tightly. 'I've got them!'

'Let's get out of here, then,' said Eileen. 'Don't try to stop us, Lolly, or I'll run you through, I swear it. They won't even put me away for it. Self-defence, you see. And I've got a witness.'

'Eileen, come on,' urged Marion, from the door.

Eileen darted for the door and Marion slammed it behind her and locked it, removing the key. They ran for the front door, Marion searching for the key with fumbling fingers. She found it, unlocked the door and out they went.

Eugene had tied the keys for the car onto the house keys, the silly man. Eileen laughed out loud. 'I told you he was a brainless chancer!'

Marion found the right key and opened the car door. Eileen lowered herself into the passenger seat and waved to Eugene, who was now trapped in the ensuite bedroom of his dream cottage, with his own blood seeping into the collar of his best coat, pounding at the window in rage. Marion flopped in behind the wheel, and started up the engine. Then she reversed down the drive, completed a near-perfect three-point-turn, and swung out onto the main road, holding her breath all the way.

Eileen cheered and clapped. What a turnaround! That horrible creature, Lolly, was locked into a house with triple-glazing. Like a goldfish in a bowl, he could not get out. Marion moved the driver's mirror a little bit, and looked out for the signs for Belfast. A couple of hours at least, it would take. They ought to telephone home, of course, but they had no money with them. Eugene had taken their handbags. And anyway, they were afraid to stop the car in case it would not start again. That was the kind of thing that happened in some TV dramas. Eugene might catch up with them somehow if they dallied at all. And so, they drove on towards the city, only taking a couple of wrong turns.

At seven o'clock, they parked right outside Eileen's

home on Eglantine Avenue, and tooted the horn loudly, and hugged each other.

'Thank you, Marion, you've been brilliant,' Eileen said.

'We made it,' said Marion. 'We really made it!'

James's lovely face appeared between the linen drapes, and Eileen waved at him and blew him a kiss. The glossy front door flew open, and down the path he came, all tears and laughter, and bewilderment.

'Thank God. Thank God,' he said. 'Oh, my heart, is it really you?'

'It is,' she said. 'I'm home.'

'Oh, Eileen! My love. We couldn't raise the money on our own, and the bank was no help. I've been out of my mind with worry. Where have you been? Did they bring you back?'

'We escaped under our own steam. That fool, Eugene Lolly, did it.'

'The one who shot himself, years ago?'

'The very same.'

'Eugene Lolly. On his own?'

'Yes. The rotten leech. I wore him down, day by day. He fell asleep, and we escaped.'

'How?'

'He was careless. No doubt I'll have to tell the police all about it so time enough for you to hear the gory details then. We got the keys off him and locked him in. Now, run me a hot bath, would you? I hated that modern shower, the pressure was far too strong. Oh, and ask Johnny to bring me a cooked chicken from the super-market. I've been living on prime steak for days, and I'm heartily sick of it.'

Marion waved them inside and raced off for her own dear home in Derryvolgie Avenue. She couldn't wait to see Eddy's face. And her children, too.

James and Eileen were hugging in the hall.

'Eileen, you were so brave!'

'It was no trouble to escape that cockroach! His brain is smaller than a walnut.'

'You could have had a heart attack.'

'Now, don't fuss, James. Didn't we lose our only son in the war? If I can survive that, I can survive anything. Phone Johnny right away and tell him not to bother with the ransom money – and ask for that cooked chicken. And then phone the police in Donegal and tell them that Eugene Lolly is hopefully still stuck in a big, modern, pink bungalow on the coast road. There's a big hedge round the house, and two stone eagles on the gateposts. And oh, maybe it belongs to an artist because it's full of big paintings.'

'I can't believe all this. I feel quite weak all of a sudden,' he said, sitting down on the sofa. Eileen came and put her arms round him, and they sat like that for half an hour.

James made several phone calls, while Eileen relaxed in the bath, and the media frenzy started up all over again. The big house on Eglantine Avenue was full of policemen, reporters, friends, family and neighbours. Eileen was magnificent, giving endless interviews, and telling the story of her daring escape over and over again. Johnny was delighted, and the two of them posed for photographs on the sofa. James finally ushered everyone out of the front door at eleven o'clock so that Eileen could go to bed and get some rest. Within seconds, she was sleeping soundly. James lay beside her, holding her hand, tears of happiness in his eyes.

Back in the elegant sitting room of Derryvolgie Avenue, Eddy was still holding Marion's hand, and he wouldn't let it go. Twice now, he had almost lost the love of his life. But he wouldn't be so careless for a third time. He promised himself that. And if Hogan ever came near Marion again, Eddy knew that he would kill him. He didn't allow himself to dwell on what might have happened during the women's ordeal with that deranged fool Eugene Lolly. They were both dizzy from a lack of sleep and food. Marion kept bursting into tears and hugging him, and telling him how much she had missed him. That was the only good thing that had come out of the kidnapping. Eddy now felt sure that he had finally supplanted that gigolo, Hogan, in Marion's affections. She wasn't even remotely interested in how Johnny was feeling. She hadn't mentioned him once.

Declan, Shirley and the girls were in the big modern kitchen, cooking up a celebration dinner of spaghetti and garlic bread and pizza, as they hadn't been able to eat anything during the days that Marion was missing. Poor Shirley's face was as grey as cement, as she hadn't much of an appetite to begin with. Marion was pleased that the crisis had brought them even closer together. They seemed to realize how lucky they were to have one another. It made her very happy to see Declan fold Shirley into his arms and kiss the top of her head gently. Shirley was one of the Greenwood clan now.

*

At midnight, just as Johnny was locking up, there was a phone call. The Gardai, who had gone to the pink house beside the sea, said that the place had been thoroughly searched, and it was empty. Some empty wine bottles and a pile of steak bones was all they found. They wanted the Hogan family to be very careful for the next few days, until Mr Lolly was picked up. Johnny decided to sleep on the information and decide what to do in the morning.

22. The Moment of Truth

The mysterious disappearance of Eugene Lolly did little to dampen the high spirits that followed the daring escape of Eileen and Marion. The Hogan family and the Greenwood family were drawn together in the short burst of publicity and celebrations that followed their big adventure in Donegal.

Marion knew that it was only a matter of time before Johnny and Declan got to know each other, and before Johnny saw a reflection of himself in Declan's handsome features. Now that her son was leaving his youthful looks behind and maturing into a fine young man, he looked more and more like Johnny every day. And since he had changed his hairstyle, the similarities were impossible to miss. Marion begged Declan to go back to being a blond, but he said that dark hair was much more fashionable in the music-loving circles that he mixed in.

Johnny was organizing a big celebration dinner at a local hotel for all his friends and family, and the Greenwoods were invited, and Shirley, too. Of course, Eddy didn't want to go; he never wanted to see Johnny again. (He had postponed his plan to beat Johnny up, for the time being.) But out of respect for Eileen Hogan, they decided to attend the meal and leave the hotel as soon as it was over. Marion was still feeling very emotional and tearful, after her ordeal, and she had closed the bridal shop for a while to give herself a rest. She had been enjoying long lie-ins and hot bubble baths, and watching black and white films on the television in the afternoons; and so the party invitation was simply an unwelcome irritation to her. But it was impossible to say no.

When the day of the party arrived, Eddy had a couple of whiskeys to fortify him before they set off in Marion's car. Marion told him that Johnny had invited about one hundred and fifty people, so hopefully they could sit somewhere near the back, and keep a low profile. Eddy just shook his head and sighed. He knew that Johnny would home in on Marion the moment he saw her. Johnny Hogan never did anything nice for other people unless there was something in it for himself. Eddy knew that Johnny was planning to use the kidnapping to start building a relationship with Marion again. Right under Eddy's nose. He'd done it before, giving her a job in the ballroom and flirting with her constantly.

But with his three daughters sitting in the back seat, there was nothing Eddy could say about how he was feeling. The children did not know that Johnny and Marion had once been an item. So he wasn't able to warn his wife to stay by his side in the hotel, and to be on her guard against Hollywood Hogan and his silver tongue. He gave himself a little lecture about keeping things in proportion; the scales were weighted in Eddy's favour this time. Hogan was dealing with a losing deck. A lifetime together, and a home and children with Eddy Greenwood versus a youthful infatuation with a vain poser who still used hairspray at the age of forty-eight.

Put like that, was there seriously anything to worry about?

The hotel foyer was full of people when Marion's Mercedes pulled up in the car park. Most of the guests seemed to be over the age of fifty. There were a lot of beige slacks and walking sticks in evidence. Emily, Eve and Eloise groaned. They were bored stiff before they even got out of the car. They hated stuffy things like this, with the grown-ups chattering on endlessly about the good old days. They made a last-minute bid to be released from attending and practically had to be shoved in through the main doors by their mother.

Declan was going to drive to the hotel in his own car, although Marion had told him that he needn't bother coming if he didn't want to, which made his sisters very cross indeed. They protested that if they had to endure such a boring party, then so should Declan.

'Well, he is getting married soon,' Marion had explained. 'He might want to spend the day with his fiancée. He needs his rest before the baby is born.'

And so, Eddy, Marion and their three daughters stood in a little huddle beside an enormous flower arrangement on the reception desk, and waited to be summoned into the dining room. There was a real undercurrent of excitement in the hotel. Everyone was animated and happy, waving to old friends and telling each other to put their money away.

'I think I'll try to get a drink at the bar, though it looks very crowded. Do you all want something?' Eddy felt in his pockets for his wallet and began to make his way haltingly across the room, saying hello to people as he went. Marion could hear him saying, 'Yes, she's fine now,' and

'Yes, it was a terrible shock,' and 'Thank you, I'll pass on your good wishes.'

Just then, Johnny came in, cigarette in hand. A middle-aged James Dean, with his collar turned up against the breeze.

'There's Johnny,' said someone, and Eddy turned round to look. He saw Johnny scan the crowd, and wave to Marion. She waved back. Johnny threaded his way through the guests, shaking hands with this one and that one, working the crowd with grace and elegance. He kissed Marion and her daughters on both cheeks, and stood right beside them. As if they were a little family. Eddy bit his lip and frantically waved a ten-pound note at the bar staff, but they were all busy serving other customers. Johnny was drawing deeply on his cigarette, his cheeks pale with recent worry and concern. However, his black hair was still irritatingly thick and shiny. Eddy had offered up thousands of prayers over the years, hoping that Johnny would go bald. He'd said whole rosaries for it. Johnny Hogan might as well be castrated, if the top of his head was smooth as an egg. He had based his whole persona on his image. The luxurious quiff was his best feature. Eddy often wondered if Johnny had gone to some place in America and had his scalp preserved with chemicals.

As he watched his wife from the bar, Marion patted Johnny's arm, and smiled at him. They began to talk. Johnny leaned in very close to her, to catch what she was saying. The girls got bored and slipped off to the ladies' room. When Eddy eventually attracted the attention of a barman, he asked for two small whiskeys, and three colas, and told the lad to keep the change. He hurried back to his wife, to rescue her from Johnny. But she sent him straight back to the bar to get a drink for Johnny, and two glasses of stout for James and Eileen who had just arrived also. Eddy was totally fed up. Stout would take ages to settle in the glasses. And the queue at the bar had trebled. He'd be there for half an hour at least. He was filled with impotent rage.

By the time Eddy had the drinks assembled on a little round tray, the guests were already taking their seats in the function room. It never ceased to amaze Eddy how quickly people could move themselves when there was free food involved. Within seconds the crowd had moved from the foyer to the dining room and were organizing themselves into groups of eight.

Eddy hovered in the doorway, looking for Marion's blonde curls in the crowd, and was dismayed to see Johnny pulling out a chair for her at his table. James and Eileen were already sitting down, and had the decency to look uncomfortable with the arrangement, but Johnny was starting to relax. Taking off his coat, handing out cigarettes, and saluting friends and relatives at nearby tables. Before Eddy could make his way over to them, all the other seats at Johnny's table were taken. Eddy stood alone, with his little tray, and wanted to roar. Then, he saw Emily waving him over to a table at the very back of the room and he darted over to her, grateful at least to be able to sit down. He sent Eve over to Johnny's table with the drinks for Johnny and his grandparents and with a message for Marion that they had kept a seat for her at their table. But of course, by that time, Marion and Eileen were deep in conversation about their kidnapping ordeal, and Eileen was holding Marion by the arm and telling her all about the police questioning her, and that they were going to press charges against her for wounding Lolly, when he was eventually found. But that she would get off with a caution. And that James had nearly gone berserk when he was told that his wife had been brandishing a weapon. Then, the empty seats that Eddy had been saving for Marion, Declan and Shirley were taken by some late arrivals and Eddy had to resign himself to dining without his beautiful wife by his side.

Naturally, Johnny had to make a big speech about the whole thing, and there was a wave of applause that went on for five minutes. Eileen put her hand up several times, to signal to the crowd to stop clapping, but they went on and on and even cheered hooray as well. It seemed like a hundred years had gone by when all the fuss was over and the food could finally be served. Johnny raised his hand to the head waitress, like some sort of Roman emperor from two thousand years ago, and then she motioned to the younger waitresses to get the party under way.

Halfway through the meal, Eddy left the room and went to sit in the lobby, nursing a large drink. The girls had told him they were going to shake hands with Eileen Hogan after the teas and coffees had been served, and then they were going to phone Declan to pick them up. Thank goodness Declan and Shirley hadn't turned up for the party. Declan didn't go to Hogan's ballroom very often, and so far, Johnny hadn't spoken to him for any length of time. But in broad daylight at a family function? Well, that was another matter. Eddy considered moving house briefly, but there were just too many things tying them all to the city. Two successful businesses, a lovely house that would cost over a million pounds in London, and the girls were doing very well in school. He sighed. Sixty minutes later, Marion came out of the function room, and spied her husband slumped in his armchair, staring into the dancing flames.

'There you are,' she said. 'Sorry about that, sweetheart. Once Eileen gets talking, you can't stop her. I just couldn't get away. The whole thing seems to have given her a new lease of life. In fact, it's taken far more out of me than it has of her. I wish I had her bravery.'

'It doesn't matter. Can we go home now?'

'Oh, Eddy. You're cross with me. I thought you'd be fine with the girls for company.'

'You thought nothing of the sort. You were too busy comforting Johnny Hogan. I was far more upset than he was. I nearly went out of my mind. But I had to hide my feelings in front of the children. Not rock the boat. As usual. You still care for him, don't you?'

'What?'

'I saw you laughing with him. You still love him, don't you?'

'Eddy, I do not. Don't be absurd. How many drinks have you had?'

'I'm going home.' He got up and nearly stumbled on the hearth; his jealousy making him more drunk than the whiskey.

'Don't be silly, Eddy. Don't leave. Come in and say hello to Eileen, and have some coffee, and stop behaving like a spoilt teenager. I don't want to be here, either, but it's nearly over.'

'I can't stop you and Hogan making fools of yourselves, Marion. But I'd rather not be here to witness it, if you don't mind. I think I saw a taxi out there. Excuse me.'

'Eddy, please! Stay with me. I can drive us home, I didn't finish my drink.'

'I'm telling you now, if I go into that room, I'll reach for Hogan and I'll bloody well kill him. He has no respect for me, whatsoever. I am your husband, and he treats me like some kind of a chauffeur. What did you ever see in him anyway?'

Marion laid her hand on Eddy's shoulder and massaged his neck. Eddy loved her to do that when he was tired after a long day working in his restaurant. But it was not enough to pacify him today.

'I'm beginning to wonder if I ever knew you at all, Marion.' He shrugged his wife's hand away, and stormed out of the hotel without looking back.

Some people sitting nearby saw the entire incident and Marion was very embarrassed. She hurried to the ladies' room, and wept for a while in an empty cubicle. She knew she should have listened to Eddy and cried off the party altogether. God knows she had the perfect excuse. She could have said she was still in shock and it was half true. But then, Eileen would have been very offended. And if it hadn't been for Eileen's quick thinking, they might still be locked in the pink house by the sea, with that madman drinking his way through a hefty supply of wine.

It was so hard to please everyone. Some days, she wondered how she had found the strength to keep going for all these years. Bringing up four children, running her boutique, and keeping the secret of Declan's real father to herself.

She needed Eddy. Just as much as she loved him. He was such a good and wise man. She was deeply shocked at his display of bad temper.

And she knew that Eddy was right about Johnny. Johnny was insensitive and vain and obsessed with his ballroom, and he dressed like an eccentric, and acted like he was famous. And he did ignore Eddy. That was true as well. Johnny had a smile and a good word for every stranger on the street, but he barely acknowledged Eddy whenever they met.

She was stuck at the main table of this party with everyone clapping for her, and she wasn't even feeling very well. Her nerves were in tatters. God, she had to get out of here! She would just collect her jacket and handbag, say her goodbyes to Eileen and James, and go straight home. Thank goodness she had refused all those drinks. She longed to feel her trusty car keys in her hand once again!

When she returned to the table, Johnny noticed that she had been crying. He dabbed her eyes with a napkin and gave her a gentle hug. She told Johnny that Eddy had gone home with a migraine. James caught Johnny's eye, and shook his head. *You're treading on thin ice*. But Johnny ignored him. It was perfectly acceptable to speak to an old flame at a party. Some of the younger guests came over to the table then, shook hands with everyone, thanked Johnny for the lovely meal, and went home. The majority of the older relatives retired to the bar, to make a night of it. Who knew when they would all be together again? James and Eileen decided to go home and put their feet up. Emily, Eve and Eloise went to the foyer to wait for Declan. Johnny and Marion were left alone in the function room. They chatted for a few minutes, until Marion was sure that Declan and the girls would be on their way home. Then she tried to say goodbye.

'I'm feeling a little fragile, Johnny. It's been lovely but I'll head on now.'

'Would you like to go for a walk, Marion? To get some fresh air?'

'No, I'm fine. Thanks, Johnny. I'm going home.'

They stood up and he helped her into her jacket. Johnny gave all the waitresses a tenner each and told them they were great girls, and they were delighted with him. Marion wondered again why he hadn't used his charm to get himself a wife. Maybe Johnny did derive a certain pleasure from keeping the men of Belfast in a permanent state of anxiety. (That was Eddy's theory.) As they were going through the foyer, someone called out to them.

'Mum!'

Johnny and Marion looked up to see Declan standing there with Emily and Eve. His black quiff was the mirror-image of Johnny's. Johnny said nothing but he looked thoughtfully at Declan, as if seeing him for the first time. There was a tangible silence in the air. Marion's heart seemed to turn inside out.

'Eloise is powdering her nose,' Declan explained. 'We're waiting for her.'

'Declan, I didn't see you there,' Marion croaked. 'Your father's gone already.' Surely Johnny hasn't twigged, she thought. God knows, he's seen Declan enough times before now in the ballroom.

'Gone where?' asked Declan brightly.

'He went home already,' said Marion, although her mouth had dried up. The words came out in a husky rasp. A hateful red flush began to burn on her neck, and slowly spread up towards her cheeks. She pulled some of her lovely blonde curls forward in an attempt to hide her blushes, and took her pink tweed jacket off and folded it over her arm. 'Isn't it cruelly hot in here?' she said quietly.

'Dad went home? Without you?' The concept was unthinkable to Declan.

'He had a headache, pet. I didn't have any wine myself, so I could have taken the girls home. Sorry to bring you out for nothing. I should have thought to call you . . .'

'It's okay, Mum. Are you leaving now, too?'

'Yes, I am. My car's just outside.' She stepped forward and opened one of the heavy glass doors, and a cool breeze flowed in and soothed her bright red face.

'Give your grandparents my best wishes, Mr Hogan,' said Declan, politely.

'Thank you, Declan. I will,' he said.

Then, Eloise joined the little group and they went out together, laughing and joking.

Johnny turned to Marion. She couldn't tell if he was even remotely suspicious, or if he could be so self-obsessed that he had never wondered about her pregnancy. But she couldn't speak to him. Her throat had dried up completely. They waved to Declan and his sisters as they drove away.

When they had gone, Johnny turned to Marion again and said, 'Is there something wrong?'

'What do you mean? What could be wrong?'

'You don't look well.'

'That's a first. You, worrying about my health.'

'Are you going to faint?'

'No, I'm exhausted, if you must know. For heaven's sake, I thought I was going to be killed by that madman. How would you feel?'

She was wondering if she should simply make a dash for the car, and blank out this awful moment from her memory. Oh, why did she leave Eddy in the first place? What had she ever seen in Johnny? And when would the guilt that hung around her neck like a stone, ever go away?

'Declan doesn't look like Eddy much, does he?' said Johnny. 'He's a good-looking boy.'

'Don't be bitchy, Johnny. It doesn't suit you.' She made a huge effort to act normally, putting the pink jacket back on and making for the doors.

'How long were you married to Greenwood when Declan was born?'

'Nine months,' she whispered.

'Are you sure?' He was trying to work it out in his head. Was it July, or August or September? He couldn't remember. But Marion's horrified expression told him what he wanted to know. He decided to chance it. 'He's my son, isn't he?'

'No! He's not. Are you crazy?'

'Marion, he is. Admit it.'

'He's Eddy's. He was born early, that's all.'

'I thought you said nine months?'

'Oh, God, leave me alone,' she snapped. 'What does it matter? You didn't want to marry me anyway.'

'So, he is mine?' There was a lengthy pause.

And then she said, 'Yes. He is.'

Marion didn't expect him to cry, but he did. Johnny thought he had no more reserves of emotion left, after the drama of Eileen's kidnapping. But he had. He staggered out through the hotel doors and stood in the car park with his hands over his face. Tears flowed down his cheeks and soaked his silver-tipped shirt collar. Marion linked arms with him and told him she was sorry, over and over again. The two of them idled round the hotel gardens, and eventually found a little bench in the shelter of a huge oak tree. Johnny wept, and smoked, and wept again. Sometimes his shoulders shook with noisy sobs and sometimes he cried silent tears as he gazed up at the sky.

'Why?' he said. 'God in heaven! Why did you not tell me?'

'I couldn't. I was in a pure panic, at the time. I couldn't think straight.'

'But, *why*? You knew I would have done the decent thing!'

'I did not know. You had no notion of getting married. You never even talked about getting engaged. Five years, we were together.'

'I would have married you. I would have, Marion.'

'I couldn't take that chance. Once the news was out, it would be too late to marry anybody. No other man would have wanted an unwed mother, Johnny. And I didn't want to be alone.'

'I had a right to know.'

'Look, I was going to tell you. It was the day of the robbery.'

'What?'

'I was all set to tell you. That's why I came into the ballroom that night. Anyway, the whole place was in chaos for days. You know it was. And afterwards, I lost the courage. Time was running out for me.'

'I can't believe it. You should have told me, Marion.'

'How many times do I have to explain? I couldn't tell you. You have no idea how hard it is to say those two little words: *I'm pregnant*. Why didn't *you* notice I was ill? Why is this all my responsibility?'

'I'm sorry. You were always kind of pale. I didn't notice.'

'It's all in the past, now, Johnny.'

'So that's why you married Greenwood so suddenly. And I thought you were just trying to make me jealous.'

'Johnny, I didn't mean to hurt you. I didn't think you'd care. Can't you see? I dropped all kinds of hints about settling down. You never once picked up on them. You would have made a terrible father, anyway. It was a kind of miracle, when the robbery stopped me from telling you.'

'How can you say that? We would have made a great couple, Marion. We could have set the world on fire. We could have had a chain of dance halls!'

'Oh, please! I didn't want that kind of life, Johnny. Not with a baby on the way. Will you never understand? I wanted a quiet life, and a husband who was at home with me in the evenings.'

'Did you love Greenwood?'

'Not in the beginning. Not in the way I loved you.'

'But, then you did?'

'Yes. He was so kind. He *knows* me, Johnny. He cares about every little thing I do and feel.'

'And you still love him?'

'Yes, I do. More than ever. He's the gentlest man on the planet. I should never have left him in the first place.'

'Did he know about the baby?'

'Of course he did. He could tell I was expecting, just by looking at my face.'

'And he saw his chance to steal you away from me?'

'Please, Johnny. It wasn't like that.'

'Wasn't it? The coward! He couldn't take me on, and fight me for you?'

'Johnny, where do you get your logic from? You can't go around beating people up for love. Be reasonable. Would you have given up the ballroom for me? If I'd asked you to?'

'What else could I have done with my life? It's the only thing I was good at.'

'Well, then.'

Johnny lit another cigarette, and sighed. 'He's a handsome lad – Declan. He takes that after me.'

'He is good-looking. And clever, too. He's going to be a doctor.'

'Really? That's great. I knew he was at college but I didn't know what he was studying. Doctor, eh? He didn't get his brains from me, then.'

'He loves music, though. Like you.'

'But he doesn't know about me? That I am his –'

'No. I never told him. It's funny how you can never escape the past, isn't it? You can kid yourself that certain things are over and done with. But then, one day, they come back to haunt you. I was going to tell him lots of times, but I couldn't. It was too hard. He adores Eddy.'

'And now, I'll never get to know him.'

'It's too late, Johnny. He has his own life now. A baby of his own on the way.' A cold breeze came whistling

round the corner of the hotel and made them both shiver.
Marion looked at her watch.

'We would have made a great little family,' Johnny said,
as they stood up.

'Please don't tell Eddy about this.'

'Why not?'

'He thinks you still carry a torch for me.'

'I do.'

Marion shook her head. 'Johnny, you don't. I'm just a
reminder of your youth.'

Silence.

'Will James and Eileen be okay?' asked Marion. 'When
you leave for America?' It was a roundabout way of
checking that he was still leaving.

'Yes. They're going to move to a small bungalow in
Portstewart, actually. It was Gran's idea. She likes the
seaside, she's decided.'

'They really love each other, don't they? Eileen and
James?'

'Yes, they do. I hope to God they both don't drop dead
with delayed shock. The doctor says these things don't
always sink in, right away. Months later, they can affect
you, he said. The body buries powerful feelings, you see,
until it's ready to deal with them.'

'I know what you mean.'

'I'd like to meet Declan again sometime. Talk to him,
just once. But I won't tell him I'm his father. I don't want
him to think I abandoned him. Or you.'

Marion's whole body shook with relief. Thank God,
she thought. Now, Eddy never has to know our secret is
not a secret any more.

'Well, I'll go home now. I'm really sorry, Johnny. I didn't mean to hurt you. You do understand? And like you said yourself, you didn't want to settle down to an ordinary kind of life. It was all for the best.'

They hugged each other briefly. Johnny kissed her softly on the cheek. Long-buried feelings stirred within her. He was very attractive, even with the passing years chipping away at him, leaving lines around his eyes. And maybe he was slightly too thin. But still, there was something about him, something magical. Marion broke away first, and walked quickly across the lawn. She didn't want Johnny to see her breaking down in tears. Her heart was in turmoil. She thought she did still love Johnny, just a little bit. Just for old times' sake. They *had* been such a glamorous couple, the best dancers in the city. She with her jaunty neck-scarves and false eyelashes, and Johnny with his endless supply of blue suede shoes. And Johnny was right: they could have taken on the world, together. She hadn't given him the chance to show her what kind of husband he might have been. Why did life have to be so complicated?

And then, she thought of Eddy, and her heart almost broke with shame. She had left him standing in the foyer like a servant, with his tray of drinks. After all he had done for her over the years. Waiting for so long to take her to bed. Getting up in the night to help feed the children when they were babies. Setting her up in her own business so she could feel independent. Telling her he loved her every single day. He looked like a Victorian gamekeeper in those crumpled tweeds, and the tousled curly hair that no comb could tame, and yet he was always there for her and the children. He'd die for her.

She unlocked the car and jumped in. Dear, sweet Eddy. Still so possessive of her, after all this time. Drinking himself into a jealous rage like that. She would go straight home and make it up with him. And then, she remembered her promise to Johnny: he wanted to meet Declan properly. What would Eddy say if he knew about that?

23. A Bundoran Cafe

Eugene Lolly sat in a tiny back-street cafe in Bundoran and considered his options. It didn't take him very long. His picture was all over the papers. The story of the Bonbon Gang was on every front page. He looked tough and mean in the old mugshots they had managed to get from the police files. That gave him a bit of a buzz, anyway. At least he wasn't a nobody any more. Of course, now he had to be careful about being seen by the public. He was wearing a disguise of thick reading glasses and a cloth cap, stolen from an unlocked car earlier on in the day. But the owners of the cafe, an elderly couple, didn't give him a second glance. Likely they thought he was some lonely farmer in from the country on a pay-day bender. He looked down at the story in the local paper and pulled the glasses down to the tip of his nose so that he could read over the top of them.

There was a recent, though particularly unflattering, picture of Eugene at the bottom of the article. It said, *Eugene Lolly, 46, hapless leader of the Bonbon Gang.* Hapless! No one had worked harder, to get on in life, than Eugene Lolly! If his plans rarely worked out, it wasn't his fault. And now, just when he thought things could not get any worse, they were calling him names in the papers! Eugene was many things, but he wasn't hapless.

He remembered his rage as the women drove away that

fateful day, Eileen Hogan laughing at him from the car; and he had to accept that he had been outwitted by an old woman with one foot in the grave. And her silly friend, who was as jumpy as a firecracker on a trampoline. Yes, it pained him to admit that. He'd been outwitted, good and proper, by a couple of females. Left locked in the pastel-painted bedroom of a seaside bungalow. And no way of knowing how long it would be until he was arrested.

Hogan's old girlfriend had taken the key of the door away with her, so he couldn't try the old trick of pushing it out onto a piece of paper, and sliding it in towards himself, under the door. He tried to force the door, wrenching the handle constantly, but he succeeded only in bruising his palms very badly. The language that he went over that afternoon was absolutely sinful. And then, a couple of hours later, he heard the sound that he had been dreading. A police car came revving up the drive and he knew it was all over. There was no hiding place in the sparsely furnished room. He briefly considered popping into the wardrobe, but knew it would buy him only an extra few seconds, at most. He might have tried hiding in the hollow bed-base, but ruled that out for the same reason. The shabby prison walls and the hopeless clang of the metal doors flashed into his mind. He'd spent enough time there, over the years. It was a long time in coming but he had finally learned his lesson.

He just wanted to be free, and he would have given all the money in the world to find a key to the solid pine door that held him prisoner. Timothy Tate had told him it was never too late to pray, that no situation was ever too hopeless. And he was surely without hope of any kind at that point. But he just couldn't bring himself to pray. And then, a curious thing happened. He spied a little blue glass bottle, in the shape of the Virgin Mary, on a high shelf in the corner. And he knew it was one of those novelty containers for holy water that people bought at the Knock shrine. And the sight of it made him so angry that he climbed up on a chair to get it and break it into small pieces. And that was when he saw the spare key, at the very back of the shelf. He couldn't believe it. It was like a miracle. It *was* a miracle. He grabbed both objects tightly, in case they disappeared before his eyes. He jumped down again and tried the key in the lock right away, and it worked. So he nipped out through the door and locked it again behind him, just to confuse the police. His mind was in such a state of confusion that he dropped the key twice before he was finished.

At the end of the hall, through the stained glass of the front door, he could see the dark shape of one of the Gardai, fumbling with a bunch of keys. He knew there was no point in trying the other windows and doors in the house for an escape route – he had locked them all himself. He looked up to heaven for further guidance, and saw the hatch to the attic directly above him. In a heartbeat, he was up on a plant stand and through the hatch, pulling the mahogany stand up behind him. The guards came in just as he dropped the hatch back into place. He could hear them searching the house, and even coming up to the attic, but they didn't find him because by that time he was hiding in the water tank. Stone-cold, that water was. His very soul was shivering. They had a good rummage round; he had to hand it to them. They were very thorough. They found the plant stand and wondered aloud why such a fine piece of furniture was left lying on a pile of insulation felt in the corner of the attic. But they didn't look in the tank, and Eugene had already removed the overhead light bulb, so they wouldn't see his mean little face just beneath the water level.

Much later, when they had gone, he crawled out of his watery hiding place, and ripped a hole in the roofing felt. He lifted off a few slates, crawled out, replaced the slates and then slid down the roof into some bushes at the back of the house. He ran across a dozen fields, dripping wet, followed all the way by two curious horses. He found a secluded beach and went for a rest in the long grass near the sand dunes. Although he was very tired and very cold, it was pleasant to listen to the cries of the seagulls as they wheeled overhead. He took off his shoes and felt the sand between his toes, thinking of the little glass bottle and how it had led him to the key and freedom. It was probably the weirdest thing that had ever happened to him.

He felt in his pocket for the statue, and was reassured to know it was still there. He wasn't converted or anything like that, but he was intrigued. Was all religious faith just an ancient form of positive thinking, he wondered. And were the ancient monks in their beehive huts simply a bunch of peace-loving lads like himself; who made up the whole palaver about God, because they desperately wanted to get away from women and their endless chatter?

They were interesting questions to ponder as he hung around the outskirts of Bundoran, waiting for something to happen. He was barely aware of the hours passing.

He had been sleeping rough since his miraculous

escape, slipping into Bundoran when it got dark, to buy fish suppers and bottles of milk. By now, the police in Belfast would be watching the hostel, the unemployment office, and the post office. What on earth was he going to do? He was nearly out of money.

In his old life, he might have decided to bump off Timothy Tate. And Johnny Hogan too, for good measure. (The pair of them had brought him nothing but bad luck.) Go out on a blaze of glory. Back to jail for the rest of his days, his place in the criminal hall of fame assured. But he didn't feel like that any more. Even Tate and Hogan were not worth a lifetime of prison stew. To his surprise, he decided he wanted a peaceful future. Some little luxuries would be nice, yes. A bottle of good whiskey now and then, sandalwood soap, comfortable shoes. But peace of mind was definitely his number-one priority now. He thought he might hitch a ride to Spain – give his wife a little surprise. Ask her for some cash to tide him over. A little favour, for her old man. No strings attached. Or maybe just make his way to South America and try to find work there. And so, his head full of half-baked plans, he pulled his by-now shabby jacket tightly around his shoulders and ordered a hamburger and chips, and a large pot of tea.

24. Something New, Something Old, Something Blue, Something Gold

April arrived in a series of blustery rain showers. Eileen Hogan was feeling fine, although James caught the flu and blamed it on all the stress he had suffered. Marion Greenwood decided to pull herself together for the sake of her family, and also because Declan and Shirley's wedding could not be delayed another minute.

Everyone was relieved when the original date was confirmed. There would be no postponement. The tumultuous concept of a double wedding finally began to sink in, and the girls' mother wondered what she had done with all her free time before the big announcement. Relatives they hadn't seen for years were calling in to visit, and they would often stay talking and reminiscing until midnight. Martha became something of a celebrity on the street. People would say, 'There goes your woman with the two daughters getting wed,' every time she went by their window. And the amount of shopping that had to be done was serious. Even though the Greenwoods were arranging the buffet reception and the wedding cake, Mrs Winters had to choose outfits for herself and her husband, flowers for the wedding party and the church, and dresses for the bridesmaids. The pile of gifts for Kate and Shirley had grown so large that they were afraid to leave the house unattended. Mr Winters was usually left behind to guard them while the women went shopping.

Shirley had developed a craving for the scent of fabric conditioner, and spent a lot of time doing the laundry. She had a selection of bottles on the kitchen window sill, and she sniffed each one delicately before making her choice and pouring a capful into the drawer of the washing machine. She was also eating a lot of fresh fruit, since anything remotely oily made her stomach heave in protest. Strawberries were her favourite, although they weren't as filling as her mother's pies and stews. She lost weight, and went to see her doctor about it, but she reassured her it would be okay. Declan took to bringing punnets of fruit and boxes of peppermint tea to the house when he came to visit. He was very polite to Shirley's parents, but he was not allowed to see Shirley alone in her room. They had to sit downstairs in the lounge, while the rest of the family waited in the kitchen. Shirley thought it was very sweet.

'The horse may have bolted already,' said her father, 'but there's no call to get rid of the gate altogether.' No one was quite sure what he meant by that but they said nothing because he *was* coping much better than they'd expected. 'I told you, it's the quiet ones,' he said from time to time, tapping the side of his nose.

Then Shirley was summoned to Romance And Ribbons for another attempt at choosing a gown. Marion was feeling much better by then, and was back behind the counter of her boutique, although she had installed a state-of-the-art security system in the building and customers now had to ring a doorbell to get in. Kate went along too, with orders from her father not to take advantage of

Mrs Greenwood's very generous offer of a bargain-price gown. Kate said nothing at the time. She didn't think Romance And Ribbons would have anything grand enough for her. She was already getting quotes from three bridal-wear designers in England, and five hundred pounds would barely cover the deposit.

Shirley was a little nervous when she arrived at the salon. Kate was with her, which was good, but she was still slightly worried when her big sister rang the doorbell. Shirley didn't want Mrs Greenwood to think she was not worthy of her handsome son. She had no reason to feel that way but the notion was making it hard for her to choose a dress. And now, her bump was starting to show, which left simple silhouettes out of the running altogether. A puffball of a skirt, it would have to be. And Shirley hated fussy clothes. The whole world knew she was pregnant, but she didn't want to *look* pregnant on her wedding day. Not that she was ashamed of the baby, or anything. She was actually getting used to the idea of having a child, and she talked to her bump when she lay in bed each night. It was like having a little friend with you all the time, so that you never felt alone. She hoped the baby was a girl, so that they would have lots of things in common, as the child grew up. She also hoped that if the baby was a boy, he would grow up to be as gorgeous as Declan, and not take after his grandfather, Eddy, who was a little on the plain side. Kate had told Shirley that genetic characteristics could skip the generations, and her child could be as plain as a barn door, but that was just Kate stirring the pot.

She sighed and was glad that Kate would be doing most

of the talking today. Sometimes it was good to have a motor-mouth for a sister. It took the pressure off Shirley, when she wasn't in the mood for conversation. They hadn't met Marion for a while, as Shirley was beginning to feel tired in the evenings, as well as trying to cope with the morning nausea. She fell asleep on the sofa all the time. It was only lunchtime now, and she was yawning already. The door clicked open and they went in.

Mrs Greenwood, herself, was looking like a film star with her white, bubble curls and her heavy make-up. She wore very strong perfume, a pinstripe suit, and a pretty little silver bracelet on her left wrist. For the want of something to say, Shirley commented on the bracelet.

'Oh, this,' Marion said. 'I've had this little thing for years and years. It's only costume, but of great sentimental value.'

The truth was that Johnny had only recently given it back to her. Just two weeks ago, in fact. He'd kept it on his bedside table for twenty years, waiting for the opportunity. Marion had decided to wear the bracelet during the run-up to the wedding, as a way of including Johnny in the preparations. She knew it was a silly notion, but it felt the right thing to do.

'Now, let me fetch some teas, and we'll have a little chat about styles. You go ahead and have a look round. You're very pale, Shirley. Have you had any lunch? I'll see have I any cookies.'

Shirley was looking extra-pale today, because she had wisely decided to leave off the black eye-pencil and the red lipstick, so as not to stain the bridal gowns. But she was too tired to bother explaining that to her future mother-in-law.

While Marion was busy in the tiny kitchenette, Kate and Shirley walked along the rails, looking at the gowns. There were dresses of every size and description, and a huge cupboard full of glass tiaras and satin shoes, pretty drawstring handbags and silk flowers. Shirley was overwhelmed, but Kate was disappointed.

'The thing is, this is all far too fancy for me,' whispered Shirley.

'Are you mad?' said Kate. 'There's nothing here I would even consider wearing. It's all far too plain. I want a *fairytale* dress.'

'Do you think we should buy similar dresses?' asked Shirley. 'Something from the same range? So that we match?'

'Oh, no.' Kate was sure about that. 'We're not identical twins. I'm going up the aisle like a flower-show float. I want a train on the back, and a crown on my head, and a full skirt, and beading and bows and frills and covered buttons and –'

'Here we are,' said Marion, coming back with a little tray bearing three elegant china cups of tea, and a plate of fancy biscuits. 'Any thoughts so far?'

The sisters tried on gowns, all afternoon. The shop was closed to the public that day, so they had plenty of time. But nothing seemed to work. The girls' pale skin looked almost blue beside the bright whites, pale creams and shimmering ivories of the dresses. Even the magnificent gown Marion adored did not suit either of them. Kate tried it on first, then Shirley. They tried adding shawls, fabric roses, and clip-on collars. But the results were always disappointing. Even Marion had to admit that she was beaten. The two sisters would have to be dipped in a bath of fake tan, to give them a bit of colour. Marion suggested a little trip to a new tanning salon in East Belfast, but the sisters weren't interested. Kate declared that fake tans were as common as muck, and Shirley worried about the baby getting radiation poisoning or feeling too warm.

Then Shirley spied a navy velvet evening dress at the very back of the rail. It had long sleeves, a scoop neckline and a full skirt. The dress was the same colour as the sky on summer nights. Shirley felt a spasm of happiness in her chest. She excitedly announced that she had found her dress.

Marion was not impressed. 'Oh, dear, I don't think so, Shirley, pet. It's blue!'

'It's beautiful. I love it.'

'But it's *blue*.'

'I think it will suit me.'

'It's an evening gown, Shirley, not a bridal gown.'

'Can I try it on? Please?'

'Well, if you like. But I don't think . . .'

Shirley disappeared into the fitting room with more enthusiasm than she had felt all afternoon. The dress was a perfect fit. You couldn't see the bump at all, and the colour made her eyes look much bluer than they really were. She began to feel optimistic about the ceremony for the first time. She came out from the curtained changing room and gave them a little twirl.

'I'd like this one,' she declared. 'If that's all right.'

'Oh,' said Marion, flatly.

'If it's not too expensive?' said Shirley.

'No, it's not too expensive. Not that cost was ever going to be a problem.'

'Are you disappointed?' asked Shirley.

'Well,' said Marion, thinking of her own modest wedding dress, 'I wanted you to have a very special day, that's all.'

'I will have,' said Shirley. 'Thank you very much.'

'It is a *bit* plain,' Kate observed.

'Oh, but I'll wear several strands of beads. A pearl choker, maybe? And I'll have a big bouquet of flowers,' said Shirley. 'Sunflowers!'

'Sunflowers? Real ones?' Marion was shocked. 'Those big, untidy things?'

'Yes, a big bunch of sunflowers. I don't mind if they're real or artificial.'

'Will you wear a tiara?' said Kate. 'You'll have a tiara, surely?'

'We'll see.'

'So, you're definitely *not* going to wear white?' Marion wanted to be sure.

'I'm pr– I mean, I'm expecting. Everyone knows I'm expecting. It just wouldn't be right,' said Shirley. 'It would be a fraud.'

'You don't have to be a virgin to wear white!' cried Kate. 'It's not a rule of law. Is it, Mrs Greenwood? Even if you're not preggers?'

'No, it's not a *rule*,' said Marion, moving the silver bracelet round and round on her wrist. 'But it is traditional.'

'Well, then,' said Shirley. 'Let's be different. Let's have a big splash of colour. I feel confident in blue. I just feel silly in the other dresses. Like a little girl playing with the dressing-up box. I'm sorry, but that's how I feel.'

'Okay, then. If you're really sure,' said Marion. She

hadn't the energy to fight about it. Shirley's hormones must be going haywire; that was the reason for this madness. Oh, well, she thought. Let her get married in blue, if it makes her happy. Marion had stopped fussing about little things since the kidnapping. Her priorities had changed. The fact that Declan was getting married at all was the main thing. The details were not important.

'I'm definitely sure. I always thought white wedding dresses were boring, anyway,' said Shirley, admiring herself in the huge mirror. 'And patronizing to women. I mean, the men don't have to wear white, do they?'

There was an awkward silence in the room. Dozens of white gowns, hanging in their protective plastic covers, seemed to shrink away from Shirley's declaration that they were boring. Marion coughed nervously. A hot flush began to spread over Shirley's face and shoulders.

'Well, maybe they *should* wear white,' faltered Shirley. 'The grooms. And all the guests, too. Everybody in white. Like film stars . . .'

'You know what, Shirley?' said Kate, eventually. 'I think you might be onto something here, with this colour thing. Mrs Greenwood, do any of these dresses come in gold?'

'Now that you come to mention it, I do have one gold dress. It's very lavish – you might not like it. I ordered it some years ago for an actress, but then the wedding was called off. It cost a fortune, I remember. She paid half and we called it quits.'

'An actress, eh? I'd love to see it.' Kate was thrilled.

'I'll get it. One moment, please.' Marion went off to the stockroom with a spring in her step, hoping that this marathon session would soon be over.

'Are you sure it won't bring you bad luck, Kate? A cancelled wedding, and all that?' Shirley whispered.

'Not at all. You make your own luck in this world,' said Kate. 'Someone else's loss is my gain.'

Marion brought the gown into the salon. It was absolutely dripping with frills and lace and glitter-tipped rosebuds, with a long train and matching veil.

'What do you think?' she said brightly. 'I thought it was very Princess Diana.'

'I'll take it,' said Kate, checking the label. 'It's the right size. How much will you take for it?'

'Not a penny. It's a gift.'

'Oh, I couldn't. Really.' But she could.

'Sure, take it. I was going to give Shirley a gown costing a thousand pounds. And the blue one costs only two hundred. So, you might as well get the benefit of the saving.'

Kate tried on the gold dress and flounced around in it for over an hour until the talk dried up completely, and Marion had to chase the two of them out of the door, so she could get home to safety and Eddy and the children. The thought of Shirley looking shy in a *blue* dress, with her new baby on the way, and thirty-year-old Kate simpering like a spoilt child in her outrageous *gold* creation, was just too much for Marion to cope with by herself.

25. A Ghost at the Feast

'So, you haven't told him? I know I said not to but I thought perhaps you might have changed your mind? I had my hopes up, waiting for you to get in touch.'

Silence.

Johnny and Marion sat in the shade of a rose-covered trellis, in the Botanic Gardens. It was mid-April. Declan's wedding was just days away.

'I haven't told him, Johnny, and I don't think I can.'

'I know it's very hard for you, Marion. But why not?'

'Well, we were talking about the wedding, recently, just Declan and me. I wanted to be sure that he's happy to be getting married so young. And he said that myself and Eddy were an inspiration to him. How happy we are, and how much we still love each other. It's one of the reasons he's getting married to Shirley.'

'So?'

'He really believes in marriage, Johnny, which is a very unusual quality in a young man, these days. They normally say they don't want to be tied down. Not at twenty, anyway. They seem to have some misguided notion that they are going to play the field for a decade before settling down with a world-famous glamour model.'

'Are you trying to say that I would be a bad example to him?'

'I just don't want him to become disillusioned with marriage.'

'Oh, Marion, he won't.'

'How do you know? You don't know anything about him. When he finds out I got married because I was desperate, there's no telling what he'll do. Children are very emotional at that age. Every feeling they have is exaggerated by their hormones.'

'You weren't exactly desperate, Marion. Come on! Eddy was an old flame. He wasn't a stranger.'

'I *was* desperate, Johnny. You have no idea. I was worried sick. And Eddy saved me from God knows what. Adoption? Poverty?'

'But you love Eddy now?'

'Yes, of course I do. I loved him all along and just didn't know it. But I wasn't *in love* with him, the day I accepted his proposal.'

'You don't have to tell Declan that. Tell him you loved Eddy very much.'

'If that *was* true, why would I be carrying another man's child? What would that say about me and you? What we had together? That it was just based on physical attraction? I betrayed Eddy completely. You must see that.'

Silence.

'You're wearing my bracelet.'

'I don't know why. I'm too sentimental, I suppose.'

'You still care for me a little bit? Don't you?'

'As a friend, I do. We went out together for five years.'

'Then, do this one thing for me.'

'Please, Johnny, I can't do it. I just can't. Please, can we put our son first? Surely you don't want to upset him on the eve of the service?'

'So that's it? He'll never know?'

'It would ruin everything. He could have a breakdown.'

Silence again.

They listened to some birds singing in the empty band-stand, and the breeze stirring in the sycamore trees. Johnny took a deep breath.

'Can I come to the wedding?' he asked, suddenly. 'Just as an ordinary guest? You could ask Eileen and James, too? It wouldn't seem strange to Eddy, seeing what you and Eileen went through together.'

'Oh, Johnny! Eddy would never allow it. It's close family members only. We've already had to make space for Kevin McGovern's family, for heaven's sake. There isn't going to be room for another table.'

'I'm his *father*, Marion! Look, could I provide the music, or something?'

'We're not playing records. I've booked a classical quartet.'

'Well, there must be some way I can help?'

'Johnny, there isn't.'

'I want to give him a present, you see.'

'Oh, God! Why, Johnny? Why play the big family man, now? This is ancient history. You can't be involved in his life, at all. Can't you see how profound all this is? We don't know what might happen. You can't go around dropping bombshells like this on people. We need advice from the experts, at the very least.'

'Look, I've been doing a lot of thinking recently. I want to retire, as you know. And Eileen doesn't want to see the ballroom flattened by developers. It means a lot to her. So! I want to give the ballroom to Declan. I'm leaving for America soon, you see. And I could show him how to run it before I go.'

'You what? Give him the *ballroom*? I'm speechless. God, but you were always impossible!' And why have you taken so long to go to America, anyway, she thought. I'm beginning to think Eddy is right; he's invented the whole damn thing just to get some attention.

'I *want* him to have the ballroom.'

'I want him to be a *doctor*. And that's what he wants, too, despite his doubts. Otherwise, I wouldn't push him.'

'Sure, why go through with all that study, when there's a good business, ready and waiting, for him? Years, at Queen's, he'd have to endure. He needs money now, with a child of his own on the way. The kid will be in school by the time Declan gets his degree.'

'That doesn't matter. We have the money to help him support Shirley and the baby. We're going to pay their mortage until he's working. It's all in hand. They're flat-hunting at the moment but they'll soon get fed up with that idea. Anyway, you said the ballroom was becoming a headache. You're going to retire early, for heaven's sake.'

'It's too much for *me*, yes. But a young fella like Declan would have no trouble. He'd know the scene. What the young people want.'

'This is your big plan? Declan takes on the gangsters and the council bores and the staff problems, while you sun yourself in Florida? This is just *madness*. Have you forgotten that Eileen and I were kidnapped recently?'

'You said he liked music.'

'Listen, Johnny. He *does* like music. He loves it. The

house is full of records. But that won't last for ever. He's grown up, now, getting married. *With a child on the way.* He should have a proper career.'

'Something respectable, you mean?' he said, bitterly. 'A doctor is better than a glorified DJ.'

'Frankly, yes. Yes, it is. He'll be important in the community. He'll have a sense of belonging, people around him all the time.' Not like you, she thought suddenly. No wonder Johnny had lost touch with the real world, spending his life in the shadows of the ballroom; having short and superficial conversations with total strangers. It was a sad kind of life to have lived. She pitied him, in a way.

'You've changed, Marion. You've become middle class.'

'I want the best for my son. I want him to mix with nice people.'

'*Nice* people? What about his own people? James and Eileen? He'll never know I'm his father. I can't go to the wedding. I can't even give him a present. That's what you're trying to tell me?'

'That's right. That's the way it has to be. Now, are you going to accept that? I need to know, because I haven't told Eddy about all this. I need to know if you're going to cause any trouble on the day.' She didn't want to have to go through a second wedding ceremony waiting for Johnny to turn up in the church porch, and shout out, 'Wait!' And this time, he seemed lonely enough and desperate enough to actually do it. The shock could make Shirley faint. Marion began to panic.

'Trouble?' said Johnny. 'Am I going to rock the boat? No, I won't do that, Marion. You can have your big, fancy wedding. With all your posh friends, and the violins playing in the background. I won't turn up like a ghost at the feast and tell my son he was conceived on the back seat of a Lincoln Continental, on Portstewart Strand!'

'Oh, yes! I wondered how long it would take you to bring that up! Slander the woman's reputation when all else fails. You . . . you . . . I wouldn't have had to sleep with you in the back of your car if you had married me and given me a proper home. This is so typical of you, Johnny, to string me along for years, and then make out it was my fault for being an easy kind of girl!'

'Yes, a Lincoln Continental for a bed, and a picnic rug for a blanket. I'll tell him that. And that his parents ate a fish supper before the deed, from Mickey Mac's chip van. And two 99s with raspberry topping, afterwards. We took off our shoes and walked along the water's edge and you said you would always love me and no one else.'

'You're being ridiculous. You shouldn't talk about personal things like that to your children. What have chips and ice cream got to do with *anything*?' She was furious with him now.

'You weren't so la-di-da in the good old days, Marion Evans. I was good enough for you, then.'

'My name is Marion Greenwood,' she said. 'I should never have told you about Declan. You're crazy, Johnny. You haven't changed at all. Always, you put yourself first. You just want to show off. You were never any different.'

'It's not for me. I want to help him to make something of himself.'

'You want to muscle in on *my* son's wedding. Because you were too selfish to get married yourself, and now you're lonely. That's the truth, isn't it?

'Look! Eddy is the one who collected Declan from school, and taught him how to ride a bike, and all the rest of it. And it's just too late for you to be involved in his life! Why can't you just go to Florida and leave all this in the past? I don't believe you ever intended to go away!'

'Look, I'm going home. I can't talk to you when you're like this.'

'You can't talk to me, ever again, Johnny Hogan. This is the end of it. Eddy was right about you. You're flashy and selfish and you've never loved anyone in your life. Except yourself. I *hate* you.'

'I *love* you, Marion. More than you'll ever know.'

'I don't care! Don't you get it? You're living in a fantasy world. I loved you when I had no sense, Johnny. I was stupid and immature and naive. I loved you because you were a great dancer and because you had a cool car and because you were well known about the city. They were stupid reasons to love somebody. I'll *never* get over how much I hurt Eddy when I left him for you. And then he gave me a second chance, and married me in very difficult circumstances; and raised Declan like he was his own son. And then I let poor Eddy down again by even talking to you about all this. Are you trying to split us up for good? Is that it?'

'You know how I feel about you, Marion. When I kissed you outside the hotel, I know you felt something. The way you looked at me. I know that look. You wanted me back, didn't you?'

'Look, get this straight. Even if Eddy left me today, I wouldn't take you back. Not if you got down on your knees and begged me to marry you. Not if you were the last man on earth,' she said, almost in tears. This conversation was going round in circles and getting nowhere. She could feel a huge headache beginning behind her left eye.

'I don't believe you, Marion. Come to the ballroom with me, now, and dance with me again. Just the two of us? Let's feel that old razzle-dazzle!'

'Right, that's it! Will you just go to America, and give us all some peace? If you come anywhere near my family, you'll be sorry. I'll make Declan choose between us, and we both know who'll be left out in the cold. And you might think Eddy was a pushover last time, but if I told him what you just said to me, he would kill you with his bare hands.'

And she pulled off the silver bracelet, and threw it at him. Then she grabbed her jacket and went running through the park, her chest heaving with rage. Johnny picked the delicate bracelet up off the grass, and held it in his hand. He sat on the bench for a long time, just thinking. Maybe he had lost Marion for ever, to that boring baker, Greenwood, and his silly little cake shop. But that wasn't going to be the end of the story. Oh, no. He wasn't giving up on Declan.

26. Hogan's Goodbye Disco

It was the day of Hogan's Goodbye Disco in the ball-room on Magnolia Street, and Johnny Hogan put on his legendary white jacket for the last time. Within twenty-four hours, the shutters would go up and the music and the magic would fade away, possibly for ever. Johnny felt a heavy weight in his heart, but he knew that he was just too old for the responsibilities that came with running such a big enterprise. Maybe the ballroom would continue under someone else's management, and maybe it would be sold and demolished. Either way, it would be out of his hands. He opened the curtains and the morning sun came bursting through the tall windows of the house on Eglantine Avenue. The sun shone on the new leather suit-cases that Johnny had bought for his journey to Florida.

In a few days he would be thousands of miles away, and Declan would be married, and in a few months Johnny's grandchild would be born and given the Greenwood surname. And eventually Declan would work at one of the city's five hospitals, saving lives instead of spinning records. Being the pillar of respectability that his mother wanted him to be. Unless Johnny's latest big idea could do something to change all that. Because Johnny was an ideas man, he had a great imagination. That was why he had survived for twenty years in the entertainment scene. He was always good at getting out of one trend, when it was coming to an end, and jumping on the next bandwagon before anybody else in the city.

Johnny was pleased with his reflection in the hall mirror. His hairdresser had put a little sachet of dark rinse in his hair, specially for tonight; and Johnny thought it looked almost natural. He could easily pass for forty, when the lights in the ballroom were dimmed. He wanted to look his best for his last night there. He had ordered two thousand golden-coloured tickets from the printers and they were all sold. The last night of entertainment, under Johnny's stewardship, in the ballroom, would kick off at five o'clock that evening, with a fifties-style tea dance. For the old-timers. Crooners, like Bing Crosby and Frank Sinatra, tinkling out of the speakers. A hot supper at nine, and then a quick tidy-up before the main event, a disco extravaganza beginning at ten and carrying on until three o'clock in the morning. Hits from four decades would be played: Elvis, the Beatles, the Bay City Rollers, and Spandau Ballet, to name but a few. DJ Toni had been selecting records for this night for months. Johnny would make a speech at some stage during the last hour.

The punters could dress up in period outfits if they wanted to; there would be prizes for the best costumes. Hot food and exotic cocktails would be served all night, right the way through until 3 a.m., a late licence having been reluctantly granted by the council. All the staff were coming in to work, and some extra people had been taken on as well. A professional photographer had been hired to take action shots of the big night. If Johnny had worked out his figures correctly, he should make about twenty thousand pounds tonight, on the bar alone. Half of that amount again, in the food bar. The tickets had raised a fortune. It would be enough to set him up in his new life; and, of course, when the house was sold, he would be rolling in cash.

Alex Stone would be back on door duty, and determined not to admit any troublemakers to the ballroom. Johnny had been very good to take him on again, after that little run-in with the law. And now that he was working legally and above board for the first time in his life, he vowed never to allow law-breakers over the threshold again. All the bouncers would be here tonight, in their best suits and bow ties. They had been ordered to check all the tickets carefully, and let no gatecrashers in whatsoever. The police were going to keep an eye on the street, just in case Eugene Lolly turned up, but they weren't expecting him to put in an appearance. Still, the bouncers remained on a state of high alert. A trouble-free night would result in a big bonus for them all.

James had telephoned from the bungalow in Portstewart to wish Johnny well. He would not be attending, and Eileen wasn't feeling up to it either. She would cry her eyes out, the whole night long, James whispered into the receiver. Johnny understood.

Marion and Eddy were not attending, either. That was to be expected. But Declan was coming. The lad knew most of the bar staff well, and Johnny made sure that Declan was able to get a couple of tickets. He wrote their names on the tickets himself. Declan's ticket was number 742. Marion had telephoned Johnny the day before, and begged him to leave things the way they were. Johnny could talk to Declan for a little while, when he was meeting and greeting the crowd. Would that be enough for him? Maybe have a photo taken with his arm round the boy? If Johnny was really going away, did getting to know Declan matter now? Johnny had promised that he would take his secret with him when he boarded the flight to America. He intended to keep his promise.

It was only ten o'clock in the morning. Johnny would go to the ballroom at two in the afternoon, to open up, and check on the arrangements. Until then, he hadn't much to do. The house was tidy, the little bit of grocery shopping was done. Marion was right about one thing: being a footloose bachelor was great fun when you were young, but it wasn't so exciting when you were middle-aged. Now, if he *had* married the silly woman, in 1967, he'd be looking forward to the birth of his first grand-child. And showing his fine son, Declan, how to run the family business. For the poor boy wouldn't be strolling around the neat lawns of Queen's University, with a pack of snobs, if he'd been properly raised as Johnny's son. That was for sure.

Johnny decided to go for a long drive, to steady his nerves. He was going to shake his son's hand that night and look him in the eye and talk to him for a few minutes. He hoped he could steel himself to remain calm when the overhead lights came on at the end of the night, and the crowds were filing out of the main doors for the last time. He couldn't think of one occasion in his entire life when he had actually cried in front of a crowd, and he didn't want to start today.

He would drive to Newcastle, and walk along the beach for a while and think of the many wind-blown picnics he had shared there with his grandparents. (Sand in the sandwiches, and lukewarm tea in plastic cups.) He would skim stones across the bay, and hop across the rock pools. He would call into a hotel for lunch and one small whiskey, and maybe even put some loose change into the slot machines in the amusement arcades.

Johnny wasn't a gambling man, but tonight, he would take the biggest gamble of his life. It was a plan he had entertained and dismissed dozens of times during the last few days. And he knew that Marion and Eddy would be furious with him. But he was going to keep his promise. He wouldn't tell Declan who he was. But that didn't mean he couldn't give the lad a legacy of some kind. So, he had adapted his plan slightly. He *was* going to give Declan the family business: the ballroom and all the goodwill he had built up through the years. In a raffle. *A fixed raffle.* Declan could sell the site to fund his medical studies or pay for his first home; or he could run the business himself if he wanted to. He was a grown man of twenty. He could make up his own mind. And Johnny would see if he liked America enough to retire there. And if not, he would come home and live in Portstewart with his grandparents, and maybe run a little ice-cream parlour, or a chip shop. Something like that, where he could still meet people every day. It was a good plan.

Only weeks before, Eileen had made him promise that he would never sell the ballroom. Not ever, for any reason. But she had not said he could not *give it away*. So, it would not be a betrayal of Eileen Hogan's trust. Or his late parents' memory. And Eddy Greenwood couldn't accuse him of trying to buy Declan's love. He would not tell

Declan who he really was. No one in the city knew that Johnny and Declan were connected in any way. His romance with Marion was long forgotten. It would seem, to everyone, like a genuine prize draw. Declan's ticket to the Goodbye Disco was also going to be the winning ticket in the draw. Number 742.

And Marion could do nothing about it, either. No lawyer could find fault with the draw or prove it had been fixed. Johnny was going to put his hand in the ticket drum, and pull out the winning ticket from his shirt cuff. Marion and Eddy couldn't publicly accuse him of fixing the raffle without revealing their precious secret. Declan would be the new and rightful owner of the business. He was twenty years of age. A legal adult. His overprotective mother could not intervene. She had cheated Johnny out of his son; and twenty years' worth of love and good times. Because of her obsession with respectability, and all that middle-class nonsense. But she could not cheat Declan out of his rightful inheritance.

There would be a few other prizes, smaller ones, to make it look good and sustain the party atmosphere. A few bottles of wine and whiskey, some money prizes, a huge and showy trophy for the best costume. But the highlight of the night would be the surprise announcement of a Grand Draw. For the ballroom, itself. And no one knew a thing about it. It was going to be a fantastic note on which to end Johnny's career in the entertainment industry.

'I hope you've all held on to your tickets, tonight, as advised,' said Johnny, to the hall mirror. 'Hold on to your hats, ladies and gentlemen, because you won't believe what the main prize is!' Johnny filled up his cheeks with air and held his breath for a few seconds before letting it out. Wow! Talk about going out on a high!

Then, he buffed up his blue suede shoes, ran a comb through his hair, and danced down the steps towards his beloved Lincoln Continental, which was waiting for him in the garage behind the house.

27. Accusations, Palpitations

Kate sat down gently on her handbag-festooned bed, and sighed a sigh that came all the way up from her white leather shoes. This little bedroom had been her refuge and her sanctuary for thirty years. Surrounded by her lovely things, and with the homely sounds of her mother rattling pans in the kitchen downstairs, it was the one place where she had always felt safe. When the local news was full of sickening murders and rising unemployment statistics, it was the one thing that did not disappoint. Kate had closed her mind to the Troubles, and to other sad things, all her life. Like so many other people who were bewildered by the violence that raged all around them, she had emotionally left Belfast years ago; and lived her life in a bubble of new handbags and temporary love affairs and glamorous television programmes.

She now realized her mother and father had done the same; her father retreated to his garden when he was frightened by the sectarian killings, and her house-proud mother busied herself with her many china ornaments and tasselled cushions. They went to their work in the hospital each day, and patiently cleaned up after the doctors and nurses. Even when they saw the tattered remains of people who were once young and strong being carried into hospital, they said nothing. They felt nothing.

They just got out their mops and cloths and cleaned away the blood. Shirley had often asked them why they didn't move away to England or the Irish Republic, and start a new life in a peaceful place. But they'd just shrugged their shoulders and said, 'Sure, why would we do that? We don't belong there. We'd be nothing but immigrants, to the end of our days.' Kate thought being an immigrant was not nearly as bad as having to walk to school over broken glass and burnt pavements, but as a child she was powerless to leave the city on her own.

An enormous bunch of white roses stood on Kate's dressing table in a tall, glass vase. Yet another gift from Kevin. Roses were the most beautiful flowers in the world. Kate loved them with a passion. How like Kevin to be so considerate, when he had already spent a king's ransom on the home improvements! The day he gave her the roses, they'd made love properly for the first time, in Kevin's double bed. It wasn't too bad. He did his best to satisfy her. But as she lay smiling in his arms, it was the gorgeous new headboard in their bedroom she was thinking of; not him. Kate wished she fancied him a little bit more. He did have superb legs: fully rounded muscular thighs, neat, hairless kneecaps and slender, shapely ankles. Even his feet were very acceptable; small white toenails and no bulging blue veins visible anywhere, like some men had. Normally, she'd have found a lover like Kevin a real bonus, but there was something missing. Excitement! She wanted to feel a leap in her heart when he began to unbutton his shirt! She wanted to tremble with anticipation, instead of dread.

But she had more or less resigned herself to the

marriage. She liked Kevin as a friend; and loved him enough to marry him. They got on well together. But the doubts were still there. She knew they should talk about it and maybe see a counsellor. But it seemed easier to go through with the wedding now, than to start backing out at this late stage. The half of Belfast knew the tale of how Kate Winters and Kevin McGovern had suddenly fallen so completely in love, that after only *days* into their relationship, they'd decided to get married. One of the neighbours knew a woman who cleaned the floors at the TV station, and she got her to put the word around the canteen about the lovebirds from the Lisburn Road. There was talk of star reporter Pamela Ballantine turning up on the doorstep with a camera crew, but so far, there was no sign of Pamela's elegant silver shell suit. Mrs Winters was forever polishing her many ornaments in the front room, just in case. And she never let her domestic stockpile of Mr Kipling cakes fall below twenty boxes. It was hungry work making documentaries, she said.

Kevin was going to make a good husband. Kate told herself that constantly. She would be mad to call off the wedding, just because she wasn't all moon-faced and soppy about him, like Shirley was about Declan. She was going to marry him on 21 April, and worry about the lovemaking and the babies later on. Some people said that most men only found their wives attractive for the first couple of years anyway, and that after the 'honeymoon period' was over, they'd rather lie in front of the television watching sport for sixteen hours a day and drinking beer and getting fat. It seemed to be a universal fact that once a few babies had been born, the chemistry that had attracted couples to each other in the first place had to be passed on to some other newly-weds.

Kate asked Shirley if she believed in the theory of short-lived attraction. Under a deluge of tough questioning, Shirley finally admitted that she would definitely fancy Declan until the day she died. Yes, even if he put on a bit of weight or if his hairline began to recede. Yes! Even when they were both old, she'd love him just as much. Good grief. Kate still had to come to terms with being old, in general. Never mind old, and in love! Would Shirley still fancy Declan in heaven? Yes. If there *was* a heaven, or an afterlife of any kind, she'd still fancy him. Then Shirley went all starry-eyed and declared that even if they were only wisps of smoke in a faraway universe, she'd find him and they'd drift on, together. (What utter nonsense. Kate wasn't thinking that far ahead.)

The wedding was only days away. Kate's dress, that gold-coloured and heavily beaded explosion of a thing, was hanging on the wardrobe door. The neckline was so low it would give the priest a heart attack. Well, tough Cheddar to him! Women had been pushed around for centuries: ravished in private, covered up in public. Made to feel ashamed of their bodies and their sexual needs. Why the big fuss about pure white dresses, anyway, when the whole congregation knew the happy couple were going straight upstairs to the honeymoon suite of the hotel, to throw their finery on the carpet and make love all night? Wasn't that the sole point of the entire operation? The human race couldn't continue without lovemaking; and it was time for polite society to admit it. Wedding rings or no wedding rings. Shirley was correct about that, as she had been right about a lot of things, recently. (Which was a little bit sickening.) Well, Kate might have her doubts about her future husband, but she was dead set on the dress. She was very proud of her figure, especially her chest, and she was determined to show it off.

The only problem was, the dress was so lavish it would make poor Shirley look like Kate's bridesmaid, a fact that Mrs Winters had lost no time in pointing out. Well, Shirley said that was pure rubbish. Both dresses were absolutely gorgeous. And it was good to have different dresses. They weren't identical twins, after all. So the gold dress was given Martha's blessing. And Kate had agreed to carry a posy of yellow roses, to match Shirley's sunflowers. And their two friends from the dole office had been rigged out with yellow dresses as well. They'd bought them from another bridal shop, worried that Marion would get fed up with giving out gowns for free. So, all in all, the wedding group looked very artistic and upmarket. And even Mrs Winters had to agree that pink satin had been done to death. Mr Winters said nothing at all about the style choices of his daughters. He said a dress was a dress at the end of the day; and he was only worried that the two grooms would do a runner and make bloody fools of them all. Kate told him to cheer up and pay up. So he produced his chequebook, blew the dust off it and paid for the flowers, like the dutiful father he truly was.

Next to the wardrobe, on Kate's cosy bedroom armchair,

lay a tall tiara with crystal droplets, a pair of gold satin shoes, a matching draw-string dolly bag, a pearly choker with seven rows of pearls on it, a frilly garter, a set of designer lingerie, and a new bottle of Chanel perfume, *and* the keys to Kevin's (thoroughly renovated) house. Beside the roses on the dressing table were two large tickets to the last disco in Hogan's. A very fancy design from the printers, too, with scalloped edges. Kate's name and Kevin's name were clearly handwritten on numbers 334 and 335, respectively. A note on the bottom of the tickets read: *Admittance will be refused unless ticket is presented.*

Kevin was coming round an hour early, to take her out for a quiet drink before the disco began. He had thrown himself into the role of fiancé, recently. So much so, that Kate was beginning to feel suffocated. She saw him at work, of course. And he was phoning and calling round every single evening, sometimes *twice* an evening. He had agreed to all of Kate's plans for the wedding. He had booked a luxury honeymoon, and he had agreed to wear a gold-coloured suit, with a diamanté brooch at his neck, instead of a tie. The brooch was the size of a saucer, with dangly bits swinging from it. Yellow and pink stones. It would put Liberace to shame, but no matter. It was Kate's special day, and Kevin was willing to do whatever he had to do, to make her happy.

(Kevin didn't like his outfit. It was way over the top, even by his standards. Lucky old Declan was getting away with a black suit, a white shirt and a blue tie. Anyway, never mind! Kevin was just looking forward to two weeks with Kate, in a private chalet in Barbados. Never mind the glass floor where you could watch the fish swimming under the chalet – he wouldn't be taking his eyes off Kate's tiny waist or her raspberry-pink nipples for any length of time.)

Kate was thinking about the honeymoon, too. She was worried sick about it, and she didn't know why. If only she could feel the thrill that she used to feel.

For heaven's sake, she thought, Shirley was slaving away at work, through the tiredness and the strawberry cravings, through the evil looks from Miss Bingham, through the fussing and fretting of her future mother-in-law who thought she should resign and let them buy her a house. And not one word of complaint out of her; she was as cool as a freezer full of polar bears.

Yet here was Kate Winters, spoilt madam and complete flake – having doubts about her wedding to a lovely, reasonable, caring man. There must be something seriously wrong with her, Kate decided. A brain tumour, or brain cancer, or a leaking artery that was making it so hard for her to think clearly. Shirley said she should go to the doctor again and ask for some more tests. It was probably a blood-sugar thing. Diabetes, maybe? Kate might ask for a leaflet about women and alcohol, as well, just in case her symptoms were alcohol-related.

Louise Lowry was acting strangely, too. She had actually come up to Kate in the street a few days earlier, and told her they could be friends. No mention of all that business about the glass eye and the mint imperials. Bygones will be bygones, she'd said. Alex and herself were getting on like a house on fire, she'd said. Alex was a hot lover. Red hot. With the stamina and the physique of a young bull. So, no harm done on that score. Congratulations on the wedding, too. Kevin McGovern was a great fella, even if he did make his money selling drugs in Carryduff. Drugs? Drugs! What was she talking about? Kevin hadn't said anything about drugs. He didn't even smoke cigarettes. (Kate had a thing for bad boys, but not this bad. This was really bad.)

'You've got it all wrong, Louise,' Kate had cried. 'You must be thinking of someone else with a similar name. Gosh, haven't you got big hands, by the way!'

'Well, why would he mention it to you?' Louise had fired right back at her, shoving her hands into her pockets. 'It's not the kind of thing he'd want to brag about. Sure, you've only been going out with him two minutes. How does he know he can trust you? Oh, he's known as the *Bungalow Baron* out that direction, don't you know? All his clients are homeowners, you see. Very discreet operation, he runs.'

'You're a liar, Louise Lowry. Why wasn't he ever arrested, then? Answer me that! If this is common knowledge, why wasn't he lifted?'

'Sure, the half of the cops over there are smoking joints for breakfast. They've nothing else to do. It's all owner-occupied in Carryduff. No housing estates full of thieving little beggars on the *Saintfield* Road!'

Kate didn't believe her, of course. Stupid big bitch was just trying to upset her. But the doubts were still there. How had Kevin made so much money from the garage anyway? And it *was* a little annoying that Alex was very passionate in bed with Louise Lowry, when he had proved such a terrible disappointment to Kate herself. It was quite damaging to the ego. Maybe Alex only got turned on by a common sort of girl? Some men were like that. Nice girls made them feel inadequate. Maybe Louise knew some bedroom tricks that Kate didn't know? Maybe Kate was just tired out from three months of intensive shopping. She lay down on her white lace quilt and fell into a deep sleep.

All sorts of things were rampaging through Kate's tortured mind as the hands of the clock crawled round to nine o'clock. Standing Stone and Louise Lowry, making love frantically on a broken bed full of Jelly Wellies and Fizzy Lizzies; a young red-faced priest staring down Kate's thrusting cleavage and completely forgetting the words to the ceremony; the Bungalow Baron of Carryduff in his gold jacket, slipping joints and pills to the locals at the golf club; Shirley's unborn baby who was the one person responsible for this whole ridiculous circus; and worst of all, the future children that Kevin wanted so much. Kate could picture them quite vividly. Screaming and fighting, and destroying the pristine white furniture with their sticky little hands. Would Kate get a nanny, so she could still run the garage? Or would that be even worse than minding the children herself? Would the nanny be rough with the children behind Kate's back? Would Kevin fancy the nanny, when Kate's lovely body was ruined with red and purple stretch marks? Would Kate even care if he did? If Kevin started an affair with the nanny, it would give Kate a bit of time to herself. Some blessed time away from poor old Kevin who was absolutely sex mad. Kate's breathing began to speed up. She woke up and opened her eyes wide. Her lovely chandelier was hanging just five feet above her face. She'd miss seeing it every morning. She was clutching her pillow and her back was soaked with sweat.

She had turned into Shirley, for pity's sake, wondering and questioning and philosophizing about everything. Bloody hell! In a rare moment of clarity, Kate realized that she had not taken after her pushy mother, as she'd always thought. She was exactly the same as her cowardly father! Hiding away in her bedroom, instead of the garden shed. She *liked* to hide behind Martha's apron strings. She didn't want to be all grown-up and adult, and make adult decisions. She wanted to keep going on holiday with the girls every summer. She didn't want to learn how to cook Irish stew, or have to pay boring utility bills, or breast-feed hungry children. Breasts were for showing off in tight tops, and nothing else, in Kate's book. And house-work? Kate couldn't imagine herself wielding a vacuum cleaner and a feather duster. Alone all day in Kevin's house? The very idea of it made her feel ill.

'I wish I was back in the dole office,' she said, out loud. 'Even with that she-devil, Bingham, crawling around. Life was so much simpler, then. And Shirley was with me and I wasn't ever alone.'

And that was the trigger.

She leapt up off the bed, pulling on as many handbags as she could. Some on her shoulders, some on her elbows, and even one or two round her neck. She managed to get twenty-five handbags safely attached to her person before the panic overwhelmed her. She half fell down the stairs in a pair of very high heels, shouting, '*Tell Kevin we're finished, I'm leaving the country!*' to her bewildered parents. She knocked over the hall stand and two potted plants in her panic; and even the little holy-water font ended up crashing onto the tiled doorstep, and the ceramic praying hands fell off it. Then she pelted out into the street, and ran down the road, waving for a taxi.

She, Kate Winters, was going to run away to Paris, and set up her own exclusive salon, selling designer handbags. She would design them herself. How hard could it be? Art college, and a degree in design? Who needed those silly things? Her passion for bags would see her through. It was so obvious, that this was what she had been born to do. Why had it never occurred to her before? She dropped a couple of bags on the Lisburn Road when she was leaping into a black cab. (One red bag with a picture of tulips on it, and one black velvet opera bag covered with plastic emeralds.) She banged the door of the cab shut behind her.

'For God's sake, get me to the airport,' she gasped. 'I've got a flight to Paris to catch!'

'Which airport, love?'

'It doesn't matter,' cried Kate, and she bit down on her credit card, leaving faint teeth-marks on it. 'Whichever one has the most flights. And hurry!' She sat hunched forward on the seat and her face went numb, and she was only barely aware of the houses and shops and the people walking along the street. She was trembling all over; she felt sick and dizzy. She tried to control her breathing, but she lost track of the seconds, and concentrated instead on her Parisian boutique. She would have a counter covered with silver mosaic tiles, and a big mirror like the ones in royal palaces, and she would learn French and eat baguettes and posh cheese, and maybe have a little lapdog to keep her company while she became a millionaire. She would tie a bow in the dog's hair.

'Hurry up,' she gasped. 'I'm going to miss the plane.'

'You're the boss,' muttered the taxi-driver, as he pressed the accelerator.

28. High Drama at Aldergrove

When Kate arrived at the airport in tears, the panic attack had subsided and she was left feeling worn out and very sleepy. The driver pulled up at the terminal, opened the cab door for her, and waited patiently while she rummaged for payment in several handbags. She had barely enough cash with her to pay him. And then she remembered she had no passport. She couldn't get to Paris tonight. Maybe she could fly to London and stay in a hotel and have Shirley post it over? When she went into the cafe for a cup of tea to think things over, everybody stared at her and some people thought she was a pedlar selling handbags and reported her to Security. Two grim-faced young men promptly turned up and asked her to come with them. They took Kate to a private room and she had to explain that she was getting married soon, and that she was just a bit nervous about it, and that it was all a simple misunderstanding. The young men were very sympathetic. They knew that all women could be very emotional at times. They gave her a few shopping bags to keep her handbags in, a cup of tea, and said she could make one phone call from the office.

Kate reluctantly rang her mother at home to tell her she had changed her mind about leaving the country. She didn't have the energy to open up her own salon in Paris, after all. She wanted to go home and sleep for a hundred years instead. She knew her mother would be in fine rant-mode, and she was right. Mrs Winters would have crawled down the wire and bitten Kate's head off, if she could. She had an amazing ability to talk and breathe at the same time so that there were no gaps whatsoever in her tirade. Kate held the receiver at arm's length and held her breath for the onslaught.

'Kate? Is that you? Where are you? We're all worried sick, here.'

'I'm at Aldergrove.'

'She's at the airport! Everybody! She's all right. She's at the airport. What the *hell* are you trying to do to me, you big stupid article? I thought you'd done your friggin' *nut*! Your da's in the shed and he won't come out. He says he can't take any more stress and this weddin's gonna finish him off, for sure. Kate Winters, I want you to come straight home and stop this nonsense. Declan is here and he thinks you've had an *anxiety attack* and that the cure is to have counselling and relaxation classes. *Relaxation* classes, if you don't mind. You that wrote the book on how to be a lazy lump! And Shirley says she has been *trying* to tell you to calm down for years but you wouldn't listen. You go to the doctor, if you think it will help. In my opinion, you'd be better off saying some prayers to Our Lady. And by the way, you broke the font. But off with you, to the doctor! He might put you on tablets. Although I think you may do without the tablets, my girl. Your great-aunt Betty went on the tablets when her husband, George, died in a head-on crash with a lorry full of lemonade in 1952, and she never got off them till the day she died in 1979. And if an advert came on the telly for lemonade of any kind, she had to be sedated. So I don't want you going down that road. Do you hear me? You'll have me in the grave with all this carry-on. I'm sixty-one, you know. You may go to the *relaxation* classes, and buck up your ideas while you're at it. I can-not *believe* you bolted off out of this house, without so much as a by-your-leave, and telling me you're leaving the country. When you know for a *fact* that your passport is in a biscuit tin in the hall cabinet. What's Kevin McGovern going to say about this? Will he still take you on, with a slate off your roof? That's what *I* want to know! And the dress that cost a fortune. It's a sin, what that dress cost −'

'Where is Kevin?' Kate sighed. There was no point in looking for any sympathy from her mother. If Kate were hanging off a cliff by one fingernail, being bitten on the nose by a deadly scorpion, and suffering from a brain-melting fever all at the same time, Mrs Winters would have told her to stop complaining. No, the sympathy would be in short supply tonight. Better to get the prac-ticalities over with.

'He was in his garage all day, the poor sucker. Putting in some overtime so he can support you in the manner to which you have become accustomed. A fancy house with all the latest mod cons! Gold taps, if you don't mind! And a pull-down ironing board in the kitchen. Oh, things have changed since my day. Forty-eight hours after I got married, I was back in my apron, scrubbing floors in the Royal. You've been spoilt rotten from the word go. I blame myself for this. You've always got away with *murder*. Stealing money from the church envelopes! Well, we should have seen the writing on the wall, that day. Your father wouldn't spank you, and he wouldn't let me do it either. You need help, so you do. There's poor Shirley, letting you swan about like Lady Muck, taking over her lovely wedding, and you're not even grateful. She didn't have to, you know. Mrs Greenwood didn't have to, either. And the money they've spent on the grub and the fiddle-players would turn your hair snow-white.' She paused to blow her nose, and Kate saw her chance.

'Mum, can you send someone to collect me at the airport? I've no money left.'

'That doesn't surprise me. We've been going through your room, looking for some clues, and I had no idea you had so much stuff. Knee-deep, that room is, with stuff. Honestly, I don't know what I've done to deserve this.' She turned to Shirley and Declan and said, 'She wants a lift home from the airport, Shirley. No, Declan will not go. Declan, sit down! *Sit down!*' A sigh. 'Kate Winters, do you see the trouble you're causing? Declan and Shirley are going to Hogan's for an hour or so. And they are not going to the airport at this time of the night. I'll ring Kevin and ask him to go. Although I should make you walk home, you eejit!'

'*No!* Don't tell Kevin what I did. Don't tell him where I am. It was just cold feet. I'm okay now. Honestly.' No point in telling her mother that she was having a break-down. In her mother's book, only spoilt celebrities had breakdowns and that was because they were full of drugs and champagne and had no responsibilities.

'There's no one else available, Kate. You know we haven't a car. You should have thought of this before you scared us all half to death. I'm going to the chapel to say

299

a prayer for you, right this minute, and you can think about what you're going to say to that poor creature of a man of yours, when you see him in person. Goodbye.' And she slammed down the phone.

Kate gently replaced the receiver in its cradle. Actually, that hadn't gone too badly, she thought. Her mother seemed to have got a grip on the situation. Normally she needed things to be explained to her several times before she realized what was going on. Kate sat down on a chair and rubbed her arms. She felt very cold.

'Have you someone to come and collect you, dear?' asked the kindly lady in the office. 'No need to be embarrassed. A flying phobia, is it?'

'Yes,' said Kate. 'That's all it was. I'm going home now. My boyfriend is coming to take me home.'

'Right you be,' said the lady. 'I'll leave you to your thoughts. If you'd like to take a seat over there? It's more comfortable.' She directed Kate to a small sofa behind a blue felt partition, and gave her a blanket to put round her shoulders. Kate was so grateful she hugged the smiling woman, and soon fell asleep. Forty-five minutes later, Kevin came running into the airport. Kate burst into tears when she woke up and saw him kneeling on the carpet in front of her. He looked so worried.

'Kate, are you all right?'

'Yes. I'm fine. I'm sorry about all this.'

'What happened, pet?'

'Just a funny turn I took.'

'Cold feet?'

'Not at all. Not in the sense you mean.' Her feet were like blocks of ice.

'But you were going somewhere?'

'I was toying with the idea.'

'But why?'

'It's just all the excitement. Honestly, my head's not right today.'

'But we were going to go to Hogan's tonight.'

'I'm sorry, Kevin. I'm too tired.'

'It's too late now, anyway. We'll not be back till midnight.'

'Please take me home, Kevin.' She folded the soft blanket. She laid it on the sofa and said, 'I'm very cold now. That was a nice blanket. I wonder where I could buy a blanket like that?'

'Here, take my coat.' He stripped off his leather jacket and draped it round Kate's shoulders. It smelt of engine oil.

Kate thought it was a very pleasant sensation to be enveloped in Kevin's jacket. She smiled. 'Thanks, Kevin. That's lovely.'

'Do you want to call off the wedding, Kate?'

'No.'

'Are you sure?'

'Yes.'

'Then, why are you sitting in the airport?'

Kate thought she would try blaming someone else. That's what she normally did when she was in trouble.

'Louise Lowry told me you were a drug-dealer.'

'What?'

'The Bungalow Baron, she said. That's your code name.'

'And you believed her?'

'I don't know. You have spent a lot of money on me. The house. The honeymoon. Thousands of pounds.'

'And you thought the only way I could afford that was to deal drugs?'

'I don't know, Kevin. I panicked.'

'I've taken out a massive bank loan, you twit!'

'I'm so sorry.'

She was truly miserable, Kevin noted. And it was getting late and they were both confused.

'Is there anything else that's worrying you?'

'The baby.'

'Shirley's baby?'

'Yes. And our babies. I'm scared of the pain.'

'You can have all the drugs they've got on offer.'

'Maybe you could supply me with some!'

And they both laughed, although it was a bit half-hearted.

'I'm still scared. I don't want strangers interfering with my *modesty*, as my mother would say. All those little metal tools you see rattling on the trolley in hospital dramas. I just couldn't bear it, Kevin.'

'That's just your mother talking. It will be fine when you're having our babies. You won't care about all that when the time comes. You'll be with the experts. They won't let you suffer.'

'How do you know? What if we don't make it to the hospital on time? What if I can't cope with the pain? What if I crack up and scream until my brain disintegrates? I know it's hard for some people to comprehend, Kevin, but telling a nervous person to pull themselves together, *just does not work*.'

'You can have a pre-planned C-section if you're that worried. If your doctor recommends you for one. I'll hold your hand, all the way.'

'How do you *know* things like this?'

'Kate, it's common knowledge. Look. We'll go private. They give you what you want when you go private. No labour at all. You don't need to be in labour if you're having a Caesarean. You can have your own room in the hospital, too. For privacy. And I won't leave your side throughout.'

'I don't know anything about looking after children.'

'Neither do I. We'll learn together. We'll buy a book.'

'I can't even cook scrambled eggs. They always burn.'

'Who cares? We'll have boiled eggs. I've got simple tastes. We'll take it in turns to fry chops.'

'I don't want to grow old.' Tears were running down her face.

'Is that it? You don't want to grow *up*, you mean?'

'I don't know. I'm *scared*.'

'You'll still be the same age, Kate, married to me or not. It'll be great, being married. We'll be a team, helping each other. Supporting each other.'

'I know that. It's just . . .'

'Shush, sweetheart. I'll take you home now and you can have a good rest. And we'll tell Declan that we're pulling out of the wedding. We'll get married some other time. If you still want to.'

'Kevin!'

'Well, there's no point in going ahead with it, if you feel this way. You're supposed to enjoy your wedding day, Kate. I don't want you to keel over at the altar rails.'

'Are you worried about being shown up?' she sobbed.

'Kate, I don't want to be left standing there, in front of my relations. Of course I don't. But more than that, I don't want to have to cope with a broken heart in the middle of Shirley's big day. We'll ruin it for them, too. If you change your mind at the last minute. And it's Declan's family who are paying for all this. The reception is in their restaurant. Are you not thinking straight?'

'I guess not.'

'Come on, let's go. We can't sit here all night.'

They stood up. Kate gathered her bags.

'What are you doing with all these handbags?' Kevin asked.

'I was going to open a shop in Paris.'

'I see.'

Kevin guided Kate out of the office, through the main doors and down to the car park. A cold breeze was cutting through them as they walked to the car. Kate sat in the passenger seat and stared straight ahead. Kevin covered her knees with a picnic blanket. He thought that Kate was close to collapse and that the wedding was just too much for her. It was all too soon. And he was to blame. Some people dated for ten years before they got married. If Kate ended up on medication, it would all be his fault. She didn't love him. He could see that now. He would make things easier for her. He would finish the relationship that evening, as soon as he had brought her back to her mother and father. He would tell them not to leave Kate by herself for a few days, until she was back in the real world. They drove home in silence. Kate thought that Belfast looked very peaceful at night with all the street lights twinkling in the darkness. She closed her eyes and slept for a while.

Mrs Winters was standing on the pavement, with her arms folded and her lips pursed. Kevin's heart was as heavy as a lump of lead when he saw the grim expression on her face. He hoped Kate's family wouldn't be too hard on her, in the weeks and months to come. Mrs Winters, in particular, seemed to be missing the sympathy gene.

'Here she is,' she began, as Kevin pulled up and switched off the engine. 'Here comes the runaway bride!' And she knocked on Kate's window with the back of her fist, her wedding ring making a tinny tap on the cold glass.

Kate blinked awake. Her mother's face was distorted with rage.

'Aw, Jesus wept! I can't face this now,' Kate whimpered.

It seemed to both of them that Kate couldn't face a lot of things.

'Kate, I never thought I'd say this but I think we should break up.'

'What?'

'I think it's for the best. Don't you?'

'No! You don't mean this?'

'You obviously don't feel the same way for me, as I feel for you.'

'I do. Kevin! I do.'

'I can't get married under these conditions, pet. I have feelings, too, you know. I've done everything I can think of to make you happy, and it isn't working out. Let's just have a clean break. I'm sorry I came on too strong about getting married.'

'I do love you, Kevin.'

'But not enough to marry me? You were running away.'

'It was just cold feet. A silly thing, nothing to worry about.'

'Goodnight, Kate. Your mum's waiting.'

'Kevin, listen —'

'Kate, please. Just go. If we aren't ready for marriage, at our age, we never will be. We can talk about the details in a couple of days when you've calmed down.'

Mrs Winters was pulling at the door handle. Kevin was reaching for the ignition key and shaking his head. His cheeks were sucked in with disappointment. His high-lights were falling over his lovely hazel eyes. The unthink-able was happening. *He* was leaving *her*. No one had ever left Kate Winters before.

And that was when Kate felt a huge sense of loss, even though she was exhausted and cold and absolutely fed up. She was about to lose the only man who had ever truly loved her, and she knew she would be listening to her mother reminding her of that fact, for ever and a day. Drama? Here was high drama indeed. Ten times more dramatic than hanging around with bad boys. And it wasn't pleasant at all. She never wanted a minute's drama in her life again.

'Kevin, wait! I love you madly.'

'I'm tired –'

'I want to marry you. Really I do. Take me home, Kevin.'

'Oh, Kate, don't do this to me. You're driving me crazy.'

'Please! I don't want to live in this house any more. I don't want to listen to Mum telling me I have ten O Levels any more. I don't want to have to look at all those bloody ornaments any more.'

'You need to get some sleep. You're exhausted.'

'I want to get married. I want to be grown up!'

'I don't know. I just don't know any more.'

'I *want* to be with you, Kevin McGovern. Give me one more chance.'

'Kate –'

'Please, Kevin. I've been such an idiot.' There was a touch of hysteria in her voice.

'Calm down, pet. You'll upset yourself again. We won't decide anything tonight. We'll wait for a few days before we tell people it's over. Okay?'

'Do you want me to get out onto the road, and kneel down, and beg you to take me back? Is that what you want?'

'Don't be ridiculous. It's cold –' But she was already reaching for the door handle.

'I'll show you,' she cried. 'I'll knock on every door in the street and tell people I have been a complete fool, and that I am a changed woman.'

'Kate, don't make this night any worse than it is already –'

'I love Kevin McGovern,' Kate roared into the night sky, as her mother stepped back in shock. 'I really love him, Mum.' Kate was struggling to get out of the car, her handbags spilling out into the gutter again. She got one foot onto the pavement, and tried to haul herself up. Kevin caught her round the waist and pulled her back inside.

'You'd better mean this,' he said gravely. 'I'm at my wits' end, here.'

'I mean it,' she said. 'I love you. I love you. I love you.' She opened the car window and told her mother the great news. 'I love Kevin. We're going home now.'

Mrs Winters was about to give Kate another lecture but Kate wound the window up again and waved at her mother happily through the glass.

'Hurry up, darling,' she said to Kevin. 'I can't wait to

307

snuggle up in our big bed and put all this misery behind us. Like you said before, it's now or never. And I'm ready for you now . . .'

Kevin looked at Kate for a long minute, wondering if he was crazy to give her another chance. Then, he thought of his house and how empty it seemed when she was not there. He knew he would be miserable on his own. Maybe Kate was sincere in what she said? And her attempt to leave him was just her way of dealing with the end of her single days? She did seem absolutely determined to marry him now. He decided to take a chance. If she didn't turn up for the ceremony, though, he'd have to emigrate. He'd have to go to the airport himself, then. He smiled at Kate and flicked his fringe out of his eyes, revved up the engine and pulled out smartly from the kerb. Mrs Winters, who had been lying up against Kate's window, staggered into the road and hurt her toe. She watched Kevin's car as it went smoothly down the road, and disappeared round the corner.

'I don't know how that girl gets away with it,' she complained as she went back inside the house and banged the door shut. 'In my day, they'd have lifted you, for such a disturbance of the peace.'

'How is she, Martha?' her husband asked quietly, craning his neck to see beyond his wife. 'Actually, *where* is she?'

'That Kate one! She's gone back to him. After all that drama!'

'Thank God. We're not as young as we used to be, love. If anybody can sort out our Kate, it's Kevin McGovern. He's a good lad. He's strong.'

'We'll see about that. And the house is freezing, now.

You might have closed the door, for pity's sake. With the price of coal these days,' she grumbled, as her husband sipped a large brandy, beside the dying embers of the fire.

'If you think it's cold in here, you should try sitting in the shed for two hours,' he whispered, taking off his shoes and rubbing some life back into his poor blue toes.

29. The Main Prize

It was one o'clock in the morning. Kevin and Kate were fast asleep in bed, their arms twined round one another. Kate was still wearing Kevin's leather jacket.

Hogan's Goodbye Disco was in full swing. All the showbiz greats were being played. Wham. Dollar. Rick Astley. The dance floor was absolutely heaving. Even the macho men from the Ormeau Road had thrown caution to the winds and were jiving and bopping with the best of them. Louise Lowry was very disappointed that there was no sign of Kate Winters, as she was planning some more interesting requests. But then she saw a little cardboard sign on DJ Toni's booth that said NO REQUESTS PLEASE, so she went to dance with Mary instead. Alex was on bouncing duty tonight, and he could hardly spare the time to look at Louise, let alone talk to her. But Louise didn't mind. She didn't love Alex, after all. She didn't want his conversation, or even his magnificent body. She'd lied to Kate about the red-hot sex she'd had with Alex. She only wanted his money, and Alex had told her that his uncle had a bad chest infection and wasn't responding to antibiotics.

The bar staff were mere black and red blurs, as the optics and barrels were drained quicker than they could be replaced. Customers who couldn't wait for more vodka to be brought in from the storeroom were settling for any spirits available. All drinks were reduced in price, anyway. The hot-food bar was also doing a roaring trade, and the smell of vinegar was second only to the heady whiff of excitement. DJ Toni kept saying things like, 'And now, for the last time ever, here are the Kids From *Fame* and "Hi Fidelity",' to which Declan would sigh, 'Thank God.' But some of the admittedly tipsy females would scurry to the safety of the loo and have a good sob. The emotion was simply too much for them. Some of them had met their husbands here. Some of them had met their first love here. Some of them had conceived their children in the parking lot.

Speaking of conception, Shirley was exhausted. It was very tiring, being pregnant. And she thought the music was far too loud. Funny how she had never thought that before. But tonight the noise level was giving her a headache. She was afraid to breathe too much, either, in case the thick fog of cigarette smoke reached her baby, and made it sick. She wanted to go home, but Declan was having such a great time, chatting to his friends, she didn't like to spoil things. They had agreed to go home at half-past one so it was nearly time to leave anyway. Declan kept looking at his watch and then at the DJ booth, hoping that Toni would play some good music. Iggy Pop or the Psychedelic Furs.

Just then, the club's owner, Johnny Hogan, came over to their table and asked them if everything was all right. Were they enjoying the music? Shirley said that yes, it was lovely. (She'd won a prize for the best costume, even though she hadn't dressed up for the competition. But Johnny misinterpreted her 1920s' smoking jacket and very white face for a Louise Brooks look-alike bid.) The other boys at the table nodded politely. But Declan told him he thought it was a shame that certain bands were not on the playlist, and soon he and Johnny were deep in conversation about clubs and music. Declan thought a really cool nightclub would put Belfast on the map, even though some people were trying to blow it *off* the map. Johnny Hogan was fascinated by what Declan had to say and he sat down and listened with his head to one side. Shirley wished Kate was with her. It was uncomfortable being the only girl at the table.

'I'm going to get some chips,' she told Declan. 'I want to stretch my legs.'

'Sure,' he told her. 'Are you okay to go on your own?'

'Yeah, will I get you some?'

'Yes, please. I'll be right over.'

Johnny Hogan almost said that he was hungry himself and they could all go together and sit in his private booth in the food bar. But then, he remembered the prize-giving, and knew that he couldn't be seen to be too friendly with Declan Greenwood.

There was a pause in the music, and DJ Toni said, 'And now, ladies and gentlemen, for the last time ever in Hogan's ballroom, here is FR David, and the fantastic love ballad "Words".' Cue, more women in tears rushing to the toilets. There was quite a bottleneck of mascara-streaked females in the corridor. The waste-paper baskets were overflowing with sodden tissues.

'Well, I'll be on my way,' said Johnny to Declan, and they both stood up. 'I'm trying to speak to as many people tonight as I can.' Johnny offered his hand to the younger man, and Declan shook it firmly, and Johnny looked at him for a second too long before he smiled and walked away into the crowd.

But anyway, at the time, Declan wasn't even that interested in the prize-giving. He was eating his chips and holding Shirley's hand when Johnny took the microphone and made his big announcement. Declan thought he was dreaming when the winning ticket was declared and he realized he had actually won the ballroom. Shirley looked as bewildered as he felt. They both looked around for reassurance. Yes, the ballroom and everything in it now belonged to Declan. Johnny had to announce the ticket number three times before Declan was able to move a muscle. He checked in his pocket and showed the number to Shirley. Number 742. Shirley nodded her head. Yes, it was true. Everyone was applauding, the noise was tremendous.

Johnny was looking round the hall, searching out the winner. When Declan staggered to his feet, Johnny said, 'Here is our winner! Well done and congratulations! Come up and claim your prize, young man. Hooray! Let's have a picture for the paper!'

Declan went slowly up to the stage and received the keys to his great prize, and shook hands with Mr Hogan, as if he was in a trance. All his friends were green with envy, and kept shaking their heads in disbelief. Johnny patted him on the back and Declan came down the stairs again, completely bewildered. As if by magic, he was surrounded by several pretty girls. Shirley didn't know what to think. She didn't mind if Declan wanted to go into the nightclub business; he had often spoken of it. But she knew that it would take up a lot of his time, possibly even more time than if he was a doctor. She went very quiet and left for home in a taxi, claiming exhaustion. But Declan stayed on in the ballroom and had a few drinks with Johnny, and played a few records in the DJ booth. Johnny showed him the office and the fire doors and the safe and the drinks store and the lighting switches. They barely noticed the end of the night being announced by Toni, and the balloons being released from a net on the ceiling. The crowd filed out slowly, the overhead lights in the foyer showing up their flushed and tired faces. The bar staff collected glasses, and the industrial dishwashers hummed in the steamy kitchen. DJ Toni was weeping quietly in his booth as he put his precious records back in their paper cases. Declan was dizzy with happiness, his medical degree forgotten. He kept saying he couldn't take it all in. It was like the story of Charlie Bucket and Willy Wonka and the Chocolate Factory. Johnny told him not to worry. That it was really true and that all the legal stuff would be taken care of in the morning. All he needed was a signature. At five o'clock, Declan signed his name on the deeds.

As the sun was coming up, Johnny drove Declan home to Derryvolgie Avenue and they shook hands again, but Declan was too excited to go to sleep. He began to set out plates on the kitchen table for breakfast, as soon as he had washed all the cigarette smoke out of his hair in the shower. At seven o'clock, when the Greenwoods were having breakfast, Eddy and Marion found out about the raffle. Eddy dropped a full bottle of milk on the slate floor and it exploded with a crash that made them all jump. There was milk all up the front of Eddy's suit and even some dripping off the ceiling. Declan didn't tell them that he was planning to put his degree on hold for a trial period. He'd save that news for later. First, he was going to grab some sleep and then go round to Shirley's house and talk things over. If he was really the new owner of the ballroom, they could go to the bank for a mortgage, and get a decent place to live. No need for his parents to buy him a house now. He'd buy Shirley a new kitchen and all the fancy furniture her heart desired. A new car, maybe? And all the equipment for the new baby. Their lives were transformed overnight. It was a heaven-sent coincidence, getting the winning ticket like that. Beaming from ear to ear, he grabbed a slice of toast and bounded up the stairs, to bed.

Marion went straight back to bed too, with a cup of tea and some painkillers for her sudden headache. She got in beneath the embroidered cream duvet with her dressing gown still on, and shivered violently. When Eddy came and sat on the bed and asked her gently what was going on, she just shook her head. She couldn't look Eddy in the face, and refused to speak to him. He tried to put his arms around her. But she felt rigid with guilt and could not respond to his embrace. She slipped out of bed, ran across the luxury carpet and locked herself in the ensuite bathroom. She said she was taking a long bath and he knew then that she would not come out of the bathroom for hours. Marion did not cope well under stress. There was no point in having a blazing row with her. Eddy realized that she had told Johnny the truth, and that it could never be un-told. No matter how much he shouted his head off at his wife. It was not Marion's fault, anyway. It was that hound-dog, Hollywood Hogan; sniffing around things and people that were none of his business any more. He went back down to the kitchen.

'I'm going out for a while,' he told his daughters. 'Don't be late for school.' Then, Eddy went straight round to the Hogan house on Eglantine Avenue, milky suit and all, to give Johnny the beating he should have given him in 1962.

When Johnny opened the front door, he knew what was coming. He didn't even flinch when Eddy punched him hard in the eye. Johnny didn't care. He'd been expecting some sort of scene. He staggered backwards into the hall and fell heavily on the patterned carpet. Eddy rushed in and grabbed him by the collar, punching him several times. Johnny made a token attempt to defend himself but he let Eddy rough him up a little bit. It didn't hurt that much because he was still drunk from the night before, and Eddy was a clean fighter. Eddy split Johnny's lip and blackened his two eyes, and the hall table got broken. But there was no serious damage done. When Eddy had worn himself out, he stood up and pointed straight into the face of his long-term love rival.

'You won't get away with this, Hogan,' he said. 'You won't. Do you hear me? I won't let you.'

'He's my son. And it's my ballroom. And it's got nothing to do with you! You stole Marion away from me. When she was feeling low, with the baby. You weren't man enough to get her back, on your own. I'll never forgive you for that.'

'She's mine. And Declan is mine, and I swear, I'll not let you take him away from me. You stay away from Marion, too. Whatever you're playing at, it won't work.'

'Relax, Greenwood. Marion doesn't want me. Yes, I asked her to come to America. And she turned me down flat. She'd never leave the children. So, you can settle yourself. Now, get out of my house.'

'You lost her yourself, Hogan, years ago. And the boy, too. Don't think it's only our daughters that are standing in the way of a big reunion. You had five years to wed Marion, and you didn't do it. You used her.'

'I said, get out of here. I need to sleep for a while before I see Declan.'

'You're a loser, Hogan, you're going nowhere. And you'll not take the boy down with you. He's got brains to burn, and he's set for better things than shaking hands with strangers off the street. That was good enough for the likes of you and me, but it wouldn't suit him. And if you knew him at all, you'd know it's true.'

But Johnny was halfway up the stairs to sleep off the most eventful night of his life. He halted to rub his bleeding lip with the back of his hand and his white cuff became smeared with deepest red. Johnny knew the pain would be worse when the drink wore off him. But inside, his heart was floating on a cloud of happiness. The ballroom would bring his son back to him. He was not alone any more. James and Eileen were in the twilight of their lives. Five years would see both of them into the city cemetery. But that was all right. Johnny was not dreading that day any more, because now he had a son. They would get to know each other again while Johnny showed the younger man the ropes, and when he was ready to handle the truth, Johnny would tell him, and everything would be okay. Marion had no right to keep him and Declan apart. He stared at his white cuff. Blood. Declan and himself. They were blood relations. And Shirley's baby was part of Johnny, too. His first grandchild.

'Close the door behind you, Greenwood, and go home to your wife,' he said. 'We have nothing more to say to each other. It's over.'

30. A Day to Remember

Declan didn't see Eddy when he came back from the tall house on Eglantine Avenue because he was fast asleep in bed. Eddy cleaned himself up in the family bathroom and then knocked on the door of the master-bedroom ensuite, and told Marion that he had taken care of things.

'Did you hit him?' she asked.

'Yes, I did. And it felt good.'

'Did you fight?'

'Not really. He wouldn't fight with me.'

'Is that the end of it, Eddy?'

'That's up to Declan. He doesn't know the full story. Not yet, anyway.'

'I won't see Johnny again, Eddy. I promise. He frightens me. He's living in the past. It's as if the last twenty years never happened.'

'That's okay, darling. I'm not cross with you.'

'I love you, Eddy. I'm sorry about all this.'

'I love you, too. Let me see you, darling. Let me in. Whatever happens, we'll still have each other.'

She didn't answer him but, after a while, she got dressed and unlocked the door, and they sat together on the cream sofa at the foot of the bed. There was so much to say, they didn't know where to begin. It could only be a matter of time before Declan found out that Johnny was his father, and also he might leave college and manage the ballroom. And maybe even drift away from Eddy and Marion. The thought made her feel desolate. Her mouth dried up. Marion said she was thirsty and Eddy fetched them both a cup of hot, sugary tea.

'Will we tell him together?' said Eddy. 'Explain things to him before Johnny does it for us?'

'No. Not today.'

'We can't hide from this for ever. Maybe it's time?'

'I can't. It's all right for you, Eddy. You're the hero in all this, marrying me the way you did. And Johnny doesn't look too bad, either. He was denied the chance to get to know his son. His only child, as far as we know. It's *me* who will come out of this story badly; a silly woman who couldn't make up her mind who she loved.'

There was nothing Eddy could say to that. It was true. Marion sat quietly on the sofa, too upset to even cry.

'Go on to work,' she said. 'I'll be okay.' He nodded.

She spent the day sitting in her bridal shop, but she didn't open it to the public or do anything behind the scenes, either. She just sat on her little white sofa in the middle of the room, gazing at the beautiful dress in the window, and wishing that she had worn it for her wedding to Eddy all those years ago. And that she had never left him for Johnny in the first place. And that Eddy was Declan's father. And that she'd had more sense when she was young and beautiful. At five o'clock, she locked up the building and went home to make the dinner.

The wedding went ahead as planned. Both Kate and Shirley looked magnificent as they alighted from the limousine into warm spring sunshine. Kate looked like a royal princess in her gold lace gown and Shirley was surprisingly sophisticated in blue velvet and several strands of pearls. She wore blue nail polish to match the dress, and her eyeliner was much neater than usual. She'd even been persuaded (by Kate) to use a little face powder and blusher, and to wear a pearl tiara. Of course, there were gasps of amazement from the more conservative members of the congregation when they saw the blue gown, but as a whole, the guests approved of the bridal sisters. Strangely, with their beautiful bouquets of bright yellow sunflowers and roses, they looked great together. Kate graciously said she would allow Shirley to walk down the aisle first. Just so no one could say that Shirley looked like a bridesmaid. But no one did say that anyway. Shirley looked like a film star, with her hair styled to perfection and dressed with a crown of pearly teardrops. The sisters stood in the porch of the church with their proud parents. They all held hands and hugged each other. Kate's long hair was piled up on top of her head in an elaborate knot and Mrs Winters gave it a final tweak before they all assumed their positions for the wedding march.

When the music started up, they took a deep breath and began the long, slow march to the altar. Mr Winters was giving Shirley away. They set off first, in a moving and humble kind of tiptoe. Then came Mrs Winters and Kate, in a cloud of white feathers, gold lace, heady perfume and regal nods right and left to the guests. Amanda and Julie from the DHSS brought up the rear, looking shy in their bright canary-yellow dresses and carrying small posies of blue flowers. If Louise Lowry had been there, she would have said something bitchy. But she wasn't, so that was okay.

Kevin's face was as red as a boiled beetroot when he pledged his lifelong fidelity to his new wife; partly because his outlandish diamanté brooch-pin was sticking into his neck and partly because he had never been so happy. Kate smiled at him as they stood together before the altar. She felt fine. But that might have been the Valium capsule that her doctor had given her. Just one tablet, she said, to be taken before the wedding. The priest began the ceremony by welcoming the guests to God's house, and Kate's mind filtered out his words automatically, just as it had done since she was a small child. She smiled at Kevin. She felt very peaceful.

She had conquered her commitment-phobia entirely, and was very pleased that the palpitations had been due to nerves all along and not due to alcoholism, as she'd feared. The doctor explained it all to her several times, that day in the surgery. She'd been suffering from anxiety, and all her unpleasant symptoms were due to adrenaline surges! A humble hormone. Silly old adrenaline. Nothing more. The trembling hands, the cold skin, the feeling of being trapped, the dizzy spells. She didn't need medication, either. There was no need to resort to medication, so early in the day, the doctor told her. Nine times out of ten, the doctor said gently, these things went away by themselves. No need to go getting hooked on happy pills unless there was no other option. It wasn't as if she was traumatized by any actual event. It was just an excess of everyday worries making her mind tired. Kate wondered if there was a place she could go for a couple of weeks. Some quiet place to get her head together; hopefully with celebrity inmates and twenty-four-hour room service?

The doctor smiled. No. Not unless she was prepared to pay for it herself, at any rate. Kate admitted she'd soon be on her honeymoon in Barbados. (But Kevin would be with her, so she wouldn't be able to chill out very much.)

The doctor looked at her watch. 'Just relax more and stop worrying about things,' she said. 'When you stop worrying, the anxiety will stop, and the adrenaline will stop, and the panic attacks will stop. I'll refer you for some counselling. They'll be in touch when there's a place for you. There's a very long waiting list, I'm afraid.'

Kate sighed.

She'd stood up to leave the surgery that morning as if she was a new person, she remembered, as the priest worked his way slowly through the wedding Mass. Not totally reassured. But she didn't feel all that tragic any more. Being a proper grown-up wasn't nearly as frightening as she'd always thought it was. She might even come off the pill and place herself in the hands of fate, she thought. Maybe having a child would make her less self-centred. Her credit card had been consigned to the bottom of a drawer. The shopping therapy was not necessary any more. It was twelve years late, but Kate had finally come of age.

She felt Kevin tugging at her sleeve and she snapped out of her daydream. Kevin was imploring her to say something. She looked at the priest in bewilderment. He repeated the words that Kate was supposed to have said. She said them. Mrs Winters could be heard quite clearly saying, '*Bloody hell!*' Then, they were man and wife. A warm murmur of approval rippled through the congregation.

Shirley was so happy she wasn't nervous at all, and

smiled radiantly during the marriage service. She even closed her eyes at the end of the ceremony and thanked God for the way things had turned out. It was the least she could do. When she had sat alone on her little bed with the pregnancy test in her hand, she'd thought the whole world was going to end. But it hadn't ended, and now everything was better than ever. She kissed her new husband politely. They'd agreed not to overdo the kiss in front of the guests. So as not to embarrass Mrs Winters.

Declan was impossibly handsome in his black suit, and his blond hair, which was dyed specially for the occasion. It was a promise he had made to his mother. She wanted him to be blond in the photographs. He had also promised his father he would stay at college for another six months. After that, if he didn't want to go on with it, he could give up his studies and run the ballroom with his parents' blessing. Meanwhile, the ballroom on Magnolia Street was boarded up and left to the spiders and the dust. Marion had a feeling that when Declan became a father, he would lose interest in the ballroom.

The guests spilled out onto the lawn and many boxes of confetti were thrown, to the huge dismay of the fastidious church caretaker. He tried to stop the handfuls of red and pink and yellow tissue hearts and flowers being cast into the air, but the celebratory mood was impossible to curtail. In the end, he gave up and went off to fetch a dustpan and brush from the sacristy. The sun shone down through a gap in the clouds and they managed to get a few good pictures before it went in again.

Mrs Winters cried on and off, the whole morning. Partly because she was so happy to see her daughters married to good men; and partly because Pamela Ballantine never did make a documentary, and never did get to see Martha Winters's extensive ornament collection or her magnificent furniture with adjustable glass shelving and integral lighting. Mr Winters spent his time in the flower-laden church daydreaming, and planning to buy a new shed. A much bigger one with better insulation and room for a workbench, a gas heater and an armchair. Now that his daughters were married, his wife would have plenty of time on her hands and he didn't want her to turn her attentions to him. Ballroom-dancing had been mentioned, more than once. There was a beginners' class being held in the community centre. Still, to be fair to the old bag, she wasn't the worst in the world. He smiled at her and held her hand.

Marion and Eddy also held hands throughout the wedding service, their love for each other as strong as ever. Marion didn't like to admit it, even to herself, but she thought Eddy beating Johnny up was very sexy. He wasn't just a safe bet any more. He was a man of uncontrollable passion and strong desires. A man who had fought to keep her by his side, when Johnny had let her walk away without even risking his pride by begging her to stay. A passer-by wouldn't think to look at Eddy, in his tweed jacket and his cloth cap, that he was such a hero. But that's exactly what he was. Not an accidental hero like Hollywood Hogan.

Emily, Eve and Eloise were having a great time and were already planning to help Shirley with the baby-sitting. They were throwing confetti now, and taking photographs and telling the two brides they looked absolutely beautiful.

Which, as Marion knew only too well, was by far the most important part of any successful wedding. Shirley and Kate were delighted with themselves. It was going to be a great day. A day to remember always.

31. Mavourna Moon is Born

After the wedding pictures had been pasted into thick albums and stored away safely in protective boxes, both couples finally set off on honeymoon. Kate took four suitcases to Barbados with her. Including a full set of luxury bed-linen and ten embroidered bath towels, just in case the hotel's own supply proved inferior. (They were fine, as it happened.) Kate also took seventeen jewel-bright sundresses and twelve micro-bikinis on the trip, as well as countless pairs of leather sandals and plastic-flower-coated flip-flops. She hoped she would get a chance to wear every single item of clothing in the cases, but she knew that Kevin was due some high-quality bedroom action for all he had been through in the run-up to the wedding. He'd been laughed at the whole wedding day, in his gold suit. And even the priest had made a joke about forgetting to bring his sunglasses. While he was *still standing* at the altar, and all the guests were laughing their heads off in the church; which made Mrs Winters very upset. Such disrespect for a holy place.

And so, Kate was prepared to be generous to her new husband. She would let him think he had seduced her, every time. Even though she had to psych herself up beforehand in the bathroom, occasionally, like a boxer going into the ring. And pretend that Kevin was Martin Fry on *Top of the Pops*. Kate did love Kevin, as much as she thought she could love anyone. Maybe it wasn't world-class passion and fireworks, but it was comfortable. He *was* inclined to rush matters slightly when they went to bed together. That was true. He was scoring well in the frantic-passion department, but letting himself down badly on tender eroticism. When she got to know him a little bit better, she would explain the basics of love-making to him; and show him how to get her in the mood properly. But she was wise enough to know that their honeymoon was not the right place to start telling him where he was going wrong in bed. The holiday was a great success, and they both returned tanned and happy and ready to start paying for all the nice things they had enjoyed so far.

Now that Kate was officially Mrs McGovern, she was entitled to see Kevin's bank statements, and she realized with horror that they were up to their eyes in debt. She cancelled her plans to sit at home reading glossy magazines for the rest of her life, and got back to work immediately. She hired another mechanic and advertised for more work. Nearly three months passed with barely a day off. She sometimes felt hard done by, half-hidden behind a mountain of receipts and invoices, but then she thought of Shirley. Poor Shirley. Never well dressed at the best of times, she was absolutely dreary these days; wearing shapeless jumpers and cheap black leggings. She'd let herself go completely. There was no purple lipstick in evidence any more. Shirley was painfully thin and listless. Everyone was worrying about her and trying to get her to eat little bits of food. Kate was fascinated and horrified by Shirley's pregnancy. Her bump was getting bigger by the day, criss-crossed with angry purple lines; and the skin was stretched so tightly over her abdomen, it was super-shiny. Shirley said the skin was really itchy too; like a thousand ants were crawling over it all the time. She caressed it softly with her fingernails in bed each night. Kate shivered when she heard that. She hated insects of any kind. Sometimes, the baby moved violently inside the bump, and you could see little elbows or knees sticking out and slithering under the skin. Kate almost threw up when that happened. She had a nightmare that the baby would tear open Shirley's skin, crawl out by itself, peel away the messy membranes and say hello to everyone.

Shirley and Declan moved into a rented flat while they decided what to do with the ballroom. They refused to let Marion and Eddy buy them a house. It wouldn't be fair when they had other children to look after, they protested. And anyway, when the site was sold, they would be rich enough to buy their own house. Declan had secret fantasies about reopening the dance hall and making it into the coolest club in the country. Like the hippest trend-setting nightspots in Manchester and London; crammed to the doors with genuine music-lovers in black leather jackets. Marion and Eddy said nothing on the subject, but Declan knew that *they* knew he was stalling for time. They didn't want him getting mixed up in the entertainment business. The subject was never mentioned in his parents' house. Not since Eddy gave Johnny Hogan a beating. And Shirley never mentioned it, either. She didn't say he couldn't reopen the ballroom, but she wasn't madly enthusiastic either. When he tried to talk to her about it, she just said he could do what he liked with it.

His friends thought he was mad that he didn't set himself up right away as a cool gig-promoter and regular sex symbol. They didn't seem to think it mattered that he was married. They just wanted to go around, saying, *Oh, yeah, my mate owns the ballroom on Magnolia Street.* And boasting that they could get free tickets to various events. Now it was July. If Declan was going to drop out of college, time was running out. He knew he should do the decent thing and inform the university in writing. That way, they could give his place to someone else. He spoke with Johnny Hogan on the telephone from time to time to discuss things. Johnny was currently travelling in America, but he'd told Declan to call him any time he wanted advice, and he always sent him a postcard when he moved to a new hotel. Johnny was eager for him to get the shutters off, and start the heaters running.

'A big place like that gets damp if it's left standing empty,' he said. 'Mice move in, rats too, maybe. Drunks break in to sleep rough. Vandals light fires.' Then Johnny realized he was scaring his young protégé and he told Declan not to worry. That these things could be dealt with, simply enough, by the proper authorities. Even organized crime? Yes. Just call the police if any chancers showed up. That was the sensible thing to do. No need to play the hero. Declan then went off the idea again. Until he heard a fantastic new single on the radio, and then he thought that he *could* cope with all these problems. If he wanted his own club badly enough. His thoughts swung backwards and forwards like a row of washing in the wind. The days were flying past in a whirlwind of unmade decisions.

Time, on the other hand, seemed to stand still for Shirley. She had to hold up her own bump when she was walking now, because it felt so heavy. She was always hungry but her stomach was squashed flat against her ribs and she could only eat tiny meals. Nobody would get in the lift with her at the dole office, in case the doors got stuck and she went into labour. Shirley finally felt unable to travel to work on the bus any more, when she was nearly squashed under a couple of strapping Australian tourists wearing backpacks, and she reluctantly took maternity leave. She lay on the sofa for most of the day, eating crisps and watching daytime television. (She liked the mouth-watering cookery slots best of all. Shirley couldn't be bothered to cook anything herself, but it was still very pleasant to watch other people doing it. It was relaxing and harmless.) She realized that her emotions were in tatters. She cared about everyone and everything in the world. The listeners phoning in to the TV agony aunts, with their personal problems, brought tears to her eyes, where she would previously have scoffed at their hopelessness.

'Oh, you poor creature,' she would say to the screen, 'dump that heart-scald like a hot tin bucket!' Or something like that. 'Why can't you see that this relationship is going nowhere?' Television presenters became her closest friends, like another set of parents almost. (Sane and normal parents.) She felt quite desolate when the programmes came to an end, each lunchtime. The signing-off music made her heart plummet all the way down to the floorboards. The rest of the day stretched ahead of her like a prison sentence. She hated the soaps that were on in the afternoons. They bored her. All the girls were far too pretty.

She longed to tidy the flat but couldn't summon up the energy to even open the curtains. She thought that their home wouldn't look so awful if it was painted white and had a few bright prints hanging on the walls, but unless some decorators from a makeover show came round and did it for her, it would never be done.

'I'm a mere pod. A helpless host,' she said to the hideous wallpaper one day. 'My life is in limbo until this baby is born. What a stupid, stupid, *stupid* way to reproduce! God, what were you thinking of? Why can't we just lay an egg and keep it in the airing cupboard for nine months? What is the *point* of all this stretched skin and aching tiredness and greasy hair?' Then, she was sorry. At least she had the luxury of lying about while her entire body was drained of nutrients and calcium and whatever else the baby needed. Some poor women had to work right up to labour, and immediately afterwards too. In some countries, the women had to go on working on the land, with newborn babies tied to their backs. She remembered her mother's words of comfort in times of trouble: *There's always someone worse off than yourself.* Somehow, it wasn't very comforting to Shirley to know that another person might be suffering more than she was.

Declan brought home flowers some days, small pink rosebuds and white daisies; or a parcel of breast of chicken and chips from the restaurant, all wrapped up in silver foil. Her mother called in too, to wash the dishes and criticize the decor. Marion and Eddy kept their distance, for the sake of politeness. But they told her to call them any time of the day or night, if she required any help at all. And Marion bought her some lovely pyjamas to wear in the hospital. And a brand-new dressing gown and slippers. And of course, Kate called in twice a week, just to be nosy. And to marvel over Shirley in her shabby flat with the worn carpets; such a difference to her own modern show-home.

She couldn't wait to feel the first pangs of labour, Shirley said. She was so bored she thought she might develop some psychiatric problems, just to pass the time. She might start phoning radio stations and chatting about current affairs. The sooner she went into labour, the sooner the birth would be over.

'Are you going back to work, after?' Kate wanted to know.

'Well, that's easy,' said Shirley. 'My wages wouldn't cover the cost of a nursery, so I'm giving up work.'

'Won't you be bored to death?'

'No. Not at all. We're going to go for long walks, the baby and me. And bake biscuits, and read library books and visit Mum and Dad, and lots of things.'

'Sounds fascinating. Why don't you take in another couple of kids, and make some money child-minding?'

'Holy smoke, Kate! Let me get used to my own baby first, before you plan out my life's work. I'm tired, you know?'

'You'd want to get out of this dump, Shirley. The carpet alone would be enough for me. It's filthy.'

'It's just old. You always did have a thing about carpets.'

'Why don't you let your in-laws help with a mortgage?'

'It wouldn't be right. They have other children to support.'

'Why don't you sell the ballroom?'

'Why do you ask so many questions?'

'Well, why don't you? I don't know why you hang around here, when you don't have to. That's all.'

'At the moment, I haven't the energy to cut my own toenails, Kate. I don't suppose you'd oblige me?'

'Don't even think about it, Shirley. Get your fantastic husband to do it. Mr Oh-So-Wonderful.'

'Ouch! That sounds like jealousy to me. Is there a wee problem in Paradise?'

'There is not.'

'Are you sure? You can tell me if there is.'

'Absolutely nothing wrong at all.'

But there was. Kate was still feeling anxious. And she had no idea why. But she'd rather die in agony than admit it to Shirley. Kate said cheerio to her sister, and went home to have a long soak in her luxury corner bath with gold-plated taps.

Shirley was munching her way through a six-pack of salt and vinegar crisps late one Friday night, when she felt the first sudden small contraction. A small nip that made her gasp. Just a few seconds long, she noted. Ha! Easy! She was delighted that it didn't seem to hurt very much at all. It was just like a boring old period cramp, but slightly more urgent. Good on those lucky crystals, harnessing the hidden power of the mind to resist pain. And they'd only cost her two pounds in a health-food shop! She felt suddenly at one with her ancient female ancestors – mysterious and strong as their warrior-husbands. Giving birth (without pain relief) on a bed of wet granite! Pain and hardship were bread and butter to the Celts. That was why the Irish were the toughest people on the planet.

All the weakness had been bred out of them, down through the centuries.

She confidently finished the crisps, licked her salty fingers, had a quick shower, changed into the new pyjamas and then told Declan to fetch her hospital bag from the bedroom.

'Are you sure?' he said. 'The baby's not due for another week.'

'I'm fairly sure I felt a contraction. We'll wait and see is there another one. Will we?' She sat down beside him.

'Yes. And if there is one, we'll go straight to the hospital. Okay? There's plenty of petrol in the car.' He brought the bag of night-clothes and toiletries from the bedroom and began to switch off the lights in the flat and to blow out Shirley's scented candles and incense sticks. Shirley shifted her weight on the sofa and then sat up straight.

'Oh. *Oh!* There's another one. Stronger than the last one. Should we be timing this? I can't remember.'

'Are you sure it was a contraction, Shirley? Could it be all the crisps you've eaten, giving you cramps? There was only fifteen minutes between those pains.'

'I can't explain it to you, Declan. But I just know the baby's coming. I feel really weird, and kind of motherly.'

'Okay. Come on, then. We'll go to the hospital. It can't do any harm. I'll just call Mr Kelly and tell him we're on our way.' *Mr* Kelly was Marion's consultant and he'd been more than happy to see Shirley too, throughout her pregnancy. (Shirley knew now that you didn't call consultants *doctor*.) For once in her life, she didn't mind that rich people could afford to have consultant surgeons on standby like this. Not that she'd need him, of course. She was determined to give birth naturally, all by herself. If it was good enough for other women, for thousands of years, it was good enough for Shirley Winters. She was glad it was dark when she went out into the yard in her pyjamas and dressing gown, though. What would the Celts think of her? A pink flannel dressing gown wasn't the same as a hand-woven cloak, pinned with a golden brooch the size of a bin lid.

'Are you sure you won't get dressed, Shirley?' Declan wanted to know. 'What if it's a false alarm? You'll feel daft coming home again.'

'No, these PJs are very comfortable,' said Shirley. 'And they're nice and new. And besides, after the baby is born, I'll be all ready for bed.'

When they were in the car, Shirley had another pain. This time, it took her breath away, such was the intensity of it. She began to worry, but she didn't tell her husband how concerned she was. She was the brave one after all, the no-nonsense Earth Mother. Kate was the one who caused a scene if they ran out of HP sauce or coconut hair conditioner. The Moon Goddess had brought Declan to her, and she would see their first child born safely too. She closed her eyes and began to chant some soothing words. Declan was suddenly nervous as he backed the car out of the yard. He hadn't started his medical training yet but he knew it wasn't routine to go into labour so quickly. He prayed that the baby wasn't in distress. He was barely able to remember how to drive the car. It took four turns of the key in the ignition before the engine could be coaxed into life. Then he forgot to check his rear-view mirror and knocked over three empty bins. They rolled down the drive and made a noise like thunder when they crashed into the gateposts. His nerves were in shreds as he ran down to move them out of the way. Shirley was moaning softly when he got back. She wouldn't admit to being in pain, but her face was deathly white under the street lights. Declan kept jamming the gears and jumping on the brakes at the traffic lights. Every light seemed to be red. 'Come on,' he urged them. 'Come on! Go green! Please, God, let there not be a broken-down lorry in the way, tonight of all nights.'

When they arrived in the maternity unit car park, half an hour later, Shirley was in tears. The chants hadn't worked and she'd dropped her lucky crystals in the car. And she couldn't pick them up because she couldn't bend over, or even see past her bump to the car floor. Declan was sick with worry. He was afraid to look at his watch. The contractions were becoming longer and much more powerful. In fact, each pain had barely faded away before the next one began to gather strength. Shirley was holding her breath for the entire length of each contraction, contrary to the advice of the pre-natal classes.

'You've got to breathe,' he told her.

'I can't,' she said. 'It hurts more when I breathe.'

'Little tiny breaths. Please, Shirley. You'll get dizzy otherwise. Too little oxygen is as bad as too much. Pant like a dog. Come on. *Aha, aha, aha!*'

'I can't.'

'Shirley! Please. *Breathe.*'

'All right! *Aha!* OH! It hurts!' They abandoned the car at the door and went inside. The foyer was very warm and dimly lit and smelt of furniture wax and floor polish. There was no one else waiting at the reception desk.

A nurse wrote down their details. Shirley wanted to lie down under a warm blanket and go to sleep. Preferably for a week. Declan wanted a fleet of expert medical staff to appear at the desk and whisk Shirley away to safety. He was hopping with impatience. The nurse was maddeningly calm.

'First baby, is it?' she said, politely.

'Yes.'

'Well, you're going to be here all night – if your contractions have only started. Can take a long time with first babies.'

'Please,' begged Declan, 'the contractions are very close together. And she's not breathing enough. I'd like her to be seen now.'

'We're very busy tonight. All the suites are occupied. I'll see what I can do. Please take a seat.'

'Look, I don't want to sound like a snobby git, but my wife is a private patient of Mr Kelly's, and he said he would see us as soon as we arrived.'

'Mr Kelly isn't on duty tonight, I'm afraid, Mr Greenwood.'

'He's on his way in. We've already called him. He's a family friend.'

'I see. Well, follow me. I'll see if I can fit you in somewhere, but this is probably unnecessary.' Snobby git is right, the nurse thought. But she didn't dare to offend a friend of the consultant. The three of them walked slowly down a long, shiny corridor. They could hear someone shouting, '*Push!*' and something metal crashing to the ground. Declan closed his eyes with sheer terror. Just then, Shirley doubled over with a pain so huge she thought someone had stabbed her in the back with an axe. She felt her back, in fear. Then, she turned round, very slowly. She was sure she'd see a seven-foot-tall Viking standing there in full battle regalia and a sheepskin hat. Her knees seemed to forget how to hold her up. She knelt down on the floor and stubbornly held her breath until both Declan and the nurse were begging her to breathe gently and calm down. Her face was rigid with shock.

'It's unbelievable,' she gasped. 'It just gets worse and worse and worse, and then it eases off, and then it comes back again without waiting for a rest. Why isn't there a . . . *rest*? I thought there'd be a rest between . . . *pains* . . .'

'Are you sure this began only a short while ago?' The nurse was now as worried as Declan but she didn't show it. She showed Shirley into a cubicle and carried out a swift internal examination. 'You're about four centimetres,' she said quickly.

'Four what?' cried Shirley, still squirming with embarrassment. Did that nurse just have her hand *inside* her body or was she hallucinating? Mr Kelly hadn't done that. With the scanner showing him everything, he hadn't needed to.

'Dilated. Your cervix is about four centimetres open.'

'Right! How many does it have to be open?'

'Ten.'

'Oh, my God! No way! How long will that take?'

'It's okay, pet. Look, I'll get you sorted with some painkillers, and gas and air? Just a moment, I'll have to break your waters.'

Shirley gasped as the nurse expertly tweaked and

snipped; and soon, the baby's watery home was pierced by the outside world. Warm fluid flowed over the table in a rush. Her lovely pyjamas were ruined. And the pink dressing gown, too. For a horrible moment Shirley thought she'd wet herself; she'd never again feel this embarrassed in her *whole life*. She covered her face with her arm and a little sob escaped from her lips. Declan was distraught. Shirley wasn't even talking to him any more. Or looking at him. She was all alone in her trauma. There was nothing he could do for her. Nothing at all. Kate was right. He *was* a mere schoolboy, just pretending to be a grown-up. The nurse had Shirley dried and covered up and was helping her to her feet. Together they walked to the waiting suite, only recently vacated. Shirley was weeping quietly. All her Celtic power seemed to have deserted her. She thought of her shiny pebbles on the floor of the car. Maybe she should go back outside and fetch them, but the nurse was massaging her back and there didn't seem to be enough time.

I am strong and in control, she chanted internally. *I am strong and in control. I am strong and – oh, shit, where are the drugs?*

'I think I'd like some drugs,' she told the nurse. 'If that's okay?'

'Not to worry, love,' the nurse said gently. 'It won't be long now, and then you'll forget all about it. I promise you. Come on. Here we go.' Shirley laid her head on the nurse's shoulder and surrendered herself to the older woman's experience. They proceeded along the corridor together. Declan was amazed. The two women had bonded completely and he was left holding the canvas bag of baby clothes. What he had previously thought of as the nurse's cold indifference was actually sheer professionalism of the highest order. The mothers-to-be did not want to see the staff in a panic. That was *their* job. Declan was worried that Shirley was going to panic. He was worried that *he* was going to panic. He hurried after them and offered to hop up on the table himself and have a swift vasectomy, now that the nurse had her scissors out. But Shirley didn't even have the energy to laugh. And the nurse was too busy looking at her watch. In agony, Shirley climbed up onto the delivery bed and was covered with the blanket she had been dreaming of. Declan held her hand and said, 'I love you so much,' over and over again. She didn't answer him. She just wanted this night to be over.

Just then, Mr Kelly popped his head into the room.

'Well, Declan. Shirley. How are you? How're things?'

'Coming along well, now.' The nurse was brisk. 'Quite a pace, actually.' Her face communicated a lot of things to the consultant that she didn't want to say out loud. *Patient not coping very well . . .*

'Let's get this lady some gas and air and a nice little injection, shall we?' he said, taking off his coat. 'Can you get us some tea, nurse? Sugar, anyone? That's the ticket! Any chance of a biscuit or two?'

Shirley lay on the operating table three hours later, fully dilated and ready to push. She was wearing a green paper gown and her bare legs were covered in goosebumps. Soaked in sweat, exhausted by labour pains that hadn't eased off for one minute, and feeling dizzy with too much oxygen, she was at her wits' end. She'd had an epidural, but it hadn't helped. In fact, she now regretted having it at all, as the sensation of the needle sliding into her spinal column had been most unpleasant. She wasn't sure if it was the needle piercing her bones or Declan's shoes grinding into the linoleum, but she was sure she had heard a chalky, squeaking noise. And then, when she had endured the labour as bravely as she could, and the midwife was telling her how to push out the baby, she discovered it was all for nothing. A tiny white hand had popped out from between her legs, its perfect fingers opening and closing gently, and the consultant had shouted, 'Nurse! Hand presentation! Transverse position. Prep patient for emergency section!'

And suddenly the room was full of people and someone was shaving off her pubic hair and Shirley was so tired she didn't care what they were going to do to her any more. Declan was practically shoved out of the room and told to wait somewhere close by. There was no time to put him in a green surgical gown and mask, but there wasn't even time to explain *that* to him. He was left, bewildered, in the corridor, as Shirley was wheeled away from him at great speed by a team of nurses and doctors. Someone pulled a cap over Shirley's hair and someone else was preparing her arms for tubes. He staggered to a payphone and called his parents, who said they'd come right in. He sat with his head in his hands as the minutes ticked agonizingly by.

Shirley was barely conscious as they put a pen in her hand so that she could scribble her name on a consent form.

'This form is just to absolve the hospital . . .'

'Please,' she whispered into Mr Kelly's smiling face, 'just get it over with.' And she thought, Please, God, I'm sorry I wasn't married before we made this baby. I'm sorry I said I loved sex, at the good dining table, and scandalized my poor mother. Help me now, and I'll be a good parent. I promise.

Then she felt the nip of the injection in the back of her hand and she was slipping away into peaceful oblivion, and Mr Kelly had become God, and Shirley adored him. Before Marion and Eddy were even in their car, Mavourna Moon was lifted out of her mother, and laid in a clean cloth on the weighing scales. 'Nine pounds and as healthy as a trout!' declared the silver-haired consultant. Declan was able to give them the good news as they rushed into the maternity building twenty minutes later. Marion and Eddy hugged Declan and then each other. Meanwhile, all the drama in the theatre was winding down.

'Very good,' said Mr Kelly calmly. 'Well done, everyone. Now! Let's get the placenta out of the way and we can stitch this young lady up!' He calmly carried out his work, with a happy smile on his tanned and handsome face. All the female staff in the hospital were totally in love with him, and honestly, he couldn't blame them one bit!

Declan was presented with his new daughter in one of the recovery rooms and he was amazed when he saw her perfect heart-shaped face. He cradled her gently, and touched her fat little cheeks with his thumb. A huge rush of love flowed through his veins and the hairs stood up on the back of his neck. He kissed her forehead softly. She was a lovely golden colour, but the nurse explained that was due to a touch of jaundice. Very normal in new babies. Her little wrists were fat and cracked. They'd have to rub lotion into the cracks, she told them. Marion and Eddy took turns nursing their first grandchild. Nobody thought to call Shirley's parents. Or Kate. It was as if the Greenwoods wanted to enjoy this little miracle in complete peace for a short while, before the other half of the family turned up and began to fuss and fret.

'How is Shirley?' Declan asked the midwife.

'Your wife is going to be fine,' said the nurse. 'The baby turned at the last minute. It happens sometimes. No harm done.' Although you're lucky Mr Kelly was here, she thought. We might have had to deliver her the hard way, otherwise, with *forceps*. 'Tell me when Shirley wakes up,' she said, as Shirley was wheeled into the room and made comfortable. Then she went away, and Declan and his parents were left alone to admire the new baby.

When Shirley woke up thirty minutes later, she felt glorious. There was no pain anywhere. Not even a little bit. She felt like she was floating in warm water. Floating underwater in a warm lagoon. All sounds were muffled. It was a lovely happy feeling. She was afraid to open her eyes in case she was dead. If she was dead, she thought, it wasn't so bad. Then, she heard Declan say, 'She's beautiful, Mum. Isn't she just beautiful?' And Shirley knew that she was still in the land of the living. Dear Declan. He was so sweet. Unfortunately, Declan wasn't talking about his wife. Shirley's face and neck had broken out in a horrible rash of stress-induced acne and her hair was plastered to her face with stale sweat. She opened her bloodshot eyes.

'Thank you. I feel great,' she croaked through dry lips.

'Shirley! You're awake.' Declan came over and kissed her, and tried not to breathe in the aroma of several hours of profuse perspiration.

'I feel great. Oh, *wow*! I'm floating. Is this a post-birth euphoria?' Shirley asked, delighted that something had worked out right for her.

'You're on morphine, my darling,' Declan explained.

'What?'

'In your hand. In the back of your hand. There's morphine going in, on a drip.'

'Isn't morphine heroin?' Shirley was alarmed at the thought of becoming an addict. 'Quick, stop it! Get the nurse to stop it!'

'No, it's *morphine*, sweetheart, you'll be fine on that for a few days.'

'Are you sure? Will it make me look awful?'

'Of course it won't. Relax, sweetheart,' Declan said. Thank God there were no mirrors in the room. Shirley would scream if she saw how wretched she did look. But when she had gained some weight, she would be back to her usual (gorgeous) self.

'I'll go,' said Marion. 'Well done, Shirley. You have a beautiful daughter. Well done!' She kissed Shirley on the forehead. 'You take it easy, now. Do you hear me? You have nothing to do but rest and get strong again.'

'I'll come with you,' said Eddy. 'I'm sure you two want to be on your own for a while. We'll be outside in the corridor if you want us.'

'Thanks, Mum and Dad,' said Declan.

When they had gone, Declan brought the new baby over to Shirley. He could barely bring himself to let her

345

go, but he laid her on the bed beside her mother. The baby looked up at Shirley with dark blue eyes. Shirley began to cry. A huge wave of love for her little daughter swept over her and left a lump in her throat. The drama of the birth was forgotten, just as the midwife told her it would be. Shirley knew that newborn babies couldn't focus properly for a few days, but the baby seemed to be gazing right into her soul. She knows me, thought Shirley, with a shock.

'Is she really mine?' she whispered.

'Yes,' said Declan.

'Are you sure there wasn't a mix-up in the theatre?'

'No. Look, there's her name on a little bracelet. Mavourna Moon Greenwood. Just like we agreed.'

'She's far too pretty to be my daughter.'

'Rubbish. You're beautiful.' (A whopping lie just now, but what could he do?)

'She's enormous.'

'So was your bump. Go figure.'

'Is that why she was in the wrong position? Was she quite heavy?'

'Maybe. She must have moved at the very last minute. Her shoulder was where her head should have been. They might have broken her arm to get her out, the normal way.' Shirley's face was a study in horror. Declan could have kicked himself. 'Maybe not. I don't really know,' he faltered. 'Anyway, it's all over now. And we'll all look after you until you're better. You won't have to lift a finger.'

'She knew, Declan. Mavourna knew I couldn't face the delivery and she moved, so I'd have to have a section. She knew I was too tired for any more.'

'Whatever you say, pet. Just rest for now.' The consultant had told him that Shirley's weight-loss may have contributed slightly to her being overwhelmed by the labour pains, but that it wasn't the main reason. These things just happened occasionally, he said, and that was why he wasn't a big fan of home births or natural births. (He was a man of science, through and through.)

'The Moon Goddess helped me,' Shirley smiled. 'And our holy statue. We must bring it into the sitting room.' And then she fell asleep again.

Declan laid his daughter in her plastic crib and called his parents back into the room. The three of them sat by the window, sipping sugary tea and watching the cars come and go in the car park.

'The nurses were terrific,' said Declan. 'And Mr Kelly. He was so calm, you'd think he was going into that theatre to make a sandwich, not deliver a baby in emergency conditions. He was amazing.'

'Ah, yes. Our medical heroes. Where would we be without them?' said Eddy. Marion pulled a face. She knew what he was up to. So did Declan.

'Don't worry,' he said. 'I can see how something like this makes music pale into insignificance. What Shirley went through tonight, I'll never forget it. She was so brave. And Mr Kelly was brilliant. I can't believe I even considered giving up on medicine to run a stupid nightclub. There's far more to life than easy money.'

Marion and Eddy exchanged glances.

'Does this mean what we think it means?' said Eddy.

'Yeah. I'm going to stay on at college and sell the ballroom to buy a new house for Shirley and me. And the baby. I only hope I can live up to the likes of what I saw here tonight. I hope I have it in me. I don't think I have, Dad.'

'You have, son,' Eddy said.

Then, they watched the sun come up. It was only when the ward began to fill up with day staff and cleaners and early morning visitors that Declan thought of phoning Mr and Mrs Winters to tell them about their first grand-child. They came crashing into the room half an hour later, trailing Kate and Kevin with them, and brandishing several bunches of flowers and a huge floating balloon. Mrs Winters called out to all the cleaning staff to come and see the new baby, and soon the tiny room was packed to the doors. A nurse came and ushered them all out again.

'Why didn't you call me? I would have been right by your side the whole time,' Mrs Winters began, and then she saw Marion looking a little bit superior. 'I wouldn't have been in the way,' she finished lamely.

'There wasn't any time,' said Eddy, diplomatically. 'It was all over when we arrived. Things have just begun to settle down.'

'Still, it would have been nice to be here on the night shift. It's very exciting to be in a hospital at night,' sulked Mrs Winters.

'It's one night I'll never forget,' said Declan quietly. 'That's for sure.' They all looked at him, and felt sorry for him. He was very young to have witnessed such trauma. And then they looked at Shirley, lying deathly pale on the hospital pillows, and felt sorry for her too.

'Let's see the star of the show,' said Kevin, brightly, sensing the happy mood faltering slightly. 'Let's have a peep at the new baby.' Marion and Eddy parted slowly, to reveal the crib, and then they all gathered round Mavourna in a reverential silence.

'Oh! She's lovely. Isn't she lovely?' said Mrs Winters, eventually. 'She's the living image of myself at that age. There's a photo of me at home, and you'd swear it was of this wee creature here.'

'Were cameras invented when you were a baby?' asked her amazed husband and she slapped him playfully on the arm. Marion was about to tell Martha Winters in no uncertain terms that Mavourna was clearly identical to Declan; but then Eddy gave his wife a beseeching look, and she said nothing.

Let her think that, if it makes her happy, Eddy's eyes seemed to say. Marion smiled at him. He was so kind and understanding. Martha hadn't been able to pay for the wedding, and she'd missed the birth. And in the years to come, Shirley would grow away from her mother and become the polished and elegant wife of a much-respected doctor. A likeness to herself was all Martha could salvage out of the entire saga.

'Yes, she's like your side of the family, all right,' Marion said graciously, and they all stood there together in a happy and contented group, sighing and admiring the new baby in her green and white striped outfit.

An hour later, the nurse woke Shirley up, to try to get her to breastfeed the baby. Mr and Mrs Winters went to begin their shift, and Kevin and Kate left to open up the garage. Marion and Eddy went home to sleep. With some effort, they managed to get Declan to go with them. He'd need to sleep, too, they told him. He could come back in the afternoon. The nurse gave Shirley a cup of tea. Shirley savoured every drop of the hot amber liquid. It was the most delicious cup of tea she had ever tasted. The room was wonderfully peaceful. The walls were painted a soft green and there was a framed watercolour of a bowl of wild flowers, facing the bed.

'Why can't I have some breakfast?' asked Shirley, when she saw the food trolley going past the door, with a big dinner plate of soggy toast sitting on it.

'We'll see about that,' said the nurse. 'You have stitches.'

'Why haven't I been to the loo?' asked Shirley, suddenly, feeling the sheets. She hadn't had a little accident, had she?

'Catheter,' said the nurse, casually. They both looked down to the side of the bed. 'I'll just pop a new bag on for you, love. That one's half full.'

Shirley wanted to die of shame, but then realized she had no shame reserves left.

'That's not permanent, is it?' she squeaked.

'God, no,' said the nurse. 'Just for today.'

The baby began to cry with hunger.

'You make yourself comfortable and I'll pass you the baby.'

'I'm not sure what to do,' said Shirley, weakly. She'd forgotten that babies needed to be fed. Somehow, she'd thought that when the baby was born, that would be the end of all the fuss, and she could rest for a few days. But, no, the nurse was waiting patiently for her to unbutton her pyjama top. The bottoms had been washed and returned to her during the night. Her dressing gown was hanging on the back of the door, also freshly laundered. There was a small posy of flowers from the hospital shop on the window sill. Shirley wondered who was responsible for all these lovely things. Then the baby cried again. The nurse lifted her over to her mother. Mavourna's mouth was wide open, like a baby bird waiting for a juicy worm.

'No need for you to worry,' said the new nurse, whose name was Betty. Shirley wondered if the other nurse had gone home. The one who had helped her to deliver Mavourna. Catherine was her name.

But Betty cut across her thoughts. 'She knows what to do. Wait and see. Just make sure you get the whole nipple in right away. It's hard to break the suction, once they start. If you need to reposition the baby's mouth, stick your little finger in at the side. Off you go, now.'

Shirley thought it was a beautiful experience, although it was slightly painful. The baby was hungry, and she knew what to do all right! She fastened onto Shirley's nipple and sucked with a strength that Shirley simply could not believe. It was incredible. Shirley's breasts responded to the demand for milk. They were already enormous and growing bigger by the minute. Milk ran down the other breast in a steady stream, soaking the sheets. She'd have to get breast pads and a nursing bra. The baby's fat little cheeks were going in and out with dedication. Shirley's breath came out in shudders of joy. It was worth all the pain; worth all the months of backache and itchy skin. Worth the new pyjamas getting damp again.

'Swap her over to the other breast, if you like,' said Betty. Shirley slipped her finger in at the side of Mavourna's mouth and lifted her across to the other breast.

She cried crossly for a moment, then felt the nipple against her cheek. She opened her little mouth and clamped down hard. Shirley gasped with pain and pleasure. Then, the sucking began again. The baby closed her eyes and settled into a steady rhythm. She was very content.

'There you are,' said Betty. 'You're a natural.' Shirley was delighted with herself. This almost made up for the fact that she'd wept like a lost child all through the labour and been unconscious for the delivery.

'Is everyone as hopeless as I was?' she asked Betty.

'Everyone is different,' said Betty, wisely. 'Some people feel pain more than others.' Then she changed the subject. 'That's a lovely name. Mavourna. What does it mean?'

'It means the Little Darling. It's Irish.'

'That's lovely. Well, I'll leave you to bond. I'll come back in a few minutes to change and sponge her. Then you can sleep.'

'Betty, can I have a shower? I feel really stale.'

'Tomorrow, maybe. Your stitches need time to take.'

'Can I please have some food? I'm starving.'

'Sorry.' Betty shook her head.

'Scrambled eggs, even? I think I smelt some, earlier.'

'Tomorrow. Maybe.'

'I know. My stitches.'

They both smiled. Then, Shirley noticed that Mavourna had stopped drinking and had fallen asleep.

'The wee angel,' whispered Shirley.

'The wee rascal,' said Betty. 'She'll be awake in an hour, wanting more.' Betty then carried the baby back to her crib, changed her and washed her with a lukewarm sea-sponge. A fresh nappy and the lightest dusting of baby powder and she was utterly content. She sighed in her sleep, dreaming a baby dream.

Shirley slept too. The exhaustion of the last nine months caught up with her and she felt as if she was falling backwards through space. Within seconds, she was in a deep slumber. Even when Declan came to visit, and sat beside her and held her hand, she did not wake up. Even when the trolley came clanking down the corridor at lunchtime, sending the smell of steaming carrots and boiling custard through all the rooms, Shirley and Mavourna slept on without stirring. They had survived the torment of childbirth together and were now as close as two human beings could be. Closer even than Shirley could ever be to her husband. Nothing, but nothing, will ever come between us, Shirley said to herself, as she dreamt of power-showers and turkey dinners and chocolate cakes as big as double beds. I'm not going to let this child out of my sight until she's twenty-one. Or maybe thirty-one . . .

32. Hollywood Hogan Takes a Gamble

Johnny sipped his coffee in the airport lounge. He had just landed in Aldergrove, after the long flight back from New York. America had been fantastic, he'd had the time of his life there, even enjoying a brief holiday fling with an air-hostess from Idaho. But he knew he did not belong there. The mighty skyscrapers in New York frightened the life out of him. He got vertigo in one of the roof-top restaurants when he saw a bird landing on the window sill, and had to come down again immediately. The yellow taxis seemed to go too fast and the drivers didn't all speak English. There was too much choice in the diners, and the service was too fast. He never knew what he wanted when the waitress brought him a glass of water. Even when he asked for a burger and chips, it was no use. There were still endless questions to be answered. What kind of bun did he want? What kind of pickles? What kind of cheese? What kind of salad? And as for the chips? Did he really want *potato chips* with his burger? No, he wanted French fries. He could never remember to call them fries. Americans called chips 'French fries'. And they called crisps 'potato chips'. And the fries weren't proper chips anyway. Proper chips were fat and greasy and made from fresh potatoes. Not those hard little sticks of maize in a cardboard envelope. (A good feed of proper Belfast chips would keep the hunger pangs at bay for two full days.) Even when he went to Graceland, he was glad that Elvis was dead. If he'd actually seen the King alive and walking around the mansion, Johnny knew his heart would have stopped beating on the spot. The sheer thrill of seeing Elvis in the flesh would have killed him, as surely as any no-warning bomb.

America was big and fast and furious and brutal and beautiful. And Johnny was tired of it; and hungry for the small-scale ordinariness of home. He was a small fish in a big pond. Eileen was correct about that. It was easy being a big fish in a little pond like Belfast. It was hard to admit a thing like that, even to himself. All his life, Hollywood Hogan had dreamt of riding a big, wild horse across his own ranch, and when he'd finally visited Texas, he was too scared to even get on one. He bought a cowboy hat and walked around in it for a day, and then he put it in his suitcase. As a souvenir. And then he'd made his plans to go home.

He'd spoken to Declan on the phone several times, and he knew the ballroom was still closed, and he was worried that it was getting damp and derelict. The boy had seemed so enthusiastic on the night of the raffle.

Johnny thought he was prepared for this scenario, but now he was not so sure. He missed the ballroom very badly. He wanted to get it up and running again. He'd even wept a little when he thought of the day he'd accidentally smashed the bottle of cheap champagne over his best shoes at the launch.

Johnny tipped the waitress in the airport cafe, making sure she knew the money was from him. He picked up his suitcase, and went out to the car park. Hailing a black taxi, he longed to be back in the driving seat of his Lincoln. He hoped that thieves hadn't taken it from the garage behind the house. And he decided, there and then, that he was going to call round to see Declan at his flat that very evening, and convince him to drop college for good, and open up the ballroom again. And he decided another thing as well. He was going to tell him that he was his real father. Maybe not right away, but when the time was right. And to hell with the consequences. Johnny had seen the Grand Canyon from a helicopter on the third week of his long vacation. Buzzing along the vast gorge that day, he suddenly realized that he didn't have to be afraid of Marion and Eddy Greenwood any more.

33. The Beginning and the End

In bed one night, a few weeks later, Kate kissed Kevin gently on the cheek.

'Kevin,' she whispered. 'I just wanted to tell you that I love you deeply. I didn't marry you because Shirley was getting married. Really, I didn't.'

'I never said you did, pet.'

'I know. But you thought it.' She smiled at him.

'No, I didn't,' he said.

'Yes, Kevin. You did. But that's okay. I didn't handle things very well.'

'We could have waited, you know? Planned our own wedding. I told you that, at the time.'

'Well, anyway. We had a lovely day. Didn't we? We'll always have the memory of it.'

'Yes, indeed. So, what is it you wanted to tell me?'

'How do you know there's something on my mind?'

'I just know. You're being very nice to me. Making me a nice dinner this evening, for one thing.'

'I just took the notion of doing some home cooking. It was only chicken in a bit of cream and herbs. I got the recipe from a magazine.'

'I didn't know they had recipes in *Vogue.*'

'Ha! I saw it in Mum's copy of *Family Circle.*'

'Did you? Well, it was great.'

'Kevin, have you noticed I've been a little edgy recently?'

'Yes. You told me to ignore it.'

'Yes, I did. It was just something personal I had to work out for myself. Well, I'm fine now. I mean, I was fussing about various things, that's all. But I'm fine now.'

'That's great, pet. I knew you would get over it.'

'And I did. Listen. Kevin, I do want to talk to you. But first, let's make love.'

'Sure thing.' And he took her in his arms and kissed her passionately. She wriggled free of his muscular body and laughed.

'Now, listen, stud. I want it to be different tonight. I want you to take things slowly. Kiss me first, gently. No, keep your hands on my back. Caress me very softly.'

'Like this?' He moved his palms across her waist and up to her shoulder blades.

'Mmmm. That's lovely. Touch the skin on my neck with the tip of your tongue. Softly, Kevin.'

'I thought you liked me to be passionate?'

'I do, pet. But at the very end, not at the beginning. You see?'

'Okay.'

'Tease me. Make me think you might stop at any moment.'

'Will that make you want me more?'

'Yes.'

'Women! Are you all this hard to understand?'

'Yes.'

He licked her neck as softly as he could, and kept up the caressing at the same time. For half an hour, there was no sound in the pale blue bedroom except for the ticking of the Belleek china clock on the mantelpiece, and the sensual sighs of Kevin McGovern and his dark-haired wife, Kate. It was very soothing for both of them.

'Tell me I'm beautiful,' she said, in a whisper.

'You're beautiful,' he said, and then he laughed. 'You know you're beautiful.'

'Don't laugh! Look me in the eyes and tell me I'm beautiful, as if it never dawned on you before how lovely I am. Try to keep a straight face, Kevin. Try to look serious for a minute.'

'You're beautiful,' he whispered, and he looked directly into her eyes, and he didn't laugh, and Kate felt a faint flutter of excitement stirring within her.

'Women need to feel attractive to enjoy lovemaking,' she said.

'Every time?'

'Yes. Every single time.'

'Okay, I'll remember that.'

'Now, close your eyes and kiss me on the mouth.'

'Softly?' he asked.

'Yes. Very softly. Just brush your lips against my lips.' This was slightly embarrassing, discussing sex in such detail, but it had to be done.

'With my lips closed?' Kevin wanted to know.

'Yes. And mine, too. For a while.'

'Then open?'

'Yes.'

'Who'll open their lips first?'

'I will. It's symbolic.'

'You mean, you're ready for the next bit?'

'Now, you're getting the hang of it.'

She smiled at him, and kissed his hands. They were rugged and scratched from fixing cars, but also very tender and vulnerable-looking. He was really very appealing, in a strong and physical way. And he was listening to her commands and submitting himself to her guidance. That meant he trusted her and wanted to learn how to please her in bed. She realized she did love him very much.

'Now. You can touch your favourite bits,' she purred.

He moved his hands around to her sides, and very gradually, began to touch her breasts; concentrating not just on the sensitive nipples, but on the soft mounds surrounding them. He even kissed her collarbones and breathed warm air on her neck. He said her perfume was lovely. She felt very relaxed. Kate ran her fingers through his blond highlights and over his broad back, and enjoyed their lovemaking as she never had before. He massaged her shoulders and she kissed his cheekbones and told him he was sexy and a wonderful lover.

Then, when she was ready, she turned him over onto his back and knelt over him, and guided his movements until they became faster and faster and they both reached a peak of pleasure at exactly the same time. She was delighted when Kevin kissed her hand afterwards and said, 'Thank you,' without having to be told.

They lit a scented candle, and lay in each other's arms, listening to the rain outside on the street, and Kate knew that she had married the right man. Even though she'd been on Valium when she took her sacred vows.

Several hours later, when Kevin was still sound asleep with a smile on his face, Kate slipped out of bed and went downstairs. She sat in the kitchen for a while, sipping tea and drawing up plans in a notebook. Adding up figures and calculating debts. She wanted Kevin to sell the garage and the house, pay off all their debts, and start again in New Zealand. Houses were cheaper there, and the climate was much better. Now that she was sure she wanted to stay with him for ever, it was time to tell him about her desire to emigrate. Kate Winters – Kate McGovern now – was just too glamorous for Belfast. It was the missing piece of the puzzle. She was sure she wanted Kevin. Sure she wanted to be married. But she didn't want to live in Belfast any more. The city had robbed her of her peace of mind for many years, and now she was going away to begin again. Not running away because of her anxiety. But choosing to leave, of her own free will. Starting again, just the two of them, in a new country that they could learn about together. Without their families or the neighbours looking on. Kate wanted them to be different people, not just Kate from the dole office, and Kevin from the dusty garage at the bottom of the avenue. New, shiny, modern, happy people. And in Belfast, you could never leave behind who you were, and what you had been. Life was too small and too slow. And that was why she decided the best thing would be to slip away without a big fuss, and see what they could make of their lives in a new place.

When Kevin woke from his contented slumber, Kate was freshly showered and made-up and wearing a pretty white dress. She brought him tea and toasted hot-cross buns, and congratulated him again on his prowess the night before. She lay on the bed beside him and outlined her plans. She had made extensive enquiries about emigration on the telephone earlier. It would be pretty straightforward, she was told, because they had money and skills to support their application. Surprisingly, Kevin said yes.

'Why so keen?' she said, amazed. 'Don't you want to think about it? Won't you miss anything?'

'I need you,' he said, simply. 'I was dying of boredom before you came into my life, and now I don't want to go back to the way things were. It was only a shadow of a life I had.'

'Do you really need me, Kevin? No one ever needed me before.'

'I do need you, Kate. More than you think. Don't leave me behind. Take me with you.'

'I will,' she promised. 'I'll never leave you again.'

'Well, then,' he said, hugely relieved. 'I take it you can do all the paperwork? I'm no good at that sort of thing. Just tell me when to stop taking cars in for repairs.'

'Leave it to me,' she laughed. 'The house has more than doubled in value. We'll have enough for a decent deposit on a new place, flights, maybe even a couple of months' holiday before we have to start working.'

'Fantastic. And to celebrate, let's see if I can remember what you taught me last night,' he murmured, reaching for her hand and leading her into the bathroom and towards the big corner bath with the gold-plated taps. 'We might as well enjoy this lovely big bath, while we still have the chance.'

34. Whatever Happened To . . .

A few months later, as Kate and Kevin were winging their way to New Zealand, Johnny Hogan finally told Declan the true story of his birth. They were sitting together in velvet bucket-seats in the ballroom, one bright Monday morning in December. It was the first time they'd been alone together since Johnny came back from America. Johnny had tried and failed to convince his son to reopen the ballroom. And when Declan told him that he'd had a terrific offer from a builder, and that they were going to knock down the hall and build twenty townhouses on the site, Johnny couldn't hold his tongue any longer.

Declan said nothing as he heard all the details. The way Marion had used her pregnancy to marry successful businessman Eddy Greenwood, while Johnny was busy fighting off the gangsters. How she'd used Eddy's money to set herself up with her own shop and a fancy house. And then, how she'd kept Johnny's son a secret from him for twenty years. And blocked him from attending the wedding of his only child. Declan just stared at Johnny for about five minutes, with tears of shock welling up in his dark brown eyes. Yes, they did look alike. He could see that now. But he was not happy. Far from being delighted to find his true father, Declan felt uneasy beside this man with his frayed white jacket and his out-of-date hairstyle. There was something restless about him; something that made

Declan think he was not a contented person. And he spoke to Declan as if he owned him, like he was some sort of a possession. *You're my son*, he'd said, several times. As if he had some claim on Declan's friendship and his career-choices, just because he was present at the boy's conception. And he wasn't really interested in Mavourna. He said that it would be great when Declan had a son. Then, there'd be three generations of Hogans in the entertainment business.

Declan was suddenly filled with a rush of love for Eddy. Not once, in his entire life, had he ever felt there was a distance between Eddy and himself. Not once had he ever felt less important or loved than his sisters. And he understood fully why Marion had abandoned this strange man and his dimly lit ballroom for the security of Eddy and a stable family life. Johnny Hogan might be famous, but fame was a lonely place in the daylight hours and Declan didn't want to become like this man who sat staring at him from across the table. Johnny was a prisoner in this empty hall, just waiting for the darkness to fall so that he could open the main doors and let the people in to keep him company. Without the ballroom, Johnny had no identity and Declan felt sorry for him. He couldn't sell the ballroom now. It would be too cruel. Hollywood Hogan would be like an orphan without his dance hall. A fifty-year-old orphan. Declan took the keys to the building from his pocket, placed them on the table, and slid them across the Formica to Johnny.

'I'm sorry,' he said. 'I'm really sorry to have to say this. But I think I should give these back to you. I already have a father and I love him very much. And I think you only want me to take over the business for you here. Shirley doesn't want me to do it, and neither does my mother. And neither do I. It's lonely here when the lights are out and the music is switched off. I'm sorry but there's just no future for us. I couldn't hurt my parents like that. After all they've done for me. So, I wish you all the best. But, no, I don't want the ballroom. I'll sign it back to you. Let's just pretend this conversation never took place.'

He got up then, and shook Johnny's hand, and walked out of the ballroom for ever. Johnny watched him leave, like his mother had before him, twenty years earlier. He touched the keys with his index finger. They were still warm. Johnny put them in his pocket.

He looked up at the ceiling. Yes, it was lonely when the lights went out. That was true enough. But the ballroom was beautiful when it was full of light and laughter and music and dancing and romance. And Johnny would chase out the spiders and the mice and bring it back to its former glory. He would rehire all the old gang and reopen the ballroom as a venue for old-time dancing, like James suggested. There would be no more young people fighting in the toilets and wrecking the place at weekends. The ballroom would be a *proper* ballroom, with better seating and more upmarket snacks and prestigious dancing competitions with trophies and ribbons. Johnny would get a new jacket. A blue one this time. He felt a wave of excitement in his chest. It would take a lot of work, but Johnny Hogan thrived on hard work.

DJ Toni was rescued from a drunken retirement in a Ballycastle rest home and continued to play his records in the ballroom. His heavy breathing was renowned throughout the six counties, and frequently discussed on Radio Ulster. But people were kind to DJ Toni, because they believed his horror-movie respiratory raspings were mostly brought on by asthma. He met and married a very elegant lady with her own hairpiece salon, and they lived very happily together in a cosy cottage in Saintfield with a wishing-well in the middle of the lawn. When DJ Toni retired at the age of seventy, Johnny Hogan found a young lad called Jonathan to replace him, and they worked very well together. Jonathan became like a son to him, and Johnny began to train him up to take over the business one day. As time passed, he got over the pain of losing Declan to the Greenwood family. He had lost his mother and father in the war, and he had survived that. He would survive the pain of losing his only child, too. He had made thousands of people happy, over the years. His life was not a failure, as Marion thought. He was Hollywood Hogan, and he had made his mark in the world.

Eileen and James said nothing about the ballroom being given to Declan Greenwood in a raffle. And then being handed back to Johnny, and the two men falling out for good. Eileen eventually worked the secret out for herself and James had always known it, in his heart. They enjoyed their days in the little bungalow by the sea and they knew that they didn't have much time left, and they didn't want to waste it thinking of the past. They worried about Johnny, of course. They worried that he might be lonely, living and working in Belfast by himself. But he was nearly fifty now. They had done all they could for him for half a century.

Now Johnny Hogan was on his own. That was the price he paid for his career. Success, even in small-time show business, came at a high price. They blamed themselves for allowing him to go to the cinema so often, when he was a child. Maybe, if he hadn't spent so much time in the velvety darkness, staring through the cigarette smoke at so many celluloid fantasies, he wouldn't have ended up the way he did. But then they told themselves that he was happy, and that he could have got married if he'd wanted to. But Johnny wanted to be famous. That was all he really wanted. And there was nothing anyone could do about it.

The ballroom was ready for business in a couple of months, and the whirlwind of press releases and media interviews started all over again. The TV cameras turned up, the retirement-age ballroom dancers arrived en masse for the Grand Opening, and Johnny looked fabulous beside them in a jacket covered in blue glitter. Only once did a reporter ask him what had happened to return the ballroom to Johnny's ownership after the raffle, and he just said, 'That's all in the past.' And it was.

Marion asked Eddy if they could renew their wedding vows and have a lavish party afterwards. She wanted to tell the world how much she loved him. Eddy was delirious with happiness and set to work planning the great event. Marion wore the fabulously expensive velvet dress that she had not been able to sell in her salon, and she made a very emotional speech at the party and told Eddy she loved him in front of everyone they knew. They spent a fortune on fancy food and party favours for the guests, and all manner of entertainment and frills, but it was worth every penny. They felt truly married in a way that had been lacking the first time round. They didn't bother with a honeymoon. They just went home to their restful cream bedroom, and lay in bed drinking tea, and talking about all the wonderful things that had happened that day.

The builder who was beaten on the ballroom deal bought another plot of land further up the road instead. A row of smart townhouses was built on the new site and Marion and Eddy bought one for their son. Declan and Shirley moved in with their little daughter, Mavourna Moon, before the plaster was even dry. It was good to say goodbye to the little flat with its broken taps and its creaking floorboards, and the communal front door that never stopped banging, day and night. Declan was moved to tears by his parents' generosity, now that he really knew the extent of their love for him. And so, even though he had previously refused to let them help him financially, he accepted the house with good grace. He said he would repay the debt when he was working. He knew it meant a lot to Eddy that he had given back the ballroom to Johnny; it was like a formal declaration of loyalty. He hugged and kissed them both as they all had their first cup of tea in the new house. He told both of his parents that he loved them very much.

The first thing Kate did when they moved into their modern bungalow with sea views was to hang the two tickets for Hogan's Goodbye Disco, which she'd had framed, on the bedroom wall. So she would always remember the night she had fallen in love with Kevin.

They had a dream holiday, exploring their new homeland, and enjoying the scenery and eating out, and buying furniture. Kate picked up the keys to her new shop. She spent two glorious weeks painting the boutique white and supervising the construction of some pretty cube-shelving, and attending a trade event for boutique-owners. When all the new handbags were displayed on the shelves, and the champagne had been poured, Kate unlocked the door and a small crowd of excited females came swarming in with their credit cards. The shop was going to be a great success. Kevin slotted easily into his new garage environment, and even went fishing with some of the other mechanics on a boat named the *Belfast Boy*. He didn't miss his old life for a second.

Declan threw himself into his studies, and his tutors said he would make a fine doctor some day. He rarely had time to think of the ballroom and what might have been. And although he had promised Shirley that he would never hide anything from her, he kept Johnny's revelation to himself. Shirley might be upset if she had to get to know a new grandparent for Mavourna. And he sensed that she didn't like Johnny Hogan very much, anyway. (Shirley was delighted when Declan gave the ballroom back to Hogan.) Declan never told his parents what he knew either, and they never asked him why he had given the ballroom back. As the months passed, the whole thing gradually faded into the background. He knew he had made the right decision when he lay in bed with Shirley each night. He was a family man, like Eddy. He didn't care what the outside world thought of him. All he cared about was Shirley and their love for each other, and their beautiful daughter and their lovely home.

Shirley was thrilled with the tall, echo-filled new house and they made a vow to pay back Declan's parents as soon as they were earning again. Shirley had great fun painting the freshly plastered walls in restful pastel colours, and looking in the second-hand shops and sales for nice pieces of furniture. She said she might have another child to keep Mavourna company, as soon as she had her strength back after the birth. She still didn't know if she believed in God or anything else, but she knew that she wanted a surgeon standing by when she went into labour for the second time. She decorated Mavourna's little bedroom with paintings of pink trees with pale blue leaves and pretty tree-sprites. Their statue of God's mother ended up in the spare bedroom, but Shirley dusted it regularly.

She cried a little bit, sometimes, when she thought of Kate living so far away. They should have been best friends all these years and now they should be bringing up their children together. But Kate was never coming back to Belfast. They both knew that much. Shirley made Kate promise to keep in touch. But she knew in her heart that Kate would develop a New Zealand accent, and that they would only see her a handful of times in the years ahead, if that. They would grow apart and become strangers. They would never dance together in the ball-room again, or get drunk in the Crown Bar, or laugh at Miss Bingham's madness. Kate wouldn't get to see Shirley's new blue carpet, which had just been laid in the lounge, or taste the chocolate cupcakes she had made that day. It was the end of an era. But then she looked at Declan, asleep in their bed beside her, his long eyelashes flickering in some happy dream, and she knew that she already had a best friend. She kissed him on the shoulder, and cuddled up to him, and went to sleep.

Kate kept a low profile for six months and then sent her parents a postcard and some tickets for a cruise. Mr and Mrs Winters had the time of their lives on the ship, ballroom-dancing every night, and feasting on grilled chicken and platters of watermelon and pineapple cubes. Mrs Winters wore a feather ornament in her hair, and Mr Winters squeezed himself into his old tuxedo for the cocktail hour. They returned home, tanned and worldly-wise, after visiting several European countries. They decided to save up and go on a lovely holiday every year. They thought they might not be able to afford it, but with Kate and her catalogues out of the house, there was much more money available. Mrs Winters turned Kate's old room into a sewing room, and spent many happy hours there, making cushion-covers and frilly curtains. Mr Winters was very contented, but he bought the big shed anyway. Just to be on the safe side.

Then, Hogan's began running ballroom-dancing classes, and everyone went mad for them. At first Mr Winters was reluctant to leave the shed. There were a lot of shelves to be put up, he said. But Mrs Winters threatened her husband with violence if he didn't take her dancing. So he did, and they had a great time. It was just like being back on the cruise ship, except now they were learning how to dance properly. They ended up going three times a week, and even won a little cup for the best newcomers in the month of February.

Alex Stone's uncle passed away and Alex inherited a fortune. And Louise Lowry wasted no time in marrying him and getting her giant hands on his bank account. It wasn't much of a romance. They went out for a curry every Saturday night for six months, and then one rainy evening in June, a bunch of aggressive teenagers called Alex a poof, and before he could reach for them, Louise made one of her giant hands into a fist, and punched the biggest lad square in the face. That stopped them in their tracks. They apologized immediately, and scattered. Alex proposed that night, in the Star of India Curry House on the Ormeau Road. He was very touched by Louise's brave gesture. And he was happy to hand the shops over to her, when the honeymoon was over. (Twin beds in Venice.) He had no interest in the jewellery business, he said. He left Louise to run the shops and he spent most of his free time hanging around with Sunny Jim. Louise never did find out that Alex and Jim were gay, and in love with each other. And they didn't know it, either. They had been brought up in an era that did not acknowledge or tolerate modern catch-pennies, like two gay people sharing a loving and tender relationship. They just knew that they were happy together, talking about stainless-steel hand-weights and competition briefs that cost fifty pounds a pair. And so, in a strange way, it was the perfect relationship. Mary went to work for her old friend Louise, and the two of them had great fun transforming the shops from a tacky chain of second-rate rubbish into a chain of slightly less tacky, second-rate rubbish.

The police in Bundoran were mystified as to how Lolly had given them the slip. Until the winter rain soaked through the roofing felt of the seaside bungalow and made a wet patch on the carpet underneath. The Sunday papers had a bit of fun with the story, and there were some red faces in the local police station. They vowed to lock him up for good if they ever caught him again, but he was long gone by then. Eugene Lolly left the country on a tugboat, under cover of darkness, and blagged his way to Mexico, where he found work as a caretaker in a monastery. Three years later, he renounced the modern world, and its chattering women, and joined the monks himself. He wasn't sure if he was a religious man, but he managed to convince the others that he was; and the monastery was peaceful and clean, and the meals weren't bad either. It was just like prison, but without the riots and the stress and the tattoos. Eugene was very happy there. He kept the little glass statue of the Virgin Mary in his cell, as a reminder of what the most important thing in life was: freedom. He told no one in Ireland where he was and it pleased him that he would remain a figure of mystery to the end of his days. He would finally become the legend that he had always dreamt of becoming.

Virginia Lolly divorced Eugene in absentia, and married a local man ten years younger than herself. He appreciated her belly-dancing very much, and she was delighted at his prowess with a cocktail-shaker.

*

Timothy Tate won a fortune on the lottery, and gave most of it to the gymnasium where he worked. He had no real need of the money as yellow bonbons were his only luxury. The gym was therefore saved from certain closure and everyone was delighted. They had a celebration tournament and beat each other black and blue. The manager paid off all their debts straight away and even erected a small plaque on the wall in Timothy's honour. Timothy's pastor told him that he had restored his faith in human nature. The Bonbon Gang days were over at last. Well, nearly. Timothy used the last of his winnings to buy the newsagent's shop where Louise Lowry had once worked. And he renamed it the Bonbon Gang. He could now spend the rest of his life sitting behind the old counter, reading comics and eating sweets, and wondering where Eugene was, and just being content.

Miss Bingham held on to her job in the unemployment office until she was five years over the official retirement age. She was finally pensioned off and carried out of the building by the same security guard that had escorted Kate to the front door. She went on a three-week sweet-sherry bender and was found wandering in the Botanic Gardens one day, talking to the plants about flexi-sheets. Her doctor advised her to go on a long holiday, so she spent another three weeks looking at glossy brochures and complaining about the outrageous price of single-room supplements. Eventually, she decided that she liked the look of Tasmania. Off she went, on her own, for a two-week vacation, the highlight of which was a tour of the old British penal colony buildings (featuring the world's first sensory-deprivation chamber). She had a great time. She came home to Belfast wearing a T-shirt that said: *I've been to Tassie.* She bought two neutered cats and joined the church choir. She was happy. Sort of. In her own way.

Then, one day that began just like any other day, but which turned out to be life-changing, a strange man turned up on her doorstep, wearing a polyester beige suit and aviator sunglasses. His name was Tom Raymonds and he spoke with an American accent. He told Miss Bingham that he was her son, and that the Boston Adoption Agency had given him her details. Miss Bingham collapsed on the rope-twist doormat. (She was something of an expert at collapsing, by this stage.) She wept and cried and said she was so, so sorry for giving her baby away all those years ago, but it was the done thing then. The father didn't want to know and her family didn't want the disgrace. She had not known one day's peace since the adoption people came to take her son away. All his life, forty-six years of it, she had wondered what became of him. All her life she had been jealous of modern women like Kate Winters who did whatever they pleased. He forgave her, and they hugged, and went for a walk around the city, holding hands. She showed him where she used to work, and where she went to church, and where she bought her groceries. He told her he was a lawyer, who had been brought up by good people. She told him that she had never stopped loving him. He said she was welcome to come out to Boston and live with him and his wife, Amy. They had a big house with lots of space, and five grown-up children. She said she would be delighted. And before he flew back to Boston, they had their portrait taken by the best photographer in the city.

James sat watching television one night when Eileen had gone to bed. He was thinking of everything that had happened to his little family. Declan was a married man now so he hadn't turned out to be a rolling stone like Johnny. Marion had done the right thing in marrying Eddy Greenwood, even though James knew for a fact it was Johnny she really loved, all those years ago. And Eddy had done a great job in bringing up Johnny's son to become a happily married student-doctor. Of course, the downside was that James and Eileen were not part of Declan's life and never would be.

James watched the film until the credits came up, but he wasn't really listening to it. He was thinking that real life was much more interesting and complex and tragic and wonderful than any film could ever be. Then he switched off the set and went to bed.

Sharon Owens

read more

About Sharon

I was born at home in Omagh, County Tyrone, Northern Ireland, in 1968, the second child of five. My Dad was the lead singer in a country and western showband and my Mum was a psychiatric nurse. Dad's career meant he worked long hours and was often away from home for days or even weeks at a time, but he was lucky to have a job at all. Northern Ireland in those days was suffering from the twin problems of the Troubles and very high unemployment (as high as 37% in rural areas). My family moved to Dublin in 1974 for two years before returning to Omagh because we missed our family and friends so much.

I went to the local convent school for girls, and I remember those days fondly. My class was full of comedians, so we were in stitches most of the time.

I asked my husband Dermot out when I was seventeen. We were both interested in the same kind of pop music and, also, I thought he was gorgeous. Luckily he turned out to be a very gentle, intelligent and sensitive person as well. He has always supported my artistic career, and has been buying me pens, pencils and paints for twenty years.

During my student days I had various part-time jobs: barmaid, waitress, sales assistant in a bridal boutique/ice-cream parlour/gift shop, and a care assistant in a nursing home. And they were all badly paid and very sore on the feet.

We got married when I graduated from Art College in 1992. Our daughter Alice was born in 1993 in the Royal Victoria Hospital in Belfast, and we have lived in the same house in the city since that year. Dermot has worked in IT for seventeen years now, which is extremely fortuitous for me because I have my very own live-in computer expert, on hand at all times with technical advice. And believe me, I need it. I'm beyond hopeless with computers.

After Alice was born I continued to paint and draw in my spare time, and sold a small number of pieces each year, including commissions for private portraits. I started writing fiction in 2002 and now work full-time as a writer.

Q&A

What inspired you to write *The Ballroom on Magnolia Street*?

Well, I suppose it had something to do with the fact that as a child I spent a lot of time in ballrooms, mostly during the day when the spotlights were switched off and the record booth lay eerily silent. During the daytime the halls were dimly lit with overhead pendants, and you could see the dust motes in the air when the sun was shining through tiny windows near the ceiling.

I used to go to Irish dancing lessons every week, you see, and the classes were held in local halls that were built during the showband boom of the 1960s. They were more like concrete warehouses than anything else and they were always absolutely freezing because of the high ceilings. I wasn't very good at Irish dancing, and I didn't enjoy the classes much either, but that didn't matter: all the girls in the town attended every week for years.

I wasn't very good at Irish dancing, and I didn't enjoy the classes much either, but that didn't matter

Hardly any boys went to the classes, as most of them played football or attended hurling practice in their spare time. Parents in those days didn't believe in letting their offspring turn into couch potatoes: we were so fit we could have danced or kicked ball for twenty-four hours straight. We were as skinny and wiry as terriers.

But anyway, I did used to wonder, during those interminable gloomy Saturday afternoons, what the ballrooms looked like when they were properly lit up in the evenings and the disco-ball on the ceiling was glittering and twirling. I was desperate to see the shabby old places full of fun, and grown-ups dancing with each other. Not tapping (or trebling, as we called it) in neat rows like us children, straining to hear a reel or jig on a tinny cassette player.

It wasn't always good: sometimes when the night's entertainment was over we had to run for our lives

I finally made it past the ticket booth when I was seventeen and it was incredible. Everything was transformed by the spinning spotlights and the moving shadows. The furniture looked better, the floor looked shinier, the mirrors behind the bar reflected the lights and made the hall seem twice the size. And the strong scents of perfume, aftershave, whisky, beer and cigarettes were a far cry from the leathery aroma of hundreds of pairs of steel-toed dancing shoes. And, best of all, the music, which was thunderously loud. You had to yell at your friends and even then they couldn't hear you. It was so exciting. At last I understood the attraction of the ballrooms.

It wasn't always good: sometimes when the night's entertainment was over we had to run for our lives from thugs who didn't think much of our trendy clothes. But those few magical hours each weekend in the disco made

read more

the boredom of the rest of the week bearable. We could dress up and pretend to be sophisticated creatures with endless possibilities ahead of us.

The disco was a place of refuge, like the café and the pub in my other novels.

What was it like growing up as a teenager in the 1980s?

Maybe it was just me and my boyfriend Dermot who thought this, but life in the 1980s in Northern Ireland was pretty grim. There was rampant unemployment. Towns and villages were grey and run down. The news was dominated by sectarian murders, riots and bombings. People were losing their lives on a daily basis. The churches were packed to the doors with desperate parishioners praying for peace, but nobody was actually talking about peace, or doing anything to build bridges between the two communities.

The news was dominated by sectarian murders, riots and bombings

Even as young children we were taught not to make any sudden movements near a soldier or a police officer in case we were mistaken for a young terrorist or rioter, and fired upon. Similarly, we knew not to touch any unusual devices we might find on the street, or anything with batteries or wires visible. Unattended beer kegs and sports bags, or cars that were pressing down heavily on their wheels: all these things could be potentially

dangerous. I heard two large explosions going off: the Ballygawley bomb that
killed eleven soldiers and injured many more, and the Bridge Street bomb that destroyed Omagh town. (Not the explosion that became known as the Omagh bomb: that one was much later in 1998.)

I had my long brown hair cut off at the hairdresser's, until there was only about two inches of it left

As young people living in an area of high unemployment we knew the only option for us was to go to university, and then emigrate. So there was a feeling there was no point in putting down roots and keeping in touch with one another, because when our friends drifted off to colleges and jobs around the world, we'd never see them again. I suppose we existed in a day-to-day bubble, not thinking too much of the days before or the days still to come.

When I was 16, I had my long brown hair cut off at the hairdresser's, until there was only about two inches of it left, which I promptly dyed blue-black and spiked up with Shockwaves hairspray. (I can still smell that glorious stuff in my imagination. It made your hair waterproof so that it stayed standing up even in the rain.) At last, I was allowed to leave the dreaded Irish dancing classes, because with hair like that I was no longer allowed to compete in dancing competitions.

As soon as we were finished school, Dermot and I left Northern Ireland for ever (or so we thought) and went to live and study in Manchester. That's when we got the shock of our lives when we discovered that living conditions in the student areas of Manchester were even worse than in rural Tyrone and Fermanagh, and the working-class districts of Belfast. The rooms we had rented (over the phone) were nothing short of a slum: with bricked-up windows and rising damp, eight-foot weeds in the garden and the grime of years on all the furniture. All my life I'd heard local politicians blaming Britain for the sorry state of Northern Ireland, but it dawned on me there was poverty, neglect and recession everywhere.

It was the only disco in the town where the DJ was a nice normal man

We stayed in Manchester for a week and went to the Ritz ballroom every night, and the Dutch Pancake House for lunch every day. We had a fantastic week watching films at the Cornerhouse and shopping for studded belts and biker boots in Affleck's Palace, and then we went home. Two years of dead-end jobs followed, but at least we had our families to keep us company and we were living in spotless houses with cookers and showers that actually worked.

We went to our favourite disco every Friday night: a small, intimate venue next to a clerical cemetery in the town centre of Omagh. It had black glittery wallpaper and a dance floor with tiles that lit up. It was the only disco in the town where the DJ was a nice normal man who would play requests for New Order, Soft Cell and

Human League. All the other, larger venues only played crowd-pleasers like Chris Rea and Bon Jovi, which we hated.

Ironically we felt a lot safer in Belfast than we ever had at home in Omagh

Eventually Dermot and I moved to Belfast, rented a lovely little apartment off the Lisburn Road and had great fun furnishing it and living together as a couple. We got our degrees, and then safe jobs in the Civil Service. Ironically we felt a lot safer in Belfast than we ever had at home in Omagh, because in the city we were anonymous and nobody knew what religious background we came from. Or that we had stopped going to church in favour of a Sunday morning lie-in. We also became vegetarian and that was a relief, because at home every meal would have been awkward due to the meat-and-two-veg standard of those days.

There's a lot more money and prosperity in Northern Ireland these days, but sadly just as much sectarianism and segregation. I couldn't live through another thirty-five years of conflict, though. If that looked inevitable, I would definitely leave for good.

Are Kate and Shirley based on real people? And did you have tastes like theirs?

Kate and Shirley are very loosely (and I have to stress,

very loosely indeed) based on me and my older sister Kathleen. There was only a year between us but it might as well have been a decade. She was into leather jackets, high-heeled shoes, blonde highlights, pink lipstick and ankle bracelets. She liked soft rock like Bon Jovi, and she didn't drink alcohol or smoke cigarettes. And I was a typical indie-music fan in a floor-length overcoat and spiky hair. And I did like a sip of the amber nectar and I did smoke (but not very often, as cigarettes made me feel sick).

I did fall in love with a boy in a military-surplus overcoat

But we had to go to discos together: our parents thought we'd be safer that way. Naturally, Kathleen wanted to go to big mainstream discos and I wanted to go to small trendy ones, so there were quite a few rows as we trudged around the town at weekends. Once we got caught up in a riot and had to take shelter under a chip van for an hour as the halfers (half-bricks) and bottles came raining down around us. That night, we didn't argue and fight. Not much, anyway.

So that was the seed for the idea: of the complicated interdependant relationship between two sisters who have nothing in common. But all the rest of the story is fiction. Mind you, my sister Kathleen did have a thing about handbags. She had hundreds of them. And I did love second-hand clothes and plastic beads and red lipstick. But the rest is fiction. Although I did fall in love with a boy in a military-surplus overcoat. And she was a bit bossy. But the rest is definitely fiction ...

Sharon's Top Five 80s tracks

SAY HELLO, WAVE GOODBYE by Soft Cell

That was the song that was playing the night I met my husband Dermot for the first time. We had arranged to meet at the disco at 9.30pm before it got too crowded, and we had a booth all to ourselves. There was dry ice swirling around the floor, and the Soft Cell classic playing through the loudspeakers. Dermot had a long fringe like Phil Oakey's (which was why we often had to leg it home early in the years that followed) and I thought he was gorgeous. I've always thought that song was incredibly emotional anyway, but meeting Dermot made it extra-special. I love electronic pop music more than any other kind. I just don't get classical music. It always seems very stuffy and over complicated to me. A strong, simple pop tune can instantly transport me back to a certain moment in time. This is definitely my 'first serious kiss' song.

BLUE MONDAY by New Order was the biggest-selling 12" of the 1980s

It had such a strong beat with lots of other little sound effects going on in the background. I bought it and played it non-stop; it was terrific. I was a big New Order fan and loved all their stuff especially the album *Power, Corruption and Lies*. Another great song was *Temptation*, but really they were all classics. Guaranteed floor fillers, and very energizing. A good song to play in the morning when you can't be bothered getting out of bed.

WAVES by Blancmange

From the *Happy Families* album. I love male singers with deep voices and Neil Arthur's was so rich and distinctive. A real anthem for lost youth, this one, with all the synthesizers and drumbeats that were typical of the 1980s. Strangely erotic too. It's ironic that at a time when

read more

your teenage hormones are raging, you're too young and too poor to move out of your Mum and Dad's chintzy bungalow and get a little place of your own. So you have to waste about seven years of your life (and theirs) arguing with them and listening to their endless lectures about 'their roof and their rules'.

REEL AROUND THE FOUNTAIN by The Smiths

I love Morrissey, I can't help it. I know some journalists say he glorifies and wallows in misery, but really there's a lot of misery about and you can't ignore it if you're a sensitive type like Mozzer. I went mad for The Smiths when they first appeared on the pop scene and saw them twice at gigs in Belfast. I thought Morrissey was a genius with his NHS glasses, his hearing aid, second-hand clothes and armful of fresh flowers. And Johnny Marr's swirling guitar wizardry was just so different from anything that was going on at the time. It would be hard to pick out one Smiths song in particular, but *Reel Around the Fountain* is just so poignant. The lyrics are profoundly sad and yet hilarious at the same time.

SIXTEEN DAYS by This Mortal Coil

Not a lot of people might be familiar with this one but it's so brilliant, dark, moody and atmospheric. Elizabeth Frazer had an amazing voice. I saw her in concert once and she was very upset by some idiots who were causing a disturbance in the audience. The Cocteau Twins were fabulous too; I loved all their albums especially *Garlands*. *Sixteen Days* is a great song to play to people who have mainstream tastes: they'll absolutely loathe it. Which just proves how cultured and refined your own tastes are ...

VINTAGE FINDS

Really good quality vintage finds are rare, but I'm happy enough with copies. I only like Gothic, Victorian and 1920s style clothes so I tend to bulk-buy when these things are in fashion and then buy nothing else for years! I used to be able to find terrific original pieces in charity shops, but now I think people tend to sell on good pieces to collectors rather than donate them. So high street finds are fine.

TOP TIPS

Keep your best pieces on a good-quality hanger to retain shape

Keep costume jewellery wrapped in tissue paper in a strong container such as a hatbox.

Look in independent interiors shops for hand-made handbags and hats that are unique, or at least limited-edition.

Search for bargains on the high street, especially Accessorise for handbags and hairclips.

BEST BUYS

A velvet beaded handbag with a pewter clasp for £50 in a little interiors store on Belfast's Lisburn Road.

A red glass candlestick for £40 in Anna Pink, another lovely store on the same road.

A 1930s style black coat with a fake fur collar, bought in M&S for £110 in 1994, and it still looks good today!

A big silver ring with 3 black stones that I found in an African-Indian gift shop for £35.

read more